THE
EXTINCTION
TRIALS

A.G. RIDDLE

THE
EXTINCTION
TRIALS

HEAD
of ZEUS

An Ad Astra Book

First published in the UK in 2021 by Head of Zeus Ltd
An Ad Astra book

9 7 5 3 1 2 4 6 8

A catalogue record for this book is available from
the British Library.

ISBN (HB): 9781803281636
ISBN (XTPB): 9781803281643

Typeset by DivAddict Solutions

Printed and bound in Great Britain by
CPI Group (UK) Ltd, Croydon CRO 4YY

Head of Zeus Ltd
First Floor East
5–8 Hardwick Street
London ECIR 4RG

WWW.HEADOFZEUS.COM

To the brave souls who keep going—even when it feels like the world is ending.

PROLOGUE

The dinner host tapped his champagne glass with a fork.

The *ding-ding-ding* echoed through the vast dining room, drawing the attention of the sixty guests.

"Tonight, I'd like to pose a simple question: what is the *destiny* of the human race?"

He let the words hang in the air for a moment.

"We all know the answer. At some point, our species will go extinct."

He paced the room, all eyes following him.

"How? What will be our end? Artificial intelligence? Will our undoing come at the hands of an AI project one of your companies is working on? Or maybe another one of your pet projects? Will genetic engineering splinter our species, making some of us obsolete, setting off an unimaginable war between the next humans and the ones left behind?"

The host turned and paced again, stopping in front of a pair of doors that opened onto a wide stone veranda. Beyond, waves from the ocean crashed upon the rocks, a soft symphony punctuating the speech.

"Let's assume, for a moment, that our extinction won't come at the hands of one of our inventions. After all, we're not here tonight to point fingers. Tonight, we're here to find a solution—to whatever awaits us."

Murmurs erupted around the room.

The host pressed on. "Consider how vulnerable we are. A solar flare could destroy our planet in the blink of an eye. A supervolcano could blot out the sun, and starve us and freeze us into extinction. Would we stand a chance against an alien invasion? Perhaps our end will come from an old enemy: a pandemic—maybe a more deadly version of a pathogen we've already lived through."

A sea breeze swept in through the doors, tugging at the man's white hair.

"And there's another great question that should haunt us all: why do we seem to be alone in the universe? Is that a clue to our true destiny? Tonight, I'd like to propose a simple solution to those twin enigmas that have always haunted us."

He held his hands out to the crowd, palms up.

"We know the truth: we can't stop what's coming. We can't prevent the next extinction event. What we can do... is control what happens after. That is the key to the future."

He let his hands drop to his sides.

"What I'm proposing is a new kind of experiment. A project with one purpose: to restart the human race after the Fall. A project that will witness the rebirth of our species and unravel the deepest secrets of our existence. I'm calling it the Extinction Trials, and I want you to be part of it."

PART I

THE FALL

CHAPTER ONE

Every morning, before work, Owen Watts visited the nursing home.

The halls were mostly empty. Only a few doors stood open. Residents sat outside their rooms, knitting or reading, glancing up as he passed, most staring at his uniform.

At his mother's door, he paused and peered in.

Owen had a dangerous job, but that moment every morning was easily the most frightening he faced every day. One morning, he knew he would find the room empty. The narrow bed made. His mother's pictures and belongings gone.

But not today.

She sat in a chair by the window, a book in her lap.

He breathed out as he crossed the threshold, his heavy footfalls drawing his mother's attention, and instantly, a smile.

Life had taught Owen the value of time. How precious it was. How quickly things changed.

His work had left scars on his body. Life had left a few on his soul. They were what made him cling to the time he had left with his mother.

"Reading anything good?" he asked as he took the seat across from her.

"Well, I just started. But it looks promising. An original premise. And a likable main character."

She studied him a moment. "What's the matter?"

"Nothing."

She cocked her head.

"Work," he said simply, hoping she would drop it, knowing she wouldn't.

"What about work?"

"Work... is getting weird."

"Weird how?"

"Weird as in I'm slowly being replaced by robots."

"It's safer that way."

"True."

"You're worried about what you'll do next—when the robots have completely replaced your job."

Owen smiled. "You can read me like one of those books."

"That's what mothers are for." She paused. "I know what's really bothering you."

He raised an eyebrow.

"Your limitation."

Growing up, Owen's mother and father never used the word handicap. *Limitation*—that's the word they used. Because everyone has limitations.

"Can I bore you with a piece of advice?" she asked.

He exhaled and nodded.

"Life isn't about your limitations. They matter far less than you think. You make a living doing what you're good at. That's what's important—your strengths, not your limitations."

"I'm going to put that on a t-shirt. That'll be my new job. T-shirt salesman."

She smiled. "Always a tough one. But I know you listen too. And I know you'll land on your feet. You just need a little faith. In yourself, most of all."

She reached over to the bookcase and took out a small paperback and handed it to him.

He read the title: *The Birthright*. He opened it and flipped to the first page and read it:

"Every human is born with a birthright. That birthright is happiness. Our greatest challenge to achieving happiness is not the obstacles we encounter in our life. The true barrier to happiness lies inside of us—and it's the one thing we can't ever escape: our own mind.

"From birth, we are educated on countless aspects of life, from personal hygiene to personal finance, but there is no widely accepted curriculum for understanding and managing our minds. Indeed, almost every human remains the victim of their own mind throughout their entire life, never learning to master it, or manage it, or even understand it. *The Birthright* was written to change that. This book is an owner's manual for a human mind. If you read it and do the maintenance it recommends, your mind will run smoothly. It will break down less often, and in the end, it will take you to your birthright. Indeed, a well-tuned mind is the only road to true and lasting happiness."

Owen closed the book. "It's not exactly... my type of thing."

"Your type of thing?"

"Self-help books."

"It's not a self-help book—not that there's anything wrong with them. *The Birthright* is a book about science and psychology, and most of all, understanding yourself and the world around you."

"Wonderful," he muttered. "By the time I read it, the world will probably be changed again."

"The world is always changing. Always will be. The key to success is accepting that the world will keep changing. The ideas in that book transcend worlds and time."

Owen's armband buzzed. The three fast pulses signaled an emergency alert. He activated the band and read the message.

"Sorry, Mom, my disappearing job needs me."

"An alarm?"

"Probably just a false alarm. See you tomorrow morning."

He hugged her and turned to leave, but she called to him, "Owen, don't forget the book."

Fifteen minutes later, Owen was in the front seat of the fire truck, barreling through the city, sirens blaring. The truck wirelessly shut down the traffic lights and crosswalks ahead. Driverless cars pulled to the side and waited as the hulking vehicle rumbled past.

Owen studied a tablet and called to his two teammates behind him.

"It's a kitchen fire. Oasis Park Building. Eleventh floor, unit 1107. Auto fire suppression has already extinguished it."

He was about to continue when the pleasant computer voice of the central AI came over the truck's speakers.

"The apartment building has fifteen floors and seven hundred and twenty-three registered residents. Scout drones confirm sixty-five infrared signatures currently inside. There is one adult female and one juvenile female in unit 1107. Vital signs normal."

Owen set his tablet down, annoyed. The AI didn't even trust him to give the briefing. What bothered Owen the most was that he had to admit the AI was more efficient at the briefing than him. And, in a raging fire, he was glad to have the robots there. They never panicked. They were built to withstand extreme temperatures. Most of all, they were replaceable. Humans were not.

He didn't miss the danger of fighting fires. But some days—a lot of days lately—he missed going home after his shift and feeling like he had made a difference in someone's life.

This assignment would probably be like the last ten: he'd investigate the source of the fire (likely human error), explain what happened to the resident, and provide safety tips on how to avoid future fires.

The two firefighters in the backseat had each been on the job less than a year. They were staring out the window with the same sense of excitement Owen had felt fifteen years ago when he had joined the department. He wondered what they would be doing in fifteen years. If they would even be needed.

Another alert popped up on the screen. A resident in unit 403 in the same building had just reported a gas leak. The unit's safety detector hadn't gone off. That was strange. Maybe the resident was confused.

"Selena, take 403. Confirm the gas levels and do a welfare check on the resident. Call an ambulance if they seem disoriented."

"Copy, Lieutenant." She smiled, seeming happy to have her first solo assignment.

"Cole, we'll take 1107. Pay attention. You're taking the lead on the next one."

He nodded. "Yes, sir."

On the tablet, three more alerts appeared in buildings across the city—all gas leaks. That was *very* odd. Was it a malfunction in the detectors? Or maybe a prank: kids hacking the sensors and making false reports.

As the truck rolled to a stop, the rescue drones took flight. They would circle the building, waiting, arms at the ready to take anyone who needed to be evacuated from the building.

Firebots detached from the truck and marched toward the building, clanking on four legs, long arms outstretched, fire suppression tanks on their backs like jetpacks.

Owen stepped out and led his team into the building, the sixty pounds of suit and kit barely slowing him. He climbed the stairs as protocol required, feet pounding on the concrete. At the seventh-floor landing, he was barely winded, but Cole leaned over, panting, hands on his knees. Sweat covered his face behind the clear mask.

"Gotta log more gym time," Owen called over the radio. "Training is half the job. Always—"

"Be prepared," Cole said between gasps. "Copy that, sir." A few seconds later, he said, "I'm ready."

At apartment 1107, Owen pressed the doorbell with his gloved hand and waited. Cole was still breathing heavily behind his mask. When no response came, Owen pressed the doorbell again.

"Central, confirm occupants and vitals in 1107."

"One adult female. One juvenile female. Both vitals normal."

Owen banged on the door. Maybe the ringer was malfunctioning.

"Selena, what's your status?"

He stabbed the doorbell and pounded the door again while he waited.

No response.

"Selena, do you copy?"

Silence over the radio.

"Central, confirm Selena's location and status."

"Selena is in unit 403. Vitals normal. Communication systems check failure."

Cole stepped closer. "Want me to check on her?"

"No. Let's get a status here first." Owen eyed the door. "Central, open unit 1107."

The lock clicked and Owen strode in and stopped cold.

A woman about his mother's age lay on the floor. He rushed to her, jerked the thick outer glove off his right hand, and exhaled when he felt a faint pulse.

"Central, send an ambulance. Adult female unconscious. Probably asphyxiation."

Owen glanced at his arm panel. Oxygen level normal. The panel had to be malfunctioning too. And so was central: it had confirmed normal vitals. The occupant was out cold.

Something was wrong here.

He replaced his glove and the suit re-pressurized.

"Central, I'm ordering a mandatory building evac.

Possible gas leak and fire risk. Broadcast it and have the bots execute."

"Confirmed, Lieutenant."

"Selena," Owen said, standing up. "If you read me, get out of the building."

It didn't add up. This many malfunctions? It was impossible.

The apartment was likely filled with gas. The unconscious woman indicated that. Unless she had been affected by something else? An intruder. Or a medical condition. Better safe than sorry.

"Central, vent unit 1107."

Owen stared at the floor-to-ceiling windows in the living room, waiting for one to open slightly.

Nothing happened.

"Central, I repeat, vent unit 1107."

No response.

"Vent it, Cole."

"Sir?"

"Get your ax out and make a big hole in that window. Right now."

The young man had only used his ax in training a few times—and probably never expected to use it in the field, except perhaps in the oldest homes, and only after the firebots were destroyed, and he was the last line of defense. But Owen was proud to see his younger teammate unsheathe the shiny ax and charge toward the window.

Owen dashed down the hall, throwing doors open as he went. The second door on the left opened to a child's bedroom. Posters of teen idols covered the walls. A jewelry box sat on a table, cheap imitation necklaces and bracelets spilling out as if it was a treasure chest waiting in an undiscovered cave. On the narrow bed lay a young girl, eyes closed, unmoving.

Owen moved like a man possessed, quickly, automatically. He scooped her up, kicked in the door to the bathroom, and laid her gently in the tub. He was about to check her pulse when fire exploded through the apartment.

CHAPTER TWO

If the pain didn't stop soon, Maya Young was certain she would die.

Her muscles burned.

Her heart hammered in her chest.

Her pulse throbbed in her neck.

Her body was drenched in sweat.

She wasn't alone in her misery. The cycling class was filled to capacity, thirty women pedaling their stationary bikes to the music, huffing, glancing up periodically at the instructor, who was barely winded. The woman was a mix of a suburban mom and a military drill instructor. Her friendly, housewife exterior hid a merciless personality that seemed to delight in inflicting pain on those in her spinning class.

"Come on, ladies, one final push!" the instructor yelled. "Crank it up and let's do this. No pain, no gain!"

Maya reached down and turned the bike's resistance dial—just one click. She heard others cranking even higher, the sound like a hundred camera snaps going off at once, the clicks a disembodied guilt trip saying, "Why aren't you turning yours higher like everyone else?"

She pumped the pedals, breathing hard. It felt like her

bike had bottomed out in quicksand. She better get a ton of gain for this pain. Speaking of, if she ever met the person who first said, "No pain, no gain," she would punch that person in the face. Hard.

After what seemed like an eternity, the instructor stopped pedaling and began clapping.

"Okay, that's it! Nice job, everyone. See you again tomorrow. Reminder to check the schedule online tonight. Enrollment for the next eight classes opens at six."

Maya stepped off the bike and staggered on wobbling legs to the lockers. When she had first toured the gym, she had fallen in love with the cycling studio, with its exposed rafters, antique brick walls, and shining wood floor. Now she barely noticed. It was just a really well-decorated torture chamber.

Outside, sirens blared. A moment later, a fire truck rumbled past the plate glass windows, red and blue lights flashing. Maya paused at her locker to watch.

When the truck was gone and the siren had faded, Maya's friend Zoe closed her locker and said, "Guilty confession: hoping the class is full by the time I log in tonight."

"Same," Candice said, pulling her messenger bag on. "I've got two, maybe three weeks max left in me. Remind me again why we're doing this?"

Maya, Zoe, and Candice had made the current exercise pact late one night while slightly intoxicated. At the time, it had seemed like an unquestionably good idea.

"I think," Maya said, "it had something to do with becoming more attractive, finding a mate, and advancing life stages."

Zoe glanced up theatrically as if contemplating. "If this

is the cost of mating and advancing life stages, I'm opting out. I'm okay with being slightly overweight for the rest of my life. And single."

A crackling laugh erupted from Maya, almost involuntarily. Her lungs hurt—she assumed from the exertion. The laugh turned to a cough, and she brought a hand up to cover her mouth. She froze when she saw the red specks. She stared for a moment in disbelief.

Candice moved closer, squinting at the red droplets on Maya's hand.

"Hey, are you okay?"

A wave of dizziness washed over Maya. Her legs went numb. She reached out for the locker door but couldn't grip it. The floor rushed up as her vision spotted. She felt arms around her, someone saying, "Maya?"

Then muffled voices. Someone prying her eyes open. And finally:

"Call an ambulance!"

CHAPTER THREE

The blast threw Owen against the wall.

Fire reached into the room like a hand, fingers red and orange, singeing everything they touched, racing across the floor, charring the bath mat and flowing over the lip of the tub, reaching for the girl. Her clothes burned. Her hair caught fire. Flames licked her face.

Owen's vision spotted as he watched helplessly, willing his stunned body to move.

He bent forward and reached out with his gloved hand and stamped out the fire in her hair and clothes.

"External speaker on," he said between gasps. "Can you hear me?"

Her eyelids lifted slightly, revealing bloodshot, watery eyes and a far-away look. Her lips parted, but no words came.

Another explosion rocked the apartment.

Owen leaned forward, hovering over her, his core muscles straining under the suit's weight.

No fire seeped into the room this time.

He was sure then about what the explosion had been: the apartment door had blown open. Pressure—or an explosion—in the hall had been strong enough to take it off its hinges. The building shouldn't have let that happen. It should be suppressing any fires, and venting any pressure and smoke to the roof.

There was something very wrong here.

"Hang in there," he said through the suit speaker. "I'm going to get you out of here."

The girl closed her eyes as Owen lifted her and ran back to the living room.

As he suspected, the outer door to the apartment was gone. In the living room window, there was a gaping hole where it had exited the unit. Fire raged in the hallway, sucking oxygen from the opening.

Cole sat on the floor, blinking.

"Central, I need multiple evacs at 1107. Stat."

No response came.

Cole pushed up on his legs and staggered over, mouth moving but no sound coming over Owen's radio.

"Cole, can you hear me?"

The younger man just stared. His chest was heaving, from nerves or exhaustion or both. He reached up to pull his helmet off, but Owen reached out, caught his hand, and mouthed, *No*. They needed the helmets and the suits more than they needed to communicate.

"Any firebots, do you copy?"

Silence again.

Owen mentally rifled through the options. He needed to get to the window and flag an evac drone. Still holding the girl in his arms, he marched over and peered out, expecting to see one or more of the hovering monstrous drones, arms outstretched, waiting.

But none were there.

What he did see shocked him.

And terrified him.

The city was burning.

Fires consumed every building in sight, raging behind glass and bursting through windows and sending black plumes into the sky. Apartment buildings, office buildings, stores—they were all burning. How? It was impossible. This couldn't be real. For a moment, he almost felt listless, the weight of the girl lying limp in his arms gone, his limbs wavering. His gaze drifted down to the eight-story brick building across the alley. It was burning too, but the roof was clear. Its vents hadn't worked either.

Movement at the door caught Owen's attention, snapping him out of the haze. A firebot sauntered into the room on four charred legs.

"Firebot, we need evac—"

The bot lifted an arm and sprayed sticky white fire suppressant. It hit Cole directly in the faceplate, blinding him.

Owen's first thought was that the bot had malfunctioned. It must have assumed that Cole was on fire. Then it turned its arm to fire at Owen. He turned just in time to feel the white substance coat his side and the girl.

The floor vibrated as the bot bounded forward, arms outstretched, charging toward Owen.

It was a nightmare.

The bot was built to withstand fire and carry a family from a burning building. Owen didn't stand a chance against it. On his own, he might last a few seconds. Holding the girl... it was hopeless.

Owen bent to set the girl down, ready to fight—

But the bot slammed into the floor face first, front legs mashed together.

Cole. Even blinded by the suppressant on his helmet, the young man had lunged for the bot—a desperate move that had worked. He had caught its legs and held tight.

With his arms still around the bot's legs, he reached a hand up and cleared the fire suppressant from his faceplate. The bot reached back and dug its pincers into Cole's arm. Owen saw Cole's mouth fly open, a silent scream. But still, the young firefighter held on, trying desperately to keep the bot down. He wouldn't succeed much longer. He looked up at Owen, eyes full of tears, and he mouthed a single word.

Go.

Owen bent down, picked up the girl and glanced at the open doorway. Fire raged beyond. And more firebots were waiting in the building.

Behind him, the gaping hole left by the door looked out on the burning city. And the building below.

Owen turned, gripped the girl tight to his chest, and ran as fast as he could through the window.

CHAPTER FOUR

Maya awoke to a loud droning all around her. She was lying on her back on a cold, hard surface.

Her mind was cloudy, as though she had been drugged and it was only now wearing off, its effects still lingering.

She squinted at the bright light circling her. She was in a cylinder not much bigger than Maya herself.

A woman's voice came over a speaker, booming in the small space.

"Please stay still, Miss Young. The test is almost complete."

"Test for what?" Maya shouted over the hum of the machine.

"We'll explain soon. Just lie still, please."

After that, the seconds ticked by like an eternity. The machine buzzed rhythmically. A blue light inside the cylinder's white walls moved up and down the length of her body.

Finally, it beeped, and the glow dimmed and the table holding her slid out. A man in green scrubs pushed a wheelchair in, parked it beside the table, and held out a hand for Maya.

Instinctively, she froze.

Something was wrong here.

Something about the man put her on edge. She didn't recognize him, but silent alerts blared in her mind. Was it the glint in his staring eyes? His physique?

Or was she imagining it all? Was it the haze of whatever sedative they had given her for the test?

She sat up and swung her legs off the hard platform, aware that the hospital gown would gape open. The man kept his eyes fixed on her, his hand held out. Was that another clue? Or was he a genuine human being just doing his job?

"What's going on?" Maya asked, hoping his answer might offer clues to two questions running through her mind.

"Not my department, ma'am. I'm just transport."

She took his hand and he guided her to the wheelchair. Without another word, he pushed her through the halls, where nurses both human and robotic bustled about and doctors spoke orders and questions into headsets connected to the hospital AI.

Her room held a single, narrow bed and a small bathroom in the corner. Maya's clothes hung on the back of the door. Her handbag lay on a rolling bedside table. But it was the view out the window that drew her attention. Three columns of black smoke rose across the city.

She needed to check in. The fires could be part of an attack that was related to the organization she had been investigating.

She was so consumed with the scene outside that she didn't hear the door click shut. Or the man moving behind her.

She felt a cold, flat object press against her neck.

Then, her training and instincts took over.

Adrenaline shot through her bloodstream—apparently enough to save her.

She leaned away.

Just in time.

The injector fired and clicked but didn't make contact with her skin.

Instead of trying to flee the man, she did what he least expected. He was bigger than her. And he was in a superior position. What he wasn't expecting was for her to attack.

She grabbed the injector, momentarily shocking him. He leaned forward, reaching for it, but Maya was quicker. She stabbed it into his neck and pressed the trigger—once, twice, and a third time, his eyes growing wider with the sound of each click. Then, like a switch had been thrown, his face grew slack, eyes went glassy, grip loosened. He staggered, reached up to his ear, and held a finger behind it.

"Mission... fail. Subject... escaping. Backup—"

He collapsed in a heap.

Maya stood on shaking legs and held on to the end of the bed as she shuffled to the side table that held her handbag. She had to hurry. His backup could be seconds away. She drew out her armband from the handbag and activated it.

"Ops," a female voice said.

"I'm compromised."

"Cover?"

"Blown."

Maya's head was pounding now, from the drugs or the exertion, she wasn't sure. Or from her condition, whatever that was—and she had a very good idea of what that was.

"Request?" the voice asked, still betraying no emotion. Maya wondered if it was a real person or an AI. She held the armband as she moved to collect her clothes from the bathroom door.

"Immediate backup."

"Routing request."

"And I'm sick. I think they did something to me. I think I have the Genesis Virus." She glanced at the columns of smoke. There were five now. Black clouds filling the sky. "What's happening out there? The fires?"

"Probable cyberterror attack. We're investigating—"

"It's them. It's connected. I think they tried to take me out before they launched this attack."

"Noted."

Maya was about to pull on her clothes but reconsidered. She eyed the man on the floor, his chest slowly rising and falling.

She was in no shape to run. Or fight. Without the injector, she wouldn't have stood a chance against the man.

That left one option: hiding. But there was something she had to do first.

"I need you to check on my family," Maya said. "My mom and sister live in the Oasis Park Building. In unit 1107."

"Confirmed."

At the window, she peered down. Seven auto ambulances were parked directly below. As she watched, one pulled away, lights flashing on.

The window didn't open fully, but she could push it out slightly, just enough to slip the armband and her clothes through and drop them on top of an ambulance.

Her first choice was to leave the room and put some distance between her and whoever was coming. But that was too risky, and she wasn't moving very well.

The bathroom was too exposed.

The bed was open below, offering no cover.

That left the closet. She opened the door and peered inside. It was empty, only a single metal rod and two hangers.

She pulled two sheets from the bed, wrapped one around herself, and draped the other over the rod. She slipped behind it and pulled the closet door closed.

Her legs were still shaking.

She pressed herself against the back wall and let herself slide down until she was lying on the floor. She arranged the sheet around her to cover her feet and head, then tucked her arms inside.

Beyond the closet, she heard the door to the patient room open.

CHAPTER FIVE

Owen held the girl tight and twisted, turning his back toward the roof looming below. Pain lanced through his chest when he crashed down. The girl flew from his arms as his vision faded to black.

When he came to, he wasn't sure how much time had passed. He coughed hard, lungs aching. He forced his eyes open.

Smoke swirled around him like a thousand ghosts dancing around a funeral pyre.

Through the wisps, he caught a glimpse of his surroundings. He was still on the roof, lying on his side.

The girl was ten feet away.

Unmoving.

He watched her as he drew shallow, ragged breaths.

He waited, hoping, willing her to move.

He twisted his head, drawing a shooting pain from his neck.

He tried to take a deep breath, but it was useless. One or both of his lungs were collapsed. He didn't have long.

With a shaking hand, he reached over to his arm panel,

which was flashing wildly with alerts. He was about to activate the emergency beacon, but the suit had already done it. At least that part of the AI was still functioning.

A high-pitched alarm sounded from his external suit speakers. His helmet emitted a strobe light that blasted across the roof toward the girl.

Teeth gritted, he pushed off with his right arm and rolled onto his back, letting the light shine into the air.

He doubted anyone would see it. Smoke filled the sky like a thousand dark birds circling the city, diving down to feed on the burning, crumbling buildings.

He tried to slow his breathing, fighting to keep his eyes open. But his breaths grew tighter, as though he were breathing through a shrinking straw.

He tried to turn his head, but the pain stopped him. His head broke out in sweat and his chest burned through the pain, but he pushed, turning his head. He wanted to see her. He wanted to see her roll over and look at him and for her to be okay.

He watched, but she still didn't move.

A moment passed.

Black clouds tumbled over each other and piled up, a smoky ceiling lowering down onto him, a coffin door closing.

His breaths grew shorter until it felt like he couldn't breathe at all, as though there was nothing to fill beyond his throat. Even when he forced his eyes open, there was darkness, splotches flowing together at the edges.

The suit was either torn or punctured because he tasted smoke in his mouth and nose now. The black clouds had engulfed the roof. He willed his vision to clear as he gazed through burning eyes, trying to find the girl, hoping to see her moving. He saw only a billowing black curtain.

Suddenly, the clouds parted, the black swatted away like demons reeling back. Owen couldn't believe what he saw: a helicopter—with a human pilot. He hadn't seen that in a long, long time.

Like his job, flying a helicopter was dangerous. They flew themselves now. Or most new ones did.

This helicopter was older, and it bounced as it set down on the roof, and two medics jumped out, carrying a stretcher, running toward him.

With his last strength and breath, Owen lifted his arm, held out his finger, hand trembling, and pointed away from himself, toward the girl.

CHAPTER SIX

In the closet, Maya listened to the footfalls, trying to count how many people had entered the room.

Two, she thought.

A man was the first to speak.

"Her handbag is here. Clothes are gone."

A woman spoke next. She was closer to Maya, bending over the man on the floor, perhaps.

"Leon, can you hear me?"

"Bring him around," the man said.

Maya heard a click, then a long, low groan from the man on the ground.

"What happened, Leon?" the other man asked, closer now.

"She... got away—"

"She's half your size and infected with GV—"

"That doesn't matter," the woman said flatly. "Where is she, Leon?"

The man said nothing. But Maya heard the other two moving about the room. He must have pointed. Or shaken his head.

The door to the bathroom opened. Someone stepped inside.

Then the closet door swung out. A hand reached in, snatched the sheet hanging over the rod, and pulled it out. Maya felt it tugging at the sheet that covered her below.

She held her breath.

"Just linens," the man said as he tossed the sheet back into the closet. It fell on top of her as the door banged shut.

"Polestar," the woman said. "We need a location on subject seven-four-one."

"Who cares?" the man spat out. "She's got GV. And the Change is happening as we speak."

"Great," the woman muttered. "She's in an ambulance four blocks from here."

"Just let her go," the man said.

"We can't. She knows too much. Come on."

Maya's plan was to wait in the closet until the door to the room opened again. She assumed that the next person to open that door would be her backup.

But the door didn't open.

The help she needed never arrived.

She didn't know how much time had passed, but she was starting to feel weak. She felt wetness on her upper lip—what she thought was sweat.

She wiped it away with her fingers, felt the stickiness, and knew it was blood.

She unwrapped the sheet around her and pushed the closet door open.

The room was dark. Was it night?

Had it been that long?

Then she realized: it wasn't night. Smoke blotted out the sun. The city was burning.

Another trickle of blood ran from her nose. A throb of pain erupted in her head.

Her legs buckled. She extended a blood-soaked hand to the bed, gripped the rail, and pressed the call button.

"I need help."

CHAPTER SEVEN

Owen's hearing returned first, but his vision wouldn't clear. He lay in darkness, listening to the voices around him. They were muffled and far away, flowing together, as if he were at the bottom of a well, and the people at the surface, talking about him.

One voice finally broke through the din. It was a man, his tone gruff and weary.

"... multiple fractures... punctured lung. Under normal circumstances, he's out of here in two weeks. But as things stand, I think we have to label him category ten. Nine at best."

A woman's voice: "His injuries—"

"Are quite treatable," the gruff man said. "But our issue, frankly, is time. He should be in intensive care. And he would be in there for two weeks. Minimum. We could use that bed to save thirty people in that time. Let's move on."

The woman: "Wait. Can we talk about this? What happened to him?"

"He jumped from a building."

"Third one in a row for me," another man said.

The woman again: "Wait, I just found his file. He's a

firefighter. Saved a young girl. She's probably going to make it." A pause. "Look, we've got—"

"Katarina, we can't do this all day, okay? We've got to keep moving. He's a ten."

A silent moment stretched out.

Then the gruff man again: "Fine. Fine. We'll put an eight on him and that's as far as I can go."

When Owen woke again, his vision had returned.

It still hurt to breathe. Both legs throbbed in pain. The left was far worse.

He was in a large open room. He heard voices all around him, some talking, others crying out, an unsynchronized chorus of agony. A white sheet hung from a cord that surrounded his bed on four sides, preventing him from seeing the other patients.

He tried to sit up, but the pain held him down.

He lay there, staring at the ceiling, his thoughts touching places that hurt as much as his body: first, his fellow firefighters—Cole and Selena. Had they made it?

They were in the building.

And the girl from 1107? The doctors who had argued over him had said she would make it. Had she?

Finally, his mind settled on his mother. Was she alive? Safe?

How much time had passed?

And where was he?

The ceiling above was high, and from the way the sound echoed around him, he assumed the room was cavernous. A warehouse, perhaps?

Faint footsteps approached, and he leaned his head up just in time to see a nurse bot stride into his cubicle, its body covered in shiny silver metal and milky-white plastic. The head was a weak attempt at human form: the face was nearly flat, with a glass screen that showed an image of eyes and a mouth, but could likely display vitals and other information to patients and doctors. The bot held an injector in its left hand.

"Get away from me." Owen's words came out awkwardly, as if he had a mouthful of dirt.

The bot stopped. "You are due for your pain medication—"

"If you come closer, I'll bash your glass face in."

"Are you refusing treatment?"

"Get out."

"Without pain medication, you will—"

"Get out. *Now.*"

It turned and marched away without another word. Seeing it reminded Owen of the firebot that had sprayed Cole and pinned him down. His rage built as he thought about it.

He was still stewing over that when a tall man with close-cropped hair pulled back the white sheet to Owen's cubicle and entered. The man's eyes were focused yet expressionless. He wore a ribbed black sweater that only partially hid a muscular physique. Owen figured him for military.

"Mr. Watts, my name is Parrish. I'd like to ask you some questions."

"I'd like to ask you some too."

A smile tugged at the edges of Parrish's mouth and quickly disappeared. "Mind if I go first?"

Owen nodded.

"You responded to a fire alarm in the Oasis Park Building. In unit 1107."

"That's right."

"You jumped out of a window carrying a young girl. What happened to her?"

Owen stared a moment, then laughed. "That was going to be my first question for you. She's not here?"

"No."

Silence stretched out. Then Parrish asked, "Do you know what happened to her mother?"

"She was in the apartment when we arrived, alive but unconscious."

Parrish nodded, seeming to consider that.

"Can you tell me what happened to my team? Cole and Selena?"

Parrish shook his head. "No. I'm sorry. I don't know."

"What's happening out there?"

"We think the fires were part of a widespread terror attack."

"The firebot attacked my crew."

"There have been similar reports around the world. Someone hacked the robots and AI and embedded systems."

"Who?"

"We believe a scientific terror group is responsible. But there are other possibilities."

"Such as?"

"An artificial intelligence uprising. Alien invasion. Some even think it's the government."

"Why hack the bots? What's the reasoning behind the attack?"

"That's also unknown. There are rumors that this event is the start of something called the Change. But we don't know what that is yet."

"What organization did you say you were with?"

"I didn't say." Parrish turned to leave. "Thank you for your help."

"Wait."

Parrish paused.

"Is my family okay? My mother?"

"Sorry. I don't know."

Parrish grabbed the white sheet, ready to pull it back and leave, but something caught his eye. He leaned over the chair where Owen's clothes and firesuit lay crumpled, and he picked up the paperback copy of *The Birthright*.

"This yours?"

"Yeah," Owen replied.

Parrish turned and looked at Owen with renewed interest. "Where'd you get it?"

"My mother gave it to me."

Parrish walked back to the bed, laid the book at Owen's side, and picked up the medical tablet hanging on the bed rail. Whoever the man was, his retinal scan gave him access to the information.

"Eight," Parrish mumbled as he read, his face betraying a shred of disappointment.

"What's an eight?" Owen asked. "What does that mean?"

"It means this is probably the last stop for you."

Parrish scrolled through the information, then glanced back down at the book by Owen's side.

"But it shouldn't be."

CHAPTER EIGHT

Maya woke in a hospital bed in a large open space. Curtains divided the makeshift patient rooms.

Muffled conversations and cries of pain filled the space. She listened for a moment, hoping for clues as to where she was.

Her head pounded. Moving—even slightly—caused a low, throbbing pain. She winced as she sat up.

It wasn't just the pain: her brain was foggy, probably a result of whatever drugs they had given her. They impaired her movement too. Her limbs felt three times heavier than normal. She wanted desperately to get out of bed, to get dressed, and get out of here. She needed to escape; she knew that much, but to her surprise, she didn't know why.

She felt the urge to get somewhere. An image came into her mind—of her mother. Yes, that was it. She needed to find her mother. And sister. But why? Instinctively, she felt that they were in danger. But from what?

Beyond the curtain, three figures stopped in the corridor, their shadows looming, voices low.

Maya fought to sit up, straining to make out their words.

"… scan unlike anything I've seen."

"… not equipped to deal with anything like this."

"Just put ten for now."

A machine on a metal pole by the bed beeped. Liquid flowed into the IV running to Maya's arm, and a few seconds later, sleep overtook her.

A man was standing over her when Maya awoke. Instantly, she tried to reel back, but her body still wouldn't cooperate.

He put a hand on her shoulder and pushed her down into the bed.

"Hey, relax. It's me."

The man had close-cropped hair and wore a black ribbed sweater.

"Can you see me, Maya? It's Parrish."

Her voice came out breathy and labored. "I can see you."

"But you don't know who I am?"

Maya shook her head.

His grip on her shoulder loosened as he exhaled, voice now a whisper. "What have they done to you?"

"Who? What's wrong with me?"

"We believe you're infected with the Genesis Virus. Or GV. Do you recognize that name?"

It sounded vaguely familiar, but try as she might, Maya couldn't form a thought about what it was. She shook her head.

Parrish pressed on. "What about Genesis Biosciences? Do you know what that is?"

The words triggered a memory in Maya's mind.

She saw herself walking through a security checkpoint and scanning a plastic ID. After a beep, she stepped forward and stared into a retinal scanner, which flashed green. A door ahead opened, revealing a large lobby with a wide desk, where three guards sat, watching screens. A lighted sign above read "Genesis Biosciences", with a tag line in slanted letters below: *Infinite Better Tomorrows.*

Maya wove her way through the building's crowded corridors to a locked door, where she stooped to bring her eye level with the retinal scan. It flashed and promptly gave her access to a small room. She stepped inside, and as soon as the door behind her closed, one to her right opened, revealing a locker room where two women were undressing.

"Morning, Maya," one of them called over her shoulder.

"Hi, Sydney. How's Oscar?"

"Slept through the night. First time."

"Victory!"

"I might actually get some work done today."

Maya made her way to a cubby with a digital display that read, "Dr. Maya Young."

She stripped down naked, folded her clothes neatly and retrieved a tight-fitting undergarment from the shelf and slipped it on.

The next room held six airtight suits with tanks on the back. She suited up and entered the airlock... and then the memory ended.

"I used to work there."

Parrish lifted his head, smiling quickly. "Yes." He nodded. "You did."

"I worked in a lab."

"Exactly."

"I was a scientist."

Parrish cocked his head and spoke slowly, carefully. "Yes... technically."

"Technically? What does that mean?"

"It means… your life was somewhat complicated."

"Could you possibly be any more vague right now?"

Parrish eyed the white curtain around them. Beyond, dozens of muffled conversations were interrupted by the occasional shout or wail. "This is not really the place to discuss it, Maya." He placed a hand on her shoulder, gently. "I used to call you Hazel. Because of your hazel eyes. Do you remember that? It was your… code name. Does that bring back any memories?"

"No."

Parrish nodded, seeming disappointed. "Do you remember what you were working on? Please, it's important."

Maya tried to go back to the memory, but it was gone, like a dream that was fully formed upon waking but slipped away in the moments after.

"No."

Parrish nodded, clearly disappointed. "That's okay. Do you know what the Change is?"

"The Change?"

"It's some kind of project. Or process. Or event. We're not sure. Do you remember anything about it?"

"No."

"Do you remember meeting me? The first time we met?"

"I'm sorry. I don't."

"You and I were going to meet again—today. You were going to give me something. Do you know where that item is?"

Maya focused, trying to retrace her steps. She remembered being in the hospital. Being scanned. Hiding. From whom?

"No. All I remember is getting sick. And hiding. Someone was looking for me."

"We're dealing with that."

"How?"

"We're going to get you out of here and take you somewhere safe."

"Where?"

"That's... also complicated."

Maya exhaled. "What *can* you tell me?"

"I can tell you that you're going to be okay. And we're looking for your mother and sister."

PART II

THE STATION

CHAPTER NINE

When Owen awoke, the pain was gone.

Except for his eyes. A dull ache started there and radiated into his head.

He opened his eyes, but he saw only white—and felt more pain.

He shut them tight and listened. It was utterly quiet, the only sound the soft beating of his heart. That in itself was strange—the idea that he could hear his own heart beating.

He reached up, but his hands almost instantly hit a solid wall. It didn't feel like a wall, more like a block of ice. The surface was frigid. The impact made an echoing gong sound in the space.

He realized then that the wall he had hit wasn't ice. It was glass. With each passing moment, his mind seemed to work a little better. Sensation throughout his body returned.

Carefully, he raised his hand and felt the frigid glass that surrounded him. He was in a cylinder of some sort, that much was certain. He was completely naked. Tubes were attached to both of his arms.

He tried opening his eyes again. Slowly, the white he saw resolved into a view of the ceiling and three lights there, distorted by the curvature of the glass cylinder that held him. Somewhere beyond his view, a red light flashed, strobing the room.

A loud pop sounded and the glass rose. Air hissed in— cold air, hitting him like an electric shock, making him convulse.

An alarm blared—the sharp sound synchronized with the flashing red.

The cold, the pain from the light, and the piercing alarm overwhelmed Owen, a sensory assault smothering him.

He closed his eyes and was curling into a ball when strong hands grabbed his arms and hauled him up and out of the cylinder. The person didn't even bother to disconnect the tubes in his arms. The lines jerked free with a stab of pain that was only barely noticeable over the chill pressing into him.

His feet hit the floor, which was so cold it sent a wave of shock up from his feet.

"Put these on." The voice was male, calm, serene even—a stark contrast to the alarm.

Owen cracked his eyes enough to see a young man, slender and lanky, with short blond hair. The man pressed a black sweater into Owen's hands. It was thick and ribbed, with something sewn inside. Owen pulled it on immediately. The man pressed a finger into a chest patch on the sweater, and it instantly began heating up, infusing Owen's torso with warmth.

Still, his breath came out in a puff of white fog, his voice scratchy, as if he hadn't used it in a very long time. "Who... are you?"

"Call me Bryce." The young man reached for a pair of pants and boots that lay on a silver metal cart nearby.

Without a word, Owen slipped them on. Bryce bent over and tapped similar patches on each, and the garments warmed.

Suddenly, the lights snapped off, plunging the room into darkness except for the glow of the panel beside the glass cylinder and the red strobe light.

Then the lights came back on, flickering, unsteady at first.

"Where—"

"I'll tell you what I know," Bryce said quickly, grabbing Owen's arm. "But first, I need you to help me wake the others."

The young man pulled Owen forward with surprising strength.

For the first time, Owen took in the room. There were seven glass cylinders similar to the one he had emerged from—all empty. Several metal carts were strewn about, also empty. Three screens covered the far wall, all off, one cracked.

Bryce tugged him toward the door until Owen fell in behind him, struggling to keep up. It was as though his body was slowly coming alive again.

Outside the room was a narrow hallway where the alarm droned and red light pulsed.

In the hallway, Owen glanced back at the lighted control panel beside the door to the room where he had woken up. It read "POD 12". Across the way, a door panel read "POD 13". Beyond it, the door read "POD 15", and "POD 17" past that.

The long corridor stretched out to the left and right, terminating at what looked like an airlock at each end.

"Hurry," Bryce said as he sprinted down the hall. He

paused and motioned to an open door. "I'll wake them. Please take them to this room and wait for me."

Catching up, Owen read the screen beside the door: "OBSERVATION 2".

"Wake who?" Owen asked.

"There's no time to explain," Bryce said. He rushed to a door nearby that read "POD 10", and he pressed his thumb into the control panel. The door swooshed open, revealing a room exactly like the one Owen had awoken in. Seven glass cylinders sat on pedestals. Six were open. One was closed.

Bryce rushed to the closed cylinder and placed his thumb on the panel beside it.

When Owen caught up to him, he scanned the screen, reading the log.

```
Subject:
Maya Young.
Recent Updates:
Power failure.
Initiating battery backup.
Battery capacity: 43%.
Battery capacity: 33%.
Power restored.
Charging battery backup.
Power failure.
Initiating battery backup.
Battery capacity: 37%.
Battery capacity warning: 20%.
Power restored.
Charging battery backup.
```

```
Power failure.
Initiating battery backup.
Battery capacity: 26%.
Battery capacity warning: 20%.
Battery capacity critical warning: 10%.
Battery capacity critical warning: 5%.
Battery capacity critical warning: 2.5%.
Reactivation sequence initiated.
Biological anomaly detected.
Error Code 3940.
Reactivation override accepted.
Reactivation sequence initiated.
```

The glass cylinder opened with a pop.

"Get her dressed and take her to OBS 2," Bryce said. "I'll open the remaining chambers. Help me collect the others once I open their chambers. Hurry, please."

With that, Bryce turned and barreled out of the room.

Owen's instincts took over. He had to reach the others quickly. They would be freezing and scared and disoriented. He certainly had been when he woke.

For a moment, he felt the same way he had in the Oasis Park Building as the fire swept through the apartment. That danger had stilled him. Focused him. He had felt more alive at that moment than he ever had. And that surprised him.

He felt the same way again. He sensed there was danger here. And that filled him with purpose.

"Ah!" the woman yelled.

Owen's attention snapped back to the chamber. The glass dome was hinged near the foot, and it stood completely open now, revealing a naked woman about Owen's age. She had sandy blond hair and a smooth, unlined face except for the very slight wrinkles that fanned out from her eyes toward her temples.

She was shivering, and like Owen, she squeezed her eyes shut. Her breath came out in a white cloud that hung between them. "Hello?"

"I'm here."

He took her hand in his, feeling the cold skin. His warmth flowed into her, and instinctively, he reached up and placed his left hand on her face. He glanced around the room and quickly spotted a metal cart nearby with a pile of clothes heaped on top.

"Cold," she breathed out, her shaking growing more violent.

"Hold on," Owen said, releasing her hand as he reached for the clothes.

In several quick motions, he extracted the tubes from her arm. The skin seemed to seal as they exited, perhaps by some method of nano suture or simply because the incision was so small.

With her help, Owen dressed the woman and pressed the buttons on the garments that activated the heating element embedded inside.

She was struggling to open her eyes, but Owen whispered to her, "Give it some time. Just grab onto me for now."

She wrapped her arms around him, and he hoisted her up and ran out of the room and across the hall, into Observation 2.

The room was large—a bit bigger than the pods that held the chambers—and empty except for ten metal folding chairs and a pile of thick blankets in the corner. Owen set Maya down on a blanket and wrapped it around her. Her shivering had abated some and her eyes were cracked.

"Who are you?" she asked.

"Owen."

"Where are we?"

"I wish I knew. I'll be right back, okay?"

CHAPTER TEN

A hospital. That's what the place felt like to Maya. The walls were white. And they looked plastic.

It was cold here. There were no windows. Only lights above that went out at irregular intervals—and the red strobe light that acted like a hammer hitting, giving fuel to her headache that never seemed to fade.

Owen burst into the room carrying a middle-aged man in his arms. He was wearing the same black sweater, gray pants, and boots as Maya. Owen was panting hard as he reached the blankets and set the man down, who had his eyes closed as he shivered.

Without a word, Owen turned and ran toward the door.

Maya rose, stumbling on lethargic legs.

Owen glanced back. "Stay here—"

"I'm not staying here!"

"Okay, don't stay here," Owen muttered as he left the room.

Maya couldn't help but laugh at his reply. In the hall, she noticed someone else emerging from another doorway near the end: a slender young man, moving quickly away from them and to another door, which he opened by placing his thumb on a panel.

"Who's that?" Maya asked.

"Bryce," Owen said, now jogging down the hall.

"Does he—"

"That is actually the sum total of all I know: his name is Bryce."

"Do you work here?"

He chuckled. "I don't even know where *here* is."

"Wonderful."

Owen slipped into an open room that held seven of the glass chambers like the one Maya had awoken in. On one of the beds, there was a young girl, likely just old enough to start school. She was shivering. And crying. And reaching out, her eyes closed.

Instead of rushing toward her, Owen raced to a nearby cart and grabbed some clothes, which he handed to Maya. "Help her. I'm going to get the others."

Then, he was gone.

Maya froze for a moment.

"Mom?" the girl said, her voice cracking.

Maya placed a hand on her shoulder. The girl reeled back as though the touch was a shock.

"It's okay," Maya said softly. "I'm here to help."

"Cold…"

"I know."

Maya drew the tubes from the girl's arm and pulled the clothes over her. Still, she was freezing. Maya remembered then: the touch of Owen's finger on her upper chest. She found a patch there with two buttons: a circle of red and blue and another symbol shaped like a shield.

She pressed the red and blue button on the sweater, pants, and boots. The girl's shaking subsided to shivering and then heavy breathing.

"What's your name?" Maya asked.

"Blair."

"You're going to be okay, Blair. I'm going to get you out of here. Just hold onto me."

The young girl extended her arms, eyes still closed, feeling for Maya, who scooped her up, testing the weight on her still weak legs. She took a step, then another, growing more confident with each movement.

Blair nuzzled her face into Maya's neck, the child's cold skin pressing into the warmth. The girl's breath was a blast of cold air that grew warmer with each exhale.

At the doorway, Maya paused to let Bryce and Owen pass. Both held people in their arms, eyes closed, hanging limp.

When Maya reached the observation room, she found three people lying on the blankets: a woman about her age with dark hair, a middle-aged man with thinning hair, and a young man who looked about the same age as Bryce. All were dressed in the heated clothes but still shivering, staring out through squinted eyes, no doubt trying to overcome the pain and sluggishness.

Gently, Maya set Blair down and held a hand to her head, a feeble attempt to put the girl at ease.

She opened her eyes slightly, grimacing. "Who… are—"

"My name's Maya. Just rest. I'll be right back."

As she rose to leave, Owen entered the room again, carrying an older man. He was bald, skinny, and tall. To Maya's surprise, he was fighting to get free of Owen's grip.

"Let me go!"

"Relax," Owen said, struggling to hold the man.

At the blankets, Owen set the man down, who

54

immediately drew back, crashing into the young man who now had his eyes open.

"Hey, watch it."

"Who are you?" the older man snapped.

Maya stepped toward the door, but Owen caught her arm. "That's everybody."

Bryce rushed inside the room and thumbed the panel, closing the door. He tapped several buttons on the panel, and the red strobing light stopped, and the alarm fell silent.

Through the small glass window in the door, Maya could still see the red light blinking in the hallway, but the sound was gone. Soon, she heard air flowing into the room. Heat, she thought.

Bryce turned to the group. "I'm sorry you all were awoken like that. There was no other way."

The older man staggered to his feet, eyes barely open. "What's going on here?"

"Where are we?" Owen asked.

Several others joined in, lobbing questions until Maya couldn't make out anything.

"Please. Please," Bryce pleaded. "You must be quiet. I'll explain everything. At least... what I can. First, please be aware that this station is failing. The power plant is critical—"

A new barrage of questions filled the room. Bryce held his hands up. "Quiet. Please. We don't have much time."

"Where are we?" Owen asked.

"I don't know," Bryce said.

"What do you mean, *you don't know*?" The older man asked. "How can you not know where we are?"

"Because, like you, I was unconscious when I was brought

here. What I do know is that the world you remember is gone."

"What?" Owen said. "How?"

"The coastlines have changed. The cities you knew no longer exist. Same for the states and nations and corporations and everything else. The world. Is gone."

"What are we doing here? What is this place?" Maya asked. "A hospital?"

"Of sorts," Bryce replied. "This is a facility created by my employer, ARC Technologies. We are in Station 17."

"What kind of station?" Owen asked.

"It's a bunker that's part of a network of trial locations."

"What kind of trials?" Maya asked.

"The Extinction Trials."

The room fell silent.

Bryce took a step closer. "It's an experiment to restart the human race after a catastrophic global event. That event has occurred. We call it the Change. Our goal here is to find a cohort that can survive in the world after the Change. That is the key to saving what's left of the human race."

CHAPTER ELEVEN

For a moment, the group looked around at each other.

Owen was still trying to wrap his head around what Bryce had said.

The Extinction Trials.

An experiment to restart the human race.

The older man who had struggled to get free of Owen's grasp spoke first.

"I never consented to this."

"Nor did I," the middle-aged man said.

Maya held a hand up. "Does it matter how we got here?"

The older man eyed her. "It matters a great deal. But I think what matters even more is what they intend to do with us." He turned his gaze to Bryce, who merely cocked his head.

From the corner of the room, the other adult woman spoke. "There's a more pressing issue."

All eyes turned to her.

"Our health. First, we should assess everyone and treat any injuries."

"Are you a doctor?" Owen asked.

"Yes. An ER doctor."

Owen counted that as good news.

The woman stood and stepped out from the group. "Is anyone hurt?"

One by one, each person shook their head or gasped out a response.

No.

Not really.

I'm okay.

My head hurts, but it's feeling better.

Seeming satisfied, the woman turned to Bryce. "It was cold in the other rooms. It feels warmer in here."

Bryce nodded. "I've cut power to the rest of the station and routed everything here."

As if on cue, the lights dimmed a moment, then came back to full strength.

"Why is the power failing?" Owen asked.

"Mechanical failure."

The middle-aged man scoffed. "So, fix it."

"Impossible."

"Why?"

"We lack the parts. And I lack the expertise to install them."

"Well, I don't," the man said. "I want to see the power plant."

"What makes you think you can fix it?" the ER doctor asked, her voice neutral.

"Because I fix things."

"What kind of things?" the doctor asked, seeming more curious.

"Anything."

"Anything?"

"Anything. I'm a mechanic. If it used to run, I can make

it run again. Never was any good at school, but I'm good at fixing things."

"Be that as it may," Bryce said carefully, "I remind you that we lack the parts to repair the geothermal power generation system."

"This is all irrelevant," the older man said. "We need to get out of here. Right now."

"No," Bryce said quickly. "You can't."

"Why not?" Owen asked.

"There's a storm on the surface. It's deadly."

The older man narrowed his eyes, studying Bryce. He stepped closer to the door, as if preparing to leave. Bryce moved to block his path.

The lights dimmed again.

Bryce stepped in front of the door. "Please, we must remain here for the time being."

"What's your role here?" the older man asked.

"As I said, I work for ARC. I'm a proctor in the Trials."

The man swallowed then took a step back. He glanced at the group, a thought seeming to form in his mind.

Something about the scene put Owen on edge. Something was happening here. A change he couldn't put his finger on.

Try as he might, he couldn't understand. He felt as though he were staring at a warning message written in another language, a sign he desperately wanted to be able to read but never would. Because of his limitation. What his parents called his limitation: his inability to read body language and facial expressions.

It was a language he could never master, and it was part of the reason he'd become a firefighter. Fires always behaved the same way. It was science. Once you learned what affected a fire—and how to read the scene—you could figure out what to do.

People were a black box to him.

The older man reached for one of the folding chairs leaning against the wall and set it up, then unfolded another and placed it on the floor. "It would seem that we are confined here." He glanced at Bryce. "For now."

He set out another chair, establishing the arc of a circle. "I believe there's one important thing we can do: take stock of what we have to work with."

The middle-aged man grunted. "Won't take long. We've got chairs and blankets and a busted-up bunker."

"No," the man said quietly, still placing the chairs. "We have something far more valuable."

Everyone in the room focused on him, waiting.

"We have each other." He motioned to the middle-aged woman with brown hair. "Apparently, we have a doctor—one with a background in emergency medicine. Quite fortuitous." He held out a hand to her. "Doctor…"

"Allen. Cara Allen."

The man nodded. "Doctor Allen." He waved a hand toward a chair. "Will you join us?"

Owen watched as she took a seat. Again, he had the strange sensation that something was wrong about the act. It was like the older man was maneuvering everyone, positioning them like pieces for some act.

"And luckily," the man continued, "we have a mechanic. Mister?"

"I've never been a mister in my life. Name's Alister Reynolds."

"A man after my own heart. Will you join us, Alister?"

"Don't see what choice I've got." Alister stood, sauntered over, collapsed in the chair, and exhaled heavily.

The older man unfolded another chair and turned to the younger man. "And what's your name?"

"I'm Will Carraway. Software engineer." His gaze drifted over to Bryce. "I work for ARC Technologies as well." He paused. "I guess... I used to."

Alister eyed the younger man. "Then you also work for the people who kidnapped us."

"We don't know that we've been kidnapped," Maya said.

"Don't we?" Alister shot back.

Cara held up a hand. "We're here without consent. But sick patients are routinely taken to the hospital without explicit consent. Have we been kidnapped? Or saved? I favor reserving judgment."

Alister scoffed. "Well, I favor assuming the worst. It's the only way to be prepared for it. *Assuming* people are going to do the right thing only sometimes pays off. Being a skeptic always pays off."

Cara shook her head. "That's not true. Distrust is a burden on any relationship—"

Alister reeled back. "*Relationship?*"

The older man held his hands up. "If I may. You both make valid points. Who is right? I submit that we don't know for one simple reason: we lack, frankly, enough information. So, let us learn what we can." He nodded to Maya. "And I suggest we start with you, Miss..."

"I'm Maya Young." She paused, inhaled, and simply stopped at that.

Alister raised his eyebrows. "You unemployed?"

"Well, to be quite honest, I don't recall precisely what I

did before…" She turned to Bryce, who supplied the term she was looking for: "The Change."

Maya nodded. "Before the Change."

"How can you not remember what you did?" Alister muttered.

"Reasons for memory loss are vast," Cara said. "And, I imagine, given the shock we've all had, not too uncommon."

The older man turned to Owen. "And you? What about you? You ferried me out of that tube. I assume you're another proctor for the Trials?"

Owen reeled back, caught off guard. "No. I woke up here the same as you. I'm a firefighter."

The older man squinted. "Another lucky break—someone else with experience in emergency situations. Will you join us?" He motioned to a chair.

"I'll stand," Owen said. He really didn't like this now, for two reasons. One, the man hadn't invited Maya to sit. And two, he had yet to say a single word about himself.

The older man eyed the young girl in the corner, who was still sitting on the blankets.

"And who might you be, my dear?"

Her eyes went wide, and she simply shook her head.

Maya took a step toward her and knelt, wrapping her arms around the young girl. "She's a little shaken. Her name is Blair—"

The sound of the crash shattered the quiet in the room. The noise was that of metal on metal. At first, Owen assumed someone was coming through the door. He spun around, moving his gaze from Maya and Blair, and he was horrified by what he saw.

The older man held a folded metal chair up above his

head. Bryce lay on the floor, twitching. The older man brought the chair down again, slamming it into Bryce's head.

Owen expected to see blood. But there was none.

CHAPTER TWELVE

Maya pulled Blair closer to her, burying the girl's face in her chest.

The older man slammed the metal chair into Bryce again and again until the young man lay prone on the white tile floor, unmoving.

The shock of the assault was quickly replaced by a new realization: Bryce wasn't a young man at all.

Where the chair had split his head open, Maya saw wires and hard plastic.

He was an android.

The older man was panting hard, eyes wide and wild, darting back and forth as he scanned the room, perhaps waiting for someone to attack him. When no one moved, he tossed the chair aside. "We have to get out of here."

Owen moved toward him, carefully avoiding stepping on Bryce. "Why?"

The older man spoke quickly as he inhaled, trying to regain his breath. "The Extinction Trials aren't what you think they are."

"What do you mean?"

"I'll tell you outside."

"We can't go outside. The storm—"

The older man shook his head. "Lies. I suspect there's no storm—and if there is, it's likely no harm to us."

He bent down and pulled on Bryce's arm. The heap of mangled machinery barely moved.

"Help me," he said to Owen. "Please. Every moment we stay here, we're in danger."

Reluctantly Owen helped lift the android and drag him to the door, where the older man pressed Bryce's thumb onto the panel.

The lights went off again. Blair nuzzled into Maya's neck and clung to her. Slowly, the young girl began shaking again. Maya squeezed her tight.

In the darkness, Maya heard the door to the room open. Cold air rushed in. The red light from the hall flashed and went out, briefly lighting the scene in a crimson hue. In that momentary glimpse, Maya saw Owen and the other man in the hallway dragging Bryce behind them.

For reasons she couldn't understand, Maya felt a surge of fear. This was wrong. Dangerous.

But why?

In her mind's eye, she saw a memory of herself. She was standing in a decontamination chamber, putting a spacesuit on. This memory was from a place where she had worked—similar to this one. But what did it mean?

"Cara," Maya called out in the darkness.

"Yes?"

The red light in the hall flashed, and at that moment, Maya made eye contact with the doctor. The woman appeared to be about Maya's age, maybe slightly older.

"Can you take Blair?" Maya called in the darkness.

At the next flash of red, Cara was kneeling close to Maya, reaching out, taking Blair from her arms.

"I'll be right back," Maya whispered.

Her legs still felt stiff and sluggish, but with each step, they responded better.

In the hallway, she spotted Owen near the airlock, holding Bryce's hand to the panel.

The inner hatch opened, and the older man slipped through, pulling Bryce with him. Owen followed, pushing the android over the threshold.

Maya ran as fast as she could. Above, the hallway's lights flickered on and off. In that flash of illumination, she saw the two men lifting Bryce's hand to the airlock's outer control panel, which would open the door to the outside, Maya assumed.

"Stop!" Maya yelled.

The lights snapped on again, dimmed, but stayed alight.

The two men turned to her but didn't release the android.

As Maya reached the inner hatch, she braced herself on the frame, panting, breath coming out in white puffs of fog. It was cold out here in the hallway—far colder than the observation room. The heated clothes helped, but they were losing the battle against the chill.

Owen and the older man stared at her, still holding Bryce. The airlock was painted white, like the rest of the facility, with a silver metal bench beside the door and a row of environmental suits and helmets above it. Three pipes crossed the ceiling, each with nozzles hanging down.

"You can't go out there," Maya said, gasping for breath from the exertion.

"Why?" Owen asked.

"We need more information."

The lights faded to darkness.

"Don't listen to her," the older man hissed, his voice disembodied in the blackness. "She doesn't know what she's talking about."

The red emergency light flashed on. Owen was staring at her as the older man pulled Bryce's hand to the control panel for the outer door.

"Why do you think it's dangerous?" Owen asked, now in darkness again.

"Just... a hunch. Let's wait. Please, Owen."

The red light flashed.

The older man pressed Bryce's hand to the airlock control panel.

A new alarm sounded—a beeping sound. An orange light above the outer hatch came on, and a computerized voice spoke through the speaker. "Airlock opening."

The inner hatch began closing.

Maya reached out, pressing against it, but the door kept closing.

"Owen!"

The lights snapped out.

Maya expected the hatch to spring back open due to the force she was applying—a safety measure—but it kept closing.

The red emergency light from the hall flashed. Owen was beside Maya, charging toward the closing inner hatch.

It was too late. The hatch was already closed too much for them to walk through.

Owen grabbed her and lunged through the closing doorway, spinning as they tumbled to the floor. She landed on top of him in the hallway, and in the darkness, she heard the hatch seal.

The red emergency light flashed, illuminating Owen's face staring up at her.

She held his gaze for a moment, both their breaths coming out in a fog that mixed together, creating a cloud between them.

A computerized voice pierced the moment. "Outer airlock opened."

Maya scrambled to her feet and moved to the inner hatch and peered through the narrow window. Opening the outer airlock had turned on some exterior lights. She had expected to see a tunnel of some sort beyond—something human-built. What she saw was a rocky passage, cave-like and natural.

Owen came to stand beside her, their heads close as they both watched through the window.

The older man was marching away without so much as a glance back. Up ahead, where the passage turned, a dim shaft of natural light loomed.

The outer hatch swung closed. The overhead nozzles sprayed a white mist into the airlock.

"Decontamination initiated."

When the cloud cleared, Maya spotted the man farther down the passage, but he had turned to face them, his eyes wide. He reached up and clutched at his chest, mouth open.

He clawed, shaking his head, then fell to the rocky ground, writhing.

Owen glanced at Maya, then back to the window. The man managed to make it back to his hands and knees. He crawled toward the airlock, but he only made it halfway back before collapsing to the ground, unmoving.

Dead.

CHAPTER THIRTEEN

For a long moment, Maya and Owen stared at the dead man through the airlock window.

Finally, Owen said, "That was close."

"Yeah."

"We should tell the others."

Maya glanced behind them, down the hallway. "We should. But I want to see what's beyond the airlock at the end of the corridor first. We need to know what else we have to work with before we regroup."

"I agree."

At the airlock that led to the command center, Maya pressed Bryce's severed thumb onto the control panel.

The hatch opened with a click and swung out, allowing her and Owen to slip inside. At the opposite door, Owen pressed Bryce's other thumb to the panel and a voice came over the speaker.

"Decontamination commencing."

The entry door swung closed, and a cool mist sprayed from the nozzles on the ceiling.

Unlike the airlock that led to the outside, this chamber had no suits hanging on the wall and no bench.

With the white haze still in the air, Maya asked a

question that had been bothering her since the older man had disabled Bryce with the chair.

"Did you know? About Bryce?"

Through the fog, she could see Owen turning toward her, but she couldn't make out his face. The flicker of red light from the hallway through the narrow window lit the fog intermittently.

"That he was an android? No. I had no idea. If I had, I would've bashed his plastic brains in myself."

"Sounds like there's a story there."

"You could say that."

"Care to share?"

"That story might be the reason I wound up here."

"What do you mean?"

"As I said before, I'm a firefighter. Was. Or maybe still am—I don't know, but I do know that for the last little while, my job hasn't involved actually fighting any fires."

"Then what do you do?"

"Lately, it was like a dress rehearsal. We suited up and mostly just went out on calls and talked people through safety stuff and managed the firebots."

"Sounds safer that way."

"It is. That's true. But I guess I sort of signed up for a different job than I ended up doing. Not the worst thing in the world, but it was an adjustment. Anyway, on this last call, it was a mother and her daughter—maybe a little older than Blair. They lived on the eleventh floor of this apartment building, the Oasis Park Building."

His words faded, and Maya felt her breath catch in her throat. A memory came to her then: of seeing her mother standing behind a kitchen island, talking to her and her sister. And of being in the hospital. Of being afraid. Of wanting to get to her mother and sister.

A loud pop punctured the silence as the other airlock opened toward the command center.

Owen took a step forward and snapped his flashlight on and raked it across the space. "It's empty."

The haze of fog from the decontamination chamber was drifting into the darkened room. Owen followed it out of the airlock, his story forgotten.

Maya reached out and caught his arm. "Wait. The Oasis Park Building—what unit was it? The call?"

"Uhh," he shook his head. "Maybe..."

"1107?"

He turned to her. "Yes. How did you know?"

"My mother and sister live there. Lived there... What happened?"

Owen exhaled heavily. "They were both alive when we arrived. Your mother was unconscious. Your sister was too." He swallowed. "It was a gas leak. It ignited."

Maya felt her legs weaken. She reached out, grasping the wall to steady herself.

"I got your sister out."

Maya looked up. "How?"

"We vented the apartment. Then... things got crazy. Fire alarms started going off all over the city. The other door went through the window. We were about to evac when one of the firebots attacked us. I was lucky. I got your sister out through that open window."

"And then what happened?"

Owen shook his head. "I'm not sure. I passed out. I woke

up in the hospital. I was pretty banged up." He paused. "Which is the craziest thing about waking up here. Because I'm completely healed."

"And you don't know how you got here?"

"No. I was interviewed by some guy named Parrish who asked me a lot of questions about your mom and sister."

Parrish—Maya knew that name. Yes, he had visited her too. The memory was there, just out of reach.

"My mother..."

Owen took a step toward her. "She *was* alive the last time I saw her, but things got pretty chaotic. I'm really sorry."

"Thank you... for what you did."

He shrugged. "I was just doing my job."

CHAPTER FOURTEEN

The thing Owen hated the most about his job was giving people bad news. It was something he had never been very good at, mostly because reading their expressions was like a foreign language to him.

Telling Maya about her mother and sister had come unexpectedly—and it didn't help one bit that she was someone he instinctively trusted for whatever reason. She had saved his life, and he didn't want to hurt her. Most of all, he wished he could read her face right now. He wanted some clue as to how she was processing the news about her mother and sister.

He also had to wonder if it was a coincidence that they were connected. Was he connected to the others as well?

"Do you want to go back to Observation?" he asked her.

She looked up. "No. Let's continue."

She snapped on her flashlight, and they moved cautiously into the command center, sweeping the beams of light back and forth. The room was about the size of one of the pods they had each awoken in. The far wall was covered with screens, all dark. There were two rows of workstations, each with four desks that held screens and keyboards with a thin layer of dust on them.

"Looks like nobody's used it in a while," Owen said.

"Apparently," Maya replied.

He moved along the rows of desks, looking for clues. There were no personal effects. It was as though the stations were interchangeable—unassigned and available to be used by anyone working in the facility.

Owen shined his light over toward Maya, who was still searching the room, her back turned to him. "You think it's true, what Bryce said? That we're part of some... experiment to save the human race?"

"It does sound crazy. Honestly, I don't know, but a part of me thinks it's too crazy not to be true. What would be the purpose of telling that lie?"

That made a strange kind of sense to Owen. In fact, he had felt the same thing.

"Over here," Maya called out.

At the back of the room, Owen spotted a doorway. It was the only other doorway besides the airlock.

The door opened onto a narrow corridor that was dark except for their flashlights. It ended in a door, and there were two others along the right-hand wall. One led to what looked like a storage room with prepackaged food and a silver metal cart like the ones they'd found in the pods.

"That will solve our food problem for a while," Maya said.

She was right. And it was a good thing. Food was something Owen hadn't even considered until now.

The other door along the hall was the strangest thing Owen had seen yet. Inside were three standing alcoves just big enough for an adult to stand in.

"I'm guessing this is where Bryce recharged," Maya said.

"If so, it implies that there were three of him."

"Possibly. Or simply the capacity to have three on staff. It could mean that the other two had already left the station. Or were never present here."

A thought occurred to Owen—and it brought with it fear. "Or that one or two androids are still here. In hiding. Or possibly in Observation 2."

"A fair point," Maya said. "And something to keep in mind."

Behind the last door, they found five boxes made of hard black plastic. They were sealed and locked with a simple numeric punch code.

Owen's first thought was that the boxes contained records. If so, that would be immensely helpful.

Maya bent down and typed some numbers into the first box: 171717.

The box beeped and the diode flashed red, and the lock didn't open.

She shrugged. "Worth a try."

"They can't be that hard to open. We could get some tools from the closet."

"True. But I think we should get back to the observation room. They're going to start wondering where we are soon."

"I agree."

"Before we go, I think we need to form a plan."

"A plan sounds pretty good about now."

"First things first," Maya said. "My memories." She glanced through the doorway out into the command center, where the red flashing light was very faint through the airlock. "It's like that strobing red light. I just get flashes of what happened to me. It's like when you mentioned my mother and sister. I remembered then. It was more a feeling—the emotion—of what they meant to me. Then I could see their faces. It's like if I see something or remember something, it reveals memories that are connected to it. It's so... disorienting."

"How'd you lose your memory? Injury?"

"No. Or I don't think so. I was sick. In the hospital. I think whatever made me sick had some sort of effect on my memory."

"Like some sort of neurological disease?"

"Maybe."

"Do you have any other symptoms?"

Maya shook her head. "No. Ever since waking up here, I've felt fine."

"Maybe they cured you as well. Maybe the memories will return."

"I hope so."

"In my mind, the biggest question now is what to do. If we believe Bryce's assertion that the station is going to undergo an imminent power failure, it implies environmental systems will fail and we'll need to go outside."

"We know how that ends."

"Exactly. However, we do have the environmental suits."

Maya considered that. "True. But we don't know how long the suits will last. If we could wear one of the suits to get to a region where the atmosphere is survivable, maybe it works. I think it's safe to say that we need to figure out a way to call for help."

"I see risks there as well," Owen said. "What if the people who come aren't the good guys?"

"I see your point."

"Here's what I think: we need more information. We need to know where we are, first of all. Second of all, we need to know more about ARC Technologies. I'd never heard of them before today. And most of all, we need to figure out who those people are in Observation 2."

"Suggestions?"

"First, I think I should take the doctor outside and we should do some sort of rudimentary autopsy on the old man. That might give us some clue as to what we're dealing with out there."

"I hadn't thought of that. It's a good idea." Maya glanced back toward the command center. "I was thinking the answers might be in here. The younger guy—Will—said he was a computer programmer for ARC Technologies. If so, maybe he knows how to work some of the computers. If they have an internet connection, we could use that to call for help—and figure out what's happening."

"Turning on the computers could also alert someone that we're here—and awake."

"True. It's a risk," Maya said. "But I don't think we have a choice. I think, at this point, we have to take that risk. It's either that or wait for the power to go out and for whatever is outside to come in here. Either we run out of air, or we run out of food—it's just a matter of time. We need to figure out a way to get out of here and get to safety."

CHAPTER FIFTEEN

In the observation room, Maya and Owen related what had happened to the older man outside as well as what they'd found in the rest of the station.

To Maya's surprise, the whole group took it in stride.

When Owen suggested they perform an autopsy on the older man outside, Cara quickly agreed.

Will was more than eager to try to restore power to the command center and get the computers up and running. Their first priority was to enable environmental control there. If they could do that, they could cut power to the observation room and establish a new base of operations in the command center.

Maya favored the command center as their headquarters for another reason: safety. It was behind a second airlock, which would offer time to prepare for intruders and biological protection from anything they might bring with them.

She wondered if that thought was a clue to what she used to do. She seemed to have a natural instinct for strategy and security.

Alister was the only holdout to the proposed plans.

"I want to take a look at this power plant," he said gruffly.

"You think you can fix it?" Cara asked.

"Maybe."

"What sort of mechanic are you?" she asked.

"A bus mechanic."

Cara bunched her eyebrows. "Are buses quite like geothermal power plants?"

He snorted. "Apparently, they're more alike than doctors and mechanics."

She bristled. "What does that mean?"

"It means I could keep a hundred city buses running, so what's the harm in me taking a look to see if I can fix it?"

"I guess that's where I get hung up: you fixing it. We've been told its failure is imminent. What if your *interventions* simply hasten its demise?"

Maya held up a hand. She had to stop this conversation where it was. The simple truth was that she didn't trust Alister yet. She wanted either herself or Owen to keep an eye on all the team members at all times.

"I can see both of your points of view," Maya said. "I really do. But right now, we need more information before we act. We'll get that information from the autopsy and in the command center. Time is running out. We need to move. The power plant will have to wait."

In the airlock, Owen donned the suit, attached the helmet, and secured the gloves and boots. The gear fit nicely over the sweater and pants, and he was pleased that the suit also provided some added warmth against the frigid airlock.

For his job, he was used to getting into a suit quickly. It was second nature to him.

He was surprised to see that Cara slipped easily into her suit as well. As though she were practiced at it—had done it before.

"You said you're an ER doctor?"

"That's right." She glanced up at him. Had she detected the suspicion in his voice? Owen wasn't good at reading faces—or hiding his own expressions.

"Like you," Cara said, "we had a lot of practice getting dressed quickly when there's an emergency."

He nodded.

"Ready when you are," she said.

Owen pressed Bryce's thumb onto the panel and the outer airlock began opening.

Owen assumed the suit would protect him from whatever was outside. That was a big assumption—one his life was riding on. As such, he couldn't help sucking in a breath as he waited for the outside air to rush in around him—the same air that had killed the older man.

The suit had a panel in the forearm that displayed his vitals and suit status. The seals were good. His oxygen was at 100 percent.

Owen watched, waiting for any change.

Over the suit radio, Owen said to Cara, "You all right?"

"Yeah. I think we're good."

Owen stepped out into the rocky passageway. The ground was covered in soft dirt that his boots sank into instantly.

Owen arrived at the body first, knelt down, and gently turned the man over. His eyes were open, his mouth agape, dirt pasted on his face like a cake he had face-planted into.

Cara knelt beside him. "It feels so wrong to do it out here. Like this. Undignified."

"I agree," Owen said softly. "But I don't see any other choice."

"True. Help me take his shirt off. I need to open him up."

In the command center, Maya and the others had hit a dead end.

Will's attempts to power the computers had failed. Blair sat in one of the rolling office chairs, head slouched, picking at her fingers. Maya wasn't sure if she was nervous, scared, or simply bored. Or some combination of the three.

One thing was certain: Alister was annoyed. He paced back and forth in front of the screens, still going on about being prohibited from inspecting the power plant.

The worst part was that it was getting colder. Their body heat helped to warm the room some, but the cold was like an unstoppable army that kept marching deeper inside of her.

"Ideas?" Maya asked.

"You've heard my idea," Alister retorted.

"The boxes," Will said quietly. "Maybe there's something inside that could help."

Maya lit up. "Yes, good idea." To Alister, she said, "You want something to do? There's a tool closet near the outer airlock. You have lots of tools and three boxes we need to open. Let's see if you can fix that."

The boxes, as it turned out, were quite hard to open. And to Maya's surprise, Alister relished the challenge. It seemed to her that he simply wanted something to work on and wasn't terribly particular about what that was. He enjoyed the process, and despite a near-constant barrage of curse words, he managed to open the boxes in short order.

The first box contained a portable GPS system and two medkits.

The second box contained six large envelopes slightly larger than a paperback book. Each had a name on it:

Maya Young
Owen Watts
Cara Allen
Will Carraway
Blair Aldridge
Roman Morris

"Very interesting," Maya whispered. "There's an envelope for each of us." She looked up at Alister. "Except for you, Alister. Unless your name is really Roman Morris."

"My name is not Roman," Alister said, not bothering to look at the envelopes.

"Yes," Will said. "Very curious indeed. I think we can safely assume that the older gentlemen Cara is currently performing an autopsy on was named Roman Morris."

"Then why isn't there an envelope for Alister?" Maya asked.

The older man huffed. "How should I know? Maybe it's in the other boxes. Or maybe it got lost in the mail. Or maybe our cruel robot captors didn't see fit to give me a prize. Frankly, I don't care."

Maya studied him a moment. Something about his reaction was off. But she saw no point in pressing the issue at present.

"Let's see what's in the envelopes," Maya said. She ripped

her own open and peered inside. There were two objects there. One was a personal item that, to her surprise, sparked a painful memory. Try as she might, she couldn't quite see how it connected to the Extinction Trials. The other item was a complete mystery to her—and it seemed to have even less to do with what was happening here.

One by one, Maya, Will, and Blair showed the contents of their envelopes.

"They seem to be personal effects," Will said. "Except for my item. And it doesn't appear to be much use here."

"It's probably some psych experiment," Alister said. "The Extinction Trials proctors are probably watching you all and laughing right now."

"I don't think that's the case," Will said quietly. He motioned to the envelopes for Cara and Owen. "Should we—"

"Open them?" Maya said, completing his sentence. "No. I don't feel right about it. If our items somehow fit together to build something—something we needed—then maybe I could see the urgency. But the contents seem like personal items, and I can't justify violating their privacy."

"I agree," Will said.

"Well, I can justify opening the other boxes," Alister said. "If you all are ready."

Maya nodded and watched as he took the top off the third box. At first, she thought it was empty, but as she looked closer, she realized it held a single item: a key. It was an old-fashioned metal key with jagged teeth.

Alister scoffed. "Clearly, ARC Technologies is not aware that locksmiths exist."

Maya also found the object curious. She hadn't used a

key like that since she was a child. Nevertheless, she thought maybe it could be important. She slipped the item into her pocket.

The fourth and final box held a small tablet with the letters "ARC" engraved on the back.

Will smiled. "It's an ARC terminal. Like the one I use at work."

"Use for what?" Maya asked.

"Mostly at data centers. We would use these to interface a server farm or even maintain some of our mesh devices."

"Why do you think it's in here?"

"My guess is it's a backup. In case the main system goes down, we can use this to access the embedded systems and control the station. I think we just found exactly what we need to get answers. And help."

CHAPTER SIXTEEN

When he and Cara returned from the airlock, Owen expected to find Maya and the others in the command center, with the computer active and in complete control of the station.

He found none of those things.

The group was again in the observation room and none of the computers were running. Blair was lying on the heap of blankets, while the others were either pacing or sitting in the folding chairs. While facial expressions and body language were a mystery to Owen, he could tell things weren't going that great for the group.

Maya stood as the door closed behind Owen and Cara. "What did you find out?"

Owen and Cara shared a glance, and he said, "It's... not great news. Why don't you guys go first?"

"We've hit a bit of a dead end here," Maya replied.

Quickly, she showed Owen and Cara the contents of the boxes, saving their envelopes for last.

"We've opened our envelopes," Maya said. "They all had personal items in them that didn't seem to offer any help to our current situation. It was the same for the man you just performed the autopsy on."

Owen picked up the envelope with his name on it and gently tore it open. "Well, let's see what ARC saw fit to leave for me."

He peered inside and was surprised at what he saw. "Mine has personal items too," he said quietly.

Cara had opened her envelope and was reaching inside. "There's just one item in mine." She held up a twisted piece of metal.

"I don't get it," Alister said.

"It's a personal item too," Cara said. "And I'm very, very surprised to see it. With that said, I don't think it's going to be much help to us." She shifted her gaze to the ARC tablet that was lying next to one of the boxes. "But I assume that is?"

"It could be," Will said.

"Could be?" Cara asked.

"*If* I could log in," Will said. "I've tried using my credentials, which have Level Three access to all ARC security systems, but it won't recognize me."

Owen considered that for a moment. "Maybe your account was deleted. Bryce said that it's been a very long time since the Change and the Fall of the world."

"It's possible my account was deactivated, that's true. But knowing what I know about ARC, it's impossible that the account was deleted."

"Why do you say that?" Owen asked, intrigued.

"I guess I should give you a little bit of company history," Will said, drawing the attention of all the others.

"ARC stands for Archival Records Corporation. The company's original mission was to see that no record was ever lost again. The company's founder was Victor Levy.

The cause was personal to him. When he was young, he and his brother were orphans. Victor was adopted by a family, but they refused to adopt his brother, who was soon after adopted by another family. They moved away and the brothers lost touch. As an adult, Victor tried to find his younger brother, but the records of who had adopted the boy had been lost over time. He died not ever knowing his brother. His goal with ARC was to see that something like that never happened to anyone ever again. ARC's original business was storing paper records. Mostly medical records that hospitals and doctors' offices no longer needed but had to keep for legal reasons. ARC also stored government records and paper files from companies that needed their data to be super secure. It was a sleepy company until cloud computing really started to grow. At that point, ARC expanded into big data and data warehousing and became the go-to provider for mass data storage."

Alister motioned to the group. "Apparently, at some point, they got it to archive humans."

"So it would seem," Will said. "But I never heard about anything like that, though we were big into genomic data storage. We were one of the leading cloud providers for biotech and pharmaceutical companies working on genomic medicines and breakthroughs in viral therapies. We had customized solutions and tailored security for specific industry verticals. In fact, I was dedicated to a team that worked exclusively for Genesis Biosciences."

Maya turned at that and studied Will. Owen wished he could read the expression. Was it surprise? Concern?

Owen thought she was going to ask him something, but she remained quiet.

"Speaking of security," Owen said, "how do you log into one of these terminals?"

"Access is principally biometric," Will replied. "A terminal first tries a retinal scan. If that fails, it goes to facial recognition, and then to a fingerprint. You can get basic access with a typed username and password, but you really can't access much of the ARCnet, and the ARCos systems are off-limits to users signed-in via user ID and password."

Owen glanced from the tablet to the contents of the other boxes. The solution for accessing the terminal was obvious to Owen. It was literally lying right there in front of them. He wondered if he was missing something. He had just met these people and was in no hurry to make a fool of himself if he wasn't right.

"What have you tried so far to access the terminal?" he asked, still unsure of his idea.

"I've tried my biometric access and my backup user ID and password," Will said. "We tried putting Bryce's face in front of the tablet and obviously using his fingerprints."

"Interesting," Owen said, pacing across the room over to one of the black boxes. He reached inside and grabbed the smallest of the items that had been hidden in the command center. He had decided to try his idea—but not to discuss it first. If it didn't work, he would just play it off.

He walked over to the terminal and, without a word, held up the metal key to the tablet, ensuring the terminal's camera could see it. On the screen, an image of the key came into focus. Owen held it still and moved it so that the entire key was in view.

The tablet flashed a message:

```
Access key accepted.
```

CHAPTER SEVENTEEN

Maya smiled. "How did you know that?"

"Just a hunch," Owen said, echoing her words at the airlock.

"A good one," she said, still amazed.

"I have to be good for something," he said quietly, watching Will as he reached out eagerly for the now-unlocked tablet and began tapping away at it.

"Well, it makes sense once you think about it," Alister said. He seemed a little annoyed that he hadn't figured it out. "The joke's on us. How does a company founded to store paper records secure access to its archives? A key."

"It's also practical," Maya said. "In the event that someone who didn't have a login in the ARC network ever needed access to the terminal, they have a universal key." She glanced at Owen. "Assuming you're clever enough to figure it out."

Will was scanning the screen, reading the lines of text at seemingly superhuman speed.

"Okay," he said slowly, still reading. "I have good news. Great news. Possible non-news. And super, extremely, very, very bad, terrible news."

"What's the non-news?" Maya asked. Some part of her feared that might be the worst.

"There's a very well hidden file on the terminal named *Escape Hatch*."

"What's in it?"

"That's the thing," Will said. "I don't know. It has data, but there's no application associated with it. When I try to open it, nothing happens."

"Interesting," Maya said.

"What's the good news?" Owen asked. "I think we could use some of that."

"I have full control of the station. No restrictions."

"Great news?" Maya asked.

"The station net—the local area network—is not connected to any wide area network. It's isolated from the internet, cryptonet, and cloudnet. And has been for a long time. The station has been in what it calls dark mode. So, the network hasn't sent out any data. No one knows we're awake. It's possible no one even knows that we're here."

"That leaves the bad news," Owen said.

Will looked up. "We're running on emergency power. It's a backup geothermal power plant that uses piping hot water to power a turbine. Bryce was right: it's failing."

"What about the main system?" Alister asked.

"Long gone. The emergency system isn't far behind. It keeps shutting down and coming back online. It can't even keep the station's battery array charged."

"Can we reduce the load on the system?" Maya asked.

"No. Bryce put us in Observation Two for a reason—it's the smallest room in the station. The command center would draw about 20 percent more power to environmentally condition."

"So, how long do we have?" Owen asked.

"Zero," Will said. "We have zero time. Less than that. The system is way past its critical warning levels. Even the logs are intermittent. It can't even supply enough power to keep the computer online to track its failures. It could go off at any time and stay off."

"Which means that it would stop filtering the air," Maya said. She focused on Owen and Cara. "How big of a problem is that?"

"A deadly one," Cara said. "We obviously couldn't perform anything near a full autopsy out there, but it's clear to me that the man died of something he encountered out there—likely a chemical or pathogen in the air."

"How do you know?" Maya asked.

"Frankly, I had hoped that his expiration was due to some sort of pre-existing condition. That perhaps his heart was compromised in some way or that an established neurological condition would explain his demise. We found evidence of neither."

"What did you find?" Maya asked.

"Lungs that look as though they had been shredded by something. The damage persisted throughout the torso, including the heart—"

Alister held up a hand. "What does this mean—for the simpletons like me? Use little-people words."

Cara exhaled. "It means that he likely inhaled whatever killed him. And if we inhale it, we'll suffer the same fate."

CHAPTER EIGHTEEN

In the observation room, for a moment, no one said anything.

Maya broke the silence. "The way I see it, we have two options: use the terminal to call for help and wait. Or go out there and try to find help—or an area we can survive in. I would also add that these two options are not mutually exclusive. We could call for help on the terminal and venture out to look for help."

"Let's consider what we know," Owen said. "Bryce warned us about going outside. Our deceased team member who rests beyond the air lock ignored those warnings and they proved true. At the same time, that man warned us that staying here was dangerous. So, there is some chance that he was telling the truth—and that calling whoever is connected to the ARCnet could be dangerous."

"I agree with that," Alister said.

"That leaves going out there," Maya said.

"I'll do it," Owen said.

Maya stood. "I'll come with you."

"No, you won't. When I'm out there, that leaves four suits. If the environmental systems do go offline, you'll have to get everyone into the suits so they can survive for as long as possible. I'm used to moving around in a suit and I've been out there already. I'm the logical choice. And I don't have any... really critical skills. I can't fix anything—human or machine—or hack the ARCnet or anything otherwise useful. I'm going."

Owen eyed her, silently trying to communicate the other issue: that one of them should stay with the others to keep an eye on them. He still didn't trust anyone but Maya.

"Well, I have to say I agree with that," Alister said. "But it leaves the issue at hand: four suits, a failing power plant, and five of us. Who's the odd man out?"

Owen thought he knew what the older man was going to say next. But he was wrong.

"It ought to be me," Alister said.

Maya cocked her head, a silent question.

"We all know it," Alister said. "Everyone else is useful. The doctor. The computer boy. *You*," he said, motioning to Maya. He continued, his voice more somber. "And we're not going to suit up while a child goes without. That's that. No more discussion."

In the airlock, Maya eyed the blood-covered suit.

"It was a messy autopsy," Owen said. "We had to use the tools we found in the closet. They were obviously meant for maintaining the station, not opening up bodies."

She motioned to the dried blood. "I wasn't thinking about that."

"You weren't?"

"No. I was wondering whether whatever killed him might be contagious."

"That's a good question," Owen said. "Cara waited outside while I went first in the airlock. The decon spray washed over the suit but didn't get all the blood. I took my helmet off and waited a few moments, but I was fine. The spray may have neutralized whatever killed him."

"A fair point," Maya said. "Still, if anyone is exposed out there, we should consider isolating them. So, be very careful not to get a tear in your suit."

"I'm always careful."

"I'm sure."

When he'd put the suit on, Maya leaned over and tapped the display. "What's your oxygen status?"

"A hundred percent."

"Which means…"

"That I have 100 percent left?"

"That you will turn back and return at 55 percent."

"Don't you mean 50 percent?"

"No, I mean 55 percent. You need to allow for a 10 percent margin of error. If it takes 45 percent of your oxygen to get there, it should take about that much oxygen for you to get back. Which would leave you 10 percent when you return. It's a good margin of error."

"I don't plan to make any errors."

"Very funny. But seriously. Turn back at 55 percent. Or sooner if it looks dangerous out there."

Slowly, Owen nodded. This was new for him. He wasn't used to anyone caring when he went into dangerous situations—except for his mother. That thought stabbed at him. Was she out there somewhere? Had she been… archived like him? Or was she lost to the sands of time?

Maya's voice snapped him back to the moment. "I'm

going to have Will set an alarm on the terminal—so we'll know when you should be back. Or at least, the approximate time based on an average oxygen usage."

"And if I'm not back?"

"I'll go looking for you. If you're not back by the 30 percent mark, I'm going out there—just to be sure."

Owen shook his head. "No."

"Yes, I will. You can't stop me."

He laughed. "You have me there. But let's talk about that. If I don't come back, it means it's dangerous out there."

"Or you got lost."

"Hey. I never get lost."

"Even when…" Maya tried to imitate Bryce's mild, dead-pan tone. "The world you know… is gone?"

Owen chuckled. "I never. Get lost. Period."

"Right, so it would be something truly dangerous out there. Like a monster. Or a sinkhole. Or alien invaders."

"Correct. Which brings me to my point: if I don't come back, you all should use the terminal to call for help."

Maya considered that. "Fair point."

Owen stood and prepared to don the helmet.

"Wait," Maya said. "I think we should talk about priorities."

"Priorities?"

"First priority: figure out where we are. Look for any signs, geographical markers, anything that might help us."

"All right."

"Next, I would look for animals. If they can survive out there, it might offer clues about what we're dealing with."

"That's a good idea."

"Does the suit have an external microphone?"

Owen checked the suit controls. "Yeah."

"I'd turn it on."

"And listen for what?"

"Anything that might offer clues about what's happening... and signs that there are others out there."

"What do you think I should do if I see or hear someone?"

"For now, I would hide."

Owen thought that a very strange answer. Maya must have read his expression.

"We don't know what we're dealing with here. Better safe than sorry."

CHAPTER NINETEEN

Through the narrow window, Maya watched the outer airlock door open. Owen stepped out, and as the hatch swung closed, he turned and made eye contact through the glass shield in the helmet.

He smiled. Maya smiled back. And she hoped it wouldn't be the last time she saw him alive.

A moment later, he was marching past the dead man, the beams from his helmet lighting the way. Soon, he was a dark shadow, and when he rounded the turn, he was gone, the passageway dark again except for the glow of the red emergency lights pulsing outward from the station and the dim glow at the end of the tunnel.

Maya shivered in the corridor. Her breath came out in thick clouds of white now—not the faint puffs they had been when she woke. The power had been off for some time, and it was getting colder.

With each frigid breath she expelled, she had a sense that time was running out for them. Inside, the cold was closing in. Outside, whatever deadly unseen element that had killed the older man was waiting.

They were truly trapped.

She wondered what Owen would find out there. She had

wanted to join him but knew that, logically, she had to stay to monitor the others—and that preserving the suit oxygen was critical.

She jumped a little when the decon sequence began in the airlock, the nozzles spraying forth the hazy liquid with a hiss. The airlock clearly had an automated sequence to cleanse the outside air that got in when the outer airlock was opened.

As Maya watched the mist fill the airlock, her mind drifted to her mother and sister, and of a lingering memory of a man who had visited her in the hospital: Parrish. That thought evoked another memory, of her going to work at Genesis Biosciences. Will had said that he worked for ARC Technologies on a team dedicated exclusively to Genesis Biosciences. Was there a connection? Did he know her and wasn't telling her? It seemed too random to be a coincidence.

When the decon spray had been sucked out of the chamber, Maya entered the airlock and gathered the suits, careful not to touch the blood on the suit Cara had previously worn outside.

She dragged them down the corridor and fumbled with the thumb outside Observation 2, finally managing to get the door open.

A blast of warm air rushed out, and Alister turned, annoyed. "Come on, close the door, you're letting the heat out."

"Little help here," Maya muttered as she pulled the four suits inside.

At her words, Will was on his feet instantly, helping her with them. Maya realized then that the group had been eating, and she only then felt her own hunger.

With the door closed and the suits stowed in the corner, Maya ripped open a meal pack marked ARC Rations.

Alister, still chewing, called to her, "Don't expect much."

Maya immediately saw what he meant. Where she had expected some sort of structured meal, she found only a sea of gelatinous green goo. "What. Is. This?"

"ARC's idea of fine dining," Alister said.

"I checked the nutrient report on the label," Cara said. "It will sustain us. But obviously not inspire our culinary delight."

Alister snorted. "Culinary delight. Good one. I'd love to know what's in the slime. Or who. Maybe—"

Maya held up her fork. "Don't go there. Just don't, okay? Not while we're eating."

Alister shrugged. "Suit yourself. Complaining is how I stay sane."

The lights overhead faded, flickered, and after a struggle to return, winked out. Even the red flashes from the hall went dark. It was pitch black except for the ARC tablet that lit Will's placid face. He tapped furiously, as though he were playing a video game in which he was battling for his life.

Maya felt a small, warm hand slip into hers—Blair reaching out. Maya pulled the girl close and wrapped her arms around her, rubbing her hand up and down the child's bony back. She pressed her mouth and nose into the top of Blair's head and let the warmth of her exhales flow into her hair.

Maya expected the power to flip back on, but this time, it didn't.

The soft rumble of the air supply duct overhead fell silent.

By small degrees, Maya felt the temperature dropping. Blair snuggled into her as the shivering began.

Caring for the girl seemed to come naturally to Maya, but she couldn't remember if she had any children of her own. Instinctively, she felt that she didn't, that she had been alone, and that the lack of a family had been an area of regret and longing in her life. In a strange way, in this bizarre place, she felt closer to having something she had wanted in the world before.

In the dim light, Alister rose and moved toward Maya and Blair, stooping close to them, reaching for something—a blanket—which he wrapped around the girl. "We should put her in the corner and use our body heat."

Maya couldn't have been more surprised. The burly man continued to be an enigma. "Not a bad idea, but I think we should get her into the suit."

"No," Blair whispered. "I don't want to."

"You have to, dear," Maya said. "It's okay. We're all going to wear them. It will be warm and... safer."

They had all suited up—except for Alister—when the power came back on.

"What did you do?" Cara asked Will, who continued to work the tablet awkwardly through the gloves.

"Nothing," he replied over the suit radio. "I can't take credit. The system just came back on."

Overhead, Maya heard the air supply rumble to life. Alister moved over and stood below it, tilting his head toward the warm air drifting down. Despite the system being off, Alister hadn't gotten sick like the man outside.

It stood to reason since the station was sealed off from the air outside (Alister had merely been breathing the oxygen already in the station, albeit a dwindling supply).

"Is it safe to take the suit off?" Blair asked, her voice quiet.

Maya and Cara shared a glance. The doctor merely shrugged and said, "Just take the helmet off for now. Alister seems fine."

The older man laughed. "Nothing like being a sacrificial lab animal who is then used by other sacrificial lab animals. I feel so special."

"You are special," Cara said.

Alister closed his eyes and nodded dramatically. "Your words give me reason to live, doctor, if only to be your disposable signal bird."

"You volunteered."

"Hey," Will said, "I've got something."

"Please tell me you've discovered that this is all a bad dream," Alister muttered.

"It's a video," Will said.

"What is?" Maya asked.

"The file marked *Escape Hatch*. It's a video. I thought it was, but it wouldn't play."

"How'd you fix it?" Maya asked.

"Renamed it, then re-encoded it." He rotated the tablet to the group. "Want to see it?"

CHAPTER TWENTY

At the beginning of his career, Owen had spent a lot of time in firesuits. First, in training, and then, in fires.

The first time he had donned the suit, he had known that he had found his one true calling. Inside the suit, a sense of serenity had descended upon him. It was as though the constant background noise of his mind had gone quiet, leaving only his true self and the work before him. In the case of firefighting, that work was mostly carrying people out of harm's way. And he liked that. He liked the way it made him feel.

In the passageway beyond the airlock, wearing the environmental suit, he felt that sensation again—for the first time in a long time. And it felt just as good. That was strange. Here, in a time when everything had fallen apart, he felt more at home than he had in ages. He was doing work that mattered, work he was especially qualified for. He was glad it was him out here, wearing the suit, taking the risk—and not one of the others.

Here and now, his mind was quiet, focused only on the task at hand: discovering what was outside.

As he marched up the rocky path, he was careful on the

loose ground beneath his feet. A fall—and a rip in the suit—could be deadly.

Gently, Owen panned his helmet back and forth, allowing the lamps to rake over the walls and floor, looking for any clues about where he was—or who might be waiting outside the cave. He found only rock and dirt.

The wind whistled in the passageway. The soft howl outside the airlock grew stronger as Owen climbed. The tunnel turned, and as he rounded the corner, the howl grew louder.

Out of habit, he wanted to activate his radio and check in with Maya, as he might have done with his team if he were out on a call. But they had decided that radio silence was prudent.

He wasn't even sure if the suit radio would reach from the cave opening back to the station, and even if it did, broadcasting would give away their position to anyone listening. It was a risk they couldn't take. Not yet. They needed to know more.

So, Owen walked in silence, making another turn in the passage, watching as the faint light ahead grew brighter. To Owen's surprise, it seemed to flicker every now and then, not unlike the emergency strobe light in the station. Out here, however, the pulsing light seemed to follow no pattern. What was it? A searchlight of some kind? A beacon that was also losing its power?

The mystery made him hasten his pace. Soon, he was pumping his legs up the incline. With each step, the wind grew stronger. Owen heard—and felt—a gentle gust that made him slow slightly, careful not to lose his balance.

He expected the tunnel to grow wider as he neared the exit. Instead, it narrowed.

The passage made an abrupt right turn, and around that bend, Owen glimpsed the exit and the soft glow of filtered sunlight shining through. The cave entrance was partially covered with rocks stacked up like a makeshift grave. The wind blew through the opening forcefully, tugging at his suit. He leaned forward, steadying himself as he marched to the rocks and began moving them aside. As he worked, rain lashed into the cave, carried by the wind, drenching the suit and stones, causing several to slip from Owen's grip.

He was panting by the time he had cleared the last rock. He peered out, taking stock, but saw only thick fog and sheets of rain and wind.

One thing was certain: Bryce had told the truth about there being a storm. But was it deadly? Or was it something else in the air that had killed the older man?

Owen realized then what had caused the light's pulsing effect: the storm and the fog. Both drifted past the cave entrance in sheets, blotting out the sun and letting it through in a random pattern.

The cloud of fog shifted, revealing massive trees clustered near the cave opening. They were thick and dark, with limbs that stretched out and merged with each other as though they were a group of people clamoring together to withstand the storm, their own resilience magnified by their shared strength.

Owen wasn't exactly a tree expert, but he didn't recall any species quite like what he saw. The dark, massive trunks reminded him of something prehistoric, of a world untouched by humans. And so was the ground: he found no signs of roads or civilization of any sort.

He saw only trees ahead, shrouded by fog, and rock to his left and right and behind him. It was clear now that he had exited at the side of a mountain. The ground ahead descended sharply.

Owen listened but heard only the wind. No people. No birds. No machines.

Carefully, he crept out from the cave, surveying the landscape. A gust of wind blew through the trees. It bent the thick limbs aside and brought with it a blast of light from the hazy sun. The gust blew through, and the limbs whipped back into place, blotting out the sun's harshest rays, restoring the semi-darkness around the cave.

Ahead was only dense fog, thick trees, and a near-vertical drop. Things weren't any better to the left or right.

Owen turned and tilted his head back as far as the helmet would allow, gazing up at the mountain. He thought going up the mountain might give him a vantage point to figure out where they were—and if there was any help nearby.

He checked the panel in the suit arm: 79 percent oxygen left. Plenty of time to check it out and get back.

CHAPTER TWENTY-ONE

In Observation Two, Maya and the others crowded around Will as he held up the tablet and hit play on the video marked *Escape Hatch*.

In the video, a man was standing in a command center—one Maya assumed was the same as in their station.

The man was a mirror image of Bryce. Perhaps he was an android. That seemed a safe assumption to Maya.

Two other "Bryces" were sitting at the workstations in the command center, staring at screens, typing. Maya thought that was odd. If they were indeed androids, wouldn't it be more efficient to communicate wirelessly to control the computers? There had to be some reason, but like just about everything since she had awoken, it was a mystery.

"Station 17, Emergency message. Proctor Bran recording. I am the station chief PI."

"PI?" Cara whispered. "As in principal investigator?"

Will hit the pause button. "Maybe. When we used the term at ARC, it was for pseudo intelligence."

"Instead of AI?" Cara asked.

"Yes."

"Why?"

"I think because of the limits of the programs. Our PIs

couldn't really exceed the bounds of their programming—they could simply iterate and improve within pre-set functions. And... I think some of it was marketing. Everyone was scared of AI back then—because of the potential for unexpected consequences and because it was taking a lot of jobs."

"I believe," Alister said, "that it's safe to assume Bryce was only pseudo-intelligent. After all, the poor sod got his brains bashed in by some random guy he was trying to help."

"If," Cara said, "Bryce was indeed trying to help us."

Alister held a hand to his chest, feigning shock. "It's an Extinction Trials breakthrough: the doctor and I actually agree on something."

Cara rolled her eyes. When no one said anything, Will pressed the play button, and the android that had introduced himself as Proctor Bran continued speaking.

"I have been asked to record this message—by Garden Station—and go dark afterward. I'm not entirely sure what to say. Perhaps I'll start with a confirmation: we have followed the instructions issued to us by Garden Station. We are currently manually deleting our logs, not via wireless instruction as specified. We are also disabling all wireless communications and deleting the subroutines that operate the embedded systems."

Maya leaned closer to Will. "That explains some of what you found."

He nodded, studying the screen, where the proctor continued.

"As instructed, we've also taken inventory of the remaining six cohorts here at the station, which include forty-four

Trials participants. At the time of this recording, all have been restored to health, and the specified interventions have been administered to each participant."

Alister reached forward and tapped the pause button. "I don't like the sound of that—interventions."

"Nor do I," Cara said. "It implies that they've done some sort of experimentation on us."

The words hung in the air a moment. "For my part," Maya said, "I was healed. I remember being sick in the hospital. Now I feel fine—except for my memory."

She had hoped the others would elaborate on their own experiences, but strangely, no one said anything.

"Well," Maya said finally, "let's find out what else he has to say."

"To date, we have lost a total of sixteen participants to medical issues that pre-dated Trials enrollment or due to adverse events encountered during Trials execution. To date, twelve cohorts containing fifty-nine participants were successfully released and no further contact has been made with any cohort. Per the Trials protocol, the most promising cohorts were released first. Our operating assumption has simply been that the interventions administered were unsuccessful at resolving the Trials' stated outcome. We have made adjustments to the interventions based on Garden Station directives. Finally, I'd like to note that our staff of three proctors remains functional and operating within specified parameters."

The proctor paused. "As further dictated in Garden's terminating message, we have assembled the requisite items and will be sealing the station and activating biological controls. Finally, as I'm unsure who will encounter this message—perhaps a proctor from another station or a Trials participant from this station or another station, I will simply warn you to please exercise caution. Remember, sometimes the answers we seek are right in front of us."

CHAPTER TWENTY-TWO

As Owen climbed the mountain, rain fell in sheets, and the wind tugged at his suit.

The trees swayed and shed pieces of themselves—leaves that drifted down and coated the ground. The spongy leaves reminded him of pieces of fabric—green, purple, and blue. Walking across them was like climbing a carpeted mountain.

It was like nothing he'd ever seen.

He proceeded slowly, careful of his footing, knowing that one misstep could be deadly and that the others were depending on him.

Being alone out here was a bit like some of his early assignments as a firefighter when he had been cut off from his teammates. Strangely, the people back at the station already felt like that to him: teammates. That was strange, he thought. But it was also a source of strength and drive for him—having people that were depending on him.

As he climbed, the fog grew thinner, the wind weaker.

At a rock outcropping, he stopped and turned and looked, but saw only the wall of trees and fog behind him. He needed to get higher.

He trudged farther up the mountain, breathing hard now. He wondered if the exertion of the climb would elicit pain from the previous injuries he'd endured at the apartment building. But he felt fine, as though his body were new again, young, as healthy as he had been when he'd begun his career as a firefighter.

When he stopped to gather his breath, he tapped the display on his forearm and checked the oxygen reading:

73%

He could keep going a while longer, but the climb was making him use oxygen at a faster rate. He needed to hurry.

He ascended with a renewed vigor then, urgent, desperately wanting to return with some piece of information that might help the team.

He stopped again to catch his breath and glanced at the forearm panel:

67%

Time was slipping away.

He pushed even harder then, pumping his legs, stumbling over the loose rock as he drove himself up the mountain. Occasionally, he glanced over his shoulder, but the view was always the same: trees and fog that hid any clues as to what this place was.

The next time he stopped, the panel read:

59%

Up ahead, the forest was thinner, the trees shorter, with more space between the limbs. The ground was rockier. Fog still shrouded whatever was beyond, but Owen felt that he was close, as though he were surrounded by smoke and that salvation lay on the other side.

He bounded forward, pushing himself even harder.

He slipped on a rock, but luckily, he reached down with a gloved hand and caught himself before he fell. He stayed still a moment, chest heaving. Finally, he stood and inspected the glove for any puncture. He was fine. And he needed to hurry.

He took it slower then, watching the ground more carefully.

As if it had been a mirage, the fog cleared. Ahead was an outcropping of stone, and above it, a plateau of rock that seemed to be the summit of the mountain. Owen saw only blue sky beyond.

He had done it.

He had reached the peak.

He sprinted forward, seeing the end in sight, a grin forming on his face, the anticipation of possibly discovering, finally, where they were and what they were dealing with.

In his mind's eye, he couldn't help thinking about returning to the station and telling the others. In that place of imaginary future memories, for whatever reason, he saw himself telling Maya first and hearing her celebrating the good news he had risked his life to bring back. He thought it strange that she was the one he thought of first. Why was that?

At the wall of rock, he used his hands and feet to climb, careful to find his footing. He stopped to rest halfway up and glanced at his arm panel:

51%

He told himself that it would be faster going back, that he'd used more oxygen and more time to climb the mountain. The downhill dissent would use a fraction of that. He still had time. Plenty of time.

The rocky plateau was bare except for a few shrubs. The wind whipped forcefully here, a gale force that tugged at the suit and howled in the helmet speaker.

Owen crept to the precipice opposite the way he'd approached and gazed down. For a moment, he was shocked at what he saw. Taking it in, he shuffled along the edge, making a circle, looking out. What he saw sent a wave of shock and fear through him.

The storm was certainly strongest in the direction he had come from—and the fog was thicker there. The other side was clearer, but that didn't help much.

As he completed the loop, he spotted something that just might be their salvation.

He was leaning forward, trying to get a better look, but a gust of wind threw him off balance. The rock below his feet rolled and crumbled and he fell to his knees. Another gust of wind and rain hit him just as he was rising, rolling him off the plateau. He reached out with his hands, but he was too late.

For what felt like an impossibly long moment, he flew through the air, landing on a small outcropping before he bounced off and he was in the air again, freefalling. He turned and held his hands up to brace himself for the impact he knew was coming. But the pain didn't come. He hit the ground hard enough for everything to instantly fade to black.

CHAPTER TWENTY-THREE

Alister slammed the heel of his hand into the floor. "Useless. Completely and utterly useless message. What's the meaning of even naming it Escape Hatch? The video just rambles on: we have this many participants and we released this many, and this many in this many cohorts are still here and here's how many died before that. Who cares?"

Maya had to admit, the message had been a disappointment. And a bit confusing. She'd expected it to be some sort of plan that would help them. Or directions on how to get help or where to go.

On the tablet, an alarm sounded. The timer had run out. Owen's suit was down to 30 percent oxygen.

Maya had hoped that he would be back by now.

She rose and moved out of Observation Two, down the corridor, and to the outer airlock. She peered through the narrow window into the dark cave tunnel where the dead man lay, his body illuminated only by the flashing red light.

She waited, chewing her lip, debating what to do. Cara arrived beside her and stared out the narrow window as well. "Are you going out there?" the doctor asked.

Before Maya could answer, the power flickered and went off again.

"I think I should," Maya said in the pitch darkness. "We're out of time. Whether we use the suits in here or out there, we're running out of time and breathable oxygen. I'd rather take our chances trying to survive—not waiting. We need to look for help or a way out."

"I agree," Alister said from behind them, his voice disembodied in the dark. "I'll come with you."

"No," Maya said. "We shouldn't risk anyone else. If neither Owen nor I come back—"

"If neither of you comes back," Alister said, "we're no better off. If he's hurt, you'll need me to help you carry him back."

"And I'll need to help him if he's hurt," Cara said.

"You can't do much through the suit," Alister said.

"We don't know that," Cara replied. "And for all we know, we can take the suits off beyond the cave—perhaps Owen discovered that."

"I'll take care of Blair," Will said, another voice in the darkness, quiet but confident. "You know it's the right move, Maya. The longer we talk about it, the less time— and oxygen—Owen has left out there."

In the cave tunnel, they marched single file, Maya leading, Cara behind her, and Alister bringing up the rear. They maintained radio silence, as they'd agreed.

There was one bit of good news: Owen's footsteps were very clear in the muddy passage. Maya traced them out of the winding cave, the wind growing stronger and the light growing brighter with each step.

At the mouth of the cave, they found rocks piled around

the entrance. She wondered if Owen had unblocked the passage or if someone else had. And why had it been covered up to begin with?

Outside the cave, clouds of fog drifted through the towering trees. In the presence of the massive trees, Maya felt as though she had been shrunk and placed in a world out of size, an ancient place that was dominated by beings far larger. She had expected that the station would be in the middle of a city or at least near a road. There was no sign of civilization here.

She felt a hand on her shoulder and turned to find Alister pointing at the ground, at Owen's footprints. His meaning was obvious: *come on, we're running out of time.* Even after knowing him only a short amount of time, she could almost mentally hear his unspoken words in her mind. And he was right.

They had agreed that they would use the suit speakers and microphones to communicate, but that breaking their silence would be a last resort. Being quiet was safer, at least until they knew more.

Maya led them back toward the cave, following Owen's steps in the soft ground. They climbed up the mountain, snaking through the trees. The footprints were fainter higher up—the ground was shallower and the trees were thinner, which allowed the wind to wipe the tracks away. Maya felt as though she were following a map that had been dipped in water and was slowly dissolving before her eyes.

She checked her forearm panel. Owen was at 17 percent oxygen now. Was it already too late?

She pumped her legs harder. Soon, her chest was pounding. Sweat rolled down her face. The sound of her breathing in the helmet fought a war with the sound of the wind through the speaker. She felt as though she was in an echo chamber.

Finally, she stopped and put her hands on her knees, bending over to try to catch her breath. Soon, Cara arrived beside her and Alister shortly after. He was in the worst shape of them all. But he was easily the strongest.

Without a word, Maya resumed, but she had only taken a few steps when she encountered a problem: Owen's tracks were gone. The last of them were so faint she wasn't even sure they were indeed Owen's boots in the ground and not some natural indentation. The wind was stronger here, and the trees had taken more damage. Leaves covered the ground, preventing anyone from making any tracks.

Catching her breath again, Maya glanced at the others. Alister motioned ahead impatiently, silently saying, *let's just keep going.*

The ground changed as they went. With each step, the soft, rain-soaked dirt covered by leaves went away, leaving rocky terrain that was bare except for a few shrubs. Ahead, a sheer rock face loomed, almost vertical. There was no sign of Owen. Would he have climbed up it?

A cloud of fog cleared, and Maya stopped in her tracks. For the first time, she saw the sky beyond. It was a stark contrast to the wind and rain and fog that surrounded her, as if another world lay ahead.

For some reason, Maya felt certain about what Owen would've done if he had come this way: ascended the cliff and gazed out from the peak. Even if he wasn't here, she might find answers up there. She might be able to find him—and see where they were.

Carefully, she climbed, Alister and Cara behind her. At the top, she paced across the stone plateau and peered down, aghast at what she saw.

She wanted to be certain, so she made her way around the plateau, at times waiting until the fog rolled by like a curtain unveiling the world beyond.

On this high perch, strong winds came and went, a barrage that hit without warning. Twice, the gusts threw Maya off balance.

At the edge of the plateau, she felt a strong hand around her arm, and she turned to find Alister beckoning her away from the precipice, toward the center where Cara stood waiting.

Alister's gruff voice came over Maya's helmet speaker. "I think we can safely use the radios."

"Yes," Maya said quietly.

"I didn't see any sign of Owen," Cara said. "Did either of you?"

Alister shook his head and looked away.

"No," Maya said. "But he has to be close by. After all, we're clearly on a very small island."

CHAPTER TWENTY-FOUR

Owen woke to the sound of voices.

At first, he couldn't make out the words. They were scratchy and garbled and interrupted intermittently by the sound of an alarm.

Owen raised his arm and read the panel:

```
OXYGEN LEVEL CRITICAL: 9% REMAINING.
```

He tapped the panel, silencing the alarm and listening to the voices over the radio.

"There's no sign of a helipad or landing strip." It was Maya speaking.

"And no boat docks," Alister said. "Or buildings, for that matter. It's like a deserted island."

"Maybe it hasn't been an island for that long," Cara said. "We're clearly in the mountains. This looks to me like an untouched mountain range that was flooded. This station was lucky enough to be near the peak."

"Hey," Owen said, voice scratchy. "Can you hear me?"

"Owen," Maya said urgently. "Where are you?"

"I'm..." Owen sat up, trying to get a bearing, but it was

no use. "Oh, you know, over here with the rocks and fog and massive trees."

"Very funny," Maya said, her voice annoyed but also a little amused. "What happened? Are you hurt?"

"No. Or, I don't know. I don't think so. A gust of wind caught me and rolled me off the plateau."

For a moment, Owen took stock. His right arm and leg ached. But the suit had provided some cushion.

The suit.

A bolt of fear ran through him: if the suit was punctured...

Quickly, he sat up and scanned it. He was caked in the dark mud, but based on the oxygen level and no signs of tears, he thought he was ok.

"Owen," Maya said. "We're on the plateau. Grab a fallen limb and wave it around."

He complied, and soon, Maya said, "We see you. Stay put, we're coming down."

A moment later, three suited figures emerged from the cloud of fog passing by, Maya leading the way.

She held up her arm panel. "It says you have less than 10 percent oxygen left."

Owen showed her his forearm panel. "I'm at 9 percent. Plenty."

"You must have been unconscious," Cara said. "Your body would have used less oxygen during that time. Nevertheless, we're all still over 60 percent oxygen. We'll use the transfer adapter to even out the supply between the four of us. And then head back."

With that, Alister set about hooking Owen's tank to Maya's. He opened the valve and Owen watched as his oxygen level rose.

"I saw something from up there," Owen said. He motioned toward the forest and the shore beyond. "A boat. Did you all see it?"

"No," Maya said. She turned to him, her tank hooked to Cara's. "What kind of boat?"

"It's small. With a solar-paneled roof. It's beached. Not far away. We should check it out while we're here. It may be our only way off this rock."

"It may be," Cara said. "But we need to get you back to the station. I want to do a thorough examination."

"I'm fine."

"You could have a concussion. Or internal bleeding."

Owen exhaled. "Okay."

"We'll take a look," Maya said, motioning to Alister, who shrugged and added, "Why not? I always wanted a boat. The Apocalypse sounds like a great time to get one."

CHAPTER TWENTY-FIVE

Maya strode through the dense forest, dodging trees and traipsing over fallen limbs and leaves with ease. It wasn't just because she was going downhill. Or because she'd gotten used to the terrain, though she had.

She felt as if a weight had lifted, Owen was alive. And they had found a boat. A boat that might be the key to their survival—to getting off the small island.

The vessel wasn't a large ship, more like a small yacht. That's what it reminded Maya of. The hull was white and sleek, the roof arched and black, covered with solar panels which appeared undamaged. That was a good sign.

It was beached in the soft dirt bow first. Alister climbed aboard using a small ladder that hung down to the ground, then turned back and offered Maya his hand, helping her aboard.

They walked the length of the small vessel to the rear, where two large outboard motors sat in the water. The sitting area nearby featured four swivel chairs bolted to the deck and vertical pipes that looked like they might hold fishing rods.

Ahead, under the solar roof, lay the main deck. To the left, there was a small kitchenette with a sink, a small stove, and what looked like a refrigerator under the counter. Maya bent over and peered through the glass door of what she thought was the refrigerator, but it was empty. An L-shaped couch lay across from it.

Beyond the couch was an open cockpit, with two plush seats side by side and a steering wheel to the right that reminded Maya of the old cars before they became self-driving.

On the left, there was a dining table with banquette seating.

What Maya didn't see struck her most: people, blood, or any signs of habitation.

Between the dining table and the cockpit, there was a small door just shorter than she was. Alister moved toward it. "Let's check below decks."

The door creaked as he pushed it open, revealing a small staircase leading into the darkness.

Alister switched his headlamps on as he descended, and Maya did the same. They stepped single file into the darkness, their beams raking across the narrow corridor.

Dead ahead lay a closed door. There was another door directly to the right. The small landing switched back, turning toward the rear of the ship. In that short hallway was another small flight of stairs that descended further into the bowels of the vessel.

Alister pushed open the door to his right. It was a stateroom with two narrow beds just big enough to hold an adult. Both empty.

Alister stepped back and pushed open the door ahead. It was another stateroom, also empty, with a single larger bed. The room was wider near the door and grew more narrow toward the far wall, which was closer to the bow of the ship.

Maya retreated into the hall, allowing Alister to pass her and move toward the staircase that led deeper into the ship. It was darker here—the dim light that had filtered in from the stairway to the main deck now faded to a soft glow.

Maya checked her oxygen level:

52%

They needed to head back soon.

On the right side of the hallway, there was a narrow table with U-shaped banquette seating. A single door ahead was the only exit from the hallway.

Alister turned the handle and pushed the door open, panning his helmet lights left and right. Maya knew instantly from his body language that something was wrong. He drew back a step, still holding the door as if ready to slam it shut.

He waited a moment before charging into the room, swiveling about, searching. Maya saw it then: two figures lying on the largest bed she had yet to see on the ship. They were wearing suits—ARC Technologies environmental suits just like the one she wore. The two figures were unmoving. And they were holding hands.

"Stay there, Maya," Alister said, his voice more serious than she had ever heard it.

He darted toward the corner of the room and jerked open the door and stepped back. Over the radio, she heard him exhale. "It's just a bathroom. It's empty."

Maya ventured closer to the couple and leaned over the bed, bathing their faces with light. It was a man and woman. They appeared to be about her age. And Owen's age. Their eyes were closed, and their faces showed no signs of distress. They seemed, in a word, peaceful.

She felt awkward about it, but she knew what she had to do. She reached out and took the woman's arm, and turned the panel toward her and tapped it. The suit still had power—it had apparently gone into sleep mode—but the tank was out of oxygen.

Gently, she placed the woman's arm back on the bed. Alister did the same for the man. "His oxygen is at zero."

Maya checked her own panel. "I'm at 49 percent, Alister. We need to hurry."

"True. But I should make sure the boat's operational first."

Maya cocked her head. "Do you know much about boats?"

"Well... Not really. But it's sort of like a city bus floating on the water. If it's got an engine, I can make it run."

Maya smiled. "I hope you're right."

Alister motioned to the man and woman on the bed. "It feels wrong, but we need the suits. We're one short, and it would be nice to have an extra and a spare tank."

"You're right," Maya said quietly. "I'll get the suits while you check the ship. And we really should hurry."

As Maya was removing the suit, a question occurred to her: how had they died? Surely, they hadn't asphyxiated. If so, Maya imagined that they wouldn't have gone this peacefully.

She found the answer—she thought—on the bedside

table. There was a small pill bottle with an ARC Technologies label, though she didn't recognize the medication name.

Beneath the bottle was a small notebook. The first page contained a simple message: *To Someone More Fortunate Than Us.*

Maya flipped through the pages. It was a journal. As soon as time allowed, she'd read it. For now, she tucked it in the pocket of her suit.

In the darkened room, staring at the deceased couple, she felt a pang of sadness. Had they been Extinction Trials participants like her? Had they come from Station 17 as well? Were they from one of the cohorts previously released? If they were from the station, why didn't they take their suits and oxygen tanks back to the decontamination chamber, which could have refilled the tanks?

Had they run out of food? She hadn't seen any. In fact, the ship had been devoid of anything resembling a last meal. Perhaps animals or insects and time had washed away that evidence. The suits likely preserved the cadavers, making it hard to tell how long they'd been dead.

Maya felt wetness beneath her nose and instinctively knew that it was blood. Without a thought, she reached up, only then realizing she couldn't get to it while wearing the suit. It flowed across her lips and chin unabated, a savage and bizarre feeling—blood on her face that she couldn't wipe away.

A headache began then, a low pulsing pain of pressure with nowhere to escape. The hurt brought a memory.

Maya was standing in a large room with floor-to-ceiling windows. People strode by on the sidewalk outside. She was sweaty and lightly winded in the memory. She felt the same nosebleed then—right before she collapsed. Yes, she had been sick—that's why she had been brought to the hospital.

Was whatever had sickened her before returning? Or was she never truly healed?

She was so lost in the thought that she didn't realize Alister had returned.

"Something wrong?" he asked over the radio, his voice urgent.

She turned to him. "No."

"You're bleeding."

"It's nothing."

"Is your suit failing?"

"No. It's fine. It's just... I'm fine."

"Well, the ship isn't."

"What do you mean?"

"The engine won't turn on." Alister motioned to the couple. "We're as stranded here as they were."

CHAPTER TWENTY-SIX

Back at the station, Owen and Cara waited in the decontamination chamber as the nozzles above sprayed their suits down. When the process was complete, they hooked their oxygen tanks up to the replenishing alcove.

It was frigid in the main hallway and only slightly warmer inside Observation Two, where Will and Blair were sitting in the corner, wrapped in blankets. Will held up the tablet, reading aloud to the girl, who was wearing the environmental suit that was far too big for her. The helmet lay to her side, ready for her to put it on at a moment's notice.

"You're back," Will said as he stood. "Is everything all right?"

"We'll know more soon," Owen said, hoping the meaning was clear to Will.

The younger man cut his eyes toward Blair. "Right. Well, we found a cache of books on the tablet, so that's kept us busy."

"Why's it so cold in here?" Owen asked. "Power problems?"

Will shook his head. "No. Surprisingly, the power has been somewhat steady while you were gone. I just cut it back to take some pressure off the power plant."

"That's a good idea," Cara said. She motioned Owen to one of the folding chairs. "Now, I need to perform that medical eval."

Owen groaned as he took a seat.

When Cara had finished the examination—and relented that Owen was in no imminent danger of dying—Will played the *Escape Hatch* video they had found on the tablet.

"I don't get it," Owen said.

"Neither do we," Cara said.

Owen paced the room, thinking for a moment. "Play it again."

After the third time watching it, the dots connected in Owen's mind. He saw it—what the video actually meant. In a strange way, it all made sense.

Why didn't the others see it? It was the key that unlocked the tablet. It seemed obvious to him, in the same way the video did. It was just how his mind worked.

Before he could explain, the tablet lit up with a notification:

```
Airlock Opening.
```

Owen bound into the corridor, his bruised leg slowing him slightly. Maya and Alister were in the decontamination chamber, and they had brought two more suits with them. Amazing. That was a lucky break. Had they found the suits outside? Or on the boat?

In the small chamber, they hooked all the tanks up to the replenishing alcove, and when Maya turned back toward the window, Owen's mouth fell open. There was blood covering her mouth and running down her neck.

She was hurt. What happened?

She seemed to sense his concern because she reached up and wiped the blood away with her shirt.

As soon as the inner airlock opened, Owen said, "What happened? Are you okay?"

"I'm fine. It's just a nosebleed."

Owen studied her a moment, not sure what to say, wishing again he could read her expression.

Alister put his arms around himself. "Has it gotten colder in here?"

"Yes," Will said. "Power conservation."

"That's great. Assuming we don't freeze to death."

In Observation Two, Alister and Maya quickly related what they'd found on the boat.

Maya held up the journal. "I haven't had a chance to read it yet, but I'm hoping the answers as to why these two were stranded here and what happened to them are inside."

"I think the bigger question," Cara said, "is whether the boat is any use to us."

"I can fix it," Alister said. "But I don't think you're going to like the solution."

All eyes turned to him.

"I'm pretty sure I can use parts from the power plant to repair the boat's engine. But the power plant will be out for good after that. Once we fix the boat, we need to go."

"Yes, but go where?" Cara said. "Do we even have enough food to make it to another island or the mainland?"

"Well," Maya said, "we certainly don't have enough to stay here. And I didn't see any animals out there. With the power situation, I feel like the longer we stay here, the more danger we are in. If the power is out, the scrubbers won't run, and we won't be able to refill the oxygen tanks. Our choices, frankly, are either running out of food here or running out of food out in the ocean. What we truly lack is a destination once we leave on the boat."

"I think I have a solution," Owen said. "I watched the *Escape Hatch* video."

Alister rolled his eyes. "The *Escape Hatch* video," he muttered. "What a crock."

"Maybe not," Owen said as he opened the door and hobbled out into the hall. He glanced left and right, then stalked toward the outer airlock, silently counting the pods. At the end of the corridor, he turned and walked the length of the hall, all the way to the control room, continuing to count.

When he re-entered the observation room, he paused, double-checking his math. When he was certain, he smiled. "There's one very big problem with the video."

"Yeah," Alister said. "It's useless."

"No. It's quite useful. The problem is the math."

"Explain," Cara said.

"The math doesn't add up."

Maya crossed her arms. "How so?"

"Specifically, the numbers of the Trials participants don't add up."

"How do you know?" Cara asked.

"I just counted them to make sure," Owen replied. "There are twelve pods, each with seven chambers. That's a total of eighty-four potential participants. In the message, the proctor said that they had released a total of fifty-nine participants, that sixteen had perished during the Trials, and that they still had forty-four here at the station. That's 119 total participants. They don't have that many chambers—not even close. They're short by forty-five."

The group was quiet for a moment.

"Interesting," Alister said quietly. "I never would've thought to check that. That's genius."

"Not genius," Owen said. "Just professional habit. I'm used to hearing numbers of people in a building and instinctively checking those numbers, locating all those people. It's how my job has trained my mind to work."

"They could've gotten additional participants here at the site," Cara said, "after some were released."

"That's true," Owen said. "But the other issue is that it doesn't make sense that the proctor would record a message like this talking about how many participants there were. Especially if he was in contact with Garden Station—which sounds like it was a central command. If so, it conceivably would've had real-time data up until this message was recorded. There would be no need to recount the numbers."

"A fair point," Maya said.

"Now," Owen said, "if the proctor had created a running file that had data on the Trials, that makes sense. But as it stands, the video simply tells whoever finds it what Garden Station would've already known at the time that they sent their terminal message. The last line is what I find most telling: sometimes the answers we seek are right in front of us. I think he's talking directly to us with that message—encouraging us to look for the deeper meaning in his message."

Maya cocked her head. "And you think you know what that deeper meaning is?"

"I do. I think Escape Hatch has nothing to do with the Trials—or not really. Sure, telling us about the previous cohorts and their procedures gives us some sense of what they were doing here—running experiments on us and releasing cohorts out into the world to see what happened—if they could survive in the world after. But I think the file is something else entirely."

"Which is?" Cara asked.

"A map."

Will's eyebrows knitted together. "I don't follow."

"Let's back up," Owen said. "First, a simple question: what's the strangest thing about the video?"

When no one answered, he went on. "The strangest thing is that the numbers don't add up. And as I said, it doesn't make sense for him to put the numbers in there in the first place. So, the numbers mean something. There are six numbers mentioned. But how do we use them? Again, the answer we seek is right in front of us. In the boxes we found, there were several critical items: the tablet, the key, and importantly, one other item that could help us get some help."

Owen waited, watching all eyes on him. "A GPS. I think those six numbers mentioned in the video have nothing to do with what happened here. I believe those numbers are GPS coordinates. And whatever is waiting for us at those coordinates might be our only hope of survival. The numbers—specifically, the coordinates—are our Escape Hatch. And now we have what we need to reach them: a boat."

CHAPTER TWENTY-SEVEN

Maya was tired and scared.

And for the first time since she had awoken in this strange place, she was hopeful. For the first time, they had a way off this island. And a destination. What waited there, she didn't know, but it had to be better than here.

The team worked urgently then, and in sync: worked together as never before.

Owen, Maya, and Cara suited up and carried the packaged meals and their supplies to the ship. Alister and Will studied the power plant, then trekked out to the boat to inspect the broken engine again.

When they returned, the rest of the group was eating in the observation room.

"How sure are you that you can fix it?" Owen asked Alister.

"Pretty sure," the middle-aged man replied. Maya could see that he was dead tired.

"I just need to rest a bit," Alister said. "I'll get one shot at it. If I break the parts to fix the boat, then we're stuck here."

"Once we take the power plant offline," Will said, "we'll need to stay in our suits. We may as well journey to the ship together and—"

"Make our stand there," Owen said. "That's what it is."

Silently, the others nodded. With those words, the course was set.

Alister and Will ate dinner together, quietly reviewing their plan until both were so weary, they could barely keep their eyes open.

Cara lay on a bed of blankets, holding the small item she had found in the envelope with her name on it. She stared at it, marveling. It was something she had seen hundreds, perhaps thousands, of times in pictures. But she never thought she would ever hold it. A single thought ran through her mind: *I'm free now.*

In the corner, Owen was reading the book he had found in the envelope with his name on it: *The Birthright.* His face was a mask of concentration that made him look younger, like a schoolboy struggling with a new subject. Maya found it endearing.

Blair placed a hand on Maya's shoulder, and she turned to find the young girl holding the tablet. "Will you read to me?"

"Of course," Maya said, smiling.

She didn't know if Blair could read herself—the child looked like she might be at the age where she was learning—or if she simply liked the comfort of Maya reading to her. Either way, Maya was more than willing to do so. They sat in the corner, reading until Blair's eyelids stayed closed. Maya wasn't far behind her.

The next morning, they suited up and waited by the airlock as Alister and Will removed the parts they needed from the power plant.

The pulsing red emergency lights winked out, plunging the space into darkness. One by one, their helmet lights snapped on, six sets of beams cutting into the darkness.

"We're ready," Alister said over the radio.

They marched single file out of the cave and into the forest. The storm was gone, leaving only the morning fog. Still, no one risked removing their helmet.

On the uneven ground, Blair held hands with Maya and Owen, who were both prepared to catch the girl if she stumbled. A fall—and a tear in her suit—could be deadly.

At the boat, they climbed the ladder and walked along the narrow path to the open-air portion of the deck.

At the station, they had decided they would stay here, in the open portion of the deck, while they had the suits on. Cara had reasoned that if whatever deadly agent was on the island could cling to the suits, it was best not to track it deeper into the ship.

With Will's help, she had also extracted the decontamination liquid from the station's chamber. The plan was to leave the suits on the lower deck, then wipe down the ship. They didn't want to take any chances.

Alister and Will descended the short stairway to the lower deck, where they began their work in earnest.

Maya had learned that Alister was a hard worker, but he wasn't a particularly happy worker. He cursed and muttered complaints in a near-constant stream as he fitted the parts from the power plant into the engine. Chief among his complaints was having to work with the suit on. But he didn't dare take it off, or so much as mention the idea of trying to take it off.

The first time Maya glanced at the oxygen reading on her suit, it read 62 percent.

When she looked at it again, the sun was high in the sky, and the oxygen was down to 43 percent. Time was running out.

All eyes focused on Alister and Will when they trudged up from the lower deck. "We're ready," Will said.

In the cockpit, Alister tapped the control panel with his grease-covered fingers, unbothered by getting the shiny boat dirty. "Here goes nothing," he mumbled as he tried starting the engine.

It only clicked.

Alister threw his hands up. "This hunk of junk is too complicated for its own good! Probably designed to fail so they could sell some rich idiot another one."

With Will in tow, he returned to the lower deck and toiled some more.

Maya made eye contact with Owen, and she could instantly tell what he was thinking: *this isn't going according to plan.* But there was not much they could do except place their faith in Alister and Will—and wait.

Blair, despite her youth, was clearly aware of the danger they were in. Her face displayed the fear they all felt but were trying hard to hide.

Maya felt as if they were standing in a pool watching the waterline rise, knowing soon there would be nothing they could do—except remove their suit helmets. And even if they survived that, they would still be stuck on the island.

Maya took out the tablet. "Let's read, Blair. What do you say?"

Inside the suit that was far too big, the girl nodded, a hint of a smile forming at her lips.

If Maya's reading over the suit radio bothered Alister, he didn't say it. No one complained. They sat in silence, the occasional rapid whispers from Alister and Will over the shared line interrupting the storytelling.

Maya's suit panel read 27 percent when the two men returned to the cockpit to try the engines again. This time, like the last, there was only a clicking sound.

Alister didn't utter a word. He merely marched back to the lower deck, where Maya heard a furious banging. It sounded like the man was trying to beat the boat into compliance.

"Will you give me some room?" Alister yelled, his voice grating over the radio. "I can't think with you breathing down my neck!"

In her peripheral vision, Maya saw Will step away from the engine area and drift toward the back of the boat.

"And I don't like being watched like some animal in a cage," Alister said. "Go. Get out."

With that, Will climbed the stairs to the main deck and waited there, a resigned look on his face.

Maya kept reading, continuing to act like everything was fine.

Alister emerged from the lower deck again. At the cockpit, he jabbed the control panel and it lit up. Water churned where the giant outboard motors met the water.

"Hang on!" Alister yelled. He was trying to hide it, but Maya could hear the excitement beneath his words.

The boat lurched and slid into the water, the propellers sending waves onto the beach as it dragged the ship from the shore.

Soon, the rocky, wooded island was drifting away.

They were free.

They had done it.

Maya stood and watched, taking the island in. It truly looked like the top of a mountain surrounded by water, not like some equatorial paradise. It looked, in a word, unnatural to her. As strange as it was, she wondered if what waited for them beyond was even stranger.

Owen clapped a hand on Alister's back. "Never doubted you. Not even once."

The older man bit off a laugh. "That makes one of us. I doubted me a lot more than once."

"Congratulations, sir," Will said, a serene smile on his face.

"Maybe you are good for something," Cara said, hands on her hips.

Maya looked down and found tears running down Blair's face. "Are you okay, dear?"

She nodded. "I thought we were going to have to stay there. I hated it there."

Maya's eyes met Owen's as she said, "Well, we're never going back."

PART III

THE SEA

CHAPTER TWENTY-EIGHT

The boat sailed into the sunset. Behind it, the island shrank, swallowed by the sea and the darkness that chased away the sun.

The group stayed on the main deck, their suits on, waiting, everyone knowing what would come next—and dreading it.

Owen glanced at his arm panel. His oxygen tank had 12 percent left and there was no way to replenish it.

On the island, clean oxygen had been their lifeblood. They had brought a finite supply of that clean oxygen with them in the tanks, and they were using it up as they moved away from the island.

Was the air out here breathable? It would have to be.

At some point, someone had to take their helmet off and see if they could survive. What hadn't been discussed was *who* that person was going to be.

When his arm panel reached 6 percent, Owen stood and said, "Let's move to the lower deck."

The others complied. They knew it was time. There was no sense running the clock down. The island was gone. Night surrounded them. Only the ship's lights lit their surroundings.

Owen waited, watching the others as they descended the stairs. When he was alone on the main deck above, he quickly removed his helmet.

Maya surged forward. Alister caught her, moving faster than Owen had ever seen the middle-aged man move. She struggled in his arms, mouth moving, the sound lost in the suit helmet.

Staring at her, Owen breathed in.

He waited, wondering if the hurt would start, if his fate would be the same as the man who had died in the cave passage.

He felt only a cold breeze on his face, the smell of saltwater in his nose, and fresh air in his lungs.

Maya reached up to remove her own helmet, but Owen held a hand up, urging her to stop. She froze.

He put his helmet back on.

"That wasn't the plan," she said over the helmet speaker, her voice angry.

"I couldn't watch any of you be the first. This was the best way."

Maya stared at him. "We didn't agree to it."

"It's done," he said simply. "Now, I'll wipe down the ship. Then we'll find out what's out there."

After Owen had removed the suit and tossed it down to the lower deck, he moved through the boat, wiping it down. One by one, the others came up and removed their suits and breathed in the fresh air.

In a strange way, to Owen, it felt like they were being born, taking their first true breath in a new world after being trapped in the dark protective bowels of that subterranean lair.

Once Maya had shed her suit, she moved close to him, where the others couldn't hear.

"That wasn't part of the plan."

"There was no use planning it. One of us had to take the risk. Talking about it would have just added more stress and worry. I did it. It's done."

"This discussion isn't about what's done. It's about next time. Next time, we talk about any potentially fatal, unexpected moves. Agreed?"

He smiled. "Sure."

"I'm not feeling convinced."

"Look, in my line of work, doing deadly things that you know need to be done—without talking it over with your team—is pretty common."

"Well, your job is gone. According to Bryce, so is the world we knew. So, let's make some new rules."

He laughed. "All right."

"All right."

The boat, for all its mechanical problems, was quite advanced. After they had entered the GPS coordinates, it charted a course and managed its speed based on the amount of power the batteries held (and could collect via the solar panels in a given day).

The ship even had a subscription to satellite data that included weather. But none of the information would download. Owen wondered if the weather satellites were even still up there. Thankfully, the GPS satellites were.

When the sun had set, weariness seemed to settle on the group. With the danger of the island behind them, the adrenaline was fading, fatigue taking its place.

There was some discussion about the sleeping arrangements, but they came to a quick resolution when Alister held his hands up. "Look. We all know it. I snore. I snore loudly. You heard it back at the station. Which of you want to sleep in a room with that?"

No one said a word, and Blair drifted closer to Maya, placing her small hand in hers. Maya pulled the girl closer to her. Owen wondered if Maya had kids of her own. She seemed to be a natural at it. He wondered if he was too. He had always imagined himself having children, but it had never happened. He'd never met the right person. In a way, work had always been his first love. Until recently.

After Alister's speech, they settled on sleeping assignments. He got the loud room at the bow, where the waves crashed, and there was a single bed that suited him well.

Owen and Will took the room with two narrow beds. Maya, Cara, and Blair took the largest room, with the wide bed and a daybed beside it and a large bathroom.

They made a watch schedule for the night, with Alister taking the first shift, Will taking the second, and Owen taking the third and final before sunrise.

It had been a long day, but Owen still felt the urge to open the book—*The Birthright*—and read before bed. It was like gravity drawing him in.

Will, on the other hand, lay on his narrow bed, closed his eyes, and his breathing slowed almost instantly. Owen watched him, wondering if his reading light would bother—or wake—the younger man, but he didn't stir. He had had a long day. He was out cold.

The door slowly opened, revealing Maya's face peeking in.

She smiled. "Good night."

And then she was gone.

CHAPTER TWENTY-NINE

Maya had expected to have trouble getting to sleep. The boat rocked as it powered toward the GPS coordinates, the motion almost as bad as the noise of the waves in the bedroom she shared with Cara and Blair.

To Maya's surprise, sleep came almost unbidden, moments after she lay down. She slept deeply, the sort of rest that came only with the absence of worry—a sleep born of relief, from the weight of their troubles on the island having lifted away.

She awoke on the edge of the bed. Blair had fallen asleep on the other side of the bed, and somewhere in the night, she had moved closer to Maya, and closer still, wedging herself in, pushing as she snuggled.

Maya placed a pillow where her body had been, gently set Blair's arm around it, and crept out of the bedroom and up to the main deck.

The sunrise was a dim haze on the horizon, and Owen stood watching it, a small smile on his face.

"How'd you sleep?" he asked, his tone cheerful.

"Not bad, actually." She studied him. "Oh no. You're a morning person."

He laughed. "I sort of am."

"That's terrible."

"I take it you are too?"

"Me and mornings don't get along."

"Luckily, you have me here to keep the peace." He held up a pre-packed meal with the ARC logo on it. "How does green goo sound for breakfast?"

"Exactly what I was about to order."

They sat together at the banquette, watching the sunrise like two honeymooners on vacation, not a care in the world. It was, in Maya's mind, a perfect moment. Serene. Effortless. If she could, she would have stayed in it forever.

But the horizon loomed, and with it, she hoped, answers— and safety.

"I was too tired to ask last night. How long to reach the GPS coordinates?"

"The ship's nav system says about six days."

"Do we have that much food?"

Owen grimaced. "Just about. We'll have to stretch a bit, but I don't think it will be a big deal."

"It won't be a big deal assuming we find more food at those coordinates."

He nodded solemnly. "That's true."

They were both silent a while then, Maya eating the goo, Owen staring into the sun on the horizon as it climbed out of the sea and took flight.

"You're thinking about what we'll find at those coordinates, aren't you?" she asked.

"Am I that easy to read?"

"A bit."

"I envy you that."

"Reading people?"

"Yeah. I've never been able to do it."

Maya cocked her head. "What do you mean?"

"Facial expressions. Body language. It's like... well, it's like a foreign language to me. I had to study it as a kid like a subject in school. Memorize patterns. But the expressions change so quickly, it's... sort of like a flashcard that's there and gone and you have to match it with something you've memorized and decode it."

"Sounds tough."

"It could be a lot worse."

"Still, it's hard for me to imagine."

"It's my limitation. That's what my mom called it. Because everyone has limitations. We just all have different ones, and some are easier to see than others."

He took out the pin they had found in the envelope with his name on it at the station. It was a firefighter's pin, with a banner that said "10 YEARS", and three phrases wrapping around the other ring: "SERVICE", "INTEGRITY", and "THE THIN RED LINE".

"Is that why you became a firefighter? Because your limitation wouldn't matter in that field?"

"No," he said, exhaling heavily. "It's one of the reasons it was a good job for me—but as to why I became a firefighter... That's a completely different story."

She sensed that he was uncomfortable, and she instantly regretted pushing so far, so fast.

"I—"

"You asked if I was thinking about what we'll find at

those coordinates. I was. I've been thinking about it all morning."

"What do you think is waiting there?"

"My best guess is that it's another ARC facility. Maybe a station. Maybe this Garden Station. My *hope* is that we find a city at those coordinates. And that it's a bustling, normal metropolis, full of people waiting to help us."

"It could be another island."

"I hope not. I've had it with islands for a while."

"If it is a city, or an ARC station, what do you think we'll find?"

"I have no idea. I just hope that my mother is waiting there."

Owen's mention of his mother reminded Maya of her own mother and sister. "Me too."

Will appeared in the stairway, peering out. "I hope I'm not interrupting."

"Not at all," Owen said, rising and grabbing a meal and holding it out. "Interest you in green goo?"

Will smiled and shook his head. "No, thank you. I never eat breakfast."

"It's the most important meal of the day."

"For some," Will said mildly. "I've come to believe that every human's metabolism is truly unique, that generalizations are only sometimes helpful. For myself, I find that eating in the morning tends to make me hungry and tired all day."

Owen smiled. "Well, since you put it that way, I guess more goo for the rest of us."

When Will was seated, Maya went below to check on Blair and retrieve the journal she had found on the boat. She settled back into the banquette and began reading.

"How far have you gotten?" Owen asked.

She flipped through the pages, making an estimate. "I'm maybe... a quarter of the way finished."

"What is it?"

"It's a journal kept by the woman we found."

"Starting when?"

"Right about the time she woke up—in a station that sounds almost identical to the one we were in."

Alister emerged from below, looking groggy, face puffy. He collected some goo and ate slowly as he lounged on the U-shaped couch.

To Maya, Owen said, "So the journal writer was in the Extinction Trials?"

"Yes."

"In a cohort?"

"Yes. Of seven. Just like us when we woke up—before the old man went outside."

"But you and Alister only found two people, right?"

"That's right," Maya said quietly.

"What if they had an Escape Hatch video like us... And it led them to our island?" Owen asked.

That was an idea that hadn't occurred to Maya, and she hadn't read it in the journal, not yet.

"Interesting..." she said. "If so, they may have come from wherever we're going."

"Correct. I think you should read the journal aloud to the group."

"Blair..."

"Is young," Owen nodded, "but she is also out here in this weird world, and we can't fully protect her from it. She's better off knowing more about it. She's safer that way. The truth is, there may come a time when we're not around to protect her."

CHAPTER THIRTY

Once Cara and Blair had come upstairs, Owen stood before the group. "I had the morning watch, so I'll give a report. The ship sailed through the night without incident. Power levels never dipped below 50 percent. We're an estimated six days from our destination."

"Did you see any ships?" Alister asked.

"No. Or any lights on the horizon. No buoys. No lighthouses. And we received no transmissions."

"So," Alister said. "Crazy night."

"Action-packed," Owen replied.

"If the next six days are like that," Alister said, "it's going to get boring."

"After that station, I'm okay with boring for a while," Cara said.

Owen held up the journal Maya had found. "Actually, I think we may find what comes next quite interesting. This journal contains the account of another Extinction Trials participant. I'm assuming it's one—or both—of the people we found on the ship. It may hold clues about what we're going to find out there, which might save our lives."

Owen handed the small book to Maya. "As I'm not the

greatest reader-out-louder, I've asked Maya to read it to us."

Maya laughed. "Is everyone ready for the designated reader-out-louder to begin?"

With the sun burning bright ahead and a cool breeze blowing through the main deck, Maya sat on the couch under the shade of the solar roof and began to read:

Day 1

I don't know who will read this. I hope it's a historian, studying a time when our world was at its lowest point, a crossroads where we turned back from the brink of oblivion and survived.

At the moment, our odds don't look great from where I sit. As I write this, I feel like I'm perched on the precipice. All I see is the looming darkness below. But I choose to believe there is a light down there somewhere. Because that's always been my philosophy. Believing there is a better future always helps you—no matter what awaits. With that said, I am preparing for the worst. For doom— for trouble—because they say trouble is what's waiting for us outside this station.

Let me back up.

This morning, I awoke in a glass tube in Station 13. That's what they call this bunker. Because, of course, "station" is what a group of scientists would call a place like this. Bunker is what I call it. The bunker (or station) is small, with a single corridor, rooms on each side, and two androids running the place. Waking up here is a shock, to say the least.

They asked us to keep a journal of what happens to us, and to write it out. What a strange thing. Who writes anymore? Bodycams and biosensors would be more accurate and less burdensome. Apparently, there have been some issues with digital storage. They can build underground bunkers with robots running them, but they can't protect their data. Add that to the list of mysteries.

When they thawed us out, they gave us warm clothes and herded us into an observation room where they held a briefing. They called it orientation, but let's face it: orientation is for summer camp, briefings are given to people going into harm's way—which is the case with the Extinction Trials. It certainly isn't summer camp.

The long and short of it is that our world is gone. Over. Ruined. In the toilet bowl.

Around the room, the reactions were as different as the people. Some crumbled. Others were so shocked they could hardly move. A few had these expressions of *I told you so! I knew we were blowing it!*

I told you so is only advantageous if you live to revel in your superiority. Most of the human race didn't. That was the first gut punch. And they kept coming.

The question we all asked is the one that the proctors didn't have a good answer for: how did the world end?

They're vague on that point, but the bottom line is that a group of innovators and scientists had a vision for our world, and our species, that just didn't sit well with the powers that be—specifically, the governments around the world. This new reality—the Change, they call it—would have upended everything. Changed everything, if you will.

The Change—why would they even name it that? I mean, if you're a brilliant scientist, can't you come up with a better name? How can scientists be so good at inventing things and so bad at assigning a sensible title that is user-friendly and indicative of what it is? Or maybe I'm just too dense to understand the genius of the name "the Change." Or maybe it's ambiguous for a reason—to keep simpletons like me from knowing what's going on. If that's the case, it's working.

Change. If there's one thing I know about it, it's that people in power don't like change. I'm not a brilliant scientist. I'm one of the little people who do the work the big brains think up, but I know that the people at the top of the food pyramid don't like any changes to the way that pyramid works. Changes are dangerous for them. Changes have the potential to move them from the top to the bottom, and in a hurry. Apparently, this was that kind of change.

So that's how the world ended: in a disagreement about the future. One group had their vision. The other group had a different vision. The group trying to change things, well, as mentioned, they weren't a political party. Or volunteers collecting signatures door to door. They were scientists. And inventors. Whatever they invented, it had the power to change everything—without permission of the powers that be or the consent of the little people.

These scientists changed the world. Someone didn't like it. They fought back. In that war, the collateral damage was our world. That's how the world ended, with two groups fighting over the future.

What's left? We're told that the planet we've awoken to isn't conducive to human life. Here's the crazy part: that's not even the worst news.

The worst news is that I'm part of the solution to this ruined world problem. It turns out ARC was able to save a small percentage of the human race. Those chosen few are waiting to re-inhabit this world—when we figure out how to do that. How do we figure that out? By running experiments. By modifying humans in different ways and releasing them into the world and seeing if they live.

That's the grand plan. Trials. Tests to see if we survive.

Frankly, I was hoping the plan was more solid than that—safer than that.

It's not.

Look, I'm all for trial and error, just not with my own life.

For all their big words and white coats and sophistication, it turns out the scientists running the world are just gamblers. Well-educated guessers. They use known science as a guide to make guesses about what might work. And then they test it, analyze what happened and make another guess. It's a game of darts. Eventually, if they have enough time and funding—enough darts— they hit the bull's eye. Well, it turns out, in this game of biological darts, I'm what they're throwing at the board. And that board is waiting outside this station.

Day 2

It turns out the station (bunker) is just a glorified meat locker. We can't stay here. There aren't any bunks. Or a mess hall.

They designed it this way—so we'd have to leave. Want the rats to run the maze? Give them nowhere else to go. And no food.

After a night spent on blankets in the observation room, our robotic captor-saviors gave us each three pre-packaged meals and a GPS and coordinates of a dead drop. We're told that the dead drop contains supplies and further instructions.

I can't tell if the term dead drop is an inside joke for the higher-ups in the Extinction Trials. If so, it's not funny. Why? Because there were seven people in my cohort yesterday. Today, when we ventured out into the world, we found a bombed-out city, strange animals, and by night, three of us had dropped dead.

It began with headaches. Then nosebleeds. Memory loss followed. Over the course of a few hours, those three unlucky individuals simply forgot who they were and where they'd been. It was deeply unsettling. As our group trekked through the city, I think all of us had the same thought: will I be next? Am I going to get sick?

The real question is: what is this sickness? I'm terrified of it. So far, I seem unaffected. Maybe the rest of us are the cure—maybe we were given some therapy that makes us immune. Or maybe that's what's waiting at the dead drop. Whatever it is, we'll reach it tomorrow. Assuming we survive.

* * *

Owen held up a hand. Maya stopped reading and set the book on the table.

"Headaches. Nosebleeds. Memory loss." He studied her. "What happened to them is happening to you."

Maya took a deep breath. "Seems that way."

Cara stood and paced the deck. "We don't know that."

"The symptoms are the same."

Cara nodded. "That's true. But these members of the cohort died on day one. We're on day two."

Owen considered that. "Good point. And good news."

"The implication," Cara said carefully, "is that whatever... interventions they applied to us may have been better than this previous cohort. We may have been cured."

"But Maya still has the nosebleeds. And headaches," Owen said.

"Maybe," Maya said, "whatever they gave me only slowed down the disease."

"There's another point," Alister said. "Maya, your memory loss started before the Extinction Trials."

"True," Maya said. "It's possible I was among the first infected. Or maybe... somehow the virus started with me."

CHAPTER THIRTY-ONE

"Well," Owen said. "I think we should find out what happened to the other cohort from the journal. Maybe there are clues about what we're dealing with."

"I agree," Maya said. When no one objected, she opened the journal and began reading again.

Day 3

When we woke this morning, two things were gone—the food and one of our team members.

It's either quite a coincidence or a cause and effect. I'm jaded enough to quickly know the truth.

The other members of the team were unsure.

They proposed the innocent conclusion: the person left, then a scavenger came along and took our food. Or the inverse: a scavenger stole our food and then the person left—possibly even to search for more food—without telling anyone.

Yeah. Right.

I endured their debate about what had happened

until they arrived at the inevitable conclusion: does it matter? We have no food.

Therefore, we pressed on toward our destination.

We slept under a bridge. Like the whole world around us, it was hard and gray and crumbling and worn away with time. It was a bad night of fitful sleep.

The last thought I had before the fatigue overtook me made me feel more guilty than I ever have in my life: why didn't I think of it—taking the food and leaving? That person who got away with the supplies is sleeping right now with their belly full. They'll have a meal in the morning. And at lunch. And dinner and at all the meals after. They saw the future and planned for it. They did to us what we might be forced to do to others. They just did it first.

Tonight, they are evil.

Tomorrow, they are survivors.

The next day? They are visionaries.

I don't know what the Change is, but to me, this is how the world ends. The strong don't survive. The cunning survive. The people who slit throats and slink away—they survive. That's the world we live in now. Maybe it was the world we lived in before, but there was enough to go around, so no one realized it.

Not anymore.

Day 4

Upon waking, my first thought was even darker: what am I missing? What's the next surprise? Because I have only one chance of survival, I want to be the one who surprises the others this time. I don't want to be the one who is surprised.

In this ruined world, you can only be surprised so many times until you're dead. I've been surprised twice. My time is slipping away.

And I was surprised again today.

Here is what the world after the Change is like:

Gray

Desolate

Empty

The streets have no names. The signs are gone. Even the cars are crumbling. How much time has passed? Who knows? How would we even speculate?

The world feels, in a word, like slime. It's a world that is dissolving in the sands of time, washing away.

Every place we encounter is broken down. It feels old. Fragile.

There are no animals that I can see. Have they all died out? If so, what does that mean for us?

Our destination looms ahead. Does salvation wait there? I'm a cynic. My vote is no.

We stopped to rest by the roadside. The quiet is deafening. The world before was never like this. There was always *some* sound.

My heart is as hard and as hopeless as this world, but even I can admit this: I care for one person in our group. No names. I don't know who will read this or what will happen. But I do care. So, there's that. There's something still left alive inside my heart.

What I'd like most right now is to live in a world where I can love with my whole heart. This is not that kind of world.

Day 5

Two more are dead.

They were the strongest.

What happened?

Should I even write it down?

Why?

I guess it's the same old weakness: believing in a better world, doing what little I can, when I can. And so, that's why I'm writing this, in this shelter, trying to understand what happened, hoping that maybe you'll find this, and it will help you survive out here.

The city is a mess. A crumbling ruin. We marched through it, uncaring. Stupid.

We learned.

The hard way.

At the GPS coordinates, we found nothing but a collapsed building. The walls were a mottled gray that were grown over with fungus and low grass.

We're too late—that was our first thought.

But at the exact coordinates, we spotted something waiting there for us: a hatch, like you might find on a submarine. It stuck out of the ground like a giant metal mushroom.

One of us went to turn the wheel on top. He was dead the moment he touched it.

An arrow speared through him.

I spun.

The woman beside me fell—an arrow in her heart.

I ran then, not caring, not knowing where I was going.

I heard voices scream after me: "Drop it! Drop everything."

I did. I dropped every last thing I was carrying.

And I kept running.

I think, looking back on it now, the only thing that kept me running was the person running beside me. If they had fallen... I might have given up.

We ran. Together.

I stopped when I felt as though my heart was going to burst. I doubled over, grabbed my knees, and panted. One of the members of my cohort zoomed past me, then stopped, looked back, and turned to me.

"Are you all right?"

"Fine. Just winded."

The last living member of our group arrived then, also panting, glancing back, afraid. We all were.

"What happened?" he said, voice so loud it made us wince.

"Quiet," I hissed.

He gulped air, staring at me.

"It was a trap," I told him, and upon seeing his surprise, I continued: "They were waiting for us. With bow and arrow. They're probably still chasing us."

He ducked down and swiveled his head to look back. "I don't think so." He thought a moment. "I think they got what they wanted. We're dead out here without food."

Day 6

Hunger is our enemy. It hunts at night. Keeping me from sleep. It is waiting at dawn, ready to gnaw away at my humanity, a feral animal that knows no code of decency. It makes us crazy. Rude. Unreasoning.

It is the maker of dark thoughts.

We don't have any destination, only this dark road littered with the ruined remains of a world that feels alien to me.

How much time has passed? I don't know. Too much or not enough? Will this world ever be right again?

Even the animals have gone into hiding, it would seem.

Maya turned the page and noticed the subtle gap at the binding. She ran her finger into the fold and felt the rough edges where pages had been torn out.

She turned the page and the handwriting continued.

"I think someone removed some pages," she said.

"Why would they do that?" Owen asked.

"The pages missing," Alister said, "could have been gone before the person started writing in the book."

Maya thought that an odd response.

"Keep going," Cara said. "Maybe it explains."

With that, Maya continued reading aloud as the boat motored across the sea, the breeze tugging at her hair, the sun high in the sky.

★ ★ ★

I'm not sure what day it is anymore. I stopped counting a while back. What I can tell you is what happened since my last entry: we were rescued. Or so they would have us believe.

We awoke to figures in suits surrounding us. They offered us prepackaged food, and we ate it greedily.

With our bellies full, we were quite receptive to their next offer: to go back to their camp.

And quite a camp it is. They call it the Colony. It's rumored to be the last city in the world. They have everything here: farms, schools, and importantly, defenses against everything we encountered out there.

The Colony has a single goal: to reunite the human race. I have to say, it's the most meaningful work I've ever done in my life. I've signed on to be one of the scouts. The job is simple: I go out and I find people. It's the same job the people who saved me were doing.

My first assignment is on a boat crew. The Colony has been surveying the islands nearby, and some have yielded good results (and some trouble). I won't be chronicling my travels (for obvious reasons), but I do want to leave one last piece of information: the location of the Colony. If you're reading this and you need help, you can go there. There are good people there, waiting for you, ready to help.

"That's it," Maya said. "It ends with a set of coordinates."

"Do they match the Escape Hatch coordinates?" Owen asked.

"No. It's a different location."

CHAPTER THIRTY-TWO

Owen paced the deck, thinking, trying to wrap his head around the information from the journal. Frankly, it raised more questions than it had answered. That was nothing new.

One thought in the back of his mind loomed over all others: his mother. Was she still out there? She likely couldn't have survived that collapsing world. If the Extinction Trials had enrolled her and she had awoken in the world after, Owen didn't think she could have survived there either. Her best chance of survival was if she was at the Colony. But how much time had passed? She could have lived and died generations ago, if the journal was any indication of how long it had been since the Change.

The reality was, there wasn't much he could do about it now. Worrying wouldn't help.

Alister rose from the white leather couch. "Well, I'll just say what we're all thinking: let's change course and go to this Colony."

"That's not what I was thinking," Maya said, staring at the journal.

Alister shrugged. "Why not? They're what we're looking for—a way to survive." He held his arms out. "They even want to rebuild the human race—just like our beloved ARC Technologies and the Extinction Trials. And there's the obvious: when those poor saps in the journal went to their station's Escape Hatch, they got mugged. Food stolen. Killed. Shot with an arrow, for crying out loud. That is likely *exactly* what is waiting for us at our Escape Hatch location."

"We don't know that," Will said.

"What we know," Alister said, "is that we have two locations. The Escape Hatch, which we know nothing about. And the Colony, which is a paradise. Oh, and P.S., the only Escape Hatch we have any data about was a trap. A deadly trap. *And*, for all we know, their Escape Hatch location was *the same location* as our Escape Hatch." Alister eyed the group. "Is this not flashing any warning signs for any of you? *Hello*? Maybe the Extinction Trials intervention you all got left you people without good sense."

"And perhaps," Will said quietly, "it's made you believe everything you read."

Alister reeled back. "What does that mean?"

Will cocked his head to the side. "That we should consider the most obvious thing of all: that the journal could be fake. That it is itself a trap."

Cara turned her head to gaze out at the ocean. "No. I think it's true. Or at least, some of it. The voice. The way the person wrote it. It was too authentic. I don't think it's made up."

"I meant the coordinates," Will said. "Consider this: if you are a pirate in this ruined world, you have two options for raiding and looting. You can hunt. Or you can set traps. Hunting is inefficient. If the journal is to be believed, someone set a trap at that cohort's Escape Hatch. They waited for people to show up and they robbed them. The coordinates could simply be the same thing. You set a trap, but you need people to show up. So, you leave these... sort of... messages in a bottle, send them out into the world and wait for people to find them—desperate people like us who come looking for salvation. For all we know, pirates found the ship and placed the journal there."

Maya set the journal on the table. "Will has a point. A very good one. There's also the fact that we don't know when this was written. The Colony could be gone, for all we know. Or under new management that isn't friendly to guests."

Alister shook his head. "We know the journal is fairly recent—the bodies we found weren't decomposed."

"They were in suits," Owen said, "that were out of oxygen. They would have served as a sort of preservation capsule, minimizing oxidation. And as Will pointed out, we don't know for certain that either of those two individuals wrote the journal."

Alister glanced toward the sky. "Okay, now we're making assumptions about how the suits preserve cadavers and whether the journal was left by literary pirates. This is useless. Let's just skip to the end and go to the Colony and live happily ever after."

"It's too suspicious," Will said. "It just strikes me as wrong."

"I have to agree," Maya said. "Something about it bothers me as well. I can't put my finger on it."

Cara steepled her fingers. "For me, it's a simple decision. We have two destinations. Both are risks. Both unknowns.

But we have more reason to believe that the Colony will have what we need than the Escape Hatch. And, assuming you believe that part of the journal, we have reason to avoid the Escape Hatch destination. I vote to go to the Colony."

Alister focused on Owen. "That's two for the Colony and two for the Escape Hatch. What'll it be, Owen? Make a smart decision here."

Owen didn't like being pressured. He also sensed something going on here. It was the same feeling he'd had in the observation room when the old man maneuvered everyone into talking about themselves before he moved to kill Bryce. Or destroy Bryce.

But what was happening here?

"I dispute the premise," Owen said quietly.

"What premise?" Alister shot back.

"That we need to decide right now."

"Of course we do," Alister said. "We have a limited amount of food, and we need to enter those coordinates for the Colony and change course—immediately."

"We have something else," Owen said. "Something that can help us decide." He paused, then said, "Information."

Alister laughed. "I don't get it."

"We have information about the world before," Owen said. "We have information that might help us figure out what to do. It's right here and we should go through it before we make a decision."

Will cocked his head. "I don't follow?"

"The information is inside of each of us," Owen said. "We have our stories. Each of us has a story about how the world ended. We saw it from different angles. And we have the stories of where we came from, what we did before the Change. Somewhere in there, maybe there's a clue about what the Extinction Trials really are, about what ARC Technologies is truly up to—maybe even what the Colony is."

Alister plopped down on the couch and let his face fall into his hands. "That's your solution? Let's all share? This… is a waste of time. A complete and utter waste of time."

"No," Owen said, his voice firm. "It's not. It's the most important thing we can do right now."

He took a step into the main deck, out of the sunlight. "Think about this: why did that cohort die?"

Alister glanced up. "You're kidding, right? Arrows? Stolen food? Weird virus." His eyes drifted to Maya.

"No. Those are how they died. Not why."

Maya held up a hand to Owen. "All right. I'll bite. Why'd they die?"

"Because they simply ran the maze. From the time they exited their station chambers to the moment they were killed or captured or rescued, all they did was try to survive."

"Sounds like a good plan to me," Alister said.

"Look at where it got them."

Cara leaned forward at the table. "What exactly are you proposing?"

"I propose we take a different path. What I think we need to do is solve the fundamental problem: what is the Change and what happened to the world? Once we know that, it'll help us figure out what to do, maybe even where to go and who to trust."

"Wonderful," Alister said. "That's great. Why didn't I think of that brilliant breakthrough?"

"Simple," Owen said. "We were doing the same thing

they were: just trying to survive another day. Look at what happened to them. They died because they betrayed each other. Didn't trust each other. Part of that is because they didn't know each other. They didn't share their stories. They didn't see themselves in each other. Imagine if they had gotten to know one another? What might they have learned? Could they have changed their fate?" Owen paused. "If you ask me, the root mistake they made is not coming together as a team. When it was tough, they pulled apart. They didn't work together. And if we don't get to know each other and start working as a team, our fate could be the same."

CHAPTER THIRTY-THREE

For a long moment, the group fell silent. Wind blew through the boat as the outboard motors purred and the waves crashed on the hull.

Maya's mind was reeling from what the journal had revealed—and the discussion among the group. She had to admit, she was torn on which destination to favor.

She knew she needed medical attention. Soon. More than that, she wanted to know what had happened to her sister and mother. Were they at the Colony? Had they even survived the Fall?

Not having her memories was a bit like being out on this ship at sea: lost and unmoored, with no bearing points to guide her. It was an unsettling feeling that defied words. But she did have one anchor out here, and she stared at him then, standing tall on the boat's deck, confident, a lighthouse in the darkness.

Owen stared back at her, and a small smile tugged at his lips. Maya knew he was trying to read her expression, to get some idea of what she was thinking.

In a way, they shared that unique connection: a mental limitation that wasn't obvious but always evident to them. For Owen, it was being in the dark about what people were feeling or thinking. For Maya, it was being in the dark about her past.

In a sense, they were in the dark together. Even though she hadn't known him for long, Maya felt a strong bond to Owen. It wasn't just that he had been the one to wake her and pull her out of that tube in the station. It was deeper than that. A feeling she got—one she couldn't describe. She didn't mind being in the darkness with him. It felt more manageable with him in her life.

And she wondered: did she have an Owen in her life before the Fall? Or was this new?

More than that, she wondered if he felt the same way. In that moment, she got a glimpse of what life might be like for him, of constantly wondering what people were thinking.

She would have to sort that out soon. She sensed that their time on the boat might be the only opportunity. What lay ahead was uncertain, and she wanted to know where she stood with him before they reached the shore.

Alister stood and paced toward the cockpit. For a moment, Maya thought he might be about to type in the coordinates to the Colony and change the boat's destination.

Instead, he turned back and eyed Owen. "What exactly are you proposing?"

Owen held his hands out. "Simply that we share our stories. See if we can piece together what's going on here. And after that, we'll make the call on where to go next. The Colony or the Escape Hatch."

Maya felt a sudden wave of nervousness. Since she couldn't remember her own story, she would be the weakest member, with the least to contribute. As if on cue, a headache faded in.

Alister leaned against the double chair in the cockpit and crossed his arms. "Okay. But let's make it quick. We all know what we need to do here."

"I'll go first," Owen said.

Maya expected him to begin telling his story, but he walked toward the stairs and descended below deck. He returned with the large envelope with his name on it that they had found in Station 17's command center.

Owen held up the brown envelope. "They left each of us one of these. Except for Alister."

The older man inhaled sharply. Maya couldn't tell if he was insulted or annoyed. He didn't like that Owen highlighted this fact, that there had been no envelope for him. Maya again had the feeling that his lack of an envelope was an important clue. But what did it mean?

Owen reached into his envelope. "The question is, why give us these envelopes? We don't seem to need the items to survive. Or do we? I think the items they gave us are clues of some kind. Or items meant to help us. Understanding them—and what they mean to us—could be crucial."

Owen pulled his hand out of the envelope and showed the group a firefighter's service pin. It was small and round, the kind that could be pinned to a lapel. He held it out and walked around the main deck, the wind tugging at his hair, the sun burning bright in the sky behind him.

In the center of the pin was a firefighter's helmet, a ladder, and something Maya couldn't make out. Around the perimeter were three phrases: "THE THIN RED LINE" was stamped at the top, "SERVICE" on the left, and

"INTEGRITY" on the right. At the bottom was a small banner that said "10 YEARS".

"How wonderful for you," Alister said. "Let's all show off our trophies and service pins while the world goes down the drain."

Owen let the pin drop to his side and stared at Alister. For a moment, Maya half expected Owen to punch the older man. He seemed to be gathering his breath, suppressing the urge.

Alister shifted uncomfortably.

"It isn't my pin," Owen said quietly. "I have one like it. And a fifteen-year pin. But I got this one thirty years ago, and it changed my life."

He crossed his arms and took a deep breath. "When I was a kid, I wanted to be an astronaut. I dreamed of exploring space." He smiled. "In fact, I would have done anything to be in space. Asteroid mining. Shuttle mechanic. You name it. I wanted to wear that suit and float in the darkness and wake up every morning knowing there was danger and wonder and something new. I had this vision of making discoveries that could change everything."

His smile transformed, becoming somber. "It was probably the right career for me. As a kid, I was in the top percentage for my height, and I was physically strong. Had good instincts. Excelled at sports. And I was good at spatial ordering and puzzle-solving—pattern recognition."

"As we've seen," Maya said.

"Correct. But I had a big limitation: reading people. Body language. Facial expressions. It's still a problem for me. In space, it wouldn't have mattered. Maybe that was part of the allure for me. In space, you mostly read computer readouts."

Owen held the pin up and studied it, watching it glint in the midday sun. "It's funny how you see your life as a kid. And how it can change in an instant.

"The day I got this pin, I went to school and then played in my backyard. I had dinner that night with my family, my whole family—mother, father, and older sister. For the last time. I went to bed in a home we'd never live in again. I woke up coughing. My eyes burned when I opened them. The smoke was so thick it was like a blanket of soot trying to smother me. I heard screams. I got up and called out. It was like the smoke swallowed my words up. I could barely stand still, the floor was so hot. I can still remember that panic, the warmth overtaking my feet and crawling up my legs. I opened my bedroom door and the wall of heat hit me and I screamed. Someone grabbed me and pulled me close. The suit pressed into my face. It was rough, the threads deep, rubbing into me like sandpaper as he carried me. I reached up and grabbed what I thought was a button on the firefighter's suit."

Owen held out the pin. "It was actually this. It was hot as blazes when my little hand closed around it, but I held on because in my mind, I thought if I fell, I'd hit that hot floor and burn up instantly."

Owen flipped the pin over in his fingers, as if touching every part of it would bring the rest of the story back. "When he reached the front yard, the firefighter set me down, gently but quickly. I held on to him and he pushed me away, and the pin came off in my hand. He never even noticed. Only turned and ran back inside. He was the only one there. I think he lived nearby. The house was collapsing. That's what trapped my dad and sister inside. By the time he brought my mother out, the house was in a shambles. The trucks arrived a few seconds later. There were people everywhere then. Medical technicians. More firefighters. It was madness."

Owen took a deep breath, still staring at the pin. "The guy who carried me out came by to check on me. His face was covered in soot and grime. His suit was torn and singed. I was wrapped in a blanket. I could barely speak from the shock. I held out the pin to give it back to him. He looked at it a moment. I think he was surprised I had it. Keeping up with that lapel pin probably wasn't high on his priority list that night. He slowly glanced back at the ruin of our little house and then turned and pushed the pin back toward me. 'Keep it, kid,' were the only words he ever said to me. And he was gone. I never even found out his name. I think he looked at me and saw someone who had lost everything, someone with no toys, one less parent, one less sister, and no place to live, and he couldn't bring himself to take one more thing from me. At that moment, the pin was the only thing I had left. Besides my mother."

Owen slipped the pin in his pocket. "That night, I decided that I didn't want to be an astronaut anymore. I wanted to wear a different kind of suit. I wanted to be that guy—I wanted to be the guy who ran into a burning building when there was no one else. I wanted to be that person who arrived in the night when no one else was coming. I saw it clearly that night. That I could do that. Make a difference. It didn't matter if I couldn't read faces. I could recognize patterns and see logic in things others couldn't. I could be a firefighter. And a good one, I thought. And that obsession gave me something to focus on. I needed it in the days and weeks after. They held us in the hospital for a few days. My mother was in worse shape than me. We lived with my aunt and uncle after. I wore the pin to school. Even when kids made fun of me. I wore it inside my shirt as I trained to be a firefighter. And I wore it on the inside every day I put on my suit. It was a reminder to me of what I wanted to be. Why I signed up. What it was about."

Owen paced the deck, as if grasping for the words that would come next.

"The thing is, before I woke up here, I'd begun to question whether being a firefighter was what I still wanted to do."

That surprised Maya. "Why?"

He focused on her. "The job had changed. When I first started, the firebots didn't even exist. We fought fires in about the same way that guy who saved me had fought fires. Evac drones became an increasing part of our work—especially for getting people out of tall buildings. Then the bots came along. Each year, there was less work for the humans."

Owen held up his hands. "Granted, I think some of it was a good thing. Machines doing the dangerous parts of the job makes sense. But it wasn't exactly what I had envisioned. It's funny how our minds get locked into our own vision of how things are going to be. If it's different from that, we resist, even if it's better. That was the case for me. I felt my role shrinking every year. I was becoming a human babysitter for robots and AI. I felt almost like an actor in a costume, a throwback to some nostalgic era when humans did the hard work."

He paused for a moment. "I was on the verge of reassessing everything when the Fall happened. I was at a crossroads."

He put his hand in the envelope and took the paperback book out—*The Birthright*. "In fact, I was talking to my mother about that the morning the Change occurred. She gave me this book. It's the last thing she gave me. Like the pin, it's the last thing I have from someone who made such a huge impact on my life. I received both of these items at turning points in my life. One proved to be a beacon that showed me the way. I can't help but see significance in that, though I don't fully understand the book yet."

"What's it about?" Cara asked.

"Psychology, mostly. About understanding our own minds and living a life in harmony with our strengths and limitations."

Maya saw Alister quickly roll his eyes, but he said nothing.

"The funny part is," Owen said slowly, "moments after I received this book—after I saw my mother for the last time—my life came full circle. I got to play the role I had envisioned when I became a firefighter. I was that thin red line, the only person who could help a small child in a burning building."

He made eye contact with Maya, and she knew he was hesitant to say more because that small child had been her sister. She sensed that he didn't want his words to hurt her.

"Tell them," she said.

Owed nodded. "The day the Change happened, I

responded to a gas alarm. Things happened quickly. The building caught fire. I saved a girl from the fire, and I was giving orders to evacuate the building when a firebot attacked me and my crew mate. That young man sacrificed himself to allow me to escape with the girl—who I later learned was Maya's younger sister."

All eyes turned to Maya. She inclined her head to Owen, silently urging him to continue.

"I refuse to believe that's a coincidence, though like the book, I don't know what it means yet. I do know that on that day, when I saved her, I became like that guy who had carried me out of my home and changed my life. When I was lying on that roof, busted up, I felt a sense of completion. It's hard to explain, but I felt like I had done what I was born to do."

Owen took a deep breath. "What's even crazier is that when I woke in that ARC Station, and I was called to action to help get you all out of those tubes, and when I put on that environmental suit and went out into that ruined world to try to save us, I felt it again—that sense of purpose. And it felt good."

Alister grimaced. "You're kidding."

"I know it sounds crazy. And maybe I shouldn't have felt the way I did, but it is what it is. That's who I am. When I see a building burning down, and people trapped inside, I want to be the person that runs inside."

He pointed to the journal lying on the table. "They weren't. Look at what happened to them. They saw a burning building and they got out and tried to save themselves. If you ask me, I think the world we're in now is like that: it's a burning building. ARC has the last human survivors.

They're trapped inside, and we're the only ones who can save them. What's inside of us—whatever *interventions* ARC did—might be the key to saving them. For me, I feel like I'm staring at a burning building, and I know what we must do. We have to try to help them."

He paused, making eye contact with each person sitting around the deck.

"That's why I vote that we go to the Escape Hatch. Because my gut tells me that it's the only way to get those people out of this burning building that this world has become. At the Colony, we might save ourselves. At the Escape Hatch location, we might find what we need to save everyone else."

CHAPTER THIRTY-FOUR

Alister pushed off from the chair in the cockpit. "That's the worst logic I've ever heard. Totally nonsensical."

"It makes a certain sense to me," Will said. "Often, in life, the most obvious path is not the right one."

"That sounds lovely," Alister said. "But out here—where people are getting shot with crossbows—platitudes don't help us much."

The statement instantly struck Owen as odd. Why? There was something about it… "Crossbow?"

Alister looked up quickly. "Yes." He pointed to the journal. "It was in the story. Someone was shot with a crossbow."

Owen nodded. "Right."

He picked up the book and flipped through the pages. He was missing something. He felt it, like a puzzle piece out of place.

"The crossbow isn't the point," Alister went on. "The point is, we can't be on some spiritual quest for meaning out here. We need to be practical if we're going to survive. If we don't survive, does it really matter if we fought the good fight? The practical plan is to go to the Colony. That's how to survive. If we survive, sure, I'm on board for entertaining future plans of grand rescues and world-saving nonsense. But please, let's be practical right now."

"Yes," Maya said, her voice firm. "Let's be practical."

Alister nodded. "Good, so you agree."

"I don't. I think what you see as practical is quite different from me. Specifically, I think Owen is right. About a few things, actually. The first of which is that we still need more information. We need to share our stories." She turned her focus to Owen. "Thank you for sharing yours, Owen. It was beautiful and devastating and gave me a lot to think about."

Alister put his face in his hands. "Oh, for crying out loud. At this point, I wish I had been the one shot by that arrow. Right through the heart."

Maya ignored him. "Who wants to go next?"

To Owen's surprise, no one volunteered.

"Well then," Maya said. "I'll go."

She stood from the table and left the deck, descending the stairs. A moment later, she emerged with her large envelope, which she set on the table beside the journal.

"As I said before, I don't remember what happened to me. I remember being in the hospital, being visited by someone named Parrish, and I remember, vaguely, where I used to work—Genesis Biosciences."

She paused and swallowed hard. "And to be honest, as time passes, I feel the memories slipping away even more, like this ship sailing away from the shore. They feel... out of reach, as if I'll never regain them."

She picked up the envelope. "In my mind's eye, I can't see my mother's face. Or my sister's. But I can feel what they meant to me. How I felt about them. That's something. And there's a lesson there: we don't always remember people—or what they do to us—but we remember how they make us feel. We're emotional beings, and I believe that is how our memories are stored—and often how we form our opinions."

She reached into the envelope and drew out a small gold pocket watch. "I don't know what happened to me, but I do know that when I saw—and touched—this pocket watch, it brought back a memory, clear as day."

She inhaled deeply. "My father gave this to me when I was about Blair's age. He said that his father gave it to him, and his father gave it to him. That's been going on in our family for a long time, generations that stretch back to an immigrant in a new land who saved up his money and bought this as an heirloom—as a store of value that could be easily carried and, if needed, cashed in during a time of need."

She turned the pocket watch over in her hand. "It's dented and scratched and worn, and I remember his words to me as clear as if he were sitting here with us: 'The watch isn't worth much. Not anymore. But what it represents is.'"

Maya set the watch on the table. "He asked me what I thought it represented. My first guess was tradition. Wrong. My second guess was family. Wrong again. When I didn't wager a third guess, he supplied the answer: a single word—time. The watch stopped working a long time ago, but it kept time for a while. Like we all do. But time marches on, a sea that we swim in for a short while, a force that drowns us all in the end. The central question of our life is this: how will we spend our time? Will we invest it in a better future for those that come after us? What will we pass down—like the pocket watch? A better future? Or a darker one? It seems we've woken to the darkest era in human history. What comes next, we decide. And we have one thing at our disposal: time. We say that we spend time for a reason—time is a currency. In the end, it's the only currency that matters."

Maya picked up the journal. "Look at how they spent their time. Just like Alister said: trying to survive."

Alister snorted. "That's cute. But if you don't survive, you don't get any more time to spend. Game over and nothing else matters."

"On the contrary," Maya replied. "Sometimes, how you spend your time determines if others survive. What sort of world they inherit. What sort of life we create for the people we care about. That's what this pocket watch represents to me. Sure, it's a trinket now, an antique some distant ancestor acquired, but it means more than that to me. It tells a story about my ancestors who tried to create a better life for me. They didn't spend their time always focused on their own survival. It was about more than that. About future generations."

She set the watch down. "And I remember one other thing about this watch. My father passed away a short time after giving it to me. I don't remember the details, only that it was a disease that overtook him quickly. I don't know if he knew he was sick when he gave me the watch. Looking back, he probably did. His death made the point even more clear to me: time is precious. You never truly know how much you have. How we spend it matters."

Maya locked eyes with Owen. "That's why I vote to go to the Escape Hatch location. We may not survive, but we've got a better chance at getting answers there—answers that could help those people in Garden Station and the rest of the world. I vote to spend our time trying to help leave this world better than we found it."

CHAPTER THIRTY-FIVE

For a while, everyone was quiet. Maya expected Alister to rebuff her with a quip, but even he was silent.

Maya picked up the pocket watch, but just as she was about to put it back in the envelope, she stopped. That was odd. As long as she had owned the antique, it hadn't worked. The time was stopped. The watch still didn't work, but now the time had changed. Was it a coincidence? Had it simply been knocked around? Or was it a message?

Cara's voice brought her back to the present. "Was that the only thing in your envelope?"

Maya placed the watch back in the envelope. "No. There was one other item."

She took out the blank page, slightly larger than her two hands combined.

"I don't get it," Owen said.

"I don't either," Maya replied. "I looked it over in the station, but there's no markings."

"Does a blank page mean anything to you?" Owen asked.

"Not particularly. Not that I can remember. Besides the obvious—a future unwritten, infinite choices, a sort of starting over... like having your memories wiped and beginning your life again."

Alister let his head fall back theatrically. Maya sensed another tirade coming.

"Listen to us," the middle-aged man muttered. "We're reading meaning into these trinkets where there is none! A blank page? What if it's just that—a blank page? Don't we know we're in an experiment here? What if the Extinction Trials is simply like one of those inkblots the psychologists show you? They don't mean anything. You see what's inside of you, not what's there. I bet the proctors are watching us now, sitting back laughing at us chasing our tails. It's all a big experiment, right? What if the joke's on us?"

"That fire pin isn't a joke to me," Owen said.

"And that pocket watch isn't a joke to me either," Maya said.

"Nor is what I found in my envelope," Cara said quietly.

"Which brings up a question I've wanted to ask since the station," Owen said. "Why wasn't there an envelope for you, Alister?"

The older man shrugged. "How should I know? Maybe they figured I wasn't gullible enough to fall for their tricks?"

"I don't think that's it," Will said, staring at Alister.

"Maybe someone stole it," Alister said. "I woke up in that station the same as all of you."

After an awkward silence, Owen walked over to the table and took the blank page from Maya and held it up to the sun and studied it as it flapped in the wind. Finally, he handed it back to her. "I'd hang on to it for now. I think it's interesting that you and I got two items. The rest only received one—as far as I know."

"Yes," Cara said. "One for me."

"And for me," Will said.

"Me too," Blair said.

Cara rose. "Speaking of, I'd like to share what was in my envelope."

She went below decks and returned with a small piece of metal about half the size of Owen's fire pin. She held the shard up in the sunlight for everyone to see.

"I bet I've seen a thousand pictures of this chunk of metal. Since I was a young girl, it has been like a knife at my throat." She set it on the table next to Maya's envelope. "To me, it's also a reminder of how truly precious time is."

Cara pulled her hair back, revealing a scar that ran above her right ear. "When I was a little older than Blair, I was in a car accident. Cars were going driverless, but the transition wasn't complete. My father was driving me to school for a dance. I was so excited. In the blink of an eye, the crash changed everything."

She motioned toward Owen. "I can't imagine what you went through, but when you described how you felt, I saw myself on that night. The sound of the car crash was deafening. The pain overtook me. I blacked out. When I came to, there was a woman standing over me. Her hands seemed to move at supernatural speed. She tied off the cuts on my legs and my right arm. She whispered to me, 'Don't be afraid. You're going to be okay. I'm a doctor.'"

Cara took a deep breath. "I would have died that night had she not acted so quickly. It was luck. She was an ER doctor driving home from work. She had been at the intersection, simply by chance. She saved my life and my dad's. I spent two weeks in the hospital. Months in rehab. And I never was the same."

She picked up the shard off the table and held it up.

"This piece of metal was lodged in my brain. They wanted to remove it, but the operation was too risky. The fear was that if it shifted—even slightly—it could cause permanent brain damage. Or death."

She set the shard down. "Since that day, I've lived with this deadly piece of shrapnel in my brain, knowing that at any time, it might shift and take my life. Or reduce me to a vegetable. Like that pocket watch, it was a constant reminder to me of how precious time is, that every moment we're given is a gift. And that your life can change in an instant. It was the pocket watch for me. And to me, that doctor was like the firefighter who saved Owen. She was the change I wanted to be in the world. I made it my life's mission to become a physician. Before that, I had never been a very good student, frankly. But I applied myself. I had learned the hard way that I might not get a second chance at making the right decisions in life."

Cara stared out at the ocean for a long moment. "Two things are remarkable to me. One, that ARC Technologies— and the Extinction Trials—were able to remove the shard. It implies a level of surgical sophistication that didn't exist in the world before."

"They probably had a robot cut it out," Alister said.

"Yes," Cara said. "I would bet on it. Only a robot would have that kind of precision and confidence to perform the operation."

"Only a robot wouldn't care if they screwed it up," Owen said.

"Perhaps," Cara whispered, seeming to consider the implications. "Whatever the reason or method, I'm free of it now. I have that which I have always wanted: freedom and time. In a strange twist of fate, it's come when the world is gone and there seems to be no place to spend that time. As fate would have it, I've gotten what I always wanted when I no longer need it. But I think there's a deeper meaning here."

Cara motioned to Maya and Owen. "Hearing your stories was like peering through a looking glass at my own life. Seeing the same experiences in different lives, as though we are sides of a pyramid reflecting the same light. And I see it now. The shard is like the Change. It wrecked the world like that car crash wrecked my life. Like the fire changed Owen's life. Whatever the Change is, it's wedged in the brainstem of the world, always threatening, and it could shift at any moment and finish the patient off. In this case, the patient is the entire human race. We are what that doctor was for me that night: a person at the right place at the right time. What are we going to do? Are we going to run into the crash site and try to help? Or watch as time slips away?"

She nodded. "Before, I thought we should go to the Colony. Now, hearing your stories—and remembering mine—I know we should go to the Escape Hatch location. I feel it at the core of my being."

Alister opened his mouth to speak, but Cara held up a hand. "There's something else. I believe I may have witnessed the Change. I might know what it is."

CHAPTER THIRTY-SIX

On the deck, Cara paced, as if organizing her thoughts. "I was working the late shift at the hospital when trauma cases started pouring in. Massive wounds. Lacerations. Broken bones. They were robotic accidents—and that's how we classified them initially."

A gust of wind blew across the deck of the boat, tugging at her hair.

"By the end of my shift, we were calling them what they were: robotic attacks. It was… carnage like I'd never seen, even in old movies."

Cara rubbed her temple. "There was a pattern to it: the victims were all wearing uniforms. Police and fire personnel were hit the hardest."

The words were like gut punches for Owen. "Just like me and my team at the Oasis Park Building—the robots singled out first responders," he said.

"Seems that way. They also attacked political leaders and essential workers."

"They wanted chaos," Owen said. "They wanted a world in which the masses would panic."

Cara nodded. "And they did. By morning, the ER was

full. The OR was full. And so was every bed we had. We were requesting tents to triage the cases coming in. There was also a shift in case type. At some point that morning, the trauma cases decreased. There just weren't that many more uniformed and critical workers who weren't in the hospital—or who hadn't gone into hiding. It was weird. Doctors and nurses were refusing to wear scrubs or coats. Can't say I blamed them. But none of the nurse bots ever turned. I never figured out why, but I was glad for that."

"Maybe whoever hacked the other robots considered nurses off-limits," Maya said. "As if the hospitals were a safe zone. A line the terror group wouldn't cross."

"It seemed that way," Cara agreed. "The next day, the cases were different. People were confused. Many were simply brought in by neighbors who didn't know what to do with them. At first, we thought it was simply some mass psychological phenomenon—as if the shock of what had happened was getting to people. They couldn't remember their names or even where they lived. Some had headaches. Nosebleeds."

Cara's gaze drifted to Maya. "Looking back, I think they probably had what you have."

"And what happened to them?" Maya asked, her voice steady.

"About one in ten died within two days. There was nothing we could do. We tried everything. And I mean everything. It didn't matter. It was like a bomb went off in their brains. It was scary. And it was spreading. The entire staff started getting sick. People I had worked with for years were talking to me, and the next thing I knew, they were confused, then they couldn't even tell me who they were—or who I was."

Cara swallowed. "It felt like some bizarre dream. It felt like the entire world was slipping away. The hospital was sort of... under attack by the pathogen—and it was a pathogen, it spread through the building like a storm moving through."

She plopped down on the couch, as if recounting the story was draining the energy from her. "I was scared. I remember going to the on-call room because I was so tired. The headache started then. A low pressure that built steadily. Pain meds did nothing."

She inhaled sharply. "It was the moment I had expected my whole life—what I had dreaded. I was certain that the shard in my brain was shifting and finally taking my life. But it wasn't the shard. It was the virus."

"The Genesis Virus," Maya said. "Or GV. That's what Parrish called it."

"Yes," Cara said. "I remember lying down in the on-call room and activating my band. There was a news report that called the pathogen the Genesis Virus. It was everywhere—worldwide. Containment wasn't an option. I closed my eyes. And the next time I opened them, I was in that chamber in Station 17."

She turned to Maya. "The thing is, since I woke up, I haven't had the headaches. And my memory seems fine."

"Which means the Extinction Trials cured you," Maya said. "And if they did, they can cure me."

"Yes," Cara said. "Which seals it for me. We have to get

to that Escape Hatch location. You're getting worse, aren't you, Maya?"

She nodded slowly.

"Let's hope they have a record of what they did to me. It may be your only chance."

CHAPTER THIRTY-SEVEN

Hearing Cara's story gave Maya a sense of hope that there was a cure for what had happened to her, that in unraveling the answer to the Extinction Trials, she might find what she needed as well.

Alister's gruff voice interrupted her thought process. "Fine. The Escape Hatch it is. After all, I'm always agreeable, as you all know."

"And does that mean," Cara said, "you'll also be sharing what happened to you before the station?"

Alister snorted. "Of course, I love sharing. This whole thing is right up my alley."

Maya thought he was waiting for someone to argue with him, but the group was silent. The only sound was the rumbling of the massive outboard motors, the crashing of the waves on the ship's bow, and the sound of the breeze blowing through the open deck. Perhaps they were all getting to know each other well enough to know where the fault lines were between them, those places where words set off friction.

Alister crossed his arms. "I go to work early. Every day. You want to get something done? Go to work early. My dad taught me that. About the only thing he taught me before he took off. Anyway, I go to work early because I can think early in the morning—and most importantly, there's no one there talking. I tell you what, you cut out talking, this world would have to work half as much—if that."

He paused, waiting for someone to challenge him. Of course, Maya didn't logically see how the vast, vast majority of people could do their jobs without talking—and she didn't really think Alister believed it either. He was stirring the pot, but none of them were taking the bait.

"As I said back at that station, I'm a city bus mechanic. I'll tell you one thing: those buses take a beating." He nodded. "Sure, they drive themselves and they have programming to *optimize* everything, but that's half the problem. They never miss a pothole. Never. The AI that drives *loves* hitting potholes. It's like the axle manufacturers have got a mole in the programming group that makes the blasted thing veer for them. I've complained repeatedly, but the answer is always the same: the AI prioritizes human life above mechanical wear."

He threw his head back. "Ha! What a joke that turned out to be. I knew the AI and robots would be the death of us—one way or another. Every year they take—or took—a little more of our freedom. Now, they would tell you that they were freeing us up to do other work, but it just isn't true. You want to know what's wrong with the bus? Back when I first picked up a wrench, you opened the thing up and looked and used your brain. It's pretty simple, really. Now? You hook it up to a computer for a full diagnostic. The screen tells you what's wrong. It even automatically orders the parts if we don't have them. Here's the best part: if the mechanic doesn't know how to fix it, no problem—it will activate the camera, play a video walk-through of how to fix it, and then watch you and tell you when you're screwing it up. Could that mechanic repeat the exercise without the computer? Of course not! We just sit there and follow instructions like we're the robots' assistants."

Alister motioned to Owen. "He was right—it was like a dress rehearsal, with us humans only playing a mechanic toward the end. And that's not even the worst of it. The worst is that if you screw up the repair, the robot mechanic comes by and fixes it. I'm not kidding. It's the supervisor. And it never messes up. It always gets it right. I know the city was just saving up money to buy more of those blasted repair bots and get rid of all the greasers like me. Just a matter of time."

He locked eyes with Owen. "Believe me, I sympathize with your story—those firebots slowly taking away that last bit of joy you got from your work."

Owen nodded. "Yeah."

Alister held his hand out at Will. "But frankly, the bots weren't the worst part of the job. It was the programmers. They come in there, skinny as a rail, carrying coffee that costs more than my life. Using words and acronyms nobody understands, like API and runtime exception and asynchronous request and token authentication and who knows what else. It's like doctors—they've got their own language and they like it like that, so you don't know what they're saying and they feel superior. They like to keep you in the dark."

Will frowned. "The use of syntax makes any complex job easier. Without it, you'd spend half your day using known language to describe new and specific concepts. And I believe excessive use of spoken language is one of the faults you find in workplace society."

Alister threw his hands up. "That's what I'm talking about. Even when programmers are telling you what you just said, you can't understand it. Your own words. I remember once telling a programmer that a bus stopped running. So, he fires up the diagnostic and studies it and I ask what happened. His answer? That the bus AI threw a runtime exception when it made an API call to the maps service because the maps service encountered a database timeout expiration."

Alister turned to Will. "Do you know what that means? Do you?"

"Yes," Will said. "I do."

"Well, me too—cause I finally badgered them until they told me. It means, quite simply, that the idiot bus AI was driving along and one of the roads was closed for construction, so it asked for directions, and the maps AI tried to dig it up in its database, but the database was busy, so it couldn't respond in time, and the bus didn't know what to do. The fix? Well, the fix is simple: the bus has to know that it may have to wait sometimes. So, they updated the code to have it park by the side of the road and wait—what a novel concept. It logs the wait times. They get too high; they add more servers. Why couldn't they just say that?"

"I think," Owen said, "we're getting a little off subject here."

"On the contrary," Alister snapped, "this is exactly my point. The bots and the programmers—they're how the world ended. I could've been a programmer. I didn't want to. I chose not to—because I didn't want to spend my life staring at a screen, typing stuff in and being tired all the time. I need to work on things I can see. I want to feel like I got something done every day. The buses come in broken, they go out running. That's something. And that's what I was doing the day it all ended."

Alister looked around at the group, seeing that he had their attention now. "I'm at work, early, fixing a bus. On my armband, I get a notification that a bus has had an accident—a strange one: it drove into a police precinct. My first instinct is that the only way it should have done that is to preserve human life. Or if there was some bizarre mechanical failure. There were still only a few people at work. A few minutes later, another bus slammed into a military base. And another into a fire station."

"They weaponized the buses," Maya said.

"Yes," Alister said. "I did the only thing I could think of. Something I've wanted to do for a long, long time. I picked up a tire iron and I walked into the server room, and I started bashing that thing's silicon brains in—like that old guy at the station did to Bryce. I got zapped with electricity a few times, but I kept going. It was a mess of smoke and electrical fire and suppressant squirting out of the ceiling and my coworkers yelling at me, and then I hear this deafening crash. I looked through the glass windows and realized I had made a mistake."

He shook his head and laughed. "The thing about getting to work early is that you get things done. I had managed to fix the bus I was working on. It barreled through there like a missile—right for me. I ran deeper into the server room but there was nowhere to go. Last thing I heard was it crashing through the wall. Then, I woke up in a chamber in the Extinction Trials."

Owen paced the deck, pinching his lower lip with his pointer and thumb. "Interesting. It still doesn't explain why there was no folder for you."

"Maybe I'm not special enough to leave a care package for."

"What strikes me," Cara said, "is that you stand before us, completely healthy. We all are." She eyed Maya. "Well, almost."

"Clearly, ARC is good at putting us back together," Owen said.

"Yes," Cara agreed. "And they seem to have a cure for the Genesis Virus that Maya and I were infected with. It seems clear that ARC had two potential therapies for GV, and only one worked."

Maya again felt a flare of hope. A cure was out there waiting—if it hadn't been lost to the sands of time. A headache began then, a low droning that pressed at the back of her eyes. She reached up to rub her temple, willing the motion to provide some relief.

Owen leaned closer to her and whispered, "Another headache?"

"Yeah."

He exhaled heavily. She had only known him a short time, but she could read what he was thinking. It was the same thing on her mind: *I'm running out of time.*

CHAPTER THIRTY-EIGHT

On the boat's main deck, Will volunteered to share his story next. Moving quickly, he descended the staircase to the staterooms and returned holding his envelope.

"The thing about what was in my folder," he said, "is that I've never seen it in my life. It's not like the pocket watch for Maya, the fire pin for Owen, or the shard for Cara—those were items that shaped your lives."

Will reached into the envelope and drew out a small silver metal cylinder that was about as long as his hand and as wide around as two fingers. Each end was capped with a clear glass.

"It's a monocular," Owen said, reaching out for the small device. He held it up and peered through it, expecting the sea in the distance to come into focus. But it didn't. He checked up and down the small object for controls or switches but didn't find any.

"It doesn't work," he whispered.

"It doesn't seem to," Will agreed. "It's like a prop or something."

Alister threw his head back. "Oh, please, no—don't say it." He waited for the group, but no one took the bait. "I'm just going to go ahead and guess that the point is we see what we want to see, and that glimpsing the future or far away things doesn't solve all of our problems."

Owen couldn't help but laugh. For someone who resisted philosophical thinking, Alister certainly had a lot of philosophical thoughts, albeit sarcastic ones.

"I wasn't thinking that," Cara said. "I was thinking that whatever it was built to identify isn't in sight right now. Perhaps it's a specialized night vision scope. Or infrared."

For once, Alister had a blank look. "Oh. Yeah, that's probably it."

"Why do you think they gave it to you?" Owen asked Will.

"I have a theory. It has to do with the last project I worked on. It was called Revelation."

Alister closed his eyes and rubbed his eyelids. "Why?"

"Why what?" Will asked innocently.

"Why do you programmers have to name everything so elaborately? Revelation. Insight. Transcend. I mean, get over yourself. You know what we common people call things? Wrench. Screwdriver. Hammer. Ax."

"The project nomenclature hardly seems pertinent."

"I rest my case," Alister muttered.

"What was Revelation?" Owen asked, hoping to move on.

"A big data project. It was a simple premise. If you design a system with enough processing power and you give it massive—and I mean absolutely massive—amounts of data, it will arrive at answers to questions no one even knew to ask, big conclusions that could change our understanding of everything. It was the most interesting project I ever worked on."

Alister shook his head. "This is inane."

"It's fascinating," Cara snapped. "Continue, Will, please. Ignore him."

"As I said before, I was on a team dedicated to one client: Genesis Biosciences." Will turned to Maya. "You said you worked there?"

"Yes."

"Do you remember your role?"

"Not exactly. There's only a single memory— going to work, changing clothes, and going into a clean room. I think I was a scientist working on something biological. Perhaps a pathogen. Or a dangerous chemical." She paused. "But I also remember Parrish telling me my job was complicated."

"Meaning?" Cara asked.

"I'm not sure. Maybe I was… well, I don't know."

Owen sensed she was holding back. On what, he wasn't sure.

"What I can tell you," Will said, "is that Genesis Bio, or as we called it, GB, was founded to solve neurological conditions. Their founder had a single belief: that the true threat to humanity begins and ends in our brains."

The words reminded Owen of the book his mother had given him, *The Birthright*. Was there a connection?

"GB's initial focus was on therapies to treat traumatic brain injuries and degenerative neurological conditions. Their approach to the project was radically different from other pharma and biotech organizations. Instead of creating a therapy in a lab and testing it, they bought data. Large amounts of data. From hospitals. From other groups that had run failed trials. Even from governments—from their prison systems and the militaries. It was all de-identified.

Their goal was to do a meta-analysis of existing studies and data, none of it publicly available, and to see what it told them. The principle was that the answers were there, that solutions could be derived from the data we already had but had never processed enough to see it. They hired ARC to do that data warehousing and processing. Our role was to design machine-learning algorithms that scanned and rescanned the data until it made sense. That was what Revelation was."

Will paused a moment, letting the others process what he had said. "There were several branches of the project dedicated to different outcomes. I know one was looking specifically at the brain activity of criminals. The premise was simple: do people who break the law think differently than those who don't?"

"What did you find?" Cara asked.

"We found that they indeed do."

"Nonsense," Alister said. "It's one of those... correlation and causation things."

"We accounted for that," Will said quietly. "GB had enough data to prove definitively that there are brain patterns that precede criminal activity."

"Why did I never hear about this?" Owen asked.

"A good question. It's one I asked myself while working on the project. I don't know the answer. But I think the most obvious is that this information would've turned the world upside down. What is the solution? Clearly, if you could create a device that monitored people's thoughts, then you could eliminate crime. What are the implications? A society whose thoughts are policed? What sort of society is that? And what might someone do if they could abuse that power? What I find most interesting is that Genesis didn't seem to be focused on that particular revelation. They were far more interested in memories."

"As in, erasing them?" Maya asked.

"No," Will replied, "or at least not on the project I worked on. They were far more interested in how memories were stored. Their focus was on memory alteration. On people who had experienced traumatic events. The goal was to help them come to grips with what happened. The solution was a slight modification to the memory, so that when someone recalled those events, they didn't create problems for them. GB's thesis was that bad memories altered brain composition—like a malfunctioning immune system, or how cancer might wreak havoc on the physical body."

"Fascinating," Cara mumbled, seeming deep in thought.

"Did it work?" Alister asked.

"Yes," Will said. "In the early trials they were successful at modifying memories. People who were essentially unable to live a happy and healthy life because of something that happened to them were able to completely overcome these traumas. There were no adverse effects either."

"How?" Maya asked.

"I don't know," Will replied. "I only saw the data from the trials. But I know Genesis saw these therapies as a turning point for the human race. They believed that memory modification and maintenance was the key to a happier, more sustainable future." He glanced over at Maya. "Something you said is very much like what Genesis believed, that we don't always remember what happened, but we remember how it makes us feel. And to some extent, we are the product of how our memories have changed how we see the world and how we behave."

Owen paced the deck. "The implication of what you've said—if it's true—if Genesis could modify memories, is that our own memories, what we've shared here, might not even be true. We could simply be remembering what Genesis wants us to... What ARC implanted in our minds."

CHAPTER THIRTY-NINE

Alister shook his head. "Not me. I remember that bus hitting the server room as real as we're standing here right now."

"I think we should assume," Cara said, "that we can rely on our memories. Believing anything else leads us nowhere. We can't act on that information. But it could cause uncertainty, which would harm us."

"I agree," Will said. "There's no reason for them to modify our memories—that we know of yet. But I do think Genesis was moving toward some sort of end game. They were gathering larger and larger amounts of data. Even at ARC, we were having trouble providing enough storage and processing power."

"How were they getting more data?" Maya asked.

"I don't know," Will replied. "I do know that they had formed an alliance with other corporations and possibly governments. It was called the Human Union, and the idea was to combine what Genesis was doing with other projects to effect change on a large scale."

"Change," Maya said, "as in *the* Change?"

"I don't know," Will replied. "I think we have to assume that Genesis and the Genesis Virus are part of the Change."

"If you worked for ARC," Owen asked, "how did you end up in the Extinction Trials?"

"As I said, I was working on the Revelation project. We were running out of data storage, and we were working feverishly to add processing power. I was told that I would be working at an off-site data recovery facility. That facility was Station 17. They brought me in and... It's hard to explain, but the next thing I knew, I was there in that observation room with all of you."

Maya couldn't put her finger on it, but something about the story bothered her.

"And you can't remember anything else?" Owen asked.

"Nothing that might help us," Will said.

They ate lunch then, mostly in silence. Maya reread the journal while Owen buried his nose in *The Birthright*, deep in concentration.

"Any good?" she asked.

"It's interesting," he replied.

After lunch, Maya took Blair below decks to the bedroom. "I know you may not want to, but it would help us a lot if you told us what happened to you before you woke up at the station."

She nodded. "I want to."

From the bedside table, she picked up the envelope with her name on it, and she followed Maya up to the main deck.

Maya watched as the young girl reached into the envelope and drew out small, printed picture that easily fit in the palm of her hand.

She handed the small picture to Maya. "Please pass it around."

Maya studied the photo for a moment. There was a man

and a woman and two children—Blair and what looked like a younger brother. It'd been taken some time ago. Blair had clearly grown since then. They were at what looked like an amusement park that Maya didn't recognize. The family was sunburned and looked weary and tired.

She passed the picture to Cara, who seemed alarmed by it.

"What is it?" Maya whispered. Cara simply shook her head and passed the picture to Will, who seemed even more surprised by the photo. He looked up at Blair and merely cocked his head, as if seeing her in a completely different light. Alister seemed to have no reaction to the photo. He barely looked at it.

Owen glanced at it but also seemed to have no reaction.

"There is one major difference between me and all of you," Blair said. "I knew about the Extinction Trials before I woke up in that station. In fact, I was told that it would save my life."

"By whom?" Owen asked.

"My father," Blair replied. "He's the man you see in that photo."

"He's also," Will said, "the founder of Genesis Biosciences."

"That's correct," Blair said.

"And your mother," Cara said, "is the emergency room doctor that pulled me out of that car and saved my life when I was a child."

Blair was silent for a moment. "I didn't know that. What I do know is that she is the reason my father started Genesis Biosciences. She is the reason he was so obsessed with memory. Because of what happened to her."

"Is she still alive?" Cara asked. "Or was she before you entered the Trials?"

"Yes," Blair said. "But she wasn't the same person she once was. Every year, things grew harder for her. Her job in the ER seemed to grind her down like a weight she couldn't lift off of her. She saw the worst in the world. Violence. Accidents that were nobody's fault—people that lost their lives because they were in the wrong place at the wrong time. And the people who had to use the ER to get any care at all. The people society left behind. Put simply, she had the mind to do the work but not the stomach for it. It ate away at her. My dad wanted to help her. He begged her to quit work, but she wouldn't hear of it. She felt that it was what she was meant to do."

"I know that feeling," Cara said.

"So, my dad created a new plan. He thought if he could change the way my mother's mind categorized those memories, how she felt when she remembered them, she would be free of the burden."

Blair looked at the picture again. "I don't know what's happening here, but I know that my father is a good man. All he ever wanted to do is help my mother and to help other people who are struggling with what they're going through."

She placed the picture back in the envelope. "The day before I came to Station 17, I was awoken in the night. My dad was scared. He wouldn't tell my brother and me what was happening. We got on the helicopter, and we flew until the sun rose. I don't know where we went, but I remember touching down at a landing pad and a mountain range. We hiked until we reached the station. He told me that I was going to go to sleep for a little while, and that when I woke up, the world would be completely different. That it would be a better world—a world without crime or hunger or disease or anything that I remembered. He told me that he would be there when I woke up and that my mother would too, and she would be like she used to be."

Blair paused, seeming to steel herself. "I was scared. The station was so clinical and weird to me, and then when my father wasn't there when I woke up, it took me some time to process my thoughts."

She held up the envelope. "I know why he left me this picture. The day this photo was taken, I got lost in the park. I was so scared. My father and mother were looking for me everywhere. And then, almost unexpectedly, they found me. And everything was right in the world again. I think he left me this picture because he wants me to know that he's looking for me, and that when I find him, everything is going to be okay. I think there's a chance that my father is waiting at the Escape Hatch location. If he is, I think things are going to turn out like they did that day at the park."

CHAPTER FORTY

As the sun set, the group gathered on the main deck and took their dinner of prepackaged meals.

"Getting sick of this ARC food," Alister said.

"We should be glad we have food," Cara shot back. "There are probably a lot of people out there right now whose bellies are empty, with no hope for their next meal. And they're running for their lives for what food they have."

"You're right," Alister said. "Forgive me. I work for a living, so complaining is part of my way of life."

His response was somewhere between an apology and an insult, and Owen wished then that he knew enough to read his tone to figure out which it was. Whatever the case, Cara didn't respond.

When darkness came, the ship's lights illuminated the deck, and the six team members busied themselves in different ways. To Owen's surprise, Alister and Cara played a game of cards at the banquette. Maya stretched out on the couch and read the journal again; Owen thought perhaps she was looking for clues they had missed before. He'd only known her a short time, but he knew a few things for sure: she was detail-oriented and hard-working.

Will was in the ship's cockpit, his hands dancing over the

control panel, trying to learn its systems. He seemed to be an exceptionally fast learner.

Blair lay on the couch near Owen and Maya, staring up at the stars. Owen wished he had something to give her that would entertain her—or at least distract her. He figured that she was thinking about her parents and her brother, wondering where they were and what happened to them. Since they had finished talking that afternoon, Owen himself had spent a lot of time thinking about his mother and whether she was still alive.

He had also spent more than a little time contemplating what he had heard. The others' stories had shocked him. He felt as though he had been given the pieces of a puzzle—pieces that fit together, but in ways he didn't expect. There was just one that didn't quite fit. He couldn't put his finger on exactly what that piece was, but he knew it was there. The fact that they were all connected was somehow part of understanding what was happening here. What did it all mean? What did it mean that Blair's mother had saved Cara and put her on her life path? And that Maya had worked for Blair's father's company? And the fact that Will had worked for Blair's father's company as well, perhaps in a way that was connected with the Extinction Trials?

And then there was Owen himself and Alister. Owen had saved Maya's sister's life, but he seemed to have no connection with Genesis Biosciences or the Extinction Trials. Alister also seemed unconnected. And there was no envelope for him in Station 17. What did that mean?

"Blair?" Cara called.

The young girl sat up.

"Want to play cards with us?"

She smiled and moved to the banquette, settling into a game with Alister and Cara. Owen thought that Cara's disposition toward the girl had warmed quite a lot since she had heard her story. Owen had been right about one thing: getting to know each other had potentially changed everything.

He walked to the cockpit, where he found Will staring at the control screen. He glimpsed the display right before Will exited the system. It had been the communication system, which surprised Owen.

"Are comms working?"

"No," Will said. "They're still offline. It's strange. The software is working, and the mechanical components are here. It should work. It's like there's something blocking it."

"Something like what?"

"I don't know."

"Could the previous owners have done that by design? Maybe broadcasting would have put them at risk—and it would for us too?"

Will considered that a moment. "It's quite possible. However, I think if we can get comms working, we should use them with caution."

"How so?"

"What I would suggest is finding an open location near hiding places, then sending a broadcast for help and hiding the boat in a place we can observe."

"To see who comes."

"Correct," Will said.

"It's not a bad idea."

Owen moved to the couch and considered the idea of using comms for a while. It could be their salvation. Or doom. Like just about everything in this ruined world.

Finally, he opened *The Birthright* and began to read again.

"It's an end of the world book club over here," Maya said, not looking over.

He smiled.

"It would be the first book club I've been in."

"Me too."

"End of the world or not," he said carefully, "it's one I sort of like being in."

A smile slowly spread across her lips, but still, she didn't look over. "I have to say, I feel the same."

The deck was silent then, except for the sound of the boat sailing across the sea in the night, Will tapping the control screen, and the flip-flop of cards on the table.

Owen found his place in *The Birthright* and began reading again.

"A human mind is like a set of tools. It's a set of tools that determines our destiny. It's a set of tools that determines our happiness.

"Most importantly, our mind is a set of tools we are never taught to use.

"That ends now.

"Perhaps the most powerful tool our minds possess is perspective.

"Consider its power through a real-world application of perspective. How does the world look? What is it made of? If you plant your nose in the ground, you get one perspective. Fly above it in a helicopter, you get another perspective. Launch into space in a rocket, and you gain yet another perspective.

"They are all of the same thing: our world.

"But it looks and smells and feels very different depending on which perspective you view it from.

"The same is true for the people in our lives. And our own problems.

"A person viewed in the context you encounter them in might seem irrational. But if you zoom out and look at their life in a wider view, their actions might make sense.

"The same is true of the problems you encounter. Some might not seem solvable in the narrow view that is our mind's default. But, if you change your perspective, if you step back and see the bigger picture, you may find a breakthrough. With your nose in the ground, you can't see a passage through the mountains. Climbing a mountain, you can't see the ocean beyond. In the air, you might spot the sea, but you might miss the dangers lurking on the ground.

"Perspective is a powerful thing."

When the group broke and went below decks for bed, Maya turned to Owen. "It was a really good idea to share our stories today."

"What can I say, I bring people together."

"You downplay it, but sometimes talking and under-standing each other is just as important as carrying them out of a burning building."

"Yeah, but it's less exciting."

"At this point, I'm okay with less exciting."

★ ★ ★

22

When it was time for Alister's shift to begin, Owen went down the small staircase and peered through the open door to Alister's bedroom. The older man's back was turned to Owen, and over his shoulder, he could see that he was hunched over, staring at a tattoo on his forearm. It was a tattoo Owen had never seen on the man's arm before—or at least, Owen couldn't remember seeing it.

Alister suddenly realized Owen was in the room and jerked the sleeve of his sweater over his forearm, hiding the tattoo.

"Doesn't anyone knock anymore?"

"Sorry. The door was cracked."

"Well, shut it. There is something I want to talk to you about."

Owen closed the door and stood awkwardly in the small room, which was dominated by the large bed. The noise of the waves breaking on the bow was like static all around them, unnerving.

"Do you believe her?" Alister asked.

"Who?"

"Blair."

Owen shrugged. "Of course. Why wouldn't I?"

"Well, there's the obvious."

"Apparently it isn't obvious to me."

"That's strange. I figured you for the smart one of the bunch."

"I'm a guy who runs into burning buildings. I think I'm far from the smartest person here."

"I meant good sense. I'm not sure the rest of them have good sense. I do. I think you do. And Blair's story doesn't make good sense."

"Why?"

"Think about it. If her dad is out there, why hasn't he come to get her? He clearly knew where she was."

Owen wasn't sure at all what to say about that. But Alister was right—it was a good question. And it was one of many questions he pondered that night as he lay on the narrow bed in the small bedroom with Will.

What he didn't know was that Cara, Alister, and Will had all told very big lies. Lies that they knew about.

Lies that would change everything.

CHAPTER FORTY-ONE

Once again, Maya was the first awake, and Owen was waiting on the main deck alone.

"Good morning," he said, smiling.

"Good morning."

"We should reach the Escape Hatch location late tonight," he said, a glint of excitement in his eyes.

"During your shift?"

"Right at the beginning."

"I'll set an alarm and wake up for it."

He smiled. "It's a date."

The group ate breakfast and settled into the routines they had found. Cara, Alister, and Blair played cards. Will examined the ship—everything from the engine to the computer systems. It was as though he was exploring a new land and couldn't get enough information.

Maya sat down on the couch beside Owen.

"I have a favor to ask," she whispered.

"Anything."

"There's nothing to read. I wondered if we might read together."

"*The Birthright?*"

"It might be awkward, being so close—"

"I'd love to. But I warn you, I'm a slow reader."

"Then you turn the pages."

"All right. Shall we start at the beginning?"

"No. Let's pick it up where you left off."

With that, he opened the book, and Maya began to read along.

"A mind under stress naturally resists rest. It is a machine that is always on.

"Yet, often times, the only way to overcome the stress-inducing obstacle is to recharge and achieve greater performance.

"Therefore, a new perspective must be adopted: that rest is productive, that in times of great stress, rest is often the activity of greatest value."

Maya had intended to sleep on the narrow bunk in the hallway and use the small alarm clock on the bedside to wake herself when they arrived at the Escape Hatch. Yet, she found that she couldn't go to sleep. She was too excited. Or anxious. It was hard to tell.

So, she remained on the deck, with Owen, the ship cruising through the night.

Periodically, she ventured to the ship's bow and looked out, expecting to see lights on the horizon or a coastline or even a lighthouse.

There was only darkness.

As the time ticked down, her excitement turned to fear. She wasn't the only one. Owen began pacing the deck.

"What are you thinking?" she asked.

"I'm thinking I was wrong. Maybe I completely misinterpreted the message."

"We're still not quite there."

"We're close enough to see something."

"Let's just wait. And have some faith."

He nodded, but she could tell he was still deeply bothered.

"Let's read a bit more and reassess when we reach the coordinates. What do you say?"

Without a word, he plopped down on the couch, and Maya opened the book to read again.

As a cool wind blew over them, she snuggled closer to him, and he pulled her close.

In that moment, she didn't want to read the book. She looked up at him and he peered down at her, his eyes a low simmering fire she could look into for the rest of her life—a fire that was heating her from the inside.

He shook his head and whispered, "I would give anything to be able to read your expression right now."

"I'll tell you for free."

"What?"

Maya leaned closer to him, staring into his eyes and pressed her lips to his. The kiss seemed to last an eternity, and yet, when it was done, she instantly felt a vast void where it had been, a place she wanted to get back to, an emptiness that only he could fill.

Owen glanced at the door to the stairway that led to the staterooms. "The others—"

"It's the end of the world," Maya said. "You really want to worry about someone seeing us?"

"No. If you don't, I don't care if the whole world sees us."

Owen surged forward and kissed her again and reached down and pulled her shirt off, moving urgently, like a starving man clawing his way to his last meal. And that's exactly what the moments that came next felt like to Maya—an event that satiated a hunger she didn't even realize she had.

When the ship's engine turned off, Maya and Owen were lying under a blanket on the couch, staring up at the stars. Somehow, for that brief amount of time together, the entire world had faded away. The Extinction Trials. ARC. Genesis Biosciences. And the Change—they were all finally forgotten, if for only a short amount of time.

In that moment on the ship's deck, under the stars, it felt to Maya as though she and Owen were truly the last people alive, as if the world was theirs, and it was safe, and nothing else mattered.

The alarm from the cockpit was a noisy—and stark— reminder that the other universe that they had just occupied was now over.

Owen pulled his clothes on quickly—so fast Maya had to marvel. But then she reminded herself that he was a firefighter, so it made sense. It was one of his many specialized skills, which she had just expanded her knowledge of.

He jumped up from the couch and raced to the cockpit, head moving back and forth slightly as he scanned the display panel.

"We're at the coordinates," he called back to her.

As soon as Maya had her clothes on, she stood and spun around, looking out in every direction.

Owen said what she saw and what she was thinking: "There's nothing out here."

CHAPTER FORTY-TWO

For a long moment, Owen stared out at the empty sea around him.

He was tired, terrified, and so disappointed in himself. He had made the wrong call. He had led the group here—to a dead end.

And it was truly a dead end. Soon, they would run out of food.

Where had he gone wrong? The coordinates in the Escape Hatch video—had he misread them? Or had he seen meaning and reason where there was none? Had he identified a pattern that wasn't actually there? If so, why? Was it to make himself look important to the group— to elevate his status, establish himself as an authority or leader? It was certainly part of his character. His career had constantly thrust him into that role.

Even now, as the thoughts swirled in his head, he knew he was over-thinking it, beating himself up because he was scared and disappointed.

Beside him, Maya was scanning the horizon. Owen would've given anything to have been able to read her face at that moment. Was she as scared as he was? Did she blame him?

"I have an idea," Maya said.

"Good, it's fair to say my ideas aren't as great as I think they are."

"Don't do that. We all voted to come here. It was your idea, but it was our decision. And we made it together."

For Owen, the words were like a balm on an open wound.

Maya descended the staircase, and Owen fell in behind her. At the door to the bedroom Owen shared with Will, Maya turned the handle and pushed it open slightly.

"Will," she called into the darkness.

"Yes?" he said, his voice placid. He didn't seem groggy. Owen wondered if he had been awake as well.

"Do you have that monocular?"

Owen heard him rise from the bed and join them in the small hallway. He handed the device to Maya, who charged up the stairs and held it to her eye on the main deck.

"Anything?" Owen asked.

"No."

"It was worth a try," Owen said.

It was clear to him what they had to do now. The Colony was the only other location they had. But time was not on their side. They needed to set a new course and begin moving in that direction as soon as possible.

"Should we wake the others?" he asked.

Maya was nodding, but Will shook his head vehemently. "No. Let's wait."

"Why?" Owen asked.

"You two have been up the entire night, correct?"

"We have," Maya said. Owen saw a small tinge of redness blossom on her cheeks. She was blushing. Owen figured he was too, but Will didn't seem to notice.

"As have I," Will said. "We are all tired. And we face another decision. One that may seem easy but one that I feel we should face with clear heads and well-rested bodies."

It was a good plan, one that Owen agreed to, but as he lay in the narrow bed, sleep eluded him.

He didn't know how long he tossed and turned, but at some point, he finally drifted off to sleep, probably in the early hours before dawn.

Owen woke to the feeling of hands gripping his shoulders.

He opened his eyes to find Maya staring down at him.

"What happened?" he whispered.

"Come and see."

They raced up the narrow staircase to the main deck where Will was waiting.

"Look," he said, pointing.

Owen spun around and instantly saw it on the horizon: a ship.

CHAPTER FORTY-THREE

Soon, the entire group was standing on the main deck, staring at the massive ship floating in the distance.

"It's a container ship," Will said.

"It's a trap," Alister said.

Maya shook her head. "We don't know that. But I think it is safe to assume that this ship is what the Escape Hatch message was leading us to. It's within the GPS sector. It may have simply drifted off course."

"Which implies," Owen said, "that it is perhaps not crewed—or not anymore. It's adrift."

"True," Maya agreed. "Which either bodes well or badly for us. If there's no one there, it's likely not a threat."

"Seemingly abandoned places can be very dangerous," Alister grumbled. "I remind you of what happened to those poor fools from the journal who were speared through with an arrow when they reached that hatch—which appeared to be abandoned and unguarded. This is our own version of that hatch."

"This is pointless," Cara said, frustration seeping into her voice. "We're out of food, and that ship is our best chance of survival out here. We're going aboard."

"I agree," Owen said. "I'll go."

"No," Maya said. "I'll go."

Alister shrugged. "You can both go. As long as I don't have to go."

"I have something that I think might help you," Will said before turning and going below decks and returning with what looked like an earpiece. "This is part of the radio from the helmet. I've extracted and programmed it to work with the ship's comms."

He handed it to Maya, who placed it in her ear, then he walked over to the cockpit and tapped the panel. "Can you hear me?" he asked.

Alister let his gaze drift up to the sky. "Programmers… Of course she can hear you! You're standing right there."

"Through the earpiece, I mean."

Maya smiled. "Yes, Will, I can hear you. This is great work. This will really help us on the ship."

Cara paced the deck, arms crossed, deep in thought. "Maybe you should just wear the suits over there."

"They're out of oxygen," Owen said. "Well, practically out."

"Still, wouldn't it be safer that way? In case there is some pathogen or something you might encounter there?"

Owen thought for a moment. "It's an interesting idea, but the reality is, it's harder to move in the suits. I think we're better off having more agility."

He didn't say it, but Maya thought she knew what he was thinking: they might encounter someone dangerous on the ship, and it would be far easier to fight without the suits on.

That thought brought a memory, a flash of her in the hospital, sitting in a wheelchair, rising to fight with someone in the room. She could fight. That was something. Was that part of her job? Part of her training? What did that mean?

Again, the emptiness of not having her memories struck her like an old wound that had been re-opened. It was so unsettling. And it made her want to get onto that ship even more—to distract herself and to find a cure.

At the cockpit, Will set a course for the container ship, and the boat roared to life and moved toward it.

On the deck, all eyes were locked on the massive vessel looming on the horizon.

Owen drifted closer to Maya. "What do you think we'll find?"

"Answers," she whispered. "And food. Not sure which I want more at this point."

He smiled. "Same here."

Maya watched the ship as they approached it, but she could see no movement at all. There were also no markings on the vessel, no name or numbers that she could see. Metal containers were stacked three rows high and ran the length of the ship. They were blue and red and green, and none seemed to be open.

What she didn't see concerned her most: a way onto the ship. Its deck sat high above the sea, far higher than their small craft.

Owen seemed to have come to the same conclusion. "Will, swing around the other side of the ship and see if we can find a way up."

As they rounded the cargo ship, Maya spotted a tender hanging off the side—an orange boat that was about half the size of their yacht. Beside it was a rubberized rope ladder hanging about halfway down the ship's hull. It would be a stretch to reach it from their vessel, but Maya thought she and Owen could manage.

Her next thought was what the rope ladder implied: someone had boarded the vessel while it had been at sea. She wondered if they were still alive. And still on board.

One way or another, they would know soon.

With the ship in position just below the rope ladder, Maya stood on the edge of the sundeck off the back of the yacht. Her earpiece was in, and her pockets held a flashlight and her father's pocket watch—for light and good luck.

Owen held his hands up. "I'll lift you up. When I do, grab the ladder. I'll come up behind you."

His hands were strong, and he lifted her at her waist, raising her in the air with ease.

She gripped the ladder, which was rubbery and wet from splashes from the waves. A thrill of fear ran through her as it swayed in the wind, the rubber screeching against the metal hull. She felt Owen's hands beneath her feet, propelling her up. She pulled with her hands and was glad that she wasn't wearing the environmental suit. There was no way she would've been able to lift herself.

Her foot caught the bottom rung and soon she was climbing. She stole a glance beneath her and saw Alister helping Owen onto the ladder.

At the top of the ladder, she climbed onto the deck and got her first glimpse of the ship. An open corridor ran the length of the vessel. Metal struts stuck up and curved back into the ship, like I-beams that had been bent. The paint was chipped away in many places, revealing rusty red metal beneath, as though a sea creature had been gnawing away at the vessel's flesh, revealing its ribs.

The sight reminded Maya of the journal's author, who had described a world that felt like it was dissolving, wasting away under the torture of time. That's what the ship felt like to her: a floating artifact that the wind and sea were slowly wearing away.

"Radio check," Will said.

"We read you," Owen replied.

"Where should we start?" Maya asked.

"The bridge," Owen said. "And then probably the engine room, the crew quarters, and the kitchen."

"I feel strongly," Will said, "that you should announce yourselves as you explore the ship."

Through the radio link, Maya heard Alister's voice in the background. "Terrible idea!"

"It is only prudent," Will said calmly. "We have been sent to this location. We come in peace. If there are people here, they could perceive us as a threat unless we announce ourselves."

Maya heard the two of them arguing then, voices low, indicating that Will had moved away from the microphone at the cockpit.

Owen seemed to have made up his mind. He called out in the morning sun, his voice echoing off the metal walls of the corridor. "Hello! Hello!"

It was utterly silent except for the purring of their own ship's motors.

Owen moved forward, stepping cautiously on the rubber mat that ran along the corridor. They had boarded near the middle of the ship and were now making their way to the rear, where a multistory tower rose, looming over the stacks of containers. Maya could see a few columns of containers behind it, but there were far more in front. The scene reminded her of a small skyscraper in the middle of a container yard floating on the sea.

At the tower, they climbed a rickety staircase, careful to avoid the steps that time and rust had eaten away. Near the top of the staircase, Owen turned the long metal handle of a hatch and pulled it open, the sound of rusted metal wailing, calling out into the morning.

"We're entering the bridge," Owen said over the radio. "Still no signs of life."

Louder, he called out, "Hello? Hello?"

Windows ran the length of the left wall of the bridge, looking out over the ship and the sea. There was a row of computer stations that looked antiquated to Maya.

Beyond the bank of computers were four glass chambers similar to what they had found in the station. All were open. The glass on two of the domes was cracked.

On the floor, in the middle of the bridge, was a person—a man, Maya thought—lying face down, unmoving.

Owen held out a hand to Maya as he moved toward the figure. With his foot, he kicked the body over.

It was Bryce. Or another Bryce.

"We found a proctor," Owen said. "He seems to be disabled."

"Is the ship functional?" Will asked.

Owen surveyed the control panels, wiping dust off the keyboards and switches. "Everything is off. Looks like maybe it's out of power. Nobody's used it in a while."

"Is anyone else there?" Will asked.

"Not on the bridge," Owen said.

Through the window, Maya caught sight of something that made her heart stop.

"Guys, we have a problem. There's a storm forming."

As she watched it, the storm's funnel darkened, growing more defined. It was strengthening. And it was coming directly for them.

CHAPTER FORTY-FOUR

Owen dashed to the window and studied the storm for a moment, trying to gauge its speed and direction. Both were very, very bad news for them.

It was going to hit the ship, there was little doubt in his mind.

The question was, what would happen when it did? On the island, Owen had never had a vantage point to see the storm that was lashing it, but he assumed it was much like what was coming for the ship—wind and rain.

Something in the previous storm, or the air on the island, had killed the older man who had left the bunker. The environmental suits had protected Owen and the rest of the team. They had been able to remove them out on the open sea—away from the island and the storm. But here and now, the suits were practically empty. They wouldn't be much help.

There was only one solution.

Still staring at the approaching storm, Owen said, "Maya, you need to get out of here. I'm right behind you."

She replied instantly. "No. We'll finish this together, and then we'll get out of here. It'll go twice as fast."

He held his hands out, readying himself to debate her, but

she simply turned and marched out of the bridge, calling back to him, "The longer we talk, the less time we have."

He caught up to her on the rickety staircase which she was descending more recklessly now.

They ducked through the door on the floor below the bridge and found what looked like a mess hall. The tables were covered in dust. Plates sat empty—not a morsel of food on them. Here and there, empty ARC ration packs dotted the tables.

Who had eaten those rations? Survivors from another station? Or the personnel that had staffed this Escape Hatch? And if so, what had happened to them?

The kitchen beside the dining area was empty as well, and so were the freezers and fridges. From the looks of it, they had been off for a while.

At the next level down, Owen and Maya found a maze of narrow corridors. It reminded Owen of being inside a mechanical beast, as though he were simply walking through the veins and arteries that ran deeper into the organism.

He opened the first door and found a mechanical closet. The next door opened to a stateroom with a narrow bed beneath the window that looked out on the containers. It also held a desk and a small bathroom.

"It looks like we're now in the crew quarters section," Maya said over the radio.

"Acknowledged," Will said. "Be careful."

"Hello!" Owen shouted.

There was no response.

He backed out into the corridor and opened the stateroom across the way. It was empty as well.

The next room was too.

And the next one.

Over the radio, Owen heard their ship's outboard motors roar to life.

He shared a glance with Maya.

"Are you all leaving?" she asked over the radio.

"No," Will said quickly. "We're going to move around to the other side of the ship to get a view of the storm."

At the next stateroom, they found a body. It was a woman, and she was heavily decomposed. She was wearing the same ribbed sweater Maya and Owen had been given in the ARC station after waking up. A stack of empty ration packs lay on the floor. Owen scanned the room, but there was nothing else of interest. The desk had no papers or journals on it.

"We found a body," Maya said. "Female. Looks like she passed away a long time ago."

They searched the remainder of the crew quarters but couldn't find anyone else.

The sight of the woman had unnerved Owen. Had she been stationed at this ship? If so, for how long?

Or had she traveled here on yet another vessel that was now gone—was that why the rope ladder was unrolled? If so, where was that other vessel? Did her cohort strand her here? And what happened to the proctor on the bridge? The entire scene was like a mystery with no clues.

Deeper into the crew quarters, the light from the window in the outer door was fading. Owen clicked on the flashlight and Maya did the same.

At the end of the corridor, they found an interior staircase that led down to a level that was full of mechanical equipment. Owen sensed that they had reached the belly of the beast, the guts that had once made the ship run. But they were decomposing now. The parts were dusty and quiet, some beginning to rust, wires and hoses drooping under the weight of gravity and time.

As he raked his flashlight over the scene, he felt as though he were revealing a tomb that had long since been sealed.

"I think we found the engine room," Owen called over the radio. "Or part of it."

He cupped his hands to his mouth. "Hello! Hello! We're here to help!"

Silence.

Owen and Maya's footsteps echoed on the metal decking as they explored deeper into the cavernous space. Overhead drops of water dripped into his hair every now and then, as though the ship was weeping at its demise.

At the next level down, they found the engines. There was no one here, and it looked like no one had been for a very long time.

"No one in the engine room," he said over the radio.

"Copy that," Will said. "Be advised: the storm seems to be picking up speed. I think you both ought to get out of there. Assuming it has the same effects as the storm had on the island."

Maya shined her flashlight in Owen's face. "We need to search the containers."

He considered that for a moment. "There are hundreds of them. Maybe thousands."

"Then we need to hurry."

She spun on her heel and marched away from him before he could argue. This was becoming a pattern.

In that moment, Owen felt a surge of adrenaline—the thrill of racing the clock, of having a challenge where lives were depending on him. He felt like he did back at the station. This ship was like a burning building to him. They had to find what they needed and get out—before it was too late.

At the metal hatch nearby, Maya spun the wheel and pushed, but it wouldn't budge.

"Help me," she called to him.

He added his weight and the metal doorway groaned as it cracked open. They pushed, and finally, it gave way, revealing a narrow catwalk with a metal mesh floor and railing tied together with rubberized rope. It was open to the sky above, and from that perch, Owen could see to the bottom of the ship, which was flat and held at least three rows of containers below them.

Over the radio, he said, "We're in the hold immediately off the engine compartment. We're going to start searching."

"Hurry," Will said. "Please hurry."

From the catwalk, they couldn't reach any of the containers. But Owen did notice that they were numbered. And they seemed to be in sequence. The ends facing them were labeled with words in white block letters: "ARC Technologies".

At the end of the catwalk, they found a staircase that descended. He and Maya went fast now, taking risks on the unstable metal stairs until they reached the bottom.

Owen hadn't been able to see it before, but he realized now that the nearest container was already open. The double doors were cracked just enough for him to slip inside. His flashlight illuminated the cramped space. There were at least a dozen glass chambers inside.

Maya radioed what they had found to the ship.

The next container was open as well, and it contained chambers too. And that's exactly what they found all along the row of containers.

Luckily, there was a narrow gap between the containers every seven columns. It was just big enough for them to slip through, a walkway between the towering stacks.

Quickly, Owen and Maya ran to the next row of containers. The doors to these metal boxes were also open. Inside, they found what Owen assumed were servers.

It occurred to him then what the container ship was carrying: parts for more ARC stations. That's precisely what the chambers and servers would build.

At the next row of containers, only about half were open. Inside they found the alcoves like the ones they'd found in Station 17, where Owen assumed the proctors had recharged themselves.

He turned to Maya. "We're striking out here. It's nothing but components for building a station."

"We need to keep going," she said.

"Maya, we are out of time."

CHAPTER FORTY-FIVE

Maya stared at the containers stacked in columns and rows. The answers they needed were here—she sensed it.

"Maya," Owen said, urgently now. "We need to go."

He turned and took a step toward the staircase to the catwalk, perhaps hoping his movement would inspire Maya to follow.

"Wait," Maya called to him.

The answer was there, right at the edge of her mind's grasp.

"We're out of time!" Owen called back to her, one hand on the railing now.

"Out of time," she whispered, turning the phrase over in her mind.

That was it.

Time.

She took the pocket watch out of her pocket and held it out toward Owen. "Why did they give me this?"

He bunched his eyebrows. "What?"

"They moved the hands of the watch. Time is the answer. They gave us this location—and they gave us another number, thanks to this watch. We find the container with these numbers, and we find what they left for us."

"Maya—"

"Please, Owen. You felt that we should come here. You were right. There's something here. We know this was an ARC vessel—it's got all the parts for the stations. I sense that there is something else here. ARC moved the hands of time on the watch. It's a message. I know it. They brought us to the future, and they left us a clue about what we're supposed to find."

"We're bringing the boat around," Will said over the radio. "You really must hurry. Time truly is running out. The leading edge of the storm will be here imminently."

Owen stared at Maya.

"Please, Owen."

Slowly, he nodded his head. "Okay. Let's find it."

They raced through the maze of containers, stopping at each row to read the number of the first container. Luckily, the rows continued to be in ascending order. When they found a number higher than 48151, they backed up to the row before and raced down it, reading the numbers as they went.

"Wait," Owen said, skidding to a halt on the metal deck. His head titled back, and he peered up, squinting as he read the numbers.

Maya got a sinking feeling as she followed his gaze. The container they were looking for, 48151, was sitting atop two containers, its door handles at least four times her height in the air.

Without a word, Owen planted a foot on the container behind them and then set his hands on the container ahead.

To Maya's shock and amazement, he shimmied upward, breathing heavily over the radio but making astounding progress.

When he reached the container, he grabbed the handle and let his feet swing into the base of it. Quickly, he turned the metal handle and swung the door out, the creaking metal calling out in the narrow alley of containers.

Still holding the container door with one hand, he drew his flashlight with the other, clicked it on, and swiped it back and forth.

"What do you see?" Maya called.

"Two duffel bags and a tablet."

He swung inside the container and was back at the opening a moment later, one of the duffel bags in hand.

Quickly, he lay flat on the floor of the container and lowered the bag as much as he could. Maya reached up for it and caught it when he dropped it. She immediately yanked it open and found dozens of ration packs inside.

That would solve their food problem—for a while anyway.

Owen dropped the other duffel bag, and Maya quickly pulled the cord on the top and found the same thing: ARC rations.

By the time she had finished searching the two bags—and confirming there was nothing else inside—Owen had climbed down. He reached under his sweater and drew out an ARC tablet similar to the one they had found in the station.

"Let's get out of here," he said.

Moments later, they were descending the rope ladder

that flapped against the ship's hull. The wind was already starting to pick up, the sea growing choppy. Alister and Will were waiting on the deck, ready to catch Maya when she made the small jump from the ladder.

Owen tossed the duffel bags down next, and the moment his feet hit the deck, Will raced to the cockpit and maneuvered them away at top speed, desperately trying to escape the storm.

Maya didn't know if it was the fatigue from staying up almost all night or the exertion and stress and adrenaline from exploring the ship, but she felt absolutely drained.

She went below decks and lay down, and despite the ship's rocking and the propeller's scream, sleep overtook her instantly.

When she woke, she found the group having lunch on the deck. Everyone seemed anxious, as if afraid.

Something had happened while she slept.

"What did I miss?" she asked, trying to sound nonchalant.

Owen rose from the couch. "We were waiting on you to watch the video."

"Video?"

Will held up the ARC tablet. "There are six videos on here."

Maya scanned the list:

```
1_Genesis            [16]
2_ARC Technologies   [23]
3_Revelation         [90]
4_Dark               [30]
```

```
5_Exit                    [32]
6_Next                    [51]
```

"The numbers at the beginning," Maya said. "I assume that's the order we should watch the videos in?"

"I think so," Owen replied.

"What are the numbers at the end?" Maya asked.

"Just the video length," Will said.

That seemed to catch Owen's attention. He walked over and studied the screen. Maya thought he was going to say something, but he merely nodded at Will, who tapped the tablet.

The first video began with a proctor that looked like Bryce, standing on the bridge of the ship near where Owen and Maya had found someone who looked similar. His voice was serene, his eyes unblinking.

"Hello. You have found the emergency message for Station 91. I am an ARC PI who was previously charged with logistical support for the Extinction Trials project. As of today, my primary mission has ended, and I will be stationed here to provide ancillary support as further instructed."

He paused, Maya assumed, for the benefit of any human watching the video.

"I have further been instructed to create this video to provide background information as might be needed. The first item of background concerns Genesis Biosciences. What we know at this point is that Genesis is part of a coalition called the Human Union, or simply the Union. The Union's goal has been to unleash a change of unknown effect. We know thus far that several governments were investigating the Union and Genesis specifically. We know that a deep-cover agent whose code name was Hazel discovered the Genesis component of the Change: the Genesis Virus, or GV. One thing we're certain of: GV acts to erase memories. It is effective in 90 percent of hosts who are infected. The other 10 percent perish. We believe that Genesis was planning to unleash this virus, and that Hazel learned of their plan. The operative informed the government, and the government launched a preemptive strike against Union cells and targeted Genesis locations where they believed the Change would begin. We call this event the Strike. The Strike was only partially successful. Enough elements of the Union organization survived to set in motion the Change. In fact, we believe that the Union was so devastated by the Strike that they initiated the Change earlier than planned in a desperate attempt to buy time to rebuild their organization. Further background is provided in additional videos."

The tablet went dark, and Maya held up her hand. "There's something you all should know. As I said before, when I first got sick, I was visited by someone named Parrish. He confirmed that I worked at Genesis Biosciences. He also told me that I was working as a government agent to investigate Genesis and that my code name was Hazel. Because of my hazel eyes." She stared at the group. "If what he told me is true, if I am Hazel, then my actions set all this in motion—the raid on Genesis Biosciences, the Change, and even the Extinction Trials."

CHAPTER FORTY-SIX

For a long moment, no one said anything. The boat raced across the water, away from the container ship and the storm consuming it.

Owen's mind was racing too, trying to process Maya's revelation. She was... some kind of covert operative. As he thought about it more, it made sense. Several times, in dangerous situations, her instincts had saved him—and the entire group. She had a firm handle on her fear and the courage to see her missions through.

She was pacing the deck now, head down. "This video confirms what happened to me. I wasn't just an employee at Genesis Biosciences. I was a government agent embedded there to investigate them. I figured out what they were doing, and I notified the government. They initiated the raid—and Genesis gave me the virus to wipe out my memories and keep me from providing any other information to the government. I think they expected it to kill me. When I didn't die fast enough, they sent someone to finish me off. But I fought back—and got away."

"If that's true," Alister said, "how and why did you end up in the Extinction Trials?"

"I don't know," Maya whispered.

"I think," Owen said carefully, "that we should watch the rest of the videos before we start making any more conclusions."

When no one protested, Owen motioned to Will, who clicked the next video:

```
2_ARC Technologies    [23]
```

The proctor again appeared, still standing on the cargo ship's bridge.

"Topic two: ARC Technologies. As detailed in video number one, which you should have already viewed, I am in the employ of ARC Technologies. ARC has its origin in data warehousing and archival record storage. We later expanded our business into specialized data storage and data analytics services. As such, we had key relationships with the organizations that became the principal players in the Change and what occurred after. Of particular interest is a team dedicated to Genesis Biosciences and related companies that compose the Human Union—what we called the ARC-Union group. The ARC-Union group first became aware that the Change was going to take place after the government coalition initiated the strike against Genesis Biosciences and their Union partners. I will hereafter refer to the government coalition as simply the Alliance. The following videos will detail ARC's role and what we soon learned."

Alister put his feet up on the coffee table in the lounge area. "Why? Why do they have to make six videos instead of one? Why leave all these breadcrumbs? Why not just tell us the answers we need to know?"

"I think the answer," Owen said, "will soon be obvious.

Perhaps they left clear instructions elsewhere and those efforts have failed. We were the last people to wake up in that station. It would seem that direct efforts have failed. This is their last line—essentially, ARC's last hope of success for the Extinction Trials."

"No pressure," Alister muttered.

Will tapped the tablet and started the next video:

3_Revelation   [90]

"Video number three. This video presupposes you have completed the preceding two videos. It concerns ARC's Revelation project, which was principally focused on Genesis Biosciences, as well as various government programs to improve the long-term health and longevity of citizens.

"But first, some background. For some time, ARC has been working on a project called the Extinction Trials. While ARC's expertise has traditionally been in storing data and certain biological and chemical samples, the Extinction Trials was a new endeavor for us: the archiving of human beings before an extinction-level event. It was assumed that the Extinction Trials would be activated sometime in the distant future. However, events that have previously been described—the Change and the Alliance strike that preceded it—accelerated the initiation of the Trials. ARC, fortunately, had insight into both of the organizations that were now at war in a world that was changing rapidly. And we had a particular tool that was applicable to determining potential outcomes—a project called Revelation. At the time of the Change and during the Change War that followed it, we collected large amounts of data and fed it into the Revelation program, which analyzed that data and predicted outcomes. The next video details what we found."

When the video ended, Owen gazed into the distance. The container ship was shrinking. The storm was lashing it with wind and rain, rocking it like a toy in a bathtub. Thankfully, their vessel was moving faster than the storm. Strangely, the storm seemed to slow down, hovering over the larger ship. He felt that was unusual, but he didn't know what it meant.

Will tapped the next video:

```
4_Dark                    [30]
```

The proctor once again appeared, still standing on the bridge.

"Video four. Dark."

The proctor paused a moment, perhaps allowing time for the audience to prepare for taking notes.

"After the Change swept the world, the Alliance initiated a counterstrike. With their armies crippled, they could not prosecute a conventional war. As such, they turned to the same weapon that the Human Union had used against them: technology. The governments that comprised the Alliance had one thing that was still operational: drones. And soon, they began using these high-altitude drones to initiate weather events: small storms at first and later very large storms. We soon learned that these Alliance-caused storms had a unique characteristic: they were lethal for anyone who had undergone the Change. From ARC's standpoint, this constituted a potential extinction-level event. The Extinction

Trials thus began at this moment. Our initial protocol was to wait and hope that there was a peaceful resolution to the Change War, as it had become known. Our focus at this time became very simple: gather as many humans as possible and archive them for a future when there was peace and they might survive. The obstacles were clear: create a vaccine and treatment for the Genesis Virus and create humans who could survive the Alliance Storms."

The proctor paused. "This was a turning point for ARC and the Extinction Trials. We had in our possession the last human survivors. Both groups—the Alliance and the Union—needed those survivors to form an army and to populate colonies that would reclaim the planet. They searched for our stations and raided them. As such, we went further underground and initiated additional lockdown protocols. We went Dark. And have remained in Dark protocol since."

When the video ended, Owen couldn't help but glance at the storm lashing the cargo ship. Was it one of the storms controlled by the Alliance drones? It seemed like too much of a coincidence for it not to be.

And if it was, why had it attacked the ship? Was it related to them being there? That seemed to be the logical conclusion to Owen.

Maya nodded toward the tablet. "I think the government placed me in the Trials as a way to hide me away from the Human Union—and Genesis Bio. And to potentially save me. If the Extinction Trials did find a cure, that would be my best way to receive it."

"Well," Alister said, "they seem to have abandoned you."

"So it would seem," Maya said. "And I don't think I was

the only one. Do you all remember the old man—at the beginning of the Extinction Trials, when we woke up in Station 17—the man who killed Bryce? He said to us that the Extinction Trials weren't what we thought they were. Then he ran out. He didn't believe there was a storm. I think it's safe to say now that he was a government agent. A government agent that had been told that the Extinction Trials were taking human survivors from the Alliance and refusing to return them or provide any information on a cure. He must have been collected and put in the Trials after the Dark protocol was initiated."

"Yes," Owen said, "that makes sense."

"There are two more videos," Will said. "Perhaps they will provide further insight."

He pressed a finger against the file titled 5_Exit, and once again, the proctor appeared on the screen, standing on the bridge of the ship.

"Video number five. Exit."

The proctor paused. "If you are viewing this, it means that the Extinction Trials have failed. Our attempts to find a cohort that can survive the global interventions initiated by the Alliance and the Union have proved unsuccessful to date. That leaves me at a disadvantage as to how to advise your next steps. You have exited your station and are now in search of a resolution to a war that may have ended or perhaps is ongoing. The questions you must answer at this point are: is the Union still active? Has the Change been completed? Have the Alliance been defeated, or have they triumphed? The crux of the issue is differing views for humanity and the way forward. ARC Technologies and the Extinction Trials seek only a sustainable future for the human race. Please see the terminal video in the series for further instructions."

Will closed the video and selected the last file.

"Video number six. Next steps. As is required of my role here, I am compelled to provide you with a clear path to move forward. I have already done so. Good luck."

The video closed and the tablet turned black.

Alister buried his head in his hands. "You've got to be kidding me."

"I don't get it," Cara said.

But Owen did. He paced the deck, turning over in his mind everything he had seen.

"I don't see any other choice," Alister said. "We go to the Colony now. We don't have any other option."

"But who controls the Colony?" Cara asked. "The Alliance—the government coalition—or the Human Union? And beyond that, who are the good guys in all of this?"

Alister rolled his eyes. "Oh, for crying out loud. There are no good guys! The good guys are the people who put food in your belly and keep arrows out of your heart."

"I don't agree with that," Maya said.

"Dead people make my point," Alister shot back.

Owen turned to the group. "We're not going to the Colony. We're going to Garden Station. We're going to finish the Extinction Trials."

Alister laughed out loud. "Oh really? That's wonderful. By boat or helicopter? Now or at our leisure?"

"We're going to go right now. By boat."

"You're hilarious," Alister muttered.

Maya focused on Owen. "Explain."

"It's very simple. They just told us where it is. In the videos. In a code."

CHAPTER FORTY-SEVEN

On the boat's main deck, Maya sat on the couch, studying Owen's face. He had that same look he had had back at the station when he figured out that the antique physical key unlocked the tablet and that the GPS coordinates of the cargo ship were embedded in the videos.

Owen motioned to Will. "Pull up the list of files."

Will tapped the tablet and turned it toward the group.

Maya scanned the list. Whatever Owen saw, she still didn't see it.

```
1_Genesis            [16]
2_ARC Technologies   [23]
3_Revelation         [90]
4_Dark               [30]
5_Exit               [32]
6_Next               [51]
```

Owen was pacing the deck now, seeming contemplative. "Think about how we got here. We saw meaning in the video that perhaps others had missed. We don't know what happened to the cohorts before us, but I think it's safe to assume that they were also given the Escape

Hatch location. Perhaps in the same way as us. Perhaps explicitly."

"That doesn't mean anything," Alister said.

"But it does," Owen said, staring at the storm in the distance. "It gives us a clue about what we're dealing with here. We found the coordinates to the container ship embedded in false data in the videos. Incorrect patient counts. There's something incorrect about these videos too. It's also numerical."

He turned to the group and waited.

"Maya, how did we find the container?"

"The time on the pocket watch."

"What about it?"

"It was different. From when I had it before the Extinction Trials."

"Exactly. Now take a look at the file listing."

Maya focused on the tablet, but for the life of her, she couldn't find what was wrong.

"It's the time," Owen said. "They're off. The videos were either longer or shorter than these time listings. These aren't times at all. They're GPS coordinates."

The group crowded around the tablet, studying it.

"Coordinates to where?" Maya asked.

"Where should an Escape Hatch lead? To safety. To salvation. I think we are very close to completing our mission here, to finding Garden Station and rescuing the people ARC collected."

"It doesn't feel like we're very close to me," Alister muttered.

Owen pointed to the screen. "Look at the files again. The names."

```
1_Genesis              [16]
2_ARC Technologies     [23]
3_Revelation           [90]
4_Dark                 [30]
5_Exit                 [32]
6_Next                 [51]
```

"The first letters," Owen said, "spell garden. These coordinates, I would bet, will lead us to Garden Station."

CHAPTER FORTY-EIGHT

With the boat cruising toward the coordinates of Garden Station, Owen slipped below deck and stretched out on the narrow bed in the stateroom he shared with Will. He tried to take a nap, but sleep was elusive.

His mind was in a recursive loop, obsessing over what they would find at Garden Station. Was it truly salvation for humanity? Was it the exit from the burning building that was this world?

His mind kept drifting to the last time he had seen his mother. Would she be waiting there? Or was she gone, like so much of the world, swallowed up by the Change War and the aftermath?

Another thing was bothering him. One by one, he replayed the stories from the others. Instinctively, he felt there was something he was missing.

What was it?

The door cracked open, and Maya leaned her head in.

"Sorry, I didn't realize you were resting."

"No. I was just thinking. Come on in."

She slipped inside and closed the door. "It was brilliant thinking with the times on the file list."

"It seemed obvious to me."

"I don't think it was to any of the rest of us."

"Just the way my mind works."

Maya sat down on the other narrow bed. Being this close to her stirred the fire within Owen. He wished he could pull her close, kiss her, lock the door and spend some time with her before they reached Garden Station. But he desperately needed to figure out what was wrong with the stories the others had told—deep down, he felt their survival depended on it.

Maya seemed to read him like an open book.

"Something is bothering you."

"Yes," Owen said. "I feel like I'm missing something. Can't put my finger on it."

"Such as?"

"Something about all their stories. There's something off. I know it's there, but I can't quite bring it to the surface."

"I think we're all exhausted and stressed, and maybe it's just our minds trying to find meaning where there is none."

"Maybe." For whatever reason, a thought occurred to Owen. "Have you seen Alister's tattoo? The one on his forearm?

"No. He doesn't have a tattoo on his forearm."

Owen pushed up in the bed. "Yes, he does. I saw it yesterday in his stateroom. It's quite elaborate."

"Interesting. Because I was just above decks, and it was warm enough that he took his sweater off. There's nothing there."

Owen tried to wrap his head around that. He had been exhausted when he had seen the tattoo—or thought he saw it. Had he imagined it? Apparently.

"Is that some kind of clue?" Maya asked.

"That, or I'm hallucinating."

After a pause, Maya went on. "Thank you for trusting my instincts on the ship."

"You have good instincts. They've saved us a few times now."

"So have yours."

In his mind, the piece clicked into place for Owen. "That's part of it: us. I think the six of us are like some sort of tapestry."

"A tapestry?"

"I think our stories knit together. So do our skills. And our personalities. Even our values. There's something to that. I think it might be the key to everything."

At some point, Maya and Owen had stopped talking, and she had stretched out on the bed and wrapped an arm around him. With her warm touch on his body and the waves striking the hull, Owen was finally lulled into a deep sleep.

He woke to a gentle hand on his face and shoulder.

"Owen."

It was Maya's voice.

"We're here."

He rose, bounded through the door, and raced up the stairs and onto the main deck.

The sun was setting in the distance, causing him to raise a hand to shade his eyes.

Owen expected to see an island. Or the shore and a city waiting there. Or even another container ship.

He saw nothing.
Absolutely nothing.
In every direction, it was only open sea.
He had been wrong.

CHAPTER FORTY-NINE

Maya saw the disappointment in Owen's face. She knew exactly how he felt. On the ship, when she had pressed him to search for the container, she'd put herself out there like that.

Now he had made a leap, and it had led to a dead end. A dead end on the sea. With time running out.

While they now had more food thanks to the duffel bags, they didn't have a way to get any more.

Standing on the deck, staring at the horizon, Owen had the look Maya had come to know well since waking up in Station 17: focused concentration that could break through any problem.

His voice was calm but forceful when he spoke. "Will. Bring the monocular."

A thrill went through Maya. That was it. It had to be.

Owen held the small device to his eye and spun slowly.

She waited, and on his face, she saw the truth before he spoke.

"Nothing," he muttered as he handed the monocular back to Will, who tried it as well.

"Perhaps it only works at night," the younger man said. "Perhaps when the sun sets, we'll see whatever is here."

Alister exhaled heavily. "Yes, maybe there will be a fireworks show too."

When no one responded, Alister continued: "Look, we tried it. There's nothing here. Let's go to the Colony. End of story."

"I'd like to wait," Owen said quietly. "I want to make sure there's nothing here."

An idea occurred to Maya. "Maybe waiting is the answer." She took the pocket watch out. "Time. We wait until the time indicated on the watch. Maybe it's not what's here. Maybe what we're meant to find is what's coming."

With the boat's motors off, the small vessel rocked quietly in the choppy sea, waiting.

At the dining table, Alister, Cara, and Blair played cards.

Will spent his time examining every last piece of the suits. Maya knew the sight of the storm had scared him, and he was working on a way to get more oxygen into the tanks—just in case they needed them.

Maya and Owen lay on the couch, reading *The Birthright*. She paused on a passage she found particularly interesting:

"In life, negative feedback has one role: as clues to greater success. If one can't act on negative feedback to improve, the most appropriate action is very simple: nothing."

When the sun had set, Owen tried the monocular again. "There's nothing out here."

"Yet," Maya said. "Not yet."

★ ★ ★

The group was silent as they ate the last ARC meal they had brought from Station 17, the only sound that of the ocean waves lapping along the sides of the ship.

When they were finished, they waited as the time reached the hands on the pocket watch.

The moment came and went.

Nothing happened.

No signal.

No ship.

No helicopter.

Will tried the monocular again. He didn't even bother announcing that he had found nothing. He only placed it back in the envelope, as if closing the case for good.

"I'll take first watch," he said. "I'm better rested than most of you. And besides, I believe I require less sleep."

Despite napping that afternoon, Maya still felt tired. Instead of going directly to her room, she stopped by the stateroom Owen shared with Will.

"Maybe morning will bring an answer," she said, loitering in the door frame.

"Maybe."

"What are you thinking?"

"About how empty the world is."

She entered and closed the door behind her. She didn't want Blair to hear the conversation. They were in a desperate place now, and Maya wanted to spare her from hearing the people she was relying upon expressing their fear. Fear could be contagious—an infection that could grow and sicken the group.

"In the station," Owen said, "we were boxed in. Running out of power and air." He motioned to the sound of the waves striking the hull. "All we wanted was to get out. Now we're here—with air and power in abundance. Out in the wide open. With no more clues and no ground to stand on. We're adrift. Let's face it."

"There's the Colony."

"True. But I can't help thinking something is here. I'm missing a very big clue."

She put a hand on his shoulder. "Rest. You never know. Things might look different in the morning."

He nodded. "It comes down to faith, doesn't it? Just like my job some days. You go into a dangerous and unpredictable situation, and you're not sure what's going to happen, but you keep going because that's the only thing you can do."

"Exactly."

"It's funny, I felt alive in Station 17, when we were trying to escape. I felt it again on the ship—when the clock was ticking down, and we had a goal. Out here, now, I feel like I did before the Fall. Adrift. Not knowing my place in the world."

"I think your place is being an integral part of this team. And to do that, you need to get some rest."

When she woke, Maya climbed the stairs to the main deck, where she found Will, Owen, and Alister waiting. The sun was rising on the horizon, chasing the night away.

Slowly, she turned in every direction. And saw nothing.

Owen held the monocular in his hand at his side. "Still nothing," he said quietly to her.

When everyone had finished breakfast, Owen stood and said what Maya was thinking.

"Whatever was here is gone. Or whatever was going to come for us isn't coming. It's time to go."

Alister raised an eyebrow. "To the Colony?"

"To the Colony." Owen turned to Will. "Can you chart a course?"

"I've already entered it in the ship's nav system."

"Do we have enough food to make it?" Cara asked.

"Plenty," Will said. "I estimate we'll have three days, excess—assuming the Colony is by the sea. If we must hike inland, our supplies could be taxed, but we might also find additional replenishments before we reach our destination."

Day and night, the ship motored across the sea. The family, as Maya had come to see them, settled into the routine they had found. Like a true family, they were pieces that fit together well, that clung to each other and repelled each other and were often frayed around the edges where the pieces touched. But they never fell apart for long.

Alister and Cara argued about anything they could think of to argue about.

In the moments when no one was looking, Maya observed Blair taking out the envelope and gazing at the picture of her mother, father, and brother. Maya was torn between walking over to the girl and giving her a firm hug and allowing her some space.

Ultimately, Maya had opted to give Blair time to herself. She sensed that, now, she needed that more than coddling. In a way, during this long voyage in the quiet and the expanse of nothing, each of them was confronting their own thoughts and fears and demons.

Owen seemed to be having the hardest time with it. When he and Maya weren't reading *The Birthright* on the plush couch, he was pacing or locked away in his room, brooding. Maya could almost see the wheels in his mind turning. He seemed almost haunted, a mind working on a problem with no solution. She desperately wanted to help him, but she saw no way to distract his mind or set him on a new course.

And she had problems herself—in her own mind. Each morning, she awoke to dried blood caked on her lip and cheek—and a pounding headache. Each time, she quickly ran to the bathroom and washed it away before Blair or Cara spotted it.

She didn't want anyone to know she was getting sicker.

She had learned to spot when the nosebleeds were starting and would duck below decks and wait in the bathroom until they stopped.

She found Owen waiting outside after one such episode.

"It's getting worse, isn't it?"

"No."

"You're lying. I can't read your face, but I know your bladder hasn't shrunk and the skin below your nose is raw from wiping it."

"I'm just seasick."

He exhaled. "Well, I hope you will keep me informed of any *side effects* of your seasickness."

She nodded as she thought: *what would we even do about any side effects?* There were no hospitals out here. No pharmacies. And no cure in sight.

That night, as she lay in bed thinking, she attempted to mentally retrace what had happened to her. She had awoken in a bunker. Station... She couldn't remember the number. Station 19? Yes, that was it. Or was it?

And before that... what had happened? She had been sick, she knew that, and in the hospital. Someone had visited her? Who?

The memories were slipping away as though washed away by time. And time was gaining on her. How much longer before she didn't remember anything—who she was, what she was doing out here on the sea... who the others were—who Owen was? And what they had shared on that deck before they reached the container ship. In a way, she was adrift too, and she needed to find a cure. Soon.

CHAPTER FIFTY

In his stateroom, Owen woke to shouting above.

He jumped out of bed and raced up the narrow stairs.

Will was crouched on the floor where parts of the computer console from the cockpit were strewn from the table to the couch. Owen heard the roar of the engine, so he knew they were still moving. For whatever reason, the boat seemed to be okay without the computer.

Alister was towering over the younger man, hands on his hips. "You're tearing it up!"

"I am not tearing it up," Will said, his voice calm.

Alister pointed to the parts. "Let me guess, the cockpit self-destructed because it is smart enough to know we're lost at sea."

"First," Will replied, "we are not lost at sea. Second, I disassembled the ship's computer to take an inventory of its parts to identify elements that could be extracted and taken with us when we make landfall."

Alister scoffed. "Like I said, tearing it up."

"You are not the only one who can fix things, Alister."

Owen held up a hand, stopping the argument that he knew was about to erupt. "I thought you were a programmer?"

"Yes. But I also have a working grasp of computer hardware."

Owen heard footsteps on the stairs and turned to find Maya climbing up, running her thumb and pointer finger over her eyes. "What's going on?"

"Wonder Boy tore the ship apart," Alister muttered.

"What parts are you interested in?" Owen asked Will, ignoring Alister.

"The radio," Will replied. "If I can extract the radio, maybe it will work on land. We very well might need to call for help."

Alister closed his eyes and blew out a breath. "Assuming this mutilated mess actually works on land—and I doubt that very seriously—you could just as well be calling someone hostile to us."

"A working radio gives us the option of using it," Will said. "Not a requirement. As such, I feel it should be used only when we have nothing to lose."

Owen pointed to the cockpit. "The ship's still running?"

"Yes. The nav system and engine controls are still online. Only the display is off. Removing the radio components necessitated deactivating it." Will held his hands out. "We will not need to change course any time soon—not before I'm done."

"Hurry, just in case," Owen said. "You never know what we're going to run into out here."

"If the past is any indication," Alister muttered, "we're going to run into nothing out here."

★ ★ ★

When it was time for his shift to start, Owen found Will on the deck and the cockpit computer reassembled.

"I'm sorry for the commotion," Will said.

"Not your fault," Owen said as he wiped the weariness from his face. "It's Alister. He's particular about the boat."

"Yes," Will said slowly, "he is."

Owen sensed something there—a subtext—and he would have given anything to have been able to read it.

"Any luck with the radio?"

"Yes," Will said. "We have what I believe is indeed a working radio. Time will tell. I've also extracted one of the solar panels from the roof. It may prove valuable as well."

The day passed like the ones before, with one exception. Maya was going below decks more often. When Cara went to check on her, they stayed below a long time.

It gave Owen an unnerving feeling. Maya was slipping away. Getting sicker. They were running out of time, in more ways than one.

Owen spotted it as the sun was setting: the thin line that divided the sea from the sky. Land.

The coastline looming on the horizon grew thicker as Owen called out, "Look!"

Maya was beside him, staring, a hand held at her brow to shield the sun. Owen felt her other hand slide up his back and grip his shoulder.

Behind him, the others called and shouted, and he wrapped his arms around Maya and lifted her up as they spun to the group, where Alister was hugging Cara, and Blair and Will were beaming.

They had made it.

Quickly now, the shoreline came into view. There was no city here, or any that Owen could see, only an expanse of blue-green trees dotted by rock faces every now and then, sheer cliffs that looked out like faces watching the ocean waves break upon them.

Owen couldn't see the end of the coastline, so he wasn't sure if it was an island, but it looked far larger, like a primary landmass.

"We need to find a place to put ashore," Alister said.

They brought the ship close enough to make out a small opening in the tree line.

"I think we should put ashore there at first light," Owen said.

Alister reeled back. "First light? What are we waiting for?"

"Light," Cara said flatly. "Owen's right. We should get some rest. Based on how far we've still got to go, this will be a hike. And I don't want to do it in the dark."

The next morning, they loaded the duffel bags with the food they had left, their flashlights and blankets, and beached the boat at the narrow opening in the tree line.

Will carried his makeshift radio in a shoulder pack that also had the medical supplies.

"Wish we had a key to the boat to take with us," Cara said.

Alister smiled. "It turns out we do."

275

He went below to the engine compartment and returned with a handful of parts. "She can't run without them, and I think all the marine supply houses are closed these days."

Owen thought it was a good idea—one that hadn't occurred to him. But Alister had realized it effortlessly. That was interesting.

Owen was surprised at how good the ground felt beneath his feet.

"Over here," Will called out. He was crouching to the ground, holding up a rock, which Owen soon realized was a piece of pavement.

"There was a road here," Will said.

"That ran into the sea," Alister added.

"I think the sea rose up and swallowed it. There's probably a city out there under it."

"If there's a road, it once led somewhere," Maya said.

Will held up the GPS. "For now, it leads where we're going."

PART IV

THE WASTELAND

CHAPTER FIFTY-ONE

On the road, there was nowhere to hide.

The group of six walked in silence as the sun rose behind them, peeking through the trees and slowly warming them until Maya swapped the thick sweater for a long sleeve shirt she had found on the boat.

The pavement was mostly gone, buried by the trees and shrubs that had grown up through it over time, like the hands of the planet rising up to reclaim its land.

Maya kept watch for road signs—or signs of any kind.

She saw none.

They stopped for lunch, and Will turned the radio on and listened. There was only static, but the young man seemed encouraged by it. Where Owen saw connections no one else did, Will seemed to hear something nobody else could hear.

They trekked on in the afternoon, still in silence, watchful of their surroundings. What struck Maya was that there seemed to be no animals out here—none big enough to make a noise in the forest. Bugs crawling on trees were the largest living creatures she saw, besides their group.

She worried that Blair would grow tired as the day stretched on, but the girl kept pace with the five adults admirably.

Further from the shore, the terrain grew hilly, and Maya found herself taking deeper breaths and felt a slight burn in her legs. They stopped to rest more often then, typically at Alister's request.

He was bent over, gasping. "So, this is how the world ends? Hiking through the woods until you drop dead?"

"We are vulnerable out here," Will whispered. "We should try to keep quiet."

"Yeah, yeah," Alister muttered.

When they stopped the next time, they weren't out of daylight, but they were out of energy.

"We'll make camp here for the night," Owen said. "And start again at sunrise."

With that, they laid out the blankets and prepped a meal.

"Based on our progress today," Owen asked Will, "how long until we reach the Colony?"

"Possibly tomorrow."

At Will's words, all eyes turned to him. He cocked his head. "However, it may be the next day if our rate of travel slows, which I count as likely. The way forward looks even more mountainous."

When night fell, it grew colder. Maya slipped the sweater back on and snuggled under the blanket with Blair and Cara. She desperately wished they could start a fire, but it was too great a risk. So were the flashlights. They lay in darkness, waiting for the sunrise and another day of marching toward what they hoped would be salvation.

★ ★ ★

Before she drifted off to sleep, Maya tried to think back to the first thing she could remember. It was seeing the man go out of the airlock and die. But she knew there were things before that. What were they? It was like the timeline of her memories were moving up. How long did she have? How long before she had forgotten who Cara and Blair were? Or Owen? Or what she was doing out here?

Maya woke to voices arguing: Cara and Will.

Maya glanced over in time to see the doctor pulling back the blanket covering Will, revealing the glowing panel of the radio. He didn't say a word, only stalked off into the dark forest, Cara close behind him, whispering.

Maya wanted to get up and go after them, but sleep held her down.

She felt wetness on her upper lip and reached up to find blood there. Her head swam and sleep overtook her again.

When Maya woke again, Blair was tucked in beside her, sound asleep. Cara and Will were still gone. Owen was softly snoring.

Alister was awake, his back turned to her as he stared down at his forearm. Maya was at just enough of an angle to realize that there was indeed a tattoo on his arm. Owen had been right. Alister reached down and touched the tattoo, pressing his finger in, stretching the skin and distorting it. Maya's sleep-addled brain was so sluggish she could barely comprehend what she was seeing. She closed her eyes and found she couldn't lift her eyelids again.

The next thing she heard was Cara's voice shouting in the distance, seeming not to care who heard her. "We have to respond!"

That brought Maya around. Quickly, she surveyed the camp, which was now just a pile of blankets around the duffel bags. Everyone was gone except for her and Blair. They had moved deeper into the woods, perhaps to ensure their voices didn't wake her.

"Respond to what?" Owen asked. Maya heard his voice but couldn't see him through the thick trees and morning fog.

She pushed up and stumbled through the forest and uneven terrain to a small clearing where she found Alister, Will, Owen and Cara standing around the radio on the ground.

Alister had put his sweater back on and was shaking his head. "Absolutely not!"

"What's happening?" Maya asked.

"We've received a transmission," Will said.

"From whom?"

"It's probably static," Alister said.

Will bent down to the radio and tapped the display panel. "It's not static."

A tapping emanated from the speaker—a rhythmic beating that stopped with a long beep then continued. Four taps. A short beep. Seven taps. A long beat.

"Forty-seven," Maya whispered. "I don't understand."

"It's a short-wave broadcast," Will said.

"But what does it mean?" Maya asked.

Alister threw up his hands. "Nothing. It means nothing. Forty-seven. So what?"

"It's not nothing," Cara said.

Alister scoffed. "Then what is it?"

Cara stared at him. "It's a numbers station. Broadcasting a challenge. And we need to reply."

CHAPTER FIFTY-TWO

Morning light filtered through the tall trees, and for a long moment, everyone was silent. The only sound was the tapping and beeps from the radio.

"How do you know it's a numbers station?" Alister asked Cara.

"It's obvious," she said as she turned to Will. "We need to reply, right now."

"With what?" Will asked.

"The Garden coordinates."

Will cocked his head. "Why?"

"Why not?" Cara snapped.

"That doesn't seem to help us." Will paused. "I assumed we would reply with forty-seven, a standard response to acknowledge receipt. Or perhaps forty-eight, to indicate progression."

"That doesn't help us either," Cara said. "It would only reveal our presence—and location, assuming the broadcast can be triangulated. We need to send the Garden coordinates."

Owen studied their faces and their body language, willing his mind to make sense of what was happening. He once again felt as he had in Station 17, in the observation room when the group had first met—when the older man had destroyed Bryce after moving the people into place like chess pieces. To Owen, this situation felt the same, but he couldn't see the board, couldn't discern the objective and how the players were moving. It was written in their faces and their body language, he was sure of it, but it was lost on him.

"Both are horrible ideas!" Alister roared. "There's nothing at the Garden Station location, and giving away our position and waiting will get us killed."

"We don't know that," Will said.

"Look at what happened to those poor saps from the journal," Alister shot back.

"We could broadcast and keep moving," Will said. "We send forty-seven and see what comes back—that will likely reveal whether the numbers station is run by someone friendly to us."

"Remind me again," Alister said, "what number indicates friendliness? What's the friendly number?"

A sound caught Owen's attention—a rustling deeper in the woods. Was it from the camp?

He refocused on the conversation, where Will was talking. "We must establish a working vocabulary."

"Nonsense..." Alister's voice faded as Owen turned and took a step toward camp.

Fog drifted through the trees like it had on the island. The sound came again, the crunch of a limb.

The group was arguing now.

A crash of metal and plastic breaking shattered the conversation. Owen spun around and found Alister stomping on the radio. "It's done! We're not responding. We're going now. End of discussion."

"Alister, you fool!" Cara cried. "How could you—"

Blair's scream ripped through the forest like a knife through Owen's heart.

"HELP!"

His body moved before thoughts formed. He ran in long strides, bounding toward her through the trees, jumping logs and dodging limbs.

"Get away!" Blair yelled.

For a moment, he considered calling out, but decided against it—that would only give him away. That would be a disadvantage if he needed to fight.

At the camp site, Owen slid to a halt. There were two figures with hoods on. One was lifting a duffel bag up, the other was holding Blair down, who was pushing back. Both wore the same black sweater Owen had on.

They were Extinction Trials participants.

Owen held his hands up. "Stop."

The figure with the duffel bag turned and sprinted into the forest. The one holding Blair released her and darted away.

Owen chased after them, wondering if he should simply let them go. But he couldn't. They had the only food the team had.

Behind him, he heard Maya's voice speaking softly to Blair. "Are you okay? Where did they go?"

Owen was closing on the figure, and when he was in striking distance, he lunged, burying his shoulder in their back, wrapping his arms around the torso. To his shock, the sweater kept collapsing until he was hugging a body that was unnaturally skinny, nearly inhuman.

He collapsed to the ground on top of the figure, feeling as though his body were crushing them.

Owen jerked the hood off, revealing a man's face with a gray beard and sunken, wild eyes. His cheeks were gaunt, as though he was on the verge of starving to death.

He tried to break free, but Owen held the man tight. "I don't want to hurt you."

The man cast about with his hands as though he were drowning, looking for anything to gain purchase—or perhaps a rock or stick to strike back with.

Owen studied the face. He knew this man. He had seen him once in his life before. In the hospital, during the Fall.

Parrish.

The man was older now and clearly in poor health.

Owen opened his mouth to speak, but Parrish used his momentary shock to reach out across the ground again, grab a rock, and smash it into Owen's head.

The world spun and went dark.

CHAPTER FIFTY-THREE

Maya raced through the forest toward Blair's screams. The trees and brush slowed her, but Owen blazed right through them.

He was used to running through dangerous environments—and enduring pain as he went. His body had clearly adapted to it long ago.

Soon, he pulled so far ahead, Maya couldn't even see him.

When she reached the camp, Blair was standing, clutching a duffel bag, tears streaming down her face.

Maya wrapped the younger girl in her arms. "Are you okay? Where did they go?

"I'm fine," Blair said, her voice shaking. "There were two of them. They took one of the duffel bags of food."

"Where's Owen?"

Blair pointed into the woods. "He chased them."

Without another word, Maya rushed into the woods, listening for sounds of movement, ducking and swatting at the limbs as she went. She considered calling out, but her instincts screamed for her to remain silent.

To her left, she heard someone rolling through the leaves, then voices speaking, the words too quiet for her to make out.

It was Owen.

She changed course and charged ahead, heart pounding, legs aching from the exertion, nerves overtaking her.

She stopped at the sight of Owen. He was lying still on the ground, blood running from the side of his face.

"Cara!" she screamed into the fog-filled woods, not caring who heard or who came. She would fight them if she had to.

She dropped to her knees, reached out and felt Owen's neck. His heartbeat was strong. He was alive.

She bent close to him, her lips close to his ear.

"Owen," she whispered.

He didn't stir.

She sat up and tilted her head back, and she was about to yell again when Cara's voice cut through the fog. "Maya!"

"Over here!"

Cara arrived a moment later. She dropped to her knees and methodically checked Owen over. From the medkit, she drew out a small tablet and broke it under his nose. He inhaled sharply and writhed, but Cara had a firm hand on his head.

"Easy."

His eyes opened slowly. They were watery and vacant looking.

"What happened?" Maya asked.

"Parrish. He hit me with a rock. It's like he didn't remember me."

"Who is Parrish?" Maya asked.

Owen sat up. "You don't remember?"

Maya shook her head.

"You told me you met him in the hospital. You knew him."

A new sort of fear ran through Maya. Whoever Parrish was, she had forgotten him. Not only that, but she had remembered him a few days ago—clearly, she had told Owen that she knew him.

She was losing more of her past.

"It's getting worse, isn't it?" Owen said.

"Let's focus on you right now."

Owen got to his feet. "I'm fine. But they got away with half of our food."

Alister, Will, and Blair arrived then, with the other duffel bag, the blankets, and the rest of the camp.

"We need to move," Alister hissed.

Owen pointed at him. "You destroyed the radio."

"Keep your voice down."

"Who cares? They know we're out here. They're starving. They're just hungry."

"In my book, starving people are dangerous," Alister said. "That radio would have just drawn attention to us— just like standing here talking is. We need to move right now. They'll be hunting us now."

Cara turned to Will. "Can you repair the radio?"

"No."

She raised her eyebrows. "Are you sure? Even with any of the equipment you have?"

He looked at her curiously. "I'm certain. It's broken. Besides, Alister is right. We can't remain here, and I can't fix it as we walk—even if I had the parts. We must go, and quickly."

★ ★ ★

They trekked through the woods with reckless abandon, trudging over roots and branches and hills and through shrubs and thickets. There was no sign of animals large or small. No sign of civilization.

No one said a word. But Maya felt that they were all thinking the same thing: it was a race now—to safety, to a shelter they could defend.

The attack in the woods had changed everything.

Maya kept telling herself that they would reach the Colony by sundown, that if they hurried, they could make it, and that there would be everything they needed there: safety, food, and a cure for the virus that was taking more of her memories with each step.

She felt time running out—and her past slipping away. It was a gut-wrenching feeling.

The memory she clung to most was of that night on the boat with Owen, when they had thrown caution to the wind and let themselves be together.

They stopped just long enough to take a meal for lunch. They didn't talk. Each one of them scanned the forest as they ate the ARC rations, searching for any signs of trouble. Around them, it was quiet; unnaturally quiet, Maya thought. The more she saw of this world, the less she liked it.

Their pace slowed in the afternoon. Everyone was tired. And stressed. But they trudged ahead, putting one foot after the other.

Will seemed the freshest of the entire group, and he decided to scout ahead. Soon, Maya spotted him stopped at the top of the next hill. The daylight was brighter beyond the trees there, as if they were coming upon a clearing.

When Maya reached the hilltop where Will was waiting, she realized they had a problem. In the valley below lay the ruins of a vast city. Buildings and skyscrapers lay in crumbled gray heaps of glass and concrete. It was like an expanse of destruction, the piles of ruins serving as tombstones for the fallen city. Grass and trees and blue-green lichens had begun to grow over the carcass, nature slowly reclaiming what was originally its own.

"Is the Colony located in the city?" Owen asked.

"No," Will responded. "It's beyond. Directly beyond."

"We should go around," Owen said, grimacing as he stared at the city.

"It will take time," Will said.

"We don't have time," Alister said.

"I agree," Will said quietly. "If we go through, we can make it before sundown. *If* we hurry."

No one said a word. It was clear to Maya—and apparently the others—that they might not survive a night out here. They either risked their lives crossing the ruined city or risked it sleeping in the dark of the woods. The group, it was silently decided, would take their chances on their feet, marching through the city, hoping to reach the Colony before nightfall.

With that, they descended the hill toward the ruined city.

CHAPTER FIFTY-FOUR

The road into the city had long since been overgrown by shrubs and trees. The abandoned cars were the only clue that the road was there.

The six of them marched past the column of vehicles that was four wide, their doors open, the insides filled with dirt and grime and mildew.

Owen couldn't help peering inside the vehicles as they passed, as if staring at a still parade, searching for any clues as to what the ruined city might hold.

Up ahead, he heard no sounds from the city except the occasional crumbling of concrete and glass falling to the ground. It was as if the ruins were alive, shedding tears as the time slipped by.

At the edge of the city were crumpled houses. The roofs were caved in. The windows were shattered. Doors stood open. Trees surrounded them like a group of towering beings watching, willing the homes to disappear into the ground for good.

Apartment buildings were next. The parking lots were covered in moss and shrubs and trees, except for the areas with abandoned cars. Seeing the buildings reminded Owen of the Oasis Park Building and that rescue before the Fall, of Maya's family. He wondered if she was thinking about them—if she still remembered. Time was running out for her. Would she forget him—and what they had shared on the boat?

As he passed another apartment building, his mind flashed to another memory. In it, he was walking down a hallway where older men and women were sitting outside their bedrooms. A nursing home. He paused in the doorway to one of the rooms and peered in at someone—an older woman he was visiting. But he couldn't remember who that person was. It was someone important to him, he felt that. But try as he might, Owen couldn't bring the person's face into focus. Was it a family member?

He realized then: it was happening to him too. His memories were decaying, just like the city, just like Maya's memories. He sensed that with each step he took, his past crumbled a little more.

A new kind of fear went through him, of losing his identity, his sense of self, of who he was.

Cara's voice drew his attention, snapping him out of the mental spiral.

"Over here," she called out quietly, careful not to draw attention.

She moved to a mound near a cluster of cars in what had been an apartment parking lot.

When Owen reached her, he realized what she had seen: a person, lying on the ground by the car. They were wearing an ARC Technologies environmental suit, just like the one he had worn when he exited Station 17.

The person wasn't moving.

Cara turned the body over. The glass in the helmet was

badly damaged. Through the opening, Owen saw a decayed face, though it wasn't clear to him exactly how long the person had been dead.

The suit had a torn jagged hole near the chest.

"They were shot with an arrow," Alister said.

"That fits," Cara whispered, her eyes still raking back and forth over the corpse.

"How long have they been dead?" Owen asked.

"Impossible to tell," Cara replied.

"What we can tell," Alister said, "is that someone in the city was hunting at some point. They could still be out here."

No one needed to say anything more. The group moved quicker then, knowing whoever had killed that person in the ARC environmental suit might still be out there, hunting.

They passed more apartment buildings and scattered strip malls, and gradually, Owen began to see more tall office buildings and what he assumed had been mixed-use developments with stores on the ground floor and crumbling offices and condos above.

On a wide brick wall, someone had taken strips of metal and screwed them in, forming a message:
THE CHANGE WILL SAVE US

At least someone had been optimistic about the Change. It was the first clue to what happened in the city, besides the fallen Extinction Trials participant.

Will walked at the head of the group, leading them through the city, occasionally glancing at the GPS to chart their course. From what Owen could tell, they were making the most direct route through, hoping they would come out the other side and find the Colony there.

They turned a corner and were starting down another

street when Owen saw a wrapper from some prepackaged food cartwheeling in the wind like a tumbleweed blowing through a deserted town. He bent down and picked it up and studied it. It was from an ARC ration pack.

He held it out to the others.

"No telling how old it is," Alister said.

Cara studied it. "There could be someone alive nearby."

"Do you hear that?" Will asked, seeming to have ignored the conversation.

"What is it?" Owen asked.

"The wind. It's growing stronger."

Nearby, the crumbled remains of what looked like an office building were piled four stories high.

Without a word, Will dashed toward the rubble pile and began climbing up it with near superhuman speed. Owen watched, almost in disbelief.

Near the top of the heap, Will held his hands over his eyes and gazed into the distance. Next, he drew out the monocular and panned it back and forth. He gave no indication of what he saw, only stowed the monocular and descended the stack of rubble as if he'd been practicing it his entire life. Rock and glass disintegrated as he went, and he lost his footing twice, but he recovered quickly, breaking his fall with his hands and taking each stumble in stride.

"There's a storm coming," he said as he reached the group. "We need to hurry."

CHAPTER FIFTY-FIVE

Maya's heart was thundering in her chest. It wasn't just Will's news that a storm was coming. The ruined city put her on edge. Her every instinct was screaming that they needed to get out, and right now.

Blair squeezed Maya's hand tight. The girl was scared too.

"We need to find shelter—" Alister began.

"There's no time," Will said. "And besides, I've found something better."

He handed Alister the monocular. The older man held it to his eye and panned back and forth.

"How did you know?" he asked as he handed it to Owen.

"Logic," Will said simply.

Owen held the monocular to his eye and scanned the street, then quickly handed it to Maya.

At first, she thought there was nothing to see, but then Maya realized that there were a series of very subtle beams of light shining up. They seemed to be evenly spaced out: one at the next intersection and one beyond that, shining up from the street to the right. The light must have been on a wavelength outside the visible spectrum—a frequency the monocular was built to see clearly.

Will and Alister were already moving toward the light beacons when Maya handed the monocular to Cara. Owen stood waiting with Maya, Cara, and Blair, but Cara pointed ahead and began chasing after Will and Alister. "I'll take your word for it."

Soon the group was back together, racing through the streets.

Will dropped back and held his hand out to Cara. "The monocular, please."

As she handed it to him, movement in a nearby pile of rubble caught Maya's eye. She turned to focus on it, but it was gone. She saw only decaying concrete, glass, and steel. Had she imagined it?

The momentary distraction had caused her to fall behind the group, and Blair with her, since the girl was holding Maya's hand.

Owen slowed and was soon walking beside them. Shortly, the rest of the group slowed too, allowing them to catch up.

"We're sitting ducks out here," Alister hissed. "We should pick up the pace."

Maya was about to insist that Blair couldn't go any faster when a gunshot pierced the silence.

Alister spun and tumbled to the ground.

Another shot rang out, the report echoing off the crumbling ruins of the city.

Will staggered and collapsed to the ground, catching himself with his hands, seeming unharmed.

Owen and Cara then bent down over Alister.

"Leave me!" he shouted.

Owen ignored him. Instead, he threw the man's arm

around his shoulder and began lumbering toward a partially crumpled skyscraper off the street, which looked to still be habitable.

Cara reached out to help, but Alister swatted her away. She raced toward Will then, but the young man was already up and following the group toward the building.

As they ran, shots slammed into the street and cars. Grit and shrapnel and sparks flew in the air.

Maya wrapped her fingers around Blair's upper arms and moved her in front, ensuring her own body was in the direction of the fire.

They entered the building through what Maya thought was a loading dock with a large open receiving area and an elevated platform. The double doors were closed, but Will easily pushed them open.

Inside the building, Owen set Alister on the floor, eliciting an agonizing groan from the man. He was panting, holding his shoulder, blood oozing out around his fingers.

"Alister," Cara began, but he waved her off.

"Leave me."

Owen opened his mouth to speak, but a shot ricocheted off the inner wall, forcing him to duck.

Will bent down to Alister and hoisted him up, drawing another howl from the older, heavier man. Maya was amazed at Will's strength.

Another shot dug into the concrete in the loading dock area, spraying shards into the building.

Will raced down the hall, deeper into the structure. Holding Blair's hand, Maya chased after them, Owen and Cara bringing up the rear.

To her relief, the shots stopped.

Around another turn they went, into a large open area with desks and chairs and computer screens that were covered in grime.

Will turned and fished the monocular out of his pocket and tossed it to Cara.

"In case we get separated," he said without missing a beat.

Through the next door, there was a narrow hallway that led to another loading dock where a roll-up door was open to what Maya assumed was the adjacent street.

Will raced down the metal steps and out onto the street, which instantly erupted in fire. He danced through it, dodging and weaving.

A bullet hit him.

He fell to the ground, Alister tumbling with him.

To Maya's shock, Will rose, grabbed Alister, and staggered into the building across the street.

As Maya watched the street, she saw their pursuers march out into the open. And she was shocked.

CHAPTER FIFTY-SIX

Outside, the gunfire stopped.

Owen stood on the loading dock, watching.

In the building across the street, Will and Alister disappeared into the shadows.

The army that was hunting them marched down the ruined street, swerving around patches of grass and shrubs and crawling over cars as though they were dirt mounds.

One of the killers turned and strode into the building's loading area without a hint of fear or hesitation.

Another joined. Then another. Soon there were seven, all staring up at Owen, Maya, Cara, and Blair.

No one said a word.

Slowly, quietly, Maya reached out and corralled Blair behind her.

Owen stepped in front of them. There was nothing they could do now except face their fate with courage. Though Owen was feeling his memories slip away, who he truly was remained—and in this moment, it was revealed to him as he stood in front of the others. This silent act was a testament to the sort of person he was.

The killers that had been shooting at them didn't move. They waited. And Owen watched.

The killers weren't human. They were small robots that moved on six legs. The metal of their bodies was a shiny silver that glistened even in the dim shafts of light flowing in through the loading dock door.

The robots' legs had no feet, only sharp pincers that stabbed into the concrete. A memory flashed into Owen's mind. He saw another robot charging toward him, shooting a thick white liquid, a suited figure tackling the robot, and Owen turning and running. That person had saved him. What was their name?

It was all slipping away, little by little.

As that thought gripped Owen, the group of six-legged robots turned and marched out of the loading dock, as though they had decided that he was no threat, that a man slowly losing his memory could do them no harm.

Cara ran to the metal staircase and descended, chasing after the robots. "Come on."

"Are you crazy?" Owen called to her.

She stopped in her tracks. "They won't harm us. We need to get underground before the storm comes."

"How do you know?" Maya asked.

"I just... know. Okay? Come on."

Owen didn't see what other choice they had. He caught up to Cara in the street, where she held the monocular to her eye, scanning for the invisible light beacons, the breadcrumbs that would lead them to safety... Owen hoped.

Ahead, the robots were scurrying down the street, pausing only to search cars and duck through doors and broken windows into shops.

Maya was panting as she ran beside Owen. "They're hunting Will and Alister."

"Seems so," Owen said.

"Why?"

"I don't know."

Something about the whole sequence of events bothered Owen deeply. Cara knew what the robots were. Or she seemed to. Had she seen them before the Fall? She hadn't mentioned it.

"This way," Cara shouted from up ahead, apparently unconcerned about being heard.

They turned onto a street that was almost completely blocked with an overturned fire truck and several police cars. Someone had made a barricade here—an attempt to block someone or something from advancing. This city had been a war zone. It was still a war zone.

The shiny robots crawled right over and through the mangled wall of broken vehicles.

Overhead, the sky darkened. Thunder shattered the silence and rumbled, a warning call of the storm closing in.

Cara led them into a building with concrete walls that had been ripped to shreds by bullets and withered by time. She raced through, dodging into hallways and open rooms and finally out the back into a narrow alley filled with papers and trash that was beginning to float with the wind blowing through, like ghosts rising from the dead.

Cara pointed to a brick staircase that led to a pair of double doors at the basement level. "It's here."

One of the doors was open.

Was someone already here? Was it Alister and Will? Or someone else?

Beyond the alleyway, a group of the robots strode by, not even pausing to examine Owen and the others.

They descended the stairs and slipped through the doorway into a damp basement with a low ceiling.

On the far wall was a bank of silver metal standing freezers. Owen assumed there must have been a restaurant above. Or a butcher shop.

Cara brought out the monocular, peered through it, then handed it to Owen. He brought it to his eye and scanned the room. To his surprise, the keypad on the freezer on the end was glowing green.

Cara approached it and typed two numbers. The lock instantly clicked, and she swung the massive door open, revealing a decontamination chamber almost exactly like the one from Station 17.

Cara stepped inside, and Owen, Maya, and Blair followed. When the outer door was closed, a mist drifted down from the nozzles overhead, a cool liquid that made Owen shiver. He looked in the alcove and was relieved to see five environmental suits. He checked the closest one. Its oxygen level was 100 percent. They were one suit short, but they could figure that out later—assuming they could find their other two team members.

A computer voice spoke through the overhead speaker: "Decontamination complete. Welcome to Station 47."

The inner airlock door popped open, and Cara moved toward it, but Owen caught her arm.

"How did you know the code to the door outside?"

"I guessed."

"It was a good guess."

"It was the only guess: the numbers that were broadcast. Forty-seven. I think this Extinction Trials station was also a numbers station."

They exited the airlock onto a platform with a metal staircase that led down a single flight to a subbasement where a hatch with a wheel waited. It was open, but it was dark beyond.

Owen, Maya, and Cara clicked on their flashlights and descended the damp, rickety staircase.

"Hello!" Owen called out.

No response.

At the hatch, he shined his light into the narrow corridor. There were doors on each side—just like Station 17, except this place wasn't made of white plastic and steel. It seemed to be an existing structure made of concrete and bricks that had been re-purposed.

"Hello," Owen shouted, hoping...

Alister's pained voice grumbled from farther down the corridor. "Shut up! I'm trying to die in peace over here."

Owen couldn't help but smile.

Cara took off at once toward him, medkit in hand.

Maya moved to follow her, but Owen held a hand up. "Let's take it slow. Make sure it's safe before we follow." He shrugged. "Just like when we explored Station 17."

Maya didn't respond. She only stared at him. Owen couldn't read her face, but he sensed the truth.

"You don't remember, do you? Us exploring the station together?"

Maya shook her head.

Blair reached out and placed her small hand inside Maya's.

"The first thing I remember is finding the boat with Alister."

"It's okay," Owen said. "We're going to figure this out. Soon."

He moved toward the closest door and threw it open. It was a room with seven of the stasis chambers like they had found in Station 17. All empty. The screens on the wall were turned on, displaying large white block letters that read:

```
STATION 47.
PROTOCOL ENDED.
NUMBERS MODE ACTIVE.
```

The room across the hall was another pod with empty chambers. The carts were empty.

Next was an observation room, with a small bathroom, and metal chairs strewn about. There were no blankets, but Alister was lying on the floor with Cara hunched over him, the medkit open, gauze spilling out, a blood-soaked pad lying on the floor. Will was crouched there as well, but Owen didn't see any blood. He was whispering feverishly to Cara as Alister gritted his teeth in pain.

"Need help?" Owen asked.

Cara peeked over her shoulder. "See if you can find some pain killers."

Maya gently corralled Blair out of the room, obviously not wanting the young girl to see the scene—whatever was about to happen to Alister.

Down the hall, Owen found three more pods with empty chambers and an empty observation room.

"Seems like someone has already been here," Maya said. "The place has been raided."

There was one door left—at the end of the hall. It stood slightly ajar, and inside, Owen found a small decontamination chamber. He ventured through it, to the opposite hatch, which led to a small control room with several active computer stations and a wall full of screens.

It was what he saw on the floor that stopped him cold.

A body.

At first, he thought he was imagining it.

He stepped closer, bent down, and ran his flashlight over the young man's face.

"It's Will," Maya whispered.

At first, Owen was confused. How could it be Will? He had seen the young man behind them, in the observation room with Cara and Alister. But then, he realized the truth.

CHAPTER FIFTY-SEVEN

In the station's control room, Owen rolled the body over, revealing a long gash in the back—and hard plastic and wires inside.

"He's an android," Owen said. "Will's a proctor."

"A proctor?" Maya didn't know the term.

The words seemed to wound Owen like a punch in the gut. "You don't remember?"

"Remember what?"

"Bryce."

"Who's Bryce?"

Owen swallowed. "He's part of the Extinction Trials. Or was. Will is too. He's been manipulating us."

"Why?"

Owen stood. "I don't know. But I'm going to find out. It could get messy. I think you and Blair should stay here. With the doors locked."

"That's not going to happen."

"What?"

"If he's a machine, and you think he means us harm, you'll need all the help you can get."

Will's voice was soft in the small space. "I am a machine.

But I don't mean you any harm. I'm sorry that I could not tell you before."

Maya spun to find him standing at the hatch, hands at his side, a placid expression on his face. There was a large hole in his upper chest near his right shoulder where a bullet had ripped through him. Maya could see white wires and blue light seeping out. There was another hole in the upper thigh of his left leg.

"I need you to rejoin the others. I want everyone to hear what I have to say."

In the observation room, Maya stayed by the door, holding Blair's hand. Owen stood between them and Will, his body tense.

"As you now know, I am a machine. I am what ARC calls a terminal proctor, to be precise," Will said.

"Why didn't you tell us?" Owen asked.

"My programming forbade it. I was kept in my alcove for the duration of the Trials—and provided none of the data. I was effectively an emergency backup that was firewalled off from the main Trials. In the event that the Trials failed, my role was to exit the station with the final cohort and safeguard them in the world they found."

"Well, you suck at it!" Alister roared.

"In that, you are correct. I have failed you. But I hope, in my last act, I can fulfill my function."

Owen held up a hand. "Wait. Let's back up. Why did those robots... let's just call them spiders—why did they shoot at you and Alister and not the rest of us?"

"The answer is obvious," Will said. "I believe the spiders were created by one of the groups at war—either the

Alliance or the Union—and they were programmed to kill other robots."

Maya's eyes drifted to Alister.

"Don't look at me!" he spat out. "I'm bleeding to death over here. I'm as flesh and blood as any of you!"

"Then why did they shoot you?" Owen asked.

"Like I know," Alister muttered. "Probably my artificial knee. Forgive me for working my whole life and breaking down in the service of a bunch of thankless, ungrateful animals." He pointed at Will. "I'm not the liar here. You should be asking him."

"I never lied," Will said. "Yes, I kept things from you all, but I was bound by my creator to follow those instructions. They were designed for your benefit—for the benefit of the Trials, so that we might rescue those kept at Garden."

Will's gaze settled on Cara and Alister on the floor. "But I am not the only one who has kept secrets."

"What does that mean?" Owen asked.

"It means he's a liar," Alister shot back.

"Again," Will said, "I never lied. I didn't tell you the full truth because I couldn't—until you knew, or it became necessary to inform you in order to save your lives. That time has come. There will be a time when the other secrets in this room—secrets others are keeping—must be revealed, but that time is not right now. Right now, you all must leave. I counted twenty spiders out there. If I'm right, more will come. They will wait outside until we exit."

Alister shook his head. "The spiders don't matter. They are only hunting me—and you, Will. The others can go. And they should. The storm is coming."

"The storm is precisely why you all should go," Will said. "But it's not the only thing coming."

"What do you mean?" Owen asked.

"Others."

"Other what?"

"Extinction Trials participants. They have suits and I can hear their radios. They saw us coming in and have been tracking us. They'll find us soon."

"You all need to get out of here," Alister said. "Enough talk."

Owen shook his head. "We're not leaving you."

"Yes, you are."

"We don't leave people behind," Owen said, his voice firm.

"That's cute. It sounds nice. But this is the real world—"

"Yes, it is, Alister. It's the real world. A ruined, messed up world, and all we have left is each other—in a world that is out to kill us. You know what I think is important?"

Alister exhaled heavily.

"What we do about it," Owen said. "We're the last people standing. We get to decide what the world is now. We decide what matters. This might be our last stand. We might walk out there and get taken down by the people who left the Extinction Trials before us—the people that decided that hunting each other and leaving people behind was an acceptable way to live. Maybe the storm will get us. Or the robots. Or something else. But if this is our last stand, we'll go down with the last thing that matters in this world: our dignity and our humanity. We'll die the way we lived: with our values."

CHAPTER FIFTY-EIGHT

For a long moment, the observation room was quiet. Everyone in the group seemed to be considering what Owen had said.

Cara broke the silence. "I have never agreed with anything more in my life. We go together or not at all."

"I also agree," Maya said.

"Me too," Blair said.

Alister rolled his eyes. "I really hate you people."

Owen smiled. "We feel the same way, Alister. I'll carry you if I have to, kicking and screaming."

"I can walk," Alister muttered. "They shot me in the shoulder, not the leg."

"But you'll get winded," Owen said. "And you need to tell us when you do."

"We should hurry," Will said. "My guess is that this station is merely a trap. There's chatter over the radio from the others. I think they know we're here. They obviously have another station where they're charging their oxygen tanks. I suspect they left this numbers station on as a way to draw in other Trials participants. After all, there's only one way out of here."

"What's the plan?" Owen asked.

"You all should put the suits on to protect you from the storm," Will said. "It's unclear when it will hit the city. In fact, it may already be here. I will lead the robots away. When I'm sure they're following me, I'll signal you over the suit radio. You'll exit then and try to reach the Colony. You will need to hurry. Your only hope will be to outrun the others and reach the Colony before your oxygen expires."

Without a further word of discussion, they moved to the airlock and donned their suits, Alister grunting and complaining the whole way.

Will handed Owen the GPS. "The Colony location is programmed in there."

He gripped the handle to the outer airlock door, but he paused and looked back. "Good luck to all of you. I wish I could've done more."

With that, Will opened the door and charged out, disappearing in a superhuman flash of speed.

Through the suit's external microphone, Owen heard gunfire in the distance, loud then growing fainter.

"You should go now," Will said over the radio.

Owen and Alister led the group out into the small alleyway, then crept to the opening and peered out into the street.

It was empty.

The five of them jogged down the road toward the Colony, the only sound that of Alister's pained grunting and the pops of gunfire in the distance.

Owen kept scanning for any signs of other Extinction Trials participants. He saw only crumbling buildings and abandoned cars and trees and shrubs growing through and over them.

With each step, he grew more hopeful. They were going to make it.

Above, the thunder cracked again, and the rain began—a pounding precipitation that bounced off the ground like pebbles dropping in a pond.

The wind picked up, nudging him off balance as he ran.

Owen heard a shout over the radio and turned to find Blair lying on the street. Maya was quick to react. She put her hands under the girl's shoulders and raised her up to her feet and quickly scanned Blair's suit for any tears.

"We're okay," Maya said. "Let's keep going."

They ran with a renewed vigor then, feet stomping in the growing puddles of rain, the wind whipping at the suits and through the crumbling buildings, a growing howl like a monster chasing them.

Alister's voice over the radio was labored, the sound of his panting almost as loud as the wind. "I… can't… keep up. Leave… me—"

Owen reached out and grabbed his arm—the good arm from the shoulder that hadn't been hit—and wrapped it around his own shoulders and put his arm at the man's waist, giving him a slight lift. Alister cried out from the pain, but Owen could tell that he was taking some of the strain off of his body.

The group slowed but they were still making progress. Up ahead, the crumbled skyscrapers were turning into low-rise buildings.

The sound of the robots' shooting was gone now. Owen didn't know if the noise of the rain was overpowering the faint sound of the shots or if it was because the robots had killed Will. He felt a strange sort of conflict about it. The robots had killed a member of his team and assaulted him during the Fall. He couldn't remember the man's name, but he remembered the hate he felt when his mind touched the memory—his hate for the machines that had attacked during the Fall.

But Will had helped them. He hadn't told him what he was, but looking back, Owen had to admit that it had been the only way: he would have bashed Will's brains in had he told him the truth back at Station 17.

Up ahead, the city buildings gave way to a line of abandoned cars that were slowly being overgrown by trees and shrubs and grass. The pavement of the road out of the city wasn't visible, but the outline was—the trees were gone there. The path carved through the field and inclined as it crawled into the hills.

At the top of the first ridge outside the city, Owen heard gunfire once again erupt over the radio. He turned and scanned the city. He saw Will, climbing a rubble heap that had once been a skyscraper, crawling on his four mechanical limbs faster than any human could. Another shot rang out, and Will tumbled over, but he quickly recovered and kept climbing again.

Owen saw the robots then, what looked like two dozen spiders scampering toward Will, stopping only to plant their feet in the rubble to fire a shot.

He wondered if this was what the Change War had been like—robots fighting in the ruins of a lost world.

To Owen's surprise, a suited figure came into view, sauntering out from behind the remains of another building. They wore a dark suit, and they strode confidently toward the rubble pile that Will was climbing up.

"The proctor doesn't have a chance," a man's voice said.

Owen realized then that was how he had heard the gunfire: from the man's suit. He was broadcasting on their channel, letting them hear the gunfire.

"Who are you?" Owen asked.

"I imagine I'm someone just like you. A guy who woke up in a busted-up world and is just trying to find a way to survive."

The robots were closing in now, shooting more frequently. Will's body jerked violently as the bullets ripped through him.

"What do you want?" Owen asked.

"Isn't it obvious? To help you."

"You've got a funny way of showing it. You shot one of our people. And our proctor."

Will was still now, lying on the rubble heap, the spiders edging toward him.

"Well," the man said over the radio, "you can thank me for getting rid of the proctor later."

"Why would I?"

"Because he was leading you to your deaths, just like they all do."

"How do you know?"

"I've been down the road you are traveling. It doesn't lead where you think."

"Where does it lead?"

"Nowhere."

"Prove it."

"I think you already know it's true. Let me guess: they gave you this line about saving the human race. Being our species' last hope."

"What's the truth?"

"Truth is, there is no hope. You're looking at what's left of the world, and you can either come with me and survive, or make a stupid choice."

"There's just one problem," Owen said. "You shot one of our people."

"We can explain that—after you come with us."

"I'd like an answer right now. Who are you?"

"The Alliance. We're what's left of the government, and some people who escaped the Extinction Trials and had the good sense to join the right side."

Cara spoke over the radio for the first time. "You're not from the Colony?"

"No. The Colony is controlled by the Union. If you go there, they'll implement the Change on you."

"We need to go," Alister growled over the radio. "They're lying. These people are going to kill us when they reach us."

Owen was surprised at the voice he heard next over the radio: Will. The android was still lying on the rubble heap, mouth shut, body still, yet his voice was clear over the speaker, clearly a wireless transmission. "Alister is right. Go to the Colony. Please."

The spiders arrayed around Will's body fired at close range, each unloading round after round. When they were done, they stomped toward him and began using their sharp pincer feet to rip away his synthetic skin and dismantle what was left of him.

"We should join them," Cara said over the radio. "They're the government."

"They're using a robot army to hunt people," Alister said. "We need to go. Right now."

In the city below, a second suited figure joined the other one. The new arrival held a tablet, and they seemed to have said something over a private radio channel to the other person because both figures suddenly shifted and gazed up toward where Owen and the others were standing.

It was clear they had figured out where the group was—perhaps from the suit radio broadcasts.

Owen turned and jogged deeper into the woods, holding the GPS, glancing back to make sure the others were following. Even Cara was moving away from the city, despite her insistence that they join the Alliance. But she wasn't giving up that easy.

"Can we talk about this?" she asked.

"Yes," the Alliance man's voice said over the radio. "Let's talk about this. Just stop and wait for a moment."

With his hands, Owen motioned for the others to keep going through the woods. He turned back and trekked toward the city, careful to hide himself behind a tree as he gazed down at the city. Very quickly, he saw the answer he was looking for: the robots were marching out of the city, toward the forest—directly for them.

Over the radio, Owen said, "There's just one problem."

"What's that?" the man asked.

"Your robots—which just killed our proctor—are now moving toward us. If you just want to talk, you wouldn't be hunting us."

"You don't understand what's going on here."

"I'm all ears. You talk, and if you really are telling the truth, tell your robots to stand down."

Owen watched as the robots indeed stopped at the edge of the city.

Over the radio, the man began talking. It was what Owen was expecting: words without answers, ambiguities that a more naïve version of himself would have listened to.

But Owen wasn't listening. He had turned and was dashing through the woods, racing to catch up with the others. When he had, he led them deeper into the woods, charging as fast as he could toward the Colony.

Over the radio, the man stopped talking for a long moment. "Did you hear what I said?"

Owen held a finger straight at the helmet where his lips were, silently indicating for no one to reply. He wasn't a technology expert, but he assumed they could somehow track the radio transmissions to locate the group.

"Even if you aren't convinced," the man said over the radio, "at least reply so that I know you're okay. So that we can continue this conversation."

Using the panel on his forearm, Owen turned his radio off. The others followed suit, and they hiked in silence then, through the woods, making the best time they could. The wind and rain had reached the hills, swaying the trees now and causing them to shed leaves and tiny branches, as though the forests were being shelled with heavy artillery.

Owen glanced over his shoulder several times, making sure the people from the city weren't following them, but each time, there was nothing but the dark forest, growing fog, and falling leaves.

Periodically, Owen glanced down at the GPS, watching the readout counting down the numbers, and the distance to their destination shrink.

When the count reached zero, the GPS flashed a green message that read:

DESTINATION REACHED.

Owen looked around, watching the fog move in waves. They were in trouble.

CHAPTER FIFTY-NINE

For a while, the group stood in the forest and surveyed their surroundings, hoping to spot some clue as to where to go next.

The Colony should have been exactly where they were standing.

But it wasn't.

Maya wished they could use the radio to discuss it. If not their short-range broadcast radios, at least the suit speakers and microphones. But the noise from the suit speakers was a risk, just like broadcasting. The others—who claimed to be Alliance operatives—were likely in these woods looking for them already. Time was running out.

And that wasn't the only threat closing in.

On the panel on the forearm of her suit, she checked her oxygen level:

68%

They had that long to find shelter from the storm, either at the Colony or elsewhere.

Around her, the forest seemed to be disintegrating. Parts

of the trees were falling, and the sky was growing darker overhead as the storm moved in.

Was there truly nothing out here? Had they reached the end—like when they had tried to find Garden Station?

Maya was fairly certain that members of the Alliance were searching the woods by now. What would they do when they found the group? Would their fate be the same as Will's?

Owen stomped his foot in the ground, making a shallow hole, then pointed in all directions and back at the hole. Maya wasn't sure what his meaning was at first, but then he stalked off, his head bowed, inspecting the ground at his feet. She got it then: *spread out and search and then meet back at this rendezvous point.*

Maya took Blair by the hand, and they ventured in a direction away from Cara, Alister, and Owen.

Maya stalked through the woods slowly, carefully, knowing a fall could be dangerous. A stick or a rock could easily puncture the suits, letting in the wind and storm and whatever had killed the man back at Station 17.

With each step, she felt time slipping away, the forest growing darker, the wind pulling at her suit getting stronger.

Soon, she'd lost eye contact with the others. Should she go back? Or activate a radio?

What a mess they were in—

Suddenly, Maya felt the ground beneath her feet vanish.

Blair's hand slipped from hers. She tumbled and rolled down into a hole, the ground as hard as stone slamming into her sides and thighs and ribs and shoulders.

The suit would tear from this fall, she knew it. The thought was scarier than the pain, and it was the last thought she had before her vision swam and went dark.

CHAPTER SIXTY

Owen marched through the forest, scanning left and right, searching for any sign of the Colony.

Around him, leaves and limbs drifted down, as if the trees were disintegrating. He glanced down and checked his oxygen level:

57%

In that moment, he felt the same way he had back at Station 17 when he had first exited the bunker and explored that forest that was swaying in the deadly storm, searching for any hope of survival.

He had expected the Colony to be a walled city or a camp, or at least some sign of where to go. The last thing he had expected was nothing.

But as he trekked through the woods, that's all he saw.

How long did they have out here?

Eventually, the people from the city would find them—or they would run out of breathable oxygen in the suits and be forced to take them off and face the storm.

Owen felt as though he was in a room and the walls were closing in on him. In a way, fighting fires was like that. The walls disintegrated around you and buildings fell in. His job had been to get everyone out alive before that happened. That's what he felt now—an urgency to save his team and the people counting on them at Garden Station. If they were humanity's last chance, they had to succeed.

Failure was not an option.

He glanced at his arm panel again, reading the oxygen level:

54%

He stopped in his tracks and glanced around at the towering trees and fog around him. He was easily outside the GPS coordinates now. And he had seen nothing.

There was nothing out here.

What now?

The others would look to him to devise a way forward. What door would he choose? And would there be fire or salvation behind it?

In his mind, a plan formed.

He reached down and tapped his arm panel, turning on the radio. He was opening his mouth to speak when he heard Blair's voice, panicked, calling out over the connection.

"Help! It's Maya!"

"What happened?" Owen said, his mind racing.

"She fell in a hole—"

"Where?"

"I don't know."

"Where are you?"

"I'm... I don't know."

"Go back to where I made the mark in the ground. I'm coming."

Owen spun 180 degrees and raced across the forest, a bolt of fear driving him on. In his mind's eye, he saw that moment on the boat, when they were lying on the couch together, the paperback copy of *The Birthright* in his hand, her looking into his eyes. She moved closer to him, and his world shattered and something beautiful was revealed underneath, something he didn't know existed. If she was gone, he had lost it forever. He felt that deep down.

He took risks then, bounding forward, gasping for breath, not fearing falling and tearing the suit.

Cara's voice came over the radio. "Okay, if anyone is listening, I've found nothing—"

"Get back to the rendezvous point," Owen said between breaths.

"What happened?"

"Maya is hurt."

"Coming," Cara said, her voice strained now.

Owen kept pumping his legs, dodging trees and limbs, feeling the wind tossing him about.

Alister's voice came over the radio next. "You idiots found it yet?"

"Alister," Owen said, huffing, "get back to the place where we separated."

"Won't be hard," the man replied. "I haven't gotten far."

When Owen reached the point where he had made the mark in the ground, Blair was waiting for him there.

The young girl twisted and pointed in the direction she and Maya had set out to explore. "She's over there. She's hurt. I couldn't wake her up."

"It's okay," Owen said, thinking it was anything but okay. "Let's go."

At that moment, Cara arrived. She bent over, placed her hands on her knees, and sucked in air. She had been running as fast as she could.

Alister trotted into the small clearing next, panting, but it wasn't clear to Owen if it was from his shoulder wound or his journey through the woods.

The four of them marched through the forest then, Blair leading the way, Owen close behind, and Alister and Cara bringing up the rear.

Ahead, Owen saw what he thought was a sinkhole in the earth, an almost square divot that led down into darkness.

Blair stopped on the precipice and pointed downward. Owen snapped his flashlight on and shined it down into the darkness. There, lying on the ground, was Maya, her eyes closed, unmoving.

CHAPTER SIXTY-ONE

Maya awoke to a tapping sound.

Her head ached. Body too.

The tapping noise came again, a loud rapping on her helmet visor.

She opened her eyes and instantly closed them when she saw the bright light shining down on her face.

The light shifted away, and she opened her eyes again to see Owen peering down at her. Blair stood behind him.

His voice came over the radio. "Are you okay?"

She reached for her arm panel, attempting to enable her radio.

"I turned your radio on," Owen said.

"I'm okay," she breathed out, her voice a mere croak.

"Your suit's okay too," Owen said.

Maya realized that Cara was beside Owen. The doctor reached out and helped Maya sit up, the hand on her back gently pushing, the pain growing worse with each movement.

Sitting up, Maya saw what had happened then: she had fallen down a set of concrete stairs that had been covered with limbs and leaves. The darkness from the storm blotting out the sun and the falling debris from the trees had made the steps impossible to see.

She turned and glanced behind her. There was a hatch there, with a keypad beside it.

"How'd you find me?" Maya asked, her voice steadier now.

Owen turned his helmet toward Blair. "You are very lucky. Blair came to find me, and I gathered the others."

"It was very touching," Alister grumbled, "but we should hurry now."

He moved to the keypad at the hatch and began typing in numbers.

"You know the code?" Owen asked.

"Stay. Off. The radio," Alister spat out. "In fact. Turn them off."

He reached out to his panel and tapped quickly. Then he pointed at the GPS and then at his head. Maya knew the man well enough to understand exactly what he was saying: *use your head, idiots*.

He had reasoned that the key code to the door was the GPS coordinates, and he was right. The hatch popped open, revealing a dark room beyond.

Owen helped Maya to her feet and through the hatchway, Blair following close behind. Cara slammed the door shut and Alister shined his flashlight in the space. Maya had expected to see a decontamination chamber. Instead, she saw only a cramped, dark room with concrete walls. A single small corridor led out of the space.

Owen took the lead, venturing into the passageway and the darkness. Maya followed, the rest behind her.

The passage ended at another hatch with another keypad.

Owen glanced at the handheld GPS, then typed the numbers into the pad. A red light blinked.

For a moment, nothing happened. Everyone simply stood there, staring at one another, wondering what to do next. Alister scratched at his forearm and shifted uncomfortably. Maya assumed that the exertion of the trip and the gunshot wound in his shoulder were starting to get to him. She was a little surprised he was still on his feet. She could see him sweating profusely in the helmet.

To her surprise, the hatch popped open, revealing what she had expected after the first hatch: a decontamination chamber. The group shuffled in and the door closed behind them, and the nozzles above opened up, raining down milky-white fluid.

When the shower was over, a man's voice came over the speaker. "Suits off."

Maya didn't see what choice they had. Apparently, neither did the others. At once, they all stripped the suits off, placing them in crumpled piles on the floor.

As Maya wiggled out of her suit, she pulled out the blank page she had found in the envelope from Station 17. It floated to the floor and landed in a pool of decontamination liquid.

Maya bent down, picked it up, and was about to slip it in her pocket when she noticed that faint black lines had formed on the page where the liquid had soaked through. She desperately wanted to inspect it, but she knew that would draw attention. She sensed that she should hide the new information until she understood what it was—and until she figured out if the Colony truly was a safe place.

She slipped the page in her pocket as she stood.

"Any weapons?" the voice asked over the radio.

"No," Alister barked. "I've been shot. Let us in!"

Over the speaker, the man chuckled. "Glad to see the time away hasn't changed you, Guthrie."

The inner hatch opened, and a tall man stepped through. He had short hair and a long beard, and he smiled at Alister. "Welcome back. And well done."

CHAPTER SIXTY-TWO

For a long moment, Owen could barely process what he was seeing. This man knew Alister. Alister—or Guthrie, whatever his name was—had been here before.

How was that possible? How could the city bus mechanic who had woken up with them in Station 17 have been here before?

The man advanced into the room. "We had almost given up hope."

He reached out to embrace Alister, but Alister held up his good arm. "Mind the shoulder. I've been shot."

"We'll get you patched up."

Alister stared at the man, his eyes hard. "Did you...?"

"No. She's here. Our deal is still on. We honor our promises."

Alister exhaled. "Good. Thank you." He nodded in Maya's direction. "She's infected with GV."

The man studied Maya. "Oh, we know exactly who she is and what she's infected with. We've been looking for you for a very long time, Doctor Young. We have some questions for you. We'll get those answers soon."

The man bent down and focused on Blair. "And we've been looking for you for a long time as well. There's someone who wants to see you, Blair. We're waking him up right now."

He stood again and to the group said, "Welcome to the Colony."

Armed guards escorted them to a holding room that reminded Owen of an observation room in one of the ARC Stations. There was a small bathroom, a couch, several chairs, and a wide mirror set in the wall. Owen assumed that there were people behind the mirror right now, peering into this holding room, discussing what they saw, making plans, and perhaps concocting experiments to run. He had hoped the Colony would be their salvation. So far, it seemed they had only landed in another cage.

The guards had paid Alister no mind. At the airlock, he had split from the group and walked with the man who had greeted them, talking as they went, like old friends reunited.

Who was Alister?

What was going on here?

"We need to talk," Cara whispered to Owen and Maya.

Before either could respond, the door opened, and Blair's father stepped in. He knelt down, arms held out. "Come here, B."

The girl ran into his arms, and he squeezed her tight, his eyes closing.

"Daddy," she whispered.

"I missed you so much, little one. I'm sorry I couldn't be there when you woke up."

"I was scared."

"I know. It's all over now. Everything is going to be okay."

He lifted her up as he stood and rocked her back and forth.

To the group, he said, "Thank you for returning my daughter to me. I can only imagine what you've been through to get here."

"Why are we being held?" Owen asked.

The man set Blair down and called through the door. "Melissa, can you take my daughter, please?"

A tall woman wearing a gray uniform stepped into the doorway and extended a hand for Blair to take. "Go along, B," Blair's father said. "I'll be along shortly."

Blair looked back at Maya as the woman in the gray uniform tugged gently at her hand, coaxing the girl out of the room. Suddenly, Blair broke free of the woman and ran back to Maya, who bent down to hug her.

"It's okay," Maya said, holding Blair tightly. "Everything is going to be okay."

"Where are you going?" Blair asked.

Maya swallowed. "I don't know."

Blair's father studied the scene—his daughter's attachment to Maya seemed a surprise to him. "She needs to stay here for a bit, sweetie. Doctor Young is sick." He stared at Maya. "We're going to make her better. And then we're going to have a talk about what happened."

When they were alone again in the room, Cara ushered Owen and Maya into the corner and whispered, "We need to get out of here. Right now."

"Why?" Owen asked quietly, glancing at the two-way mirror, wondering if anyone could hear their conversation.

"I can't explain. Not here. Not now."

"At that station in the city, Will said that you and Alister were both hiding secrets," Owen whispered. "I think we know Alister's secret. He was from the Colony. What's your secret, Cara?"

"I'll tell you. Once we get out of here. We need to get the cure for the Genesis Virus and get out."

"And go where?"

"Back to the city."

"To those people who killed Will?"

"Yes."

Owen was about to respond when the door opened again, and Blair's father strode through. The woman with the gray suit pushed a silver cart behind him. There were three injectors on the top shelf and a stack of sanitizing wipes.

The man smiled. "The time for secrets has passed, my friends."

Owen stepped toward the man. "I couldn't agree more. Why are you holding us here?"

"For your protection. And ours." The man placed his hands in his pockets. "My name is Darius Aldridge. I'm the founder of Genesis Biosciences." He cut his eyes to Maya. "And one of your former colleagues, as you'll soon remember."

"What do you want from us?" Owen asked.

"That will become clear to you very soon."

Owen stepped closer to the man. "I want to see Alister."

Aldridge turned to the mirror. "Who's Alister?"

A voice over the speaker boomed in the room. "His real name is Guthrie. He's the agent that brought them in."

"Oh. Okay, get him in here after they're treated."

He focused on Maya. "It's good to see you again, Maya. I know you don't remember me. Or what happened between us. We'll talk about that as soon as you remember."

He motioned to the tray and the injectors. "And that will happen very soon. This is a cure for the Genesis Virus, or GV as we called it."

"You have a cure?" Maya asked. Even Owen could hear the hopefulness in her voice.

The man exhaled and then laughed. "The irony. Yes, Maya, we have a cure. You developed it. Just like you helped develop the virus."

CHAPTER SIXTY-THREE

Maya allowed them to inject her with what they claimed was the cure to the Genesis Virus. She didn't see what choice she had. Apparently, Owen and Cara didn't either. They could have fought against it, but that would have been a useless endeavor. And besides, if the injector held an actual cure for the virus, Maya was ready.

She was also ready for answers.

And ready to remember.

And to get out of here.

Had she truly been part of the team that created the virus and the cure? If so, she was partially or perhaps even fully responsible for the Change and the war that followed the Fall. That thought weighed on her as she paced the room where they were being held.

The door opened and Alister strode in, a somber look on his face. He wore clothes similar to Blair's father—a gray tunic and pants—and the man had clearly had a bath. The arm below the shoulder where he had been shot was in a sling. Overall, Alister looked, in a word, renewed.

Owen and Cara spoke at the same time, and Alister held

his good hand up. "I know you have questions. Let me just... try to explain."

"Who are you?" Owen asked.

"My name's Guthrie."

"Not Alister?"

"No. Alister was some guy that died in the chamber. I found him in Station 17 and assumed his identity when I entered the station."

"Back up," Maya said. "Start at the beginning. I want to hear your whole story."

Alister smiled. "You already have."

"I don't understand."

"The journal."

"From the boat?"

"Yes. I wrote it."

Maya was shocked. She never saw that coming. She turned the revelation over in her mind, willing herself to remember the details.

"So, you're not a city bus mechanic?" Owen asked.

"I am, actually. Everything I told you was true. I was a city bus mechanic, and I was there the day of the Fall. I marched into that server room and nearly died when that bus crashed into it."

Alister held his hands out. "But the other part of my story was in the journal. I woke up in the Extinction Trials just like you all did. I woke up in that city out there that we just traipsed through. It was a war zone. I wrote the journal because that's what they told me to do, and back then, I was still who I was before—a civil servant who did what he was told."

He let out a laugh. "What a crock. I wrote that journal, and you know what happened. The world out there picked us off one by one. We betrayed one another. We got killed. And two of us were saved."

Alister motioned to the room around them. "By the Human Union. They brought us here, to the Colony, and fed us and protected us."

"And you joined them," Owen said.

"I had no choice."

"Why?"

"Love."

"I don't follow," Maya said.

"I put it in the journal," Alister said, turning away from them. He didn't seem to want to say any more about it.

Maya tried to remember what she had read. "Yes, you said that you'd fallen in love with one of the other Trials participants."

Alister nodded. "She and I were the only ones left. Carmen is her name. She had the Genesis Virus, just like you. They cured her. And they showed us what our life could be like here at the Colony."

"And what is that life like?" Owen asked.

"It's not perfect, I'll grant you that. But we're not running for our lives every day. And there's food. And... well, the other aspect is hard to explain."

"Where are we?" Cara asked. "Where is the Colony?"

"In truth, I don't know. It's underground, a vast bunker city with connecting tunnels to entry terminals like this one."

"Entry terminals?" Owen asked.

"Basically, holding areas where field agents like me

enter—a place to quarantine and confine anyone who might be dangerous."

"And who might be dangerous to the Colony?" Owen asked.

"Everyone who hasn't joined the Union," Alister replied. "The Change War isn't over. It's still raging. You saw it out there. It's become a global trench war, both sides in their bunkers, returning to the surface only to look for survivors and to wage war."

"Is that what you were doing out there? Waging war? Or looking for survivors?" Maya asked.

"That's the thing. There isn't a difference anymore. Whoever controls the survivors wins the future. That's what we're fighting over at this point: people."

"So, you were out there looking for us?" Owen asked.

"Not you specifically. Just survivors. And Aldridge's daughter, in particular. That was the deal I made. They would keep Carmen in a stasis chamber if I joined that scouting team. There were three of us. We went out on the boat searching for that Extinction Trials station. We had the location. As you know, ARC Technologies was once part of the Union. They betrayed the group when the Extinction Trials went dark."

Cara held up a hand. "You said there were three of you?"

"You saw the other two," Alister replied. "The dead man and woman on the boat."

"What happened to them?" Owen asked.

"When we arrived at the island, we began exploring. I stayed on the boat—my shift was ending, and I wanted to get some rest. I used the Mesh to notify the Colony that we had a lead."

"The Mesh?" Owen asked.

"Yes. You almost caught me using it once." Alister held up his forearm and pressed two fingers into the area just below his palm. An image appeared on the hairless skin of his forearm—an interface similar to an operating system on a computer. He tapped on his forearm and the interface changed, menus opening and words printing on the skin.

"You were using it on the boat," Owen said. "In your stateroom."

"Yes. I was sending the Colony an update. Specifically, I was informing them that I believe the Mesh is what summons the storms."

That caught Maya off guard. "How do you know?"

"Experience. As I said, there were three of us when we landed on that small island where we found Station 17. Two went out to search the island. I sent a message via the Mesh and then lay down to rest. I was sleeping on the boat when the storm came. The others radioed back and said they were sick. I put on one of the environmental suits and survived."

Alister paced the room. "I used the Mesh and asked for instructions from the Colony. They said not to come back without people or answers about the storms—and preferably both. They told me if I came back empty-handed, I wouldn't be admitted. At that time, I didn't know that the storms were connected to the Mesh. That's new. The working theory is that the storms are created by high-altitude drones searching for mesh signals. They create the storms and release something or modify the air to kill anyone with the Mesh."

"So that's what really happened to the older man who woke up in Station 17?" Cara asked.

Alister nodded. "I think it's safe to say that he was a member of the Union who was Meshed. I don't know when he entered the Trials, but it must've been at a point after ARC had betrayed the Union. He was probably trying to get to the surface to use the Mesh to contact the Union. I only realized that it was the Mesh causing the storms after I used it on the boat and the storm began following us and converged on the cargo ship. I didn't use it after until we reached the city out there."

"So, the storms were never any threat to us?" Owen asked.

"No. Not to you all. I was fairly certain about that, but not absolutely certain."

"They were only a threat to you because of the Mesh," Maya said. "But you let us believe they could harm us."

"As I said, I wasn't certain that they couldn't. And they provided a good reason for you to get out of that station and get to the Colony. The old man who died inadvertently made the argument I had planned on making—that we needed to find safety."

Owen shook his head. "But the proctor—Bryce—knew the storms were deadly."

"Yes. I think ARC must have had sensors on the surface that picked up the anomalies in the storm. That's the only thing that makes sense."

"And the Mesh is why the robots attacked you as well?" Owen asked.

"Yes. They attacked Will and me because they're programmed to attack ARC proctors and the Meshed—The

Alliance considers itself at war with both ARC and the Union. I knew about the robots, but I was hoping we would get by them before they converged on us."

"It was you," Maya said, realization dawning on her. "You sabotaged Station 17, didn't you, Alister?

He swallowed. "Yes."

"How?"

"I had a way to get into the station—the thumb of another proctor the Union had captured. I used it to enter, and I found the whole place shut down. Most of the chambers were empty. As I said, there was a deceased participant in one of the chambers. I couldn't tell if it had failed, or if he had simply passed away from whatever intervention they had given him. His name was Alister. I found the only proctor in his alcove in sleep mode. I found the man's folder and threw it away. I figured I would never be able to explain what was inside—and I doubted it would matter."

Alister spread his hands. "I did what I had to do, what the Colony required me to do. You heard what it was like for me and my cohort out there. I couldn't return empty-handed. I put the other two members of the team in suits and placed them on the ship. I left my journal there because it talks about the Colony, and I believed that after reading it, you all would be convinced to come here. I disabled the boat so that none of you could board it and leave the island without me. Then I entered the station and damaged the power plant, ensuring that it was in a terminal state of decline. I entered the chamber of the person named Alister and waited. I woke up, just like you all. At that point, the proctor knew I wasn't in the original cohort. I think he was probably about to expose me in the observation room when the other man did what I was going to do anyway—destroy the proctor."

"But didn't Will know your secret?" Owen asked.

"I think he did," Alister said. "Or at least I think he suspected it after we got on the boat. The parts I took from the power plant didn't fit the boat. I made him go away, and I retrieved the parts from the engine room where I'd hidden them. He may have known before, depending on how much data he had access to at the station. I'm not sure."

"Why did he play along?" Cara asked.

"I think that was his programming," Alister said. "As a terminal proctor, I think his role was to simply see where the Trials went and to try to keep us alive. Probably, by his reasoning, exposing me would've caused harm to me and perhaps some of you. The other alternative is that he thought the Colony was your best chance of survival. And I do too."

Owen shook his head. "If Garden Station is out there—holding countless humans waiting to repopulate the world—we have an obligation to find those people."

"Exactly," Alister said. "That has become both sides' goal now: to find Garden and repopulate their armies. When we find Garden, we'll cure the survivors who are infected with the Genesis Virus and bring them into the Union. We'll finally have the army we need to win this war. We've been waiting a very long time for that. Keep in mind, we have chambers like ARC Technologies used in the Extinction Trials. We can leapfrog across time too. That's what's happening now—an endless war of attrition, a slow-motion bunker war on a ruined world."

"What if you don't find Garden Station?" Owen asked.

Alister shrugged. "I don't know. The Alliance might eventually run out of food. Half of them have the Genesis Virus. It must be an unimaginable strain on their society—people who forget their past on a continual basis. They need a cure. We have it. They have robots and storms that hunt us. We both need the people ARC is holding at Garden Station to replenish our numbers if we have any hope of winning the war and returning to the surface permanently. The Colony isn't large enough to support growing our population naturally. We need space. We need adults we can train and arm to kill the robots and the Alliance. As I said, whoever finds Garden first likely wins the war and reclaims the surface and the world."

Maya sat on the couch. "Why not broker a peace?"

"It's been tried," Alister said softly. "Many times. Always ends the same: betrayal by one side or another. So many Colonists have been lost. And Alliance citizens."

"The world needs us to complete the Trials, Alister," Owen said. "To find a way to put things back together."

"Face it, Owen: the world is over. The Colony is your home now. The Change is your future."

"I don't know what the Change is, but I don't want it," Owen said.

"It doesn't matter," Alister muttered. "You've already taken it." He looked up. "It was in that injection with the GV cure. You'll all change soon."

CHAPTER SIXTY-FOUR

When Alister left the room, guards came to the holding room to escort Maya and Cara away. Owen's instincts told him to fight the guards. His good sense forced him to stand by as they were ushered toward the door.

Maya paused at the threshold to look back at Owen, and that moment seemed to stretch on for an eternity, and within it was all the things they had left unsaid and all the things he felt he might never get to say.

He wished more than anything that they had more time together, that he could go back to those days on the boat and tell her exactly how he felt. He couldn't read her face, but he knew what she was thinking: they needed to get out of here. They had to escape the Colony. But where would they go? To the Alliance outside? That seemed to be the only other option.

Once again, Owen felt like a trapped man in a burning building, staring at two doors in a smoke-filled room, wondering which one to open.

He also wondered where his mother was. Could she be here at the Colony? Or with the Alliance? Or did ARC have her at Garden Station? Those were three possibilities.

The last was that she was gone, her life taken in the Fall and buried in this ruined world like countless others had been.

When the door closed, Owen was alone in the holding room. He paced then, waiting, wondering what the Change was, when he would feel it, and if he would survive it.

He felt a strange mix of emotions about the Union's cure: thankful that he would soon recover all his memories, and apprehensive about what else the Change might do to him.

An orderly in a gray uniform brought him a meal on a floppy plastic tray: leafy greens and red slime that reminded Owen of ARC's green sludge. It seemed that good food was another casualty of the Change War.

When he'd finished eating, the orderly collected his tray and dropped off a new set of clothes—a gray outfit like the one Alister had worn. Owen removed his pants and reached for the gray ones, but he then stopped, remembering the small item in his pocket. He reached in and retrieved the small round fire pin and studied it a moment, remembering the selfless act of the man who had given it to him.

He didn't know what the Change was, but he did know what he had to do. The Colony was a burning building. He was going to get out. He was going to get Maya and Cara out too. He didn't know where they would go, but he would get them to safety—somehow.

As he pulled the gray outfit on, he sensed a presence in the room, a stranger, sitting in the corner. He turned quickly, but the club chair beside the couch was empty. And, of course, it was. The door hadn't opened. But he could have sworn someone was in the room.

As the feeling faded, he realized how exhausted he was.

He lay on the couch, telling himself he'd just close his eyes for a moment. As soon as he did, sleep overtook him.

Owen didn't know how long he'd slept, but it must have been ages. When he woke, his body was stiff and sore in places. The exertion of the trek through the city and the hills to the Colony had finally caught up with him.

He was groggy, but that feeling of someone being in the room came again.

He sat up, his eyes adjusting to the light—and found that this time, there was, in fact, someone in the room.

Blair's father.

Darius Aldridge sat in the club chair across from the couch, staring at his forearm. He pulled his sweater down when he saw that Owen was awake.

"Good morning."

Owen sat up.

Darius held out his hand, but Owen didn't shake it.

"I wanted to see you—to personally thank you for returning my daughter to me. I can't tell you what that means to me."

"You're welcome. She's a remarkable girl. But the credit goes more to Maya and Cara. And I'd like to see them."

Darius nodded. "That can be arranged... Depending on our conversation here."

"Conversation about what?"

"Your future—in the Colony."

Owen studied the man's face. Something had changed. He wasn't even sure what he was seeing.

He felt a tingling on his forearm. He pulled the sweater back and found a single word there:

LOADING...

He watched, horrified by what he saw.

MeshOS Initiating...

He felt the presence again. Of not being alone.

"What's going on here?"

A smile tugged at the man's lips. A strange thing happened then: Owen understood. He could read the expression on Darius's face. Owen knew, instinctively, that Darius didn't find what he saw funny. Or sad. He was proud—the sort of look a painter might have when inspecting his masterwork.

Owen felt as though he was hearing a foreign language, one he had heard his entire life, a language everyone spoke, one that he struggled with—a language that was now crystal clear. He imagined this was what it felt like for a person who had been partially blind their entire life to see for the first time.

He felt, in a word, complete.

"This room isn't just a holding cell," Darius said. "It's one of several suites in this entry terminal. It's a transition area for people we bring into the Colony. Alliance defectors. Extinction Trials participants. Even some ARC personnel right after the Fall. The entry terminals provide security but the most important thing they do is perform scans on anyone entering the Colony."

"Scans for what?" Owen asked.

"Brain abnormalities—that's what concerns us the most."

"Why?"

"Because they have the potential to disrupt the Change. We've found that certain minds can't handle it. Every human resists change to some degree. Some more than others. Especially those who have been indoctrinated against our ideology. And there are just those stubborn individuals who will never change. We were a little concerned about you. And not just because of your beliefs."

Darius stood. "As I'm sure you're aware, you have an abnormality in the right hemisphere of your brain. It's a genetic defect. One that I imagine has put you at something of a disadvantage your whole life. How does it manifest? Issues differentiating colors? Difficulties with language production?"

"No. Reading expressions: faces and body language."

Darius nodded solemnly. "That must have been tough as a child."

"I managed."

"Obviously. And you thrived. Tell me, did the defect manifest in other ways? Did you have any particular affinities? Or a strength? Something your brain could do that offset the deficiency."

"Pattern recognition."

"Interesting," Darius whispered. "The human mind is the most fascinating thing in the universe, in my view. Your mind saw those dead ends in that region of your brain, those neurons that took electrical input and couldn't relay it, couldn't fire, and it wired around it, like a muscle that had been cut out, growing scar tissue and strengthening the connections around it. A highway re-routed. A highway that, thanks to us, has been rebuilt. Those faulty neurons have now been replaced with a synthetic nano mesh."

"What kind of nano mesh? What are you talking about?"

"Think of it as a sort of neuro-prosthesis. We see the brain like any other part of the body. If you lost your leg, doctors would provide a prosthesis. You were born without a part of your brain. A very small part, but an important one. A part no one could see, but one that affected you every day. The Mesh has filled that gap. But the Mesh is much more."

"More how? What are you telling me?"

"I'm telling you that the Mesh is an integral part of the Change."

"Integral as in…"

"The Mesh is the answer to the oldest question in human existence: what is our future?"

When Owen said nothing, Darius moved to the door and swung it open. "Would you like to see the Colony?"

Owen followed the man into the hall, where he glanced back and forth, searching for any clues as to where Maya and Cara could be.

"They were taken to another entry terminal," Darius said. "We have… different plans for them."

Without another word, he marched to the doorway at the end of the hall where he brought up his forearm and began tapping on the interface there. The door slid into the wall, revealing what looked like a plush auto car beyond.

They got inside and Owen felt the pull of inertia. The trip was short, but Owen wasn't sure how fast the car could move. He had been hoping to get some sense of how far the Colony was from the entrance they'd found in the woods. His mind was still focused on finding Maya and Cara and escaping.

But there was another question that had been weighing on his mind since he reached the airlock.

"Is my mother here?"

Darius stared at the floor. "No."

"Is she alive? Does ARC have her? Or the Alliance?"

"I don't know that either. I'm sorry, Owen."

"What about Maya's family?"

"Same answer. They're not here and we don't know where they are."

Silence stretched out until the door to the car opened, revealing what looked like a park with walking trails lined with shrubs and trees that stood several times Owen's height. Above was a blue and white sky with a hazy yellow-orange sun. What Owen didn't see revealed what this place was: there were no birds, no bugs, and no breeze.

"We're still underground, aren't we?" Owen asked.

"Yes. And quite a bit farther underground."

Darius exited the car and led Owen down a path. They passed adults sitting on benches made of wood and steel. Children played on the grass pitches, throwing balls and playing tag. At a gazebo nearby, a group of teenagers was discussing a book called *Star Watch*.

Owen couldn't help but pause and study the faces of the group. One of the teenage girls had her hands out, speaking excitedly, describing the book. "Yes, we all love a happy ending." She rolled her eyes.

Before, Owen would've assumed that she loved the book.

But now, based on her body language and expression, he knew instinctively that she was being sarcastic.

Owen then realized that Darius was watching him.

"What you're feeling now, it's just the start," he said.

"Start of what?" Owen asked.

"Your new life."

Darius resumed walking along the path, his head bowed, studying his feet as they walked. "What do you think caused the Fall?"

"You. Genesis. The Union."

"Why do you think that?"

"It's true, isn't it? You released the Genesis Virus?"

"Yes."

"And that caused the Fall."

Darius cocked his head, studying Owen. "I was asking about the root cause. Why do you think we created the Genesis Virus?"

"You tell me."

"If you answer me, it helps us both."

"How?"

"It lets me know where you stand." Darius held up a hand. "I'll know soon, either way. It's better if you tell me."

"What do you mean, *you'll know soon?*"

"That presence you feel. It's the Mesh. It's mapping your brain. When it's done, the Mesh will know your thoughts."

Owen stopped on the path.

Darius smiled. "Don't be concerned. A guy like you has nothing to worry about."

"What does 'a guy like me' mean?"

"Someone whose thoughts are pure. A truly kind and

decent human being. Someone who has dedicated their life to serving others."

"What happens when someone thinks something you don't like?"

"That depends on what those thoughts are. We have very advanced technology in the Colony—the ability to model brain activity, to predict behavioral outcomes. If we identify brain wiring that could be dangerous to the greater good, we... fix it. Similar to the way we fixed your brain abnormality. That's how we see it. Those who might disrupt the greater good have no place here, Owen. But you do. You know first-hand the difference the Mesh makes. Look at what it has given you. You see, where before you were blind. And you have a role to play here."

"What role is that?"

"Think about it. There may be others like you out there—waiting in Extinction Trials stations, waiting for someone to carry them out of those burning buildings."

"You want me to be an agent—like Alister."

"That's your future. It's what you were put here to do. Who knows, you might even find your mother out there. Right now, as we speak, she might be confined to a chamber in an ARC station like the one you woke up in, the power slowly draining away, her time slipping away as she waits for help that might never come. But you could save her. In fact, it might be your only chance to save her."

Those words—and the possibility of rescuing his mother—tugged at Owen like an ocean current carrying him out to sea, a force of nature almost impossible to resist. But he wanted to know more first.

Owen motioned to the park and the people there. "Is this the Change? Are *they* the Change?"

Darius turned and kept walking along the path, as if gathering his thoughts. "The Union was faced with an impossible task. We knew our world was coming to an end. It was only a matter of time before a catastrophe occurred. We made the difficult decision: to do a controlled burn and restart the human race using what we had learned."

"What does that mean exactly?"

"The Genesis Virus was supposed to be a global reset."

"I don't follow."

"Think about it. If you want to defeat a global army arrayed against you, an army with nearly unlimited resources and unlimited personnel, how do you win?"

"You convince them not to fight in the first place."

Darius smiled. "That's actually a very good answer. In fact, in a way, it's the route we took. If you want to defeat a superior enemy without ever firing a shot—and keeping everyone alive—there's a simple way: erase everyone's memories. An army can't fight if they can't remember what they're fighting for."

"Your plan was to give the whole world amnesia?"

"Curable amnesia. Our plan was quite simple, really. Once the Genesis Virus had infected the global population, we would have gathered the human race together and started over. We would have administered the cure for the virus and the Mesh at the same time and begun anew."

"How would the Mesh solve the world's problems?"

"Think about it. In a world where the Mesh knows your every thought, there can be no crime, no hunger, no suffering."

Owen shook his head. "And no freedom."

"Freedom is an illusion. Freedom is nothing more than a currency—something we spend to get something we want. We've always traded some amount of our freedom for the things we need for survival. We trade our freedom for financial compensation when we take jobs. We trade our freedom for safety when we allow police to search our homes and stop us when we're walking down the street. The Mesh is no different."

"The Mesh is the Change, isn't it?"

"The *Change* is what the Mesh does to us. The Mesh creates a changed society in which your thoughts determine your destiny. It's always been that way: your thoughts determine your words and actions, and your words and actions determine your fate in life. The Mesh simply moves up the cause-and-effect chain. By monitoring thoughts, we can perfect our society. The Mesh is the eventuality of human evolution: the Union, the joining of all human consciousness. The truth is, we were always destined to be one human organism, one cohesive whole with a shared consciousness. That is the Change. That is what the Alliance are terrified of. Unity. Unlimited progress with no need for what they provide."

Darius motioned to the park around them. "You're seeing proof right here."

"I don't see how the Mesh can solve all of our problems. Linking our minds just connects us. It doesn't necessarily make us better."

He focused on Owen. "That's because you don't yet understand the full scope of the Mesh and Revelation—our predictive technology."

"Then tell me."

"I'll start with an example you'll understand. Do you know how a fire starts, Owen?"

"Of course. Combustible fuel, oxidizer, and a source of heat above the flashpoint—"

"I meant conceptually. A fire starts with a spark. A spark gives rise to a flame, a flame becomes a blaze, a blaze an inferno, and finally a wildfire that cannot be stopped. That's what bad thoughts do to our minds. They begin as a spark—a tiny thought that grows. If that thought gets enough oxygen, it can lead a person to ruin. The Mesh prevents that. It's a mental fire detector. I would think you of all people would be for that."

"I think our own minds are the last place we truly control—and they should be our domain."

"One might say the same for a home. But the government requires smoke detectors to protect the inhabitants. This is no different. In the age in which we live, a person's thoughts are the most dangerous thing in the world."

"What about *The Birthright*—it provides a framework for managing your mind. For understanding how the mind works. What about morality—a shared code of ethics?"

"Those are risks we can't take, unfortunately. Our solution—the Mesh—ensures our society's success. Voluntary adherence to a code of ethics doesn't. We're done taking risks with the human race. We saw where that road led us before."

Owen considered that for a moment. And he considered what he hadn't seen. Maya. And Cara.

"You said before that minds that were wired differently,

that might oppose the Change, would be *fixed*. What do you mean specifically?"

Darius stared at Owen, seeming to read his face. "You're asking about Maya and Cara."

"I haven't seen them here."

"You'll see them again."

"When?"

"Soon."

"What will happen to them?"

"In the past, our society has imprisoned those who didn't obey the laws—those who acted against the greater good. It's inhumane, if you ask me. The criminals often don't recover from their time in captivity. And it has an effect on the people who care about them—being separated from their loved ones. The Mesh, just as it offers you a chance at a better life, offers salvation for them."

Owen felt his body go numb. "What kind of salvation are we talking about here?"

"The same life the Mesh offers everyone else: a unified society where our minds work together. In the case of minds like Cara's and Maya's, we make a few modifications to their brain wiring to prevent them from harming the greater good. Just like you, they will be changed."

"Changed how?"

"We call the process pacification. Pacified individuals only have use of those parts of their brains that are safe. The effects are varied, but generally, you might see a pacified friend or family member doing more... basic work. Maya might be the woman wearing an apron, working in the back of a flower shop, bringing the plants in, or sweeping up.

Or wiping down the tables at a café where you have lunch. She'll enjoy the work. Her life will be a simple one—a life free of the burden of those thoughts that might harm her and all of us."

Owen swallowed hard. "Will she remember me?"

"No, Owen. She won't. That would be far too dangerous. But you could see her every day. If you wanted to."

"When will she change?"

"It's already started. First, the cure for the Genesis Virus will restore her memories. Then the Mesh will begin mapping her brain and identifying any problematic areas. The duration of the process varies from person to person, but I expect she'll be fully pacified by tomorrow morning."

CHAPTER SIXTY-FIVE

The orderlies in gray suits led Maya and Cara to a car that whisked them away to another part of the Colony, one that looked like the receiving area they had first entered: it had a hallway and several doors and a hatch at the end.

The room they led Maya to had a couch and club chairs and a full bathroom. There was also a wide mirror in the wall, similar to the previous room. It was some sort of observation area. She was pretty certain of that.

When the door closed, leaving her alone, a sudden rush of fatigue swept over her. She wondered what the cause was—if it was the cure for the Genesis Virus they had given her, or the fall she had sustained when she had found the entrance to the Colony, or simply the exhaustion from the trek from the sea.

Whatever the cause, sleep came quickly for Maya.

When she woke, she was stiff and sore—and most importantly, she was in possession of something she had been wanting since she woke in Station 17: her memories.

Finally, Maya remembered.

She remembered everything.

Leaning back on the couch, she focused her mind on the first memory of Genesis Biosciences. In her mind's eye, she saw herself wearing a freshly pressed suit, walking on the sidewalk toward the Genesis Biosciences building. A breeze tugged at her hair and stirred the faint smell of her shampoo. She clutched a portfolio in her right hand. It held a printed copy of her résumé (which no one ever asked for anymore, but she had the mortal fear of being asked for it and not having it). Also inside the small case was a notepad. She always took notes at job interviews. At home, in her small apartment, a round trash can by her desk was filled with discarded pages from prospective employers who had rejected her. And even more of those positions she had rejected.

The skyscraper's entrance was a glass revolving door that spit out people and sucked others in, and as she shuffled through, she was reminded of her mother's words to her: "For your first job, don't pick the one that pays you the most. Or the one where you like the people the most. Pick the one where you can learn the most."

"Learn about what?" she had asked.

"About yourself. It's like an investment—learning about yourself. If you figure out your strengths and weaknesses—and find the right opportunity—there's no limit to what you can accomplish, Maya."

In the conference room, the interviewer asked a series of technical and general questions. As expected, she didn't ask Maya for her résumé. Maya didn't offer. The interview ended the same way the dozen before had—with a promise that they would be in touch.

Maya received that response the same day, which she

took as an indication of what sort of organization Genesis Biosciences was: decisive, efficient, and in a hurry. She liked that. She was all of those things too.

The second interview took place the next day. The questions were more difficult. She wasn't familiar with one of the scientific questions they asked. She was nervous, but she didn't fumble her words. She simply said, "I'm not familiar with quantum genomic sequencing. But I'll begin researching it as soon as I leave this interview."

The man smiled. "It's understandable. We recently invented it. No one outside this building has ever heard of it."

"Then why—" Maya realized the reason then. "Ah. I see."

"We're looking for the best and brightest here, Doctor Young. But we're also looking for something else. We're looking for certain kinds of minds. Curious minds. People who have a thirst for this kind of work. You'll need it here. Genesis can be a brutal work environment. It's challenging in ways you can't appreciate now. And for the uncommitted, it's a hard road. But for those who are life-long learners, those who thrive on achieving the impossible, anything is possible here."

To Maya's surprise, he stood and stepped toward the door. "It's a yes from me, Maya. You'll have one more interview, though. I wish you luck."

At the final interview, there was one man waiting for her in the conference room overlooking the river. He needed no introduction, but he extended his hand and introduced himself nonetheless.

"Hello, Maya. I'm Darius Aldridge. Thank you for coming."

"I'm honored, Doctor Aldridge."

"I'm just Darius around here. And we're honored that you'd apply here at Genesis. I just have one question for you."

Maya swallowed.

"Why are you here?"

"I'm interested in the work Genesis is doing."

"Why?"

"I want to save lives. I want to create something that changes the world."

"Why?"

Maya inhaled. "My father died of a rare heart condition. They created a genetic screen for it a few years later. They would have found it during a routine physical if he had lived a few years longer. I've always wondered what my life would have been like if that test had been delivered to market a little sooner."

Aldridge stared at her. Maya felt the urge to fill the silence.

"That's what drew me to genomic medicine. I want to go home every day knowing that I might develop a test that would save someone's father. Or mother. Brother or daughter."

Darius nodded. "I know exactly how you feel, Maya. Welcome to Genesis Biosciences."

Maya's first few years at Genesis were the toughest of her life. It wasn't the long hours. Or those few times she cried at her desk. For Maya, the hardest part about the job became disconnecting. She thought about work when she was at home. In the shower. On the way to work.

She didn't date. She didn't make many friends outside of work. Her life was Genesis Biosciences and her research.

But everything changed when she met Sherman Parrish.

The first time she met Parrish was on a Saturday afternoon when he knocked on her door. He was wearing the uniform of a pest control company, and he nodded when she cracked the door.

"I'm very sorry for the interruption, ma'am, but the building HOA has asked me to do a bug treatment on your unit. You should have gotten a notification about it."

Maya nodded. "I did. Come on in."

The man breezed through the apartment, checking in hard-to-reach places and deploying small boxes, and then he was gone.

He returned two weeks later, and this time, when the door closed, he didn't venture deeper into Maya's apartment. He squared on her and said, "I have an admission to make."

Maya bunched her eyebrows. "What?"

"I'm not a pest control specialist, though I did search your apartment for bugs—and planted some myself. We've been watching you, Maya."

A bolt of fear ran through her. She cut her eyes to the door, but Parrish held his hands up. "It's not like that. I work for the government. I'm here to recruit you—that's why we've been surveilling you."

"Recruit me for what?"

"An operation that could save the world."

"I don't understand."

"The company you work for—Genesis Biosciences—is not what you think it is."

Maya put her hands on her hips. "What is it then?"

"A scientific terror organization, one dedicated to taking control of the entire human race."

Maya laughed out loud. "Oh, you are good. Who planned this? Darius?" She looked around. "Are you filming this for some kind of streaming prank show? You almost had me."

But Parrish wasn't laughing. He stared at Maya. "This is no prank, Doctor Young. It's the most serious thing you will ever be involved in, I can assure you."

Parrish reached into his pocket and took out a small data drive and offered it to Maya. "This will convince you. I'll be back tomorrow—and we'll discuss what to do about it."

When he was gone, Maya set the data drive on her dining table and paced the living room, biting her lip. What if the guy was a total lunatic—a stalker with psychotic delusions? She should call the police. Yes, that was the only prudent thing to do.

When the emergency operator answered, Maya explained the situation as best she could and waited while they connected her to the appropriate authorities.

The line clicked and she heard a deep sigh before Parrish spoke. "I told you, Maya, I'm with the government. Don't feel bad, we expected you to do this. We've built a profile on you. It's why we chose you—you are someone who does the right thing."

Maya's heart was racing. Fear gripped her. "I…"

"Just look at the data on the drive, Maya. It'll change everything. I'll see you tomorrow."

Parrish had been right. The data did change Maya's mind.

Contained on the drive was Genesis Biosciences' research data related to Maya's work into a cure for dementia. What she saw in those files kept her up the whole night. It occupied her thoughts at work the next day. She no longer saw Genesis in the same way.

That night, a knock sounded on her door again, and Maya opened it to find Parrish standing there. He didn't say a word, only walked in and turned as Maya closed the door.

"How do I know the files are real?" Maya asked.

"You know they are. You know the format. The way Genesis runs its trials. And it's related to your work on dementia."

"They're reversing my cure. Using it to create a virus."

"Yes."

"Why?"

"What do you think would happen if the entire world had dementia—a specific kind of dementia that affected mostly memories?"

"A collapse."

"Yes. For a while. And what could you do if you had the cure? If you could organize everyone and give them something that had a biological impact on their brain?"

"Anything."

"That's right," Parrish said. "You could upgrade the human race. That's what they want to do."

"Upgrade how?"

"We don't know. What we do know is that they are not happy with the current world order. They want to be in charge. And they're planning something very big to make that happen. They're using you—and your research—to make that happen. Millions will die. Maybe billions."

Maya swallowed. "What are you asking of me?"

"Only one thing: to be our eyes and ears inside Genesis. To gather data and send it to me."

"You want me to be a spy."

"Yes."

Maya pointed to the data drive on the dining table. "Seems like you already have one."

"Had one."

"What happened."

Parrish stared at her.

"I see," Maya said. "So, Genesis is aware that you're on to them?"

"Genesis is part of a coalition of companies. They call themselves the Human Union—or the Union. And yes, they know we have become aware of their plans. They're accelerating their timeline. We need more information. And you're our best chance. I know this is going to sound crazy, but the entire future of the human race could turn on what you do here, Maya. We need your help. We need you to gather data for us."

"And what if I end up like your last agent? The one who gathered the data on that drive?"

"You have my word that I will do everything in my power to prevent that from happening."

"How?"

"First, we'll train you."

"Train me how?"

"In self-defense. You'll enroll at a martial arts dojo a few blocks away. I'll be your instructor. In those sessions, we'll exchange information—and data drives, if you can smuggle them out."

"I get the feeling this is not the kind of thing I can fist-fight my way out of."

"True. But if the time comes—if you're trapped—you have my word, I'll come for you. I will do everything in my power to get you to safety, wherever in the world that may be. I promise you, Maya."

In the observation room, Maya stood, trying to process the memories she had recovered. She had known that her work had been used for the Genesis Virus and that Parrish had recruited her and enrolled her in the Extinction Trials as a way to save her, but seeing it in her mind's eye was a completely different thing.

The next memory was of the Fall.

Maya was wearing a spacesuit, working in a clean room, when a voice came over the speaker.

"Maya."

"Yes, Darius?"

"I need to see you."

"We're in the middle of something—"

"It's urgent. I'm sorry, Maya, but your life could depend on it."

Maya exited the lab, removed the suit, and made her way

to the conference room, where Darius Aldridge was waiting with two medical technicians. One took a blood sample, the other swabbed her shoulder with an alcohol pad and uncapped a syringe.

"What's this?" Maya asked.

Darius stared at her. "A vaccine."

"Vaccine for what?"

"Something we've been working on. Just in case it gets loose. We want to protect you, Maya. Just like you protect us." He watched her, waiting, and when she said nothing, he pressed on. "Don't you trust me?"

"Of course," Maya said, trying to make her voice calm, and failing.

Darius nodded to the young man holding the syringe, and he jabbed it into Maya's shoulder. She was nearly certain she knew what it was, and that they were likely watching her.

On her way home from the office, Maya opened her old-fashioned appointment book, which she had bought specifically for her work with Parrish, and wrote him a note that read, *I think they know about me. I'm going to download all the data and drop it at lunch tomorrow.*

In a park near her apartment building, she sat on a bench, chewing gum, watching until there was no one around. Casually, she took the gum from her mouth, attached it to the page, and stuck it on the underside of the bench.

That was the last night she ever spent in her apartment. At the gym the next morning, she got sick.

★ ★ ★

The door in the Colony opened and Darius Aldridge stepped into the observation room.

"Hello, Maya."

"Hi," she said quietly.

"Do you remember now?"

"Yes."

"You broke my heart, Maya."

"You broke the world."

That gave Darius pause. He stood there, studying her as if debating what words to use against her, like someone would survey a table full of sharp objects, all lethal.

"The world was already broken."

"Not as broken as it is now."

"True." Darius took a few steps toward her and turned, then sat in a club chair across from the couch.

"Do you know what we do to cancer patients, Maya?"

"I think you're going to tell me."

"If we find the cancer early enough, the patient isn't aware of it. Half the time, they feel fine. Healthy. They don't know they're sick. They don't know something is growing inside of them that will one day end their life."

"I feel an analogy coming on."

"You weren't this jaded before."

"Living through an apocalypse will do that to you."

Darius smiled. "Quite right. My point is that we did what we had to do to save humanity. We wish things had turned out differently. If you hadn't interfered, maybe they would have."

"You have the nerve to blame all of this on me?"

"I'm just stating the facts."

"Felt more like an opinion to me."

"There's no use debating it, Maya."

"Then why are you here?"

"I wanted to see you... one last time."

Maya's heart beat faster, fear growing inside of her. "One last time before what?"

"Before you change."

"Change how?"

"It's not important." Darius stood and eyed her. "Life is strange—the way people come in and out of your life, and the roles they play. Before the Fall, you cut my heart out, Maya. I trusted you like you were my own family."

He shook his head and broke eye contact with Maya. "Yesterday morning, I was alone in this ruined world. I was surrounded by people, but I had lost my daughter, the only family I had left. I sent Guthrie—who you know as Alister—to try to find her. But it was you who brought her back to me. I have no doubt of that. And I'll forever be grateful for that. That's why I wanted to see you. To say thank you."

"You say it like this is goodbye."

"It is. We'll see each other again, but this is goodbye, Maya." Darius took a deep breath and proceeded to explain exactly what the Mesh was and how it would soon pacify her mind.

When he left, Maya stared at the closed door. She wanted to cry. But she decided she wasn't going to let herself cry. She was going to get out of this room and the Colony and she was going to get the Mesh out of her body. She just didn't know how. Yet.

CHAPTER SIXTY-SIX

When Darius left him in the park, Owen wasn't quite sure what to do.

He settled on a bench and watched the citizens of the Colony as he considered his options.

Being here felt so strange to him—especially after what he had been through: escaping Station 17, the voyage across the sea, and the trek through the ruined city. Now he was underground, in a safe place. That is, if he was willing to accept the Union's vision for humanity's future.

And what they were going to do to Maya and Cara.

As the people passed by on the trail—parents and kids and friends chatting—he was amazed at how the Mesh had opened his world. He saw them. He understood them like he never had understood people before. There was something effortless about it. It was, in a word, serene. Harmonious.

With each passing moment, he felt the Mesh claiming more of his mind. He felt a bit of himself slipping away—but something wondrous taking its place.

But as he turned the question over in his mind, his thoughts flashed to Maya. And the hurt he felt there—at what they were going to take from her—was far greater than anything the Mesh or the Union could give him.

He also thought about the legions of people waiting for someone to rescue them in Garden Station. How many would the Union pacify if their minds were deemed dangerous?

Owen looked up when a young girl veered off the path and approached him.

He smiled when he realized it was Blair. She was carrying a pink flower that she held out to him as she approached. A light shade of red was creeping across her cheeks. She was embarrassed but was smiling nonetheless. Owen realized something then that he had never been able to see before: the young girl had a crush on him.

"My parents wanted me to tell you thank you—for bringing me home," Blair said as Owen took the flower. "And I wanted to say it as well," she added, her face turning even more red.

Owen reached out and pulled her into a hug.

"You're welcome, Blair."

"My dad says you're going to stay," she said, avoiding eye contact with him. "And Maya too."

Owen nodded, unsure what to say. "That's their plan. Do you know where Alister is?"

"Sure. Follow me."

They walked along the path, out of the park, and into what felt like a quaint little village. Shops lined the streets. People sat outside delis and restaurants. Lunch was apparently just starting.

Ahead, Owen heard banging and muttered curses that seemed to be the anthem of Alister working.

This shop didn't have any sort of reception area or office, only a deep workshop area with a roll-up door that opened onto the street. Alister was in the back, behind several scooters that Owen assumed had been fixed and were waiting on their owners to retrieve. Alister was banging on another near the back wall.

He looked up when Owen and Blair approached.

"Didn't figure you for a scooter mechanic," Owen said.

"I told you, I can fix anything. I told them I would fix anything—so long as it couldn't run me over like that bus did."

Owen laughed. "Can't say I blame you."

Blair turned to him. "I should get back." She smiled. "Will I see you around?"

"Maybe."

As Blair walked away, Alister stood and washed his hands at the sink, eyeing Owen as he dried them off.

"They give you the old Union sales pitch? One society. One mind, blah, blah, blah?"

"You sound less excited than you did in the observation room."

"I don't get excited about anything anymore. That's part of getting older."

"Actually, I think complaining is just part of your way of life."

"Maybe there is hope for you, Owen. And yes, you're right. I complain. And I comply. And I fix things. That's my life."

"Yet the Mesh lets you stay. Unpacified."

Alister eyed him. "It does. It knows when someone is just frustrated—knows the difference between someone planning to do the world harm and someone who just needs to vent."

"So, it knows what I'm thinking?"

Alister stared at Owen. "Not fully. Not yet. It hasn't been long enough. But it will. Right now, it's mapping your brain. It's sort of... what would Will say... installing itself."

"That's a terrifying thought. Surely, it is for you too?"

"Change is terrifying. All change, not just *the* Change. But that's life. You weigh what the Union takes from you and what they give you, and you make a call. That's how it goes."

Alister bent down and tossed some of his tools into a nearby bin. "You hungry?"

"I was hoping to find Maya."

Alister stared at him for a long moment. "Lunch is a lot easier to come by. Let's start there."

It turned out that Alister's home was above his shop. It was cozy, with an open-plan kitchen, living, and dining room, but the warmest thing inside was the woman who walked over and hugged Alister when he arrived. She was tall with long brown hair and eyes that Owen felt held a sea of kindness.

"I didn't know we were having company," she said after breaking the hug with Alister.

"Carmen, this is Owen Watts. He's a former firefighter, general do-gooder, and a naïve pain in the rear who saved my life out there."

Carmen nodded to Owen. "Sorry about the introduction."

Owen held his hands up. "Don't worry, I introduce myself that way too."

Carmen laughed and smiled. "Well, we're very happy to have you here. Belden told me he had some very good companions out there that refused to leave him behind."

Owen turned to Alister. "Belden?"

The man shot him a look. "Not another word—only she calls me by my first name."

Owen shook his head and they settled at the table, where Carmen served them sandwiches—easily the best meal Owen had eaten in what felt like ages. It was nice to have solid food again. And the normalcy of sitting at a kitchen table with friends. And Alister was a friend. Or perhaps more.

After lunch, Carmen left to run some errands and Owen returned to the main reason he had come to see Alister.

"I want to see Maya."

The older man shook his head. "Impossible."

"Why?"

"She's in one of the entry terminals."

"Why is that a problem?"

"Your mesh doesn't give you access. Not yet."

"When will it?"

"After the Mesh has fully integrated with you. When it can detect any thoughts that might harm the Union."

"It can't now?"

"No. Not yet."

"But you can take me to see her."

Alister's silent stare was all the confirmation Owen needed.

"Please. I just want to see her. You're the only chance I have. Before... before they pacify her."

Alister shook his head.

Owen glanced at the door where Carmen had just exited. "I think you know exactly how I feel right now. You've been in the same position. Kept from the person you love and running out of time. I just want to see her—to talk to her one last time."

CHAPTER SIXTY-SEVEN

In the observation room, Cara lay down on the couch, trying to see a way out of this prison.

In a way, she felt exactly as she had during the Fall.

In the hospital, the corridors had been filled with gurneys and people. As time passed, the staff disappeared as they joined the ranks of the fallen.

She had worked herself to the point of exhaustion. In fact, the last thing she remembered was collapsing in an operating room.

When she woke, she was lying on the bottom bunk in an on-call room. The hospital administrator was towering over her along with another man with short hair and a ribbed sweater.

"Sorry to wake you, Cara," her boss said.

Cara rubbed a hand across her face and threw her legs over the side of the bed. "I need to get back to work—"

He placed a hand on her shoulder. "Easy there. This man needs to speak with you first. His name is Parrish, and you're going to want to hear what he has to say."

With that, the hospital administrator exited the room.

Cara studied Parrish. He looked like military to her. His

voice was firm and efficient, like a man reading from a script on a deadline.

"I'll cut to the chase, Doctor Allen. The government needs your help."

"Help with what?"

"What we're facing is a war, the likes of which we have never encountered before. One where every piece of technology can turn against us. Where one moment we feel fine and the next we can't even remember who we are. It's a war we are losing."

"I've noticed."

"You can help turn it around."

"Me?"

"You're in the right place at the right time, and you have the right skills."

"I don't follow."

"Are you familiar with ARC Technologies?"

"Of course. Their software runs the medical records in the hospital."

"They do more than that."

"Such as?" Cara asked.

"ARC is organizing a trial to find a solution to whatever this scientific terror group is trying to do. Specifically, they're going to develop a cohort that can survive this virus and whatever else our enemy is planning."

"I don't see how I fit in."

"There's a scientist who knows what the cure to this virus is. Her name is Doctor Maya Young. She was unknowingly working on the project until we recruited her." Parrish took a deep breath. "The problem is, they discovered that she was working for us. They've infected her with the virus."

"Which means she's forgotten her research."

"Exactly."

"I still don't see how I fit in."

"We're placing Doctor Young in ARC's program. It's called the Extinction Trials. What we're looking for is a physician to place in her cohort, someone who can help keep her alive in case she needs help. We're hoping ARC can restore her memories. When they do, we need you to get her to us."

"How would I do that?"

Parrish reached into his pocket. "The other reason we're recruiting you is because you're in this hospital, right now, in the same place as Doctor Young. We need to implant this device in your leg. There's an operating room already prepped and waiting."

"What *is* that device?"

"It's a homing beacon. Your mission is very simple, Doctor Allen: keep Maya Young alive, help her recover her memories, and when you do, activate the beacon. We'll come and find you, and we'll take it from there."

"How do I activate it?"

"It'll be in your right leg. You press and hold for twelve seconds."

"And what if we don't find a cure for her? What if she never remembers?"

"Then they probably win the war. And the world will be theirs. I don't know what that world will be like, but I think there will be a lot less of us, and I would bet that their control of the ones left will be near absolute. That's what this war is about ultimately: who controls the world."

★ ★ ★

Cara had drifted off to sleep when the door opened. She sat up, feeling groggy and stiff.

Darius Aldridge stood over her, seeming to wait for her to regain her senses.

"It's the Mesh," he said. "It causes some systemic inflammation when it's integrating."

"Wonderful," Cara muttered.

Darius softly closed the door. "We've been looking for you for a very long time, Doctor Allen."

"Really?"

"We know you're an Alliance agent. A fairly recent recruit. We found your name in some files we recovered during the war."

"What do you want?"

"A simple act. One thing that can help end a war."

Cara stared at him.

"I'm assuming they gave you a way to contact the Alliance."

"I don't know what you're talking about."

"You can lie now, but it won't matter soon. Soon, the Mesh will be part of you. We'll have access to your memories, and we'll learn the truth. But... it would be better if you told us. That would be an act of support for the Union, the kind of act that might better your situation here."

"You're holding me in a cage. How does that situation improve?"

"The world is a cage, Doctor Allen. We're just making it a safer cage."

CHAPTER SIXTY-EIGHT

Maya felt a tingling on her forearm, like a bug crawling under her skin. She looked down, but there was nothing there.

She placed a finger just below her palm, and words faded onto her skin, black letters that read:

```
MeshOS Initiating.
22% Loaded.
```

She had to get out of here—and soon, while she could still think, while she was still herself.

But how? And where would she go?

For some reason, her mind drifted back to the page she had found in the envelope with her name on it in Station 17. In the airlock to the entry terminal, a drop of liquid had brought writing to the surface of the blank page—in a very similar way to how the MeshOS interface had appeared on her skin.

The item was still in her pocket. They hadn't bothered searching her. And why would they? She was trapped here, and they would soon control her with the Mesh.

She rose from the couch and walked to the bathroom,

where she closed the door and hunched over the sink, trying to hide what she was doing from any cameras inside—and she hoped there weren't any.

She turned the water on, drew the page from her pocket, and let the bubbling liquid wash over it.

Slowly, in waves, the image took form, the lines gray at first, then darker, and finally black.

Maya was shocked by what she saw. At first, she didn't understand it. Then, comprehension dawned on her. It was actually really simple. The symbols had been there all along. Guideposts standing along the road for anyone willing to read them.

She saw what they had to do.

Yes, they had a chance.

Through the bathroom door, Maya heard the door to the outer room fly open, impacting the wall in a loud crash.

They knew—the Colony had seen what she had done. They knew what she had discovered. She shook her head, regretting her actions as she stuffed the page in her pocket.

The door to the bathroom flew open and Maya staggered back. But when she saw who was standing in the doorway, her heart burst.

Owen.

He was panting, a smile growing on his face.

"Hi."

"Hi," she said, a laugh starting. "How did you get here—"

Maya caught a glimpse of the room then, of Alister standing in the living area, a resigned, surly look on his face—a very Alister expression.

"I know where we need to go," Maya said.

"You do?" Owen said, clearly surprised.

"We have to get out of here."

"You're right about that."

Owen held his hand out to her, and she took it, and they raced back into the observation room, toward the door, but Alister didn't move.

"You need to lock me in here," he said quietly.

"You're coming with us, Alister," Owen said.

The man shook his head, swallowing hard. "I'm not."

"Alister, we don't leave anyone behind—"

"Not this time, Owen. This isn't a fairy tale. They can see and hear everything I can. They're sending more guards. I've already done too much."

"Come with us," Owen said.

"My place is here. With Carmen. Go now."

"Thank you, Alister," Maya said. "Or Guthrie, rather. That's your name, isn't it?"

"Alister is fine. That's how you should remember me. Now go. And lock me in here. I don't know how much the Mesh can control me."

In the hallway, Owen locked the door with a keycard.

"Where's Cara?" Maya asked.

"She's in one of these rooms," Owen said, glancing down the hallway at the three other closed doors.

Maya realized there were two incapacitated guards near the door at the end of the hall. That must have been where Owen had gotten the keycard that opened the doors.

"They were the only guards," Owen said. "But I think more will come—they're probably in the cars right now."

Maya nodded. They needed to hurry.

"Cara!" she called out.

"I'm here," Cara yelled from behind a door nearby.

Owen raced to the door and scanned the keycard but the doorknob simply beeped and a small light flashed red.

"They know we're trying to escape," Maya said. "They've locked the doors."

Owen eyed the door as he stepped backward.

"What are you doing?" Maya asked.

"Don't worry, I used to do this for a living."

Owen ran the width of the corridor and kicked the door just beside the handle. It shook and the wall cracked, but it didn't open.

He seemed unfazed. He merely backed up and took another run at it, kicking with just as much force. The wall cracked after that, and the frame shifted. The third kick swung it open, and Cara ran out and the three of them barreled toward the end of the corridor.

At the airlock, Owen scanned the keycard, but like the door, it simply beeped and a red light flashed. The hatch was locked. And unlike the door, Owen couldn't kick it in.

CHAPTER SIXTY-NINE

For a long moment, Owen stared at the hatch. They had come so far. And now they were at the end of the road.

They had been so close. He had almost gotten Maya and Cara out. Granted, he wasn't sure where they would go, but at least out there, he had a chance at freedom—and a chance at saving the people counting on him at Garden Station.

Maya marched ahead of him and ran her hand over the white plastic wall beside the hatch.

"What are you doing?" Cara asked.

"Looking for the emergency release. All Genesis Bio airlocks had them—in case the computers failed."

"Oh," Owen muttered. Why didn't he think of that? He should have. His entire existence since waking up after the Fall had been one emergency escape after another.

Maya pulled a panel off the wall and reached in and twisted a handle. The hatch popped but didn't open.

Owen surged forward and ripped it backward. Maya and Cara raced into the airlock, moving quickly to the small window where they peered out, their heads close together.

"We have a problem," Maya whispered.

"How big of a problem?" Owen asked.

"A storm-sized problem," Maya said.

Owen came up beside her and peered through the window. Above the steps outside, the storm's winds blew through the forest, carrying leaves with it and laying down sheets of rain. If it was the same type of storm that had been on the island and the container ship, it was deadly to them now. They had mesh. They wouldn't survive out there, not without suits.

Maya glanced at the five suits in the alcove. "I don't know if we'll have enough oxygen to get clear of the storm. And now that we have the Mesh, the storm—or the drone directing it—will probably track us. Even if we escape, we can't outrun the storm."

Cara was already moving to the suits. "Leave it to me. I... have a plan."

Quickly, the three of them began putting on the suits.

Outside, the wind howled against the outer airlock door. Even if they didn't run out of oxygen, avoiding a fall—and a rip in the suits—would be a challenge.

In the corridor beyond the airlock, Owen heard a door open.

"They're here!" he yelled as he grabbed a helmet from the shelf above.

Maya eyed the two remaining suits, seeming to contemplate their dilemma.

"We could disable them—" Cara began, but Maya held up a hand.

"There's no time." To Owen, she said, "Close the door."

He pulled the inner airlock door closed and spun the wheel.

Maya and Cara affixed their helmets and Owen followed suit.

On the wall beside the outer airlock door, Maya once again searched for the emergency release and found it just in time. She turned the handle and opened the outer hatch just as faces filled the small window in the inner airlock door.

Owen felt the outside air from the storm tugging at his suit as he looked back and saw Darius Aldridge glaring at them through the small window, his mouth moving, the sound muted. The man reached down and tapped a panel by the door and his voice came over the suit speaker.

"You don't have to do this, Owen. Close the airlock, and we'll sort this out." Darius stared at Owen. "If you stay, you can be part of something."

Owen locked eyes with Maya. "I'm already part of something."

She reached down, grabbed one of the empty suits, and charged through the open airlock. Owen saw her plan then. He grabbed the other empty suit and followed Cara out.

He didn't know how long it would take Darius to get more suits to the airlock, but Owen knew he would, and when he did, someone would come after them.

CHAPTER SEVENTY

Outside the airlock, there was a set of concrete steps similar to the ones at the airlock where they had entered the Colony.

Maya raced up them, dragging the suit. The forest was dark, either from the time of night or the storm. The wind nudged her, and the trees shed their leaves in blankets as though they were weeping for what was to come.

Maya was about to activate her suit radio, but she felt Owen grab her arm. He shook his head and looked over at Cara, who saw the action too. Her stare at Maya and Owen showed confidence—her eyes silently reiterating what she had said in the airlock: *I have a plan.*

She bent down and gripped her lower leg and held it for a long moment.

Maya didn't understand what it meant. Owen didn't seem to either. His gaze drifted over to Maya, and she shrugged.

Without a word, Cara stood and motioned them away from the entrance to the airlock.

They ran single file through the woods, Cara leading the way, moving methodically but not hastily.

The suit Maya was wearing weighed her down, and so did the one she was dragging through the woods. Twice it caught on branches and logs, slowing her. But she tugged it free and kept barreling through the dark forest and storm.

At a clearing ahead, Maya spotted a shadow in the sky, moving right above the tree line.

The grass in the field was tall and swaying in the wind and rain. It parted as the object in the sky dove for the ground. To Maya's shock, it was a helicopter. It was unmarked, and her first instinct was to turn and run, but Cara charged toward it.

Owen followed her and Maya tried to keep pace, her muscles screaming from the exertion.

When they reached the helicopter, Maya realized there was no one inside—it was either operated remotely or autonomously.

Cara climbed into the cockpit, Maya and Owen into the back, and Cara hit a button on the dashboard, and the helicopter lifted off, shuddering as the wind battered it.

The motors overhead roared as the aircraft powered through the storm. Cara's hands danced over the digital display and the helo banked left, throwing Maya into Owen. He grabbed a handle next to the sliding door and wrapped an arm around her, holding tight.

What followed was a harrowing flight as the helicopter warred with the rain and wind, Cara constantly adjusting course to outrun it.

Finally, they broke through the edge of the storm into the clear night sky, the only sound that of the helicopter's blades chopping the air.

In the cockpit, Cara worked the controls feverishly. She was entering GPS coordinates for a new destination.

Maya was about to activate her radio and ask where they

were going, but Cara turned back and waved her off, the meaning clear: *avoid the radio.*

They flew on in silence. Owen searched the aircraft, for what, Maya wasn't sure. What he found was two emergency medkits, six large bottles of water, eight-round smoke canisters that could be used to provide cover for landing and pick-ups, and a pile of thick blankets. He used the blankets to dry off the suits—including the ones they were wearing and the two they had brought with them.

They were just passing the coast when he opened the sliding door and tossed the blankets into the wind. They drifted, blowing open and collapsing like ghosts set free to fall to the sea.

For a moment, Owen let the wind blow into the helicopter. Cara turned the handle and opened one of the front doors, creating a cross-breeze to air out the vessel.

Maya marveled at how well their small team now worked together—even without words.

Owen closed the sliding door, and Cara pulled the front door shut and removed her helmet.

Maya slipped her helmet off, and as soon as Owen had removed his, he said, "Cara, while I'm very thankful for that escape from the Colony, if you tell me you've had this helo on standby this whole time, I really will lose my mind."

Cara held up her hands. "I haven't. Or at least, I didn't know it would call a helo."

"What would call a helo?" Maya asked.

"I need to back up," Cara said. "There's something I need to tell you."

"Your secret," Owen said.

"Yes. What I told you on that boat was true: I was—am—an emergency room doctor. I was during the Fall. It was... carnage. It was clear to me we were in a war we were losing. I was recruited by the Alliance, by Parrish, to go into the Extinction Trials."

Maya could hardly process the words.

"They gave me a specific mission." Cara focused on Maya. "To keep you safe, Maya. To offer medical treatment if you needed it and help you recover your memories. They thought if you remembered your work, you could help them cure the Genesis Virus and turn the tide of the war. The plan was for me to get you to the Alliance after we woke up in the Trials."

"But there was just one problem," Owen said. "Maya didn't have her memories when she woke up."

"That's right," Cara said. "It seemed the Trials had failed. That's why I didn't use the beacon before."

"Beacon?" Maya asked.

"It's a device they implanted in my leg. It's what called the helo."

"How do you even know how to operate it?" Owen asked.

"It's the same model as the emergency air ambulances. I did a few rotations on them—we had to learn the manual control systems in case the computer had an error or satellite comms went down."

"So now you're completing your mission?" Owen asked. "Taking us to the Alliance?"

Cara stared at them.

Owen shook his head. "What do you think they'll do to us, Cara? They'll interrogate Maya. They'll probably dissect us to study the Mesh. They'll get the coordinates for that entrance to the Colony. And when they get the cure for GV, they'll organize their army, and the war will rage again."

"I know," Cara said quietly. "The helo was programmed to return to what I assume is an Alliance base or meeting point. I changed it."

"To what?" Owen asked. "We have the Mesh now. The Alliance has the storms. We only have so much oxygen. We're dead out here, one way or another. And so is any hope of finding Garden Station and finally ending this."

Maya placed a hand on his arm. "That's not necessarily true."

CHAPTER SEVENTY-ONE

In the helicopter, Cara and Owen stared at Maya as she drew the blank page out of her pocket. Owen thought it was the same page she had found in the envelope with her name on it at Station 17.

She unscrewed one of the bottles of water and poured it on the page.

Slowly, lines faded in, a simple illustration of rows of plants. A garden.

"What does it mean?" Cara whispered.

"It's the last clue," Owen said. "A garden. One only visible underwater."

"I don't understand," Cara said.

But Owen did. He smiled. "Well done, Maya. How did you know?"

"Luck, honestly. When we were entering the Colony, some liquid got on the page. I saw a glimpse of the image starting to form."

"Does somebody want to clue me in on what's happening here?"

"We had it right before," Owen said. "We had the location of Garden Station. It was encoded in those videos. We just got one thing wrong."

"Garden Station isn't on the surface," Maya said. "It's in the water."

Cara opened her mouth to speak, then shut it. Finally, she said, "I... did not see that coming."

"The question becomes what to do now," Owen said. "I think it's safe to say the Alliance can track this helo. And I have to wonder if the Union let us go a little too easily. I'm sure they can track us now that we have the Mesh. I bet the Union is hoping we'll lead them back to the Alliance. And I think it's a risk to lead them to Garden Station."

"Assuming," Maya said, "we can even get to the station. We're on a helo, not a submarine."

"It's a fair point," Owen said. "But I believe we have exactly what we need right here."

He pointed to the oxygen tanks connected to the suits. "Clearly, the environmental suits and controls are built for normal atmosphere. I doubt they'll work underwater, and I certainly don't want to risk it. But the tanks will. We just need to disconnect them from the suits and take them with us." He motioned to the cans of smoke. "We'll use these to help weigh us down."

Maya swallowed. "I don't like this plan."

Owen reached out and took her hand. "It's the best option we have."

Gently, he moved his thumb up to her forearm and pressed there. As Owen pulled her sweater back, lines began forming on her skin.

MeshOS Initiating.
41% Loaded.

"Do you feel any different?" Owen asked.

"No. Not yet."

"Did Darius tell you what the Mesh will do to you?"

"Yeah." Maya glanced out at the sea. "I know time is running out for me, Owen. But what if the station is too far down? As in only accessible by submarine? What if we keep falling in the sea and get crushed by the pressure? And what if the coordinates aren't exact? We'll be walking around on the ocean floor—or more likely a ledge with survivable pressure—until our oxygen runs out."

"It's a risk," Owen said. "To be exact, it's a leap of faith. I've done a few of those—out of burning buildings. It's how I saved your sister. And I think we have to take this one. For everyone's sake."

Maya nodded and squeezed his hand. "Okay."

"The only problem I see," Owen said, "is that even if we survive, the Alliance and the Union will likely come after us. They'll find Garden Station."

In the cockpit, Cara held up her hands. "I have a solution to that." She nodded to the medkits. "The strange thing, the thing I just realized, is how completely we fit together. This can't be an accident. It has to be by design."

"What are you talking about?"

"I have a role to play here," Cara said. "Before, I thought it was to get Maya to the Alliance and cure the Genesis Virus. Now, I see the truth—the bigger picture. I know what I have to do."

Cara told them her plan then, and Owen had to admit, it was brilliant, one he couldn't have seen himself.

And it just might work.

CHAPTER SEVENTY-TWO

Maya winced as the needle entered her arm. The helicopter's subtle movement didn't help matters.

Cara drew the blood into one of the tubes, then capped it and drew another tubeful. There was a pile of blood-filled tubes on the floor of the helo now. Owen was busying himself with taping the tubes to the cans of smoke and other detachable heavy objects in the helicopter, readying them to be deployed.

Their plan made a big assumption: that the Mesh was in the bloodstream. They knew it was in the brain fluid, and the Mesh could obviously change the pigment of the skin on their forearm, so it served to reason that the technology flowed in the bloodstream. They were betting their lives on it.

Cara had programmed a series of coordinates into the helicopter's nav system. At the first stop, she opened the cockpit door and dropped a canister with two tubes of blood tied to it—one from Maya and one from Owen.

At the next three stops, she did the same.

At the fourth stop, the helicopter hovered near the water, and she turned back to Maya and Owen, each of whom had oxygen tanks between their legs and weights tied around their waists.

To Maya's relief, the tanks that connected to the suits had a mouthpiece at the port—just in case they needed to be disconnected and used without the suits in an emergency. And this was that emergency.

"You could come with us," Owen said to Cara.

She smiled and shook her head once. "We all know I can't. This is the only way."

"If we find help down there," Maya said, "we'll come for you."

Cara nodded. "I know you will. But I'm pretty sure this is goodbye. And I'm okay with that. As I said before, I think this is what I was meant to do."

"We'll never forget you, Cara. Or what you did here," Owen said.

"Likewise," Cara replied. She nodded to the sliding door. "You better get going. If the stop is longer than the others, they might get suspicious."

Maya glanced out the window, then pulled back the arm of her sweater one last time and pressed her thumb into her forearm, and waited as the lines and words formed there.

```
MeshOS Initiating.
48% Loaded.
```

She hoped she had enough time left to reach Garden Station—if it was down there.

Owen pulled the door open and leaned out over the water, studying the waves below. He glanced back at Maya, and she gave him a firm nod.

He stepped out onto the helicopter's rail, still holding the oxygen tank, and slipped the mouthpiece between his teeth. His next step was out over the water, and he plunged down.

Maya ventured out onto the rail, dragging her oxygen tank, and then she was following him, down toward the water and what she hoped would be salvation for the entire human race.

CHAPTER SEVENTY-THREE

Cara watched as Owen and Maya disappeared into the ocean, leaving a small wake where they had entered, like a small scar on the vast sea that quickly healed.

In a way, she felt like she had countless times in the operating room after closing an incision. The operation—or at least her part—was done. Now, it was on the patient to survive or perish. Like she had then, she pinned all her hopes on their survival. She wished there was more she could do, but sometimes life required one to have faith and wait and do the only thing you could do.

For her, that was entering the coordinates of the next helicopter stop. She typed them into the helicopter's nav system and held on as it banked to the right. On the horizon, a storm was forming, no doubt one of the deadly amalgamations of wind and rain that was chasing the Mesh inside her body. It would catch her soon, but not, she thought, before she had a chance to play her role.

At the next stop, she once again opened the cockpit door and dropped the weighted tubes. She did that six more times before entering the coordinates she had memorized.

In a way, she was returning to where it had all begun—or at least, their first destination after the station.

Soon, the massive container ship loomed on the horizon. It grew larger with each passing moment—and so did the storm chasing her.

She set the helicopter down on the stack of metal containers and ran across the columns to the ship's control tower. At the rickety staircase, she ascended until she reached the bridge. There, she found a pair of binoculars and walked to the wide windows, and brought them to her eyes.

In the distance, she saw the storm. To the left, she saw a fleet of helicopters. They were different from the Union aircraft sitting atop the containers. There was no doubt in Cara's mind whose squadron it was: the Union. They couldn't allow the Alliance to recover Maya.

The two final tubes in Cara's pocket would lead them here. And they would turn the vessel upside down looking for Maya—or what they thought was Maya.

Cara panned the binoculars to the left and saw exactly what she was hoping for: another fleet of helicopters. They were exactly like the ones sitting on the container ship. The Alliance had sent their own force.

Soon, the two fleets would arrive at the ship and the battle would begin.

Cara exited onto the rickety staircase, descended into the bowels of the ship, and began searching out a hiding place she knew would likely become her final resting place.

CHAPTER SEVENTY-FOUR

Maya hugged the oxygen tank as the weights tied around her pulled her deeper into the ocean. She didn't know how much time had passed. And worse, there was nothing she could do except hold on and wait.

Owen had been right: this truly was a leap of faith.

As the sea above grew darker and she moved closer to the floor of the ocean, her every instinct told her to reach down and release the pieces of metal tied around her waist, inhale one last deep breath from the tank, and kick with all her might toward the surface. It took every ounce of her willpower to overcome her mind's survival instinct, to trust the plan, and bet it all on Garden Station being down there.

If it wasn't, she was finished. So was Owen. They were rapidly passing the point of no return, where they couldn't return to the surface. And besides, even if they did, what then? They'd be afloat, waiting for rescue—and by whom? The truth was, there was no safe place for them in the world anymore, a world constantly at war with no hope of compromise.

In a way, she felt as though she were returning to the beginning, to Station 17, where they had been trapped with limited options, where going forward was the only hope of survival. That's what she was doing now: going forward. Or down, to be exact.

She knew the ocean was deep this far from the shore—or at least, it had been in the world before. She didn't know exactly where they were. Was it possible that Garden Station had been above the sea before the Fall and that the rise in the water level had covered it?

It seemed that Station 17 had been in the mountains before and was an island now. If Garden Station was down there—and it was on a ridge or shelf near the surface—it would be her only hope of survival.

Most of all, she wished she could see Owen, reach out, and hold his hand as they faced their fate together. Of all the things she had found in the world after the Fall, he was the most remarkable. He had awakened something inside of her she'd thought long dead. That was one of the reasons she clung to life so tightly, as hard as she was holding the oxygen tank as the darkness around her became complete.

CHAPTER SEVENTY-FIVE

Owen didn't know how long he had been falling. A long time. Possibly too long. He felt the pressure growing, pressing into him, crushing him.

It reminded him of the head of a burning building—growing hotter, taking more of the air, closing in.

He should have said more to Maya. He should have said what he really felt, told her what she meant to him. If this was the end, that would be his greatest regret.

He was so lost in his thoughts that he was startled when his feet sank into a soft bed of silt.

He wanted to throw his head back and laugh with joy, he was so happy, but he clamped tight onto the oxygen tank. How much had he used during the descent? There was no way to know without the suit.

He needed to take stock of his surroundings. He let the oxygen tank drop beside him, and he spun around, searching.

Visibility was minimal, but in the short distance he could make out with the naked eye, he didn't see anything that might have been Garden Station. Or trees. Or the ruins of a city. He seemed to be in something quite like a desert on the floor of the sea.

He released one of the weights and paused to see if he floated upward. He kept untying them until there was a slight lift, one he could manage easily by hanging on to the tank resting beside him. He would have to drag it, and having the other weight gone would help.

He reached into his pocket and drew out the flashlight from the helicopter's emergency kit. Now was another moment of truth. He clicked it on and was relieved when it shone into the murky darkness, a beam carving into the abyss.

Again, he spun, but there was no sign of Maya. They had entered the water at about the same time and roughly in the same spot, but Owen wasn't worried. Not yet, anyway. He had expected himself to sink faster than her.

He waited, shining the flashlight back and forth, the beam like that of a lighthouse on the ocean floor.

He smiled when he saw Maya's light lance out at his. He dragged the tank across the ocean floor, his feet sinking with each step. The effort was taxing, especially after the run from the Colony through the woods, but he trudged forward, knowing there were no seconds he could waste.

When he reached her, Owen could tell Maya was smiling around the mouthpiece. There were lines at the edges of her eyes, and her lips were curled beyond the nozzle.

He couldn't take the line from his mouth, so he walked closer to her, leaned in, and pressed his forehead to hers. She pressed back. It wasn't a kiss. Or a hug. But it was sort of perfect for this moment, on the bottom of the sea in a ruined world, as if they were the only two people left, sharing a love that needed no words and had a language all its own.

When he released the gesture, she stared at him, and he stared at her, and he knew precisely what she was thinking: *Let's finish this—together, right now.*

He shined the light all the way around them. He saw only murky darkness, and no clear path to follow. But Owen had been in this situation with Maya before. And they had always found their way. Now they just had to do it again, one last time.

CHAPTER SEVENTY-SIX

Outside the boat, Cara heard gunfire and missiles detonating. A crash came soon after—what she thought was a fallen helicopter crashing into the ship's deck. She heard a giant splash in the sea, perhaps one or more containers spilling from the stacks.

The firing grew faster then, the explosions closer together. The ship shook, and she wound her way to the ship's engine and crouched down.

The ocean floor was a wilderness—barren, dark, and unending. Maya and Owen marched across it, doing the only thing they could: shining their lights left and right and putting one foot in front of the other. Maya felt almost like an explorer in an alien world.

She wasn't sure how long they had walked, but with each step, she knew their oxygen was depleting. There wasn't a way to get more. They would either find shelter, or it would all end here.

Up ahead, her flashlight raked over a lump in the sea—a very human-sized lump. She reached over, nudged Owen, and focused the beam of her flashlight on it.

He stopped and stared at it a moment, and then he marched to the small protrusion in the seabed and bent and brushed the mud and sediment away.

It was a person, and they were wearing a diving suit. Owen methodically uncovered the torso and helmet, and Maya shined her light through the glass faceplate at the dead man's face. What stopped her cold was the small bit of shirt she could see: it was a black ribbed sweater, the same kind she had been given when she woke up in Station 17.

Owen focused on the man's suit and seemed to conclude that his oxygen had depleted. That was an unnerving thought to Maya. In fact, seeing the dead man was, in a way, the sum of her fears brought to life. It told her that they weren't the first to seek out Garden Station down here. And at least one person had died searching. Was there actually nothing down here?

She would have given anything to be able to talk to Owen then, to at least voice her fears. He glanced up at her, and in his eyes, she saw her own thoughts reflected: *There's nothing to do but keep going.*

And so, they did, trekking across the seafloor, searching. They came across another body lying in the sediment. This one was wearing a slightly different kind of diving suit—more form-fitting with large goggles. Maya wondered if this individual was from either the Union or the Alliance.

They marched on, Maya's fear growing now. Her legs were tiring too.

Up ahead, the beam of her flashlight raked over a large dark object perhaps a little taller than she was. It was oblong, and it was connected to an even larger object, which towered at least four times her height.

Owen quickened his pace and Maya rushed to keep up. When they reached the smaller object, Maya realized it was a submersible. The larger object seemed to have no end—when Maya shined her flashlight to the left and right, it simply kept going like a giant building rising from the seafloor.

A sense of pride surged through Maya. She had been right: there was something down here. Would it be their salvation? Or another dead end?

Owen rounded the submersible and took a few paces back, shining his flashlight along the length of it. The beam settled on a hatch at the top, which stood open. Moving slowly, he traced his light across the vessel until he found a vertical ladder of footholds that led to the hatch.

Using hand motions, he urged Maya to stay but shine her light on the ladder as he waded forward and climbed up it, dragging the oxygen tank with him, his flashlight off.

At the top of the submersible, he once again activated his flashlight and moved to the hatch and peered inside. He studied whatever he saw for a long moment, then motioned for Maya to climb the ladder.

He held his light on the rungs as she ascended, and on top of the submersible, she joined him in glancing down through the hatch at the cramped compartment with a pile of dirt around the open hatch. Dark computer screens covered the walls, and there was no sign of the crew. Maya wondered if one of the bodies they had seen had come from the vessel. If so, it meant this might, in fact, be a dead end.

Owen switched off his light and lifted his oxygen tank into the hatch, and then he descended, shining his light up for Maya when he had reached the inside of the submersible.

When she was through the airlock, she shined her light over the interior of the vessel. It looked like some sort of small research submersible, perhaps one launched from a larger ship.

At the end of the vessel was another hatch that also stood open. Pulling his tank with him, Owen paddled and pushed toward it, Maya following close behind.

The submersible had clearly docked with this facility—or ship—here on the seafloor. What they saw beyond the hatch was what looked like an outer door to the massive creation. There was a small, oblong window, and when Owen shined his light into it, Maya saw only an inner airlock that was empty.

Running her flashlight across the outer wall, Maya saw no handle for the airlock door, no wheel to spin, and no emergency release lever. There was, however, a number pad.

Owen cocked his head as he studied it. Maya could also see the wheels turning in his head. She hoped he had figured it out, because as they stood in the submersible, she felt oxygen in her line growing thin.

CHAPTER SEVENTY-SEVEN

At the number pad on the airlock, Owen typed the GPS coordinates of the container ship. The code made sense to him—it was proof that whoever was entering had come through the waypoint at sea and had followed ARC's other directions.

The door opened with a pop and swung inward. Luckily, the chamber beyond was filled with water, allowing Owen and Maya to drift inside with ease instead of being forced in with a wave of water.

They had found the large structure here on the seafloor in just the nick of time—Owen's oxygen tank was practically empty.

He closed the door and waited as the water drained from the chamber. And as it did, he studied the walls and design. It was, to his great relief, very ARC-like: white paint, tubing above with nozzles, benches beneath alcoves that were empty but could hold suits, and an inner airlock door ahead with a small window that revealed only darkness beyond.

When the water was gone, Maya let her tank drop to the floor as she took a deep breath and began shivering. Owen wrapped his arms around her and pulled her tight, letting his body heat infuse into hers.

The nozzles above hissed and sprayed a milky-white liquid that, unfortunately, was frigid. Owen hoped there were blankets beyond the inner airlock.

It opened with a swooshing sound and Owen felt only more cold air rushing out. If anyone lived here, they liked it cold. He didn't voice it, but he counted the temperature down here as a bad sign.

Maya peered up at him, a smile on her face despite her shaking.

"We made it," she whispered.

"Thanks to you."

She shook her head. "Thanks to all of us. You. Cara. Alister. Will."

Owen released her from the hug, and he took Maya's hand as they stepped through the inner airlock door into a narrow corridor with gray metal walls, floor, and ceiling. Beady lights overhead snapped on as he walked forward.

The corridor ended in a room that was roughly the size of one of the observation rooms from Station 17. And what Owen saw there was just as strange as that first meeting in the observation room: three bodies lay on the floor, unmoving. Ahead was a single locked door. There was no window, no keypad, and no handle.

In the crew quarters of the container ship, Cara found an empty bunk room and lay down on the bottom bunk. It was fitting. The narrow bed and small room reminded her of the on-call room where Parrish had first recruited her to the Extinction Trials. It was a sort of thematic end to the beginning of it all.

Outside, the fighting raged. Gunfire pelted the ship and metal containers, dinging the outer walls of the crew quarters. Explosions cried out overhead, and the crashing of aircraft into the ship got louder by the moment.

Cara closed her eyes and listened, knowing sleep wouldn't come. Her mind knew what was next.

She clutched the tubes of Owen's and Maya's blood to her chest and slowed her breathing. She barely felt a thing when the floor above came crashing down on her.

CHAPTER SEVENTY-EIGHT

Despite the cold around her, Maya felt sweat breaking out on the hand Owen was holding. He gave her a gentle squeeze, then released her and moved to the closest body lying by the door directly ahead. It was a woman, and she was wearing a diving suit. She had taken her helmet off, which lay nearby.

From what she saw, Maya didn't know how long the woman had been dead. She wondered if this place had preserved the body somehow.

Moving quickly, Maya and Owen surveyed the other bodies. There were clues as to who the people were. Two were wearing the ribbed sweaters like the one Maya had worn after waking in Station 17. They had been in the Extinction Trials. They had made it here. Just like her. And no farther. That sent a spike of fear through her.

Was this her end? If so, it would be with Owen. That was something. They had tried. Given it all they had. What more could a person do?

She pulled back the sleeve of the soaking wet sweater she was wearing and pressed her thumb into her forearm, where words appeared.

```
MeshOS Initiating.
54% Loaded.
```

As she pulled the sleeve back down, Maya realized how badly she wanted to get out of the damp, frigid clothes. Her only option was to take clothes from the dead, and she was just about to raise the morality of that when the door ahead opened.

Owen moved between her and the door, his hands held out at the ready.

A faint white light oozed into the room and two figures stepped through the opening. They were people Maya knew.

One was a mirror image of Will. The other looked like Bryce, the proctor from Station 17.

"Hello, Maya. Hello, Owen," the Will clone said.

Maya's eyes had adjusted to the light now, and behind the two androids, she saw stacks of glass tubes similar to the chambers from Station 17. They stretched back as far as she could see, like rows in a field with no end. They were filled with human bodies, as though waiting to be harvested and released into a world that was ready to grow again.

"Congratulations," the Bryce clone said. "You have reached the end of the Extinction Trials."

CHAPTER SEVENTY-NINE

For a long moment, Owen and Maya stared at the two androids.

"We've been waiting a very, very long time for you," the clone of Will said.

"First things first," Owen said. "What should we call you?"

"The names you know are fine. Bryce and Will. We saw and heard everything you experienced."

A million questions swirled in Owen's mind. He addressed the biggest one of all first. "How could you see everything?"

"The Fall was a long time ago. Our technology has advanced quite a bit since then."

"If that's true, why haven't you saved the world?" Owen asked.

"The answer is obvious," Will said.

"Not to me."

"Yes. It is. You recognize patterns, Owen. It's what your brain is genetically wired to do. You already know the truth."

Owen studied the two proctors. When he considered it closely, the truth *was* obvious to him. But it was one he hadn't even entertained until he had seen the bodies lying in the sea and in the corridor outside—the breadcrumbs along this deadly path. He said the truth he was fairly certain of:

"You have a cure for the Genesis Virus."

"Yes," Will said. "We've had it for quite some time."

"And the storms," Owen said.

"Also true. We have found the keys to enable humanity to survive in this ruined world—biologically."

"Then why are we here?" Owen asked. "Why haven't you released the humans you have? If you're not ready to repopulate the world, why did you let us in now? Why did you leave so many to die out there in that corridor—and across this ruined world?"

Will cocked his head. "You already know. You see the pattern."

"We're different from the other cohorts."

"Yes."

"We're smarter."

"No. Smarter people than you have failed to reach this chamber. What you have is something far more important. Do you remember what Bryce told you at the beginning, in that observation room in Station 17?"

Owen thought back to that moment in Observation Room Two. "Yes. He said that the Trials were an attempt to find a cohort that can survive in the world after the Change—that whatever those differences were, they were the key to saving what's left of the human race."

Will took a step deeper into the room that held the rows of glass chambers. "We were given a simple task: to alter these survivors so that they could restart the human race. Simple tasks are not always easy tasks. Ours certainly wasn't. We had two tools at our disposal. One: Trials participants like yourselves. And two: we had the Revelation program."

"The big data modeling project our Will described to us."

"Correct. With Revelation, we were able to simulate the world after the Trials—a world in which we released the survivors with a cure for the Genesis Virus and modifications to survive the storms."

"Interesting," Owen whispered.

"Do you know what our simulations revealed?"

"I'm assuming they failed."

"Every time," Will said. "The conclusion was quite clear: the reason the world fell wasn't the Change—or the Mesh or the Genesis Virus or the Alliance or the Union. It wasn't biology or technology or the environment. It was something far more fundamental. Revelation showed us that. And your arrival here has confirmed it. Do you know what the root cause of humanity's Fall was?"

"It's how we're different from the other cohort—Alister's cohort."

"Yes, Owen."

"They betrayed each other. We didn't."

"That's a part of it. What's at the root?"

"Our values. That's how we're different."

"Precisely."

"What are you saying?" Maya asked. "That we succeeded in the Trials because... of our beliefs?"

"That's correct. In a word, you care. For each other. And for strangers. For the future. Caring isn't always the easiest thing to do. Indeed, those who don't care are often happier— unburdened by what they encounter in life. But not you all. You believed in each other. You took the time to get to know each other, to understand each other. And you cared for one another. Alister risked losing everything he loved when he helped you escape. Cara risked her own life. Time and again, you put yourselves at risk for each other. The other cohorts who arrived did so at the expense of their fellow participants—not in sacrifice and service."

Bryce held out his hands. "We're still analyzing the data from your Trial, but we believe the root breakthrough is a simple perspective: treating others the way you wish to be treated. Time will reveal further nuances."

"What do you plan to do with these... revelations?" Owen asked.

"This code that you've demonstrated is the key to creating a human race that can survive long-term—with a large population. As such, it is the true cure to what ailed your species. It will be administered like any other treatment."

"How?"

"These values that are the key to humanity's survival will be embedded in the psyche of all survivors. They will operate at a fundamental level, manifesting themselves in belief systems and mythologies that will be created over and over again. The human we release will be biologically programmed to recognize these stories and beliefs and to gravitate to them. Indeed, we believe this is not something we have discovered, but rather a phenomenon that is a component of a far greater force at work, one that predates humanity, one that operates on a grand scale we don't yet understand."

Maya squinted at the proctors. "What about the people out there—the Union and Alliance citizens?"

The proctors paused, as if communicating wirelessly with each other, deciding how much to say.

"Right now," Will said, "a final battle is raging at the container ship you found. Our models indicate that casualties will be heavy. The two combatants haven't had an opportunity like this since the Fall: an opening to end the war. They have both pushed all their forces forward. They will fight to the end, until the ship sinks."

"Can you stop it?"

"No. This was always how the Change War was going to end."

"What will you do next?" Maya asked.

"We will send proctors to the Alliance and the Union—specifically to the Colony—to collect the remaining survivors. Those populations are in terminal decline. We'll bring them back to Garden Station."

"Why not retake the world?" Owen asked.

"Consider what you didn't see out there."

"Animals."

"Correct. The world out there is ruined in more ways than you know."

"But you can fix it," Owen said.

"No. We can't. There are limits to what we can achieve. We will have to wait and see if this world can heal itself. If not... we have an alternative plan."

"What does that mean?" Owen asked.

When the proctor told him the plan, Owen felt his legs go weak. It was unthinkable.

"How can you be sure?" Owen asked.

"Revelation models confirm it."

Owen felt Maya squeeze his hand. Like him, she was scared, but she was facing the news with a brave face.

"What will happen to us?" Maya asked. "To Owen and me?"

"Once again, you have a role to play in the new world, a

role similar to the role we played in this one."

"You want us to be proctors? For trials?" Owen asked.

"Of a sort," Will replied. When he had finished telling them what ARC was proposing, Owen looked over at Maya, who was staring at him.

She nodded once, a silent confirmation.

"Our answer is yes," Owen said. "What now?"

"I believe," Will said, "that each of you has two final questions you want to ask us. For both of you, they are the same two questions."

Owen swallowed hard, knowing what those two questions were and almost dreading the answers. He glanced at Maya and whispered, "You first."

"Is my family alive?" she asked. "Are they here?"

Bryce turned and led them deeper into the cavernous room to a glass chamber that held a sleeping girl with her eyes closed, a girl Owen had seen once before in his life, lying on a bed in the Oasis Park Building, on the eleventh floor, in unit 1107. On that morning, she had looked much the same as she did now: lying peacefully on her bed, eyes closed. What Owen learned later, in Station 17, was that the girl that he had carried out of that burning building was Maya's sister. Since he had awakened after the Fall, he had never stopped wondering what had happened to her.

Joy overwhelmed him. He felt Maya slip her hand in his and squeeze. He looked over at her as a single tear rolled down her face. Before the Mesh, he would have assumed she was upset. She smiled and he knew the truth—he could almost feel how elated she was. And he felt it too. He and Maya had saved her.

Before the Fall, Owen had jumped out of that burning

building alone in a desperate attempt to save the girl.

Now, here at the end, he and Maya had jumped together, into the sea, hoping to save her and every last human left alive. They had risked it all. And together, they had come through it and triumphed. But Owen sensed that, like so many things in life, that triumph wasn't complete. What he didn't see told the story of what they had lost forever. And he knew what Maya's next question would be.

Her voice was strained and heavy with emotion when she spoke. "My mother..."

"Unfortunately," Will said, "we were not able to recover her."

Maya swallowed and nodded slowly, but that was all the response she could manage.

Owen felt her sorrow so completely that he couldn't bring himself to ask about his own mother, though he wanted to so badly.

Will spared him. He walked across the aisle to another chamber, and what Owen saw there burst his heart. His mother lay in the glass tube, eyes closed, resting peacefully.

"The facility where she lived," Will said, "had a data management and archival contract with ARC Technologies. She was one of many we were able to recover."

Owen felt Maya's arm wrap around him and squeeze.

"Thank you," he whispered.

"What will become of them?" Maya asked. "Will they... be released with the others?"

"No," Will said. "They will emerge with you, when the time is right. We've done the simulations. It's better if you're not alone. Family—the one you're born into and the one like you all formed on your journey here—is important.

It's one of the most powerful factors we encountered in our simulations."

Owen gazed down at his mother. Since Station 17, he had wondered if that morning before the Fall would be the last time he ever saw her. He had almost given up hope of ever seeing her again. Knowing he would have more time with her and that she would be there to talk with him, to listen and advise him, steeled his resolve for what he knew he had to do. She had always been his anchor in the world—that one constant he could count on—and he sensed that he would need her more than ever in the new world.

"And now," Will said, "please ask your final question. The other question that applies to both of you."

"The Mesh," Maya said. "Can you remove it?"

"Yes," Bryce replied. "For both of you."

Owen opened his mouth to speak, but Will beat him to it. "We know about your limitation, Owen. And we know the Mesh fixed it. We can too. And we will. When you wake in the new world, you'll be free of the Mesh, but you'll still have what it gave you."

Without another word, Will and Bryce marched deeper into the vast room. At two empty chambers, they stopped and motioned for Owen and Maya to enter.

As Owen settled into the tube, he looked over at Maya and smiled. She smiled back, a somber, grateful smile that said all the things he felt.

Will placed a hand on the glass dome above Owen's chamber. "And now, it ends as it began, and begins again as it did before."

"How long will we sleep?" Maya asked.

"A very, very... very long time," Will said.

PART V

THE NEW WORLD

CHAPTER EIGHTY

The glass chamber opened with a loud pop. Maya opened her eyes, but her eyelids were heavy and clung together. She felt a warm hand on her shoulder, gripping her gently. It was a touch she had felt once before—the last time she had awoken in a chamber.

She tried again, and this time, her eyes opened. She peered up and saw Owen standing over her, smiling. Bryce and Will stood behind him, waiting.

Owen helped her up and into the black ribbed sweater and pants that were an exact match to the clothes she had donned after her last awakening.

She smiled at Will. "I see you all haven't made any wardrobe changes while we were out."

Will sighed theatrically. "Doctor Young, we're apocalyptic androids, not fashion innovators."

Maya was so surprised at the joke, she laughed out loud. "You've apparently become funny while we were sleeping."

Will shrugged. "When faced with a near eternity of waiting, self-improvement—within the confines of my programming—became my only refuge."

"I see. And how much time has passed?"

"The numbers would have no meaning. It's better if we show you. Your time has come, and the new world is waiting."

Maya focused on the vast space then and realized that the glass chambers were all empty.

"So. It's started."

"It started a long time ago," Will said. "Our role was to help them stand again. You will help them fly. Our shift has ended. Yours begins now."

He and Bryce led Owen and Maya out of the sprawling room and into the corridor that was now clean, the bodies of the fallen Extinction Trials participants gone.

"Wait," Maya said. "Our family members—where are they?"

"They're waiting for you," Will said. "We've prepared everything you need."

At the airlock, there were no environmental suits, only thick coats and pants, and boots with metal teeth.

They dressed in the cold-weather gear, and when the airlock opened, Maya expected to see a submarine waiting on the other side. What she saw was open sky—an absolutely spotless, clear sky, more blue than any she had ever seen.

The ground was even more surprising. It was covered in ice and snow as far as she could see—an endless expanse of white that took her breath away. And when she did breathe out, it drifted in puffs of steam.

"Where are we?"

"At the planet's south pole," Bryce said. He crunched forward then, across the sea of ice, Owen, Maya, and Will following.

They walked in silence, the biting cold wind whipping

at them. Maya couldn't help but notice that she felt a little heavier, her gait more labored, and she tired more quickly.

Ahead, where the ice met the sea, a small boat waited. It reminded Maya of the craft they had found on the island that held Station 17, except this boat didn't have any computerized components. It was like something from a different time.

They boarded, and Maya and Owen went below decks where they found Owen's mother and Maya's sister resting in the largest stateroom. Each had a small white device attached to their temple. Maya assumed the small devices were keeping them asleep—or in a stasis-like coma.

They returned to the deck where Will and Bryce were waiting.

"How long will the voyage be?" Owen asked.

"Quite some time," Will replied. "Which is good. There is much we need to tell you. This new world is different in ways you can't imagine."

CHAPTER EIGHTY-ONE

The boat sailed across the open sea, never sighting land or any other vessels.

During the day, Maya sat in the lounge with Owen, talking and playing cards, and sometimes, just holding each other as they listened to the ship's engines and watched the waves crest and the sea life jump into the air and splash back down.

At night, they listened as Will and Bryce educated them on the world that was waiting for them—and what they had to do. When the talks were done, they retreated below decks into a stateroom where they did what she had wanted to do on the small vessel they had found outside of Station 17.

She couldn't remember ever being happier.

She felt slightly guilt at the fact that she didn't want the voyage to end. But she knew it must. She and Owen had a role to play here. For them, the Extinction Trials weren't over.

She had lost track of the days when Owen spotted land. He was standing in the cockpit, peering out with binoculars.

He handed them to her, and her jaw dropped at what she saw. To the right, a city spread out along the coast. It was situated at the edge of a peninsula, and across from it was another peninsula, one that was barren and undeveloped, with mountainous terrain covered in shrubs. But it was the sprawling creation that stretched between the two peninsulas that took her breath away. The two landmasses were joined by the largest bridge Maya had ever seen. It was red with two towers and suspension lines reaching down. Behind the boat, the sun was setting, casting a golden glow across the red bridge and lighting the fog that was drifting in from the sea.

"It's the longest suspension bridge in the world—by main span length," Will said. "At least for now."

Cars crept across the massive structure as the boat floated closer and then under it.

A wide, deep bay spread out beyond the bridge. Ahead, there were three islands: a large one to the left, a small one dead ahead, and a slightly larger island to the right, connected to the mainland and the peninsula by two bridges.

Owen pointed toward the small island. "What's that?"

"It was formerly a military base," Will said. "It's a prison now."

They proceeded slowly through the bay, Maya taking it all in. It was truly a spectacular city. She marveled at this small sliver of what humanity had built while she and Owen had slept.

They docked the boat at a marina, and the four of them went below decks.

"Their language is different," Will said. "But it won't be a problem. We've implanted the vocabulary in your minds already, so you'll be conversant, but I should warn you, this world is very different from the one you left. It will take some getting used to."

"We understand," Owen said.

"Their clothes are also different," Will said as he set two outfits on the bed.

Maya eyed hers before picking it up. "What is this?"

"They call it a skirt."

"It's just... open at the bottom?"

"Yes."

"Strange."

When they were dressed, they loaded their supplies into a van Will and Bryce had left in the marina parking lot. It was night by the time they used a ramp and wheelchair to move Maya's sister and Owen's mother from the boat into the van.

They drove through the city then, Owen and Maya sitting by the windows, taking in every detail. The terrain was hilly, and the streets were crowded. What Maya saw surprised her and, at times, broke her heart. In alleyways, she saw homeless people huddling together to stay warm. On street corners, prostitutes loitered and posed and called into the night. In the shadows, drug dealers whispered and handed off small packages to people passing by.

She also saw acts that restored her faith in humanity. Soup kitchens and homeless shelters and ambulances charging into the night to save lives when seconds counted.

At the apartment Will and Bryce had rented, they unloaded the supplies and brought Owen's mother and Maya's sister inside.

In the living room, Will and Bryce stood before Owen and Maya.

"This is where we depart," Will said.

"What will you do?" Maya asked.

"We will take the boat back to Garden Station and destroy it. Now is the time. If we wait, they might find it. They are already developing more advanced satellite technology. We've delayed as long as we can."

"Tell us about the past," Owen said. "When you released the survivors."

Will studied them for a moment. "It was difficult at first. As we told you, we weren't sure the planet would recover from the damage that occurred during the Change War. We waited, hoping it would heal itself. But it only got worse. Our models confirmed that the surface would never again be habitable for humans. As such, we proceeded with our backup plan. In your time, this world was a volcanic wasteland. The atmosphere then was low in oxygen. Frozen methane deposits on the seafloor were melting and rising up into the air. We modeled the changes using Revelation. We knew this world would be habitable for you—eventually. This planet has a slightly different atmosphere and stronger gravity, but it's easily within acceptable parameters. From a scientific standpoint, it's almost a sister to our world, one simply a few years younger. Well, younger on a geological timescale. It was a long wait, but as we are machines, time is of no concern to us."

"What did you do when you arrived?" Maya asked.

"We used a modified version of the Genesis Virus to erase the survivors' memories and embed the code of ethics deep in their psyche. They mingled with the emerging primate species on the planet, and, as expected, they flourished. There were never this many of you in the world before."

"I don't mean to be a critic," Owen said, "but I just have to say, based on what I saw out there, things aren't going that great. No offense."

"It looks that way," Will said, "but what you saw are just your species' growing pains. They will ease in time. In the long run, the outcome will be as we expect. We have a high degree of certainty."

"But not absolute certainty," Owen said. "Hence, why we're here."

Will nodded. "Correct. It would be irresponsible to ignore the unexpected—variables that can't be anticipated and factored in. You will play the role we once did: as a sort of insurance policy, in case humanity once again loses its way."

"But you had all the resources of ARC Technologies, a massive company. We're two people, starting from scratch."

"You have three very important assets," Will said. He paced to the window and looked out. "First, you know the future, the broad arc of the human race. Don't underestimate that. Second, and perhaps most importantly, you have each other. The two of you saved the world before—when so many others failed. And lastly, you have capital."

Owen shrugged. "What are you talking about? We don't have any capital."

Bryce placed a small bag on the table. "A parting gift."

Owen reached out and pulled the string and dumped the contents on the table: a hundred small rocks, clear and sparkly.

"Diamonds?" Maya asked.

"Yes. They hold great value in this world."

"You're joking," Maya said.

"I'm not."

"For lasers? They were everywhere in the old world," Owen said.

"True. But here, this new society uses them as decoration, to show importance and status and affinity for each other."

Owen picked one up and held it in the sunlight. "I don't get it."

"What you hold will give you what you need. Think about it: there are three ways to control the future. You can either create it, inspire it, or facilitate it. What you hold is key to facilitating it."

Owen smiled as he turned the diamond in his fingers. "Okay. Now I get it."

The next morning, Maya and Owen dressed and went to a jeweler, where they sold the first of the diamonds.

Back at the apartment, they sat in the living room and talked at length about the future.

"Do you think," Maya said, "that we're in over our heads?"

Owen smiled. "Probably. Definitely. But we have been since the beginning of the Extinction Trials."

"What do you want to do?"

"I've been thinking about that. And the more I think about it, the more certain I am about what we have to build."

"What's that?"

"The thing that saved us."

"Which is?"

"An Escape Hatch."

CHAPTER EIGHTY-TWO

After selling more diamonds, Owen secured a spot for his mother at a nearby assisted living facility. It was similar to the one she had known in the world before, but Owen still worried about how well she would adapt to her new environment.

That thought ran through his mind as he removed the white block from her temple.

Slowly, she opened her eyes and looked around at the light-filled bedroom in the apartment.

"Owen?"

He reached out and took her hand in his. "I'm here, Mom."

"What happened?"

"There was a war. A long one. And there are a few other things I need to tell you."

When he was done explaining what had happened, he expected his mother to be overwhelmed, for her to ask him a thousand questions. Neither of those things happened. She merely smiled at him, a knowing, contented smile, and said, "It's wild. Truly. But it's the way of the world."

"What is?"

"Change. Every generation grows up in a world a little different than their parents. For some generations, there's more change than others. For some generations, the future seems like science fiction. And then their children end up living something that resembles the stories that no one believed in their own time. That's the way of the world. Some changes are for the better. Some for the worse. But always change." She studied him a moment. "But those changes don't interest me much. It's the change in you that interests me."

Owen raised his eyebrows.

"You seem happy."

"I am."

"Care to elaborate?"

Owen smiled. "I met someone. Someone very important to me."

"I thought so." His mother squeezed his hand and stared out the window. "What about your job? Have you found something new yet?"

"I guess you could say a new job found me."

"It happens that way a lot of times. What sort of work?"

"I'm in insurance now."

When they were settled, Maya and Owen rented office space and began putting the word out that they were interested in investing in disruptive technologies—technologies that they knew would forever change the world.

Their meeting that Tuesday morning was with two engineers named Robert and Gordon. The men were in their early thirties and currently employed. Owen had heard, however, that they were unhappy with their current employer and contemplating starting a new venture.

"Thank you for being here," Owen said. "I'll keep it simple: we offer capital and guidance. The capital will be provided on generous terms. Our advice will always be just that—suggestions that you can take or leave."

Robert exhaled heavily. "Who says we're even looking for capital? Or advice, for that matter."

"We know you're not happy at Fairchild. And we think you're capable of a lot more."

Robert cut his eyes at Gordon but remained silent.

Owen held out his hands. "The world is going to look a lot different in twenty years. Twenty years after that, the changes will be even more drastic. In another twenty years, the world will be nearly unrecognizable."

"What *exactly* are you referring to?" Robert asked.

"Your invention—the integrated circuit. You know it's important, but you don't yet realize how important it will be to human civilization. This is going to sound unbelievable, but in the next ten to fifteen years, the number of transistors you can place in a dense integrated circuit is going to double every year. After that, the number of transistors in the same amount of space will double roughly every two years."

Robert bunched his eyebrows. "What do you think about that, Gordon?"

The other man was silent for a few seconds. "I think it's actually a really interesting thought."

"It's the truth," Owen said. "The unrelenting rise in the amount of processing power will make an incredible number of things possible—computing on a scale you can't even imagine today."

Owen watched the two men, gauging their reactions. "Right now, what you've created is like a ripple on the ocean, the type made by a small pebble dropping. In time, it will be a wave, and one day, when it reaches the shore, it will be a tsunami. The changes will come faster then, and the world will be harder to control. Trust me."

"Let's assume it's true," Gordon said. "That this... law of ever-increasing density will come to pass. How do you both benefit? What do you want?"

"We have learned how important it is to have a stake in companies changing the world. We've learned that sometimes, it's the only way to save it."

That night, Owen sat in the study of the Victorian mansion he shared with Maya and her sister, watching the cars zigzag back and forth down the winding, narrow street toward the bottom of the hill. Pedestrians hiked past, tourists holding maps and locals with their heads down, some bound for home, others meeting friends for drinks after work.

In the great room, Maya's sister was practicing on a grand piano, the music like an anthem for the march of civilization outside the windows.

The year was 1961, and the city was called San Francisco, and to Owen, it felt like anything was possible. He felt an immense weight for that reason, the weight of responsibility for what he knew would happen, as it had happened on his world before.

He also felt full of pride, as though he had truly found his calling—a cause that needed his unique experience and skills. The world would one day be a burning building, but it wasn't on fire now. It was dry and safe but giving off sparks. And it was his responsibility to keep it from igniting.

His life hadn't turned out the way he had planned it. Or imagined it. It was different, but that, he thought, was simply the way life was.

He walked upstairs to the second floor and then up the creaking stairs to the roof-top deck where Maya was bent over, peering through a telescope pointed at the sky.

She turned and smiled when she saw him.

"Looking at home?" he asked.

"Yeah. It helps me wrap my head around it all."

"I know what you mean. It still feels odd here. The smell. The gravity."

Maya nodded and bent over, returning her eye to the eyepiece. "Remind me again what they call our world?"

"Venus."

438

EPILOGUE

In the lavish restaurant overlooking the Pacific Ocean, Owen stood and brought a fork to his glass and tapped it three times, the ding-ding-ding echoing in the cavernous room.

The dinner guests looked up from their plates and set their wine glasses aside.

"Tonight," Owen said, "I'd like to pose a simple question: what is the destiny of the human race?" He paused, allowing his guests to consider what he had said. "We all know the answer. At some point, our species will go extinct."

He moved away from his table to a set of double doors that opened onto a veranda overlooking the Pacific Ocean. Below, waves crashed on the beach, and couples and small groups and individuals walked along the shore, flashlights guiding their way.

"What will be our end?" Owen asked his guests. "A technology one of you is developing? Nuclear war? A natural disaster, perhaps? Will an asteroid or a solar flare or a supervolcano be our undoing?" He took a deep breath. "The real question is not how our species will end. The question is what we plan to do about it. We can't fight the future, but we can plan for it. In this room are the people creating the future. We've invested in many of your companies. We've given you capital because we think you'll prosper, but more importantly because your companies and labs are building the technologies that will radically alter our society. What I'm proposing is that we collaborate on a project just as important. Let's call it... an Escape Hatch."

He walked to the placard and pulled the white sheet off it.

As Owen described his plan, a few guests gasped. Some laughed, unsure if this was a prank.

"I know it might seem fantastic now," he said, "but soon, what we're building will be a global obsession. We will be the first to do it. And we won't be doing it for the buzz or for the money. We will be creating something that will ensure the survival of the human race. You see, I believe one day soon we will need an Escape Hatch. One day, Earth will be in trouble. And we will be the light in the darkness."

As the room broke out in thunderous applause, Owen glanced over at Maya, who was clapping politely, her elbows resting on her swollen belly and the child growing inside of her.

A NOTE FROM THE AUTHOR

Dear Reader,

Thank you for reading *The Extinction Trials*.

As you now know, based on the two big twists at the end, this novel presented several major challenges to write. Imagine writing a story that took place in the distant past—on a completely different planet—without telling the reader? It was tough.

The Extinction Trials and the twist it contains is something I worked on for almost four years—writing and revising and abandoning the novel before returning to it. I do hope you enjoyed it.

While *The Extinction Trials* is a standalone novel, Owen and Maya's son does appear in another standalone book called *Lunar Park*, which focuses on a theme park on the moon (and the discovery of a pyramid buried nearby).

You can find out more at agriddle.com/lunar-park. I hope you enjoy the next adventure, and most of all, I hope that wherever you are, you're happy and healthy and that this novel gave you some escape for a little while.

Gerry Riddle
Raleigh, North Carolina

ABOUT THE AUTHOR

A.G. RIDDLE spent ten years starting and running internet companies before retiring to pursue his true passion: writing fiction. He lives in North Carolina.

www.agriddle.com